Copyright © 2015 Rob Radcliffe 2015

The right of Rob Radcliffe to be identified as the author of this work has been asserted by him in accordance with the Copyright, Designs and Patents Act 1988.

All rights reserved. No part of this publication may be reproduced, stored in or introduced into a retrieval system, or transmitted, in any form, or by any means (electronic, mechanical, photocopying, recording or otherwise) without the prior written permission of the publisher. Any person who does any unauthorized act in relation to this publication may be liable to criminal prosecution and civil claims for damages.

ALSO BY ROB RADCLIFFE

MEAT MARKET
THE RACE

THE AUTHOR

Rob Radcliffe started writing when he was four years old and hopes things have improved since then. For a while he was a ghost writer for aspiring authors across the globe and then decided he'd have a go at it himself. He lives in Manchester, UK with his partner and two children.

He spends the majority of his days with his head in the clouds, sometimes coming back down to earth just long enough to turn those daydreams into stories by actually writing them down.

Rob writes across several genres, 'lad lit' (which would be chick-lit's naughty younger brother), thrillers, and sci-fi.

The Divine, he feels, is a mixture of all three genres, but don't take his word for it, the story is but a page turn away.

robradcliffe.net

CONTENTS

THE DIVINE

PART ONE: A NEW DAWN - 3
PART TWO: BAPTISM OF LIFE - 81
PART THREE – THE SIXTH APE - 141
PART FOUR – THIEF OF TIME - 235

For John,
Without your words of inspiration
the writer inside me would still be
talking about it instead of doing it.

Thank you

THE DIVINE

BOOK ONE

PROLOGUE

To be back here in Britain, waiting, always waiting for the next posting, for that phone call telling me I ship out tomorrow, pack my stuff and be at the airport. This time I might be posted in the Congo for six months, the time before that it was three months with an Inuit community in Greenland. My families change, their faces many colours, but while I am with them I save their lives and I love them for inviting me into their lives.

I always have mixed feelings about the time in between my postings which I spend back home. Granddad leases me one of his apartments for nothing more than a promise of a visit which is nice as the apartment is in the city centre and close to any local amenities I might need. University friends still live in the area which is great when I'm back as I have people to interact with, but while I am back it feels like I'm in limbo. There are only so many lunches with the girls you can go out on before you've caught up with them all and are hearing the same stories again and again.

It is from one of these lunches I now depart, promising 'the gang' I'll ring them all in a few days to organize going out for the weekend. A new bar has just opened in the centre and the girls are on a mission to get me paired up with a man as we enter the place, have me impregnated before the second round, married by the time we move onto a club, and moving into 'our' family home before the end of the night.

Sorry girls but my family is the Red Cross, my home usually the most remote places on the planet helping those small communities which time forgot, and I wouldn't have it any other way. As a doctor I live for my patients and I guess I've never really taken the time to start a life for myself.

Walking across the square I have a flyer thrust into my hand and before I can thank the distributor they vanish. I stop and read the bright pink paper.

GET READY TO CHANGE YOUR LIFE!
Join us in the celebration of Jehovah's life

I scrunch the propaganda up in my hand and look up at the apartment building, Chesterfield Oaks Luxury Apartments. Mine is on the tenth floor.

Granddad wanted me to have one of the four penthouse suites but as nice as they all are, there is only me. What am I going to do with all that room?

Crossing the road I watch as a teenaged boy eyes me up from across the street, he is sipping a can of coke and as I reach to the other side and turn towards my building I can feel his eyes on me. I'm almost anticipating the wolf whistle but none comes and as I look back the boy has gone.

Stepping down from the curb to cross the next road I hear a blast of horns and as I turn my head I hear the boy shout 'move!'

Trying to figure out where the voice came from I turn again and then see the white van, up on the pavement and heading right for me. I try to move but like the proverbial deer stuck in headlights, I am frozen to the spot.

I close my eyes for just a moment and when I open them again I am on my back with people crowded all around me.

The teenage boy approaches me and kneels by my side, stroking my hair, I watch as his hand comes back from my head and it is stained with blood.

'I tried to warn you but it never changes, I'm sorry Sophie,' he says.

'Wait,' I try to call out to him when he stands up and backs up out of the throng of people surrounding me, but no words will come. In the distance I hear sirens getting louder and louder. I feel tired, oh so tired. I close my eyes and the boy's words circle above my head. Just before the fog cloaks my mind I ask myself 'how did he know my name?'

PART ONE

A NEW DAWN

1

SOPHIE: FROZEN

Sleep, my one true release from the harsh realities of my life. When it eventually leaves me, like a dark cloud blocking out my sun, I am filled with a looming sense of dread. For a brief moment, as my brain reconnects all the dots and then realizes there weren't that many dots to connect after all, I lie in limbo, both mind and body detached from me, and I feel peace. Those brief moments are what I try and hold on to, drifting through nothingness, but then my brain picks out something from the real world, a gentle sliver of sunlight peeping through the curtains and warming my face or maybe an orderly banging their trolley along the corridor which connects to my room. There is always something, some cruel invitation back to reality.

This morning it is Nurse Beatrix and her cheery morning humming. I can hear her arrival onto the ward as soon as she steps out of the elevator. The first few minutes of her day are always filled with 'good morning sweets' and 'what a beautiful morning' to anyone she might bump into. When she is not wishing the world a good day she is humming cheerfully, there is no middle ground; Nurse Beatrix likes to appear to be a cheery mother hen figure for her colleagues. It is only when she is behind closed doors that her demeanour evaporates and we witness first-hand the indifference this lady exuberates.

My muscles ache from sleep and I yearn to be able to stretch out and fire a little life into my limbs. Not today. There will be no morning jog around the picturesque lake which taunts me whenever I am wheeled outside when the weather is fair. It has been two months now since I have left this ward, courtesy of a young doctor who likes to touch up patients like me, and I have grown restless. I will not be leaving with Nurse Beatrix on the prowl as she isn't a toucher, and whether it be a compassionate hand caressing my brow (Nurse Bradshaw) or the more sexual deviant finger inside my vagina (young Doctor West), human contact is what I need to get out of this room and out of this body for a while.

Beside me the machines which feed me and breathe for me buzz and whir in my ear, momentarily blocking out the nurse's humming. Any moment now she will enter my room, the kind smile she wears when in the company of her colleagues will disappear as soon as the door closes and we are alone.

I move my eyes from the closed curtains and the sunshine to the crack under the door and watch as a shadow appears.

'Alright lovie, we can talk about it at first break over a nice hot chocolate,' the hummer tells some invisible staff member as she stops outside my door.

The door handle moves ninety degrees and in shuffles Nurse Beatrix, true to form her mother hen smile disintegrating the moment the door clicks shut.

'Good morning my little darling, let's get those curtains open and start a new day. How are you feeling today?'

Nope, not this Mother Hen. Instead of the customary greeting which I receive from Nurse Bradshaw each morning she is assigned to my room, I am not even acknowledged. Nurse Beatrix shuffles her squat middle aged frame around my bed without saying a word. She begins twiddling with the dials on the machines which keep me alive, and from the corner of my eye I watch her work.

She doesn't glance over to me, she just continues with her morning ritual. When she does occasionally talk to me she speaks as though I am an afterthought from her machine twiddling. She doesn't take the time or have the patience to sit with me and let me speak. She has, after all, a schedule to keep. I am not the only prisoner of their own body she has to watch over on her rounds.

'Good morning sweetie,' Nurse Beatrix sighs as though it was too much to have to communicate with this statuesque patient. She then turns and without any warning yanks open the curtains.

An explosion of light engulfs my vision and forces my eyes shut.

'*What the fuck Lady!*' I scream out internally as she switches on the TV and turns the channel over to some morning talk show she enjoys. It's not as if *I'm* going to complain about her choice of programme, room 203's resident ornament. Beatrix turns from the TV and looks me over vacantly, mimicking my own expression. She then moves around the bed to my side and busies herself with plumping up my pillows.

'*Please touch my hand, please Lord have mercy on the statue and let this fierce fake fat fucker touch me, even mop back the hair which is in my eyes.*'

The Lord isn't listening this morning and so here I remain.

'The orderly will be along soon to take you for a bath. I will pick out a nice summer dress for you to wear for when your grandparents come to visit at one,' she says almost to herself, as if reciting the morning's tasks so that she doesn't forget.

There is no chance of escape through the orderly bathing me as they always wear gloves.

'There is also a pile of letters in reception for you which I will bring up and we can read together after your bath. I believe it's somebody's thirtieth birthday today. Well many happy returns.'

So sincere.
So thoughtful.
So utterly fake.

As if reading in mono-symbolic tone from a page in front of her.

Nurse Beatrix then leaves without another word and I am left watching a panel of four ladies not unlike my nurse prattle on about grandchildren.

I close my eyes to try and sleep, the only physical function I am still able to control in this prison, but sleep will not come. My mind will not release me from this body which will not work and will not die. My only sanctuary right now are my dreams. I dream of being back at home with my grandparents. I dream of before the accident, working with the Red Cross in Africa. I dream of the carefree young girl at university and the 'lifelong' friends who, after the accident, visited the obligatory once or twice to prove they were 'real' friends and then vanished without a trace.

Most of all though I dream I am with my dad. He would have visited me every day had he been here. I dream I am still a little girl, before he was gone, and him wrapping his great big arms around me telling me everything will be alright in the end.

Oh how I yearn for the end.

2

BILLY: THE HANGOVER FROM HELL

I'm dying, my eyes feel like they're bleeding, my head is about to explode all over the lecture theatre, the cold sweats and nausea take my mind off the involuntary shaking of my hands which, I suppose, is a good thing, but now the Professor is talking to me. Of all the people he could have picked on he decides I'm the best victim. Isn't that just dumb luck?

'There is nothing any more special about you than there is the rest of this class, so why is it you cannot do what everyone else does?'

That's Professor Johnson and he doesn't like me because I'm not enjoying his class. The reason for this is because I never really wanted to study genetics in the first place. I am doing it to try and please my father, who is Professor Johnson. Imagine telling your only child he is not special, tut tut tut daddy.

'I'm not a sheep,' I tell him, and listen to a few muffled laughs echo around the auditorium.

He smiles and then turns his back on his students who are all waiting for his next move, all eager, pens poised and ready to strike down upon their notebooks to scribble whatever the master may drivel. It really is pathetic, I mean we all know that we descend from apes, that our DNA is ninety eight percent identical and at some point many moons ago we decided to swing down from the trees and walk, and then continue walking. That is fact, and I understand how people like to know where they're from and how they think studying our ascent to the planet's dominant species will ultimately hold the key to predicting where, as a species, we will go next, but come on. It's sunny outside, I'm still half-drunk from last night, and I need a top up beer down the pub to sort these shakes out.

Professor Dad turns with my essay paper in his hands and clears his throat, 'Well Mr William Johnson...'

Ouch. He knows I hate being called William.

'...on this occasion you are in fact special. When asked to discuss where next you think evolution will take this planet of ours and its species you chose superheroes and superpowers...' Another echoing of sniggers, this time at my expense, '...and for this you have received an extra special super F. Perhaps for next term you might think about switching to a Creative Writing course because the scientific world isn't yet ready for red capes and invisible men.'

Now they're *all* laughing at me.

What do they know?

Dad...errr, I mean Professor Johnson is smiling, revelling in his spotlight. He's enjoying watching his only child squirm when he should really be sticking up for his offspring. Isn't that part of the way of the world, to give life and then defend that life from all predators? Look at him, down there in front of the class. He's like the aging wilder-beast pushing it's calf towards the pouncing lion so that he can make a swift escape. The bastard. I'm telling mum.

Perhaps I should explain the essay. Having studied the evolution of life on earth, from the first single celled organism and then moving forward a couple of hundred million years to when fish heaved themselves out of the water and took their first steps on land, and then onwards still to apes and then us, it appears we have evolved as much as any species might ever hope to. I mean, what else is there for us? Are we going to one day wake up with another head? And if so what purpose would that have apart from to greatly annoy the original? My essay was a serious theory of where humans as a species might be heading (excuse the pun).

Who was it that said people typically only use about ten percent of their brains? Was it Albert Einstein? Possibly, and although I know what was meant by this is that at any one given time only ten percent of the brain's neurons are firing, it still makes you think. In my essay I asked a big 'what if', and I'm classing that what if as the same 'what if we get down from the trees and walk for a bit?' the apes once chose but...what if telekinesis, teleportation, invisibility and flight is our next step? Would it be possible to unlock some of that other ninety percent of our brain power to achieve this, fire up a few more of those neurons? And have people been living amongst us for centuries having mastered these feats? Or is this theory so outlandish that I deserve my F and need to stop watching daytime cartoons and reading comics

'Class dismissed,' Professor Johnson announces.

I stand up. No more lectures for the week, it's Friday and now I can get back to doing what University students do best...

'William, could I have a quick word please?'

A couple of my fellow students turn and smile on their way out of the lecture theatre. I sit back down, packing up my laptop case, head down flat on the table and now pounding even worse than before.

The theatre clears and dad makes his way up to where I'm sitting, smiling that sympathetic smile I remember as a boy. The Professor has disappeared now. It's just me and my dad.

'How are you Billy?' he asks.

I shrug, not really wanting to make eye contact because then his suspicions will be confirmed. Bloodshot eyes = partying too much and squandering my only chance of a decent degree following in daddy's footsteps.

'I'm fine,' I tell him, shrugging again, and he nods at me and passes across my essay paper.

'It's an interesting theory Billy...'

'It's not mine,' I tell him, 'the majority of my theory was based upon that book you gave me for my eleventh birthday.'

He smiles.

'Had this class been about dissecting comic books or following the theories of an anonymous author who penned his only work over half a century ago you'd have been spot on in your essay, but it doesn't quite cut it for this class. Just keep your head down son, get your degree, and then the world is for your taking. You don't ever have to think about another form of natural selection or DNA strand again after next year if you don't want, but please just study hard now and choose the right path.'

I nod and dad stands up, patting me on the shoulder and then making his way back down to his desk at the front of the theatre. For a while I stay seated. For how long I'm not sure. It is those last four words which dad had said to me which keeps me stuck to my seat.

Choose the right path.

A first in Genetics and then off to spend my days in some lab somewhere studying the mundane, the occasional field assignment to the greenhouse counting how many types of tomato plants evolved from their one common ancestor. It's enough to lead you to drink. Is that the path I am destined to walk down? Because I want more than that and I know somewhere inside there is more for me in this world than that, I just need to find it...but first a pint to take the edge off the day.

3

SOPHIE: ROUTINE

Routine, this is what defines my existence. At eight o'clock each morning one of the nurses or doctors will arrive at my room. My machines will be checked over, a few twiddles of knobs and buttons pushed. A clipboard with data which hangs by a hook at the front of my ventilator is consulted, something is written down and the clipboard is returned.

Some of my visitors talk to me while this task is being carried out (Doctor West, Nurse Bradshaw) others (Nurse Beatrix) prefer silence or the drone of the TV to mask that silence. My curtains are opened and I am checked over.

Because of the extremities of my condition I cannot control any of my bodily functions. A machine helps me breathe, tubes feed me, and orderlies bathe and change me each day. The only thing I can control is my eyes. I can blink and I can move my eyes around the room I have become so accustomed to, and because of this I can also communicate with the more patient staff.

I also have a computer which hangs from the ceiling above my bed. With a special pair of glasses that are calibrated to respond to my eye movement and transmit the signal to the computer I can control the on screen cursor. A pronounced blink of my eyes 'clicks' the cursor, and with this technology and the software I am able to key in text, if what excruciatingly slowly, and the audio system relays my letters, words, and sentences into the spoken word. I also have the internet which often keeps boredom at bay, but there is of course a catch, I need someone to turn the computer on and put the damn glasses on my face.

Nurse Bradshaw always switches on my computer, and has the patience to listen to me and read to me. Nurse Beatrix does not, and Doctor West, I think, almost had a heart attack the day my grandparents came to visit with this state of art piece of machinery. I will not tell anyone of the Doctor's extracurricular activities with his fingers though; he is a doorway from this prison, my day release.

Once my day has begun I am then left for a short while before the orderly comes to take me for a bath. Always wearing gloves my bather will wash me economically and it is not exactly the candle lit exercise in relaxation I had been used to in my other life, before the accident. No bubble bath, or bath salts, or soft music playing, instead I am hauled out of my wheelchair and onto a gurney which is then lowered into shallow, lukewarm water. I am quickly sponged down with as much tenderness as you might offer when washing the dirt from your car's windscreen. A quick soaping up followed by a jug of water splashed over me to wash the suds away and I am done, the gurney is lifted out of the bath and I am thrown into a thin dressing gown. Twice a week my hair is washed too, who says life isn't without its little treats?

I am wheeled back to my room, often shivering, often unnoticed. The orderly then disappears and I am left to admire whichever wall I have been left in front of. Then I wait. A lifetime can pass before anyone arrives to dress me and in this time I may shut my eyes and escape into my thoughts, living an entirely different existence, children, a loving husband, a home in the country, weekends spent at the seaside sailing and playing with the kids in the surf. The sun beats down on my fully functioning body and I can actually feel the heat, taste the salt from the water which splashes up into my face.

I often have such lucid daydreams that when I 'wake' I wonder if in fact my mind has it the wrong way around, that my dreams are actually reality and this, this room, is a night terror I cannot escape. If only that was true.

After an undisclosed amount of time my favourite nurse, Nurse Pippa Bradshaw (Pip), will often be the one to come and dress me with the same orderly who bathed me earlier. My clothes hang in the small wardrobe in the corner of my room, constant reminders of the places we have been together and the things we have seen. Now when I wear these costumes from my past they are never lived in, these days I am nothing but an oddly shaped clothes horse. Most of my clothes do not fit properly anymore and drown my frail frame. Locked in Syndrome certainly is one hell of a weight loss programme, that's for sure.

Despite the staff dressing me there is never any skin on skin contact, hospital rules says that gloves must be worn for this procedure.

If only this was not so, I would have the opportunity to escape, for mine and my host's minds to swap over and for me to be free. I have to concentrate though. The first time it happened I was daydreaming, off climbing mountains in the Andes, and I hadn't noticed Nurse Bradshaw enter the room. The next thing I knew she was leaning over me to brush my hair and…well, I don't know what happened. I woke up three days later, they said I had dropped into a coma after a violent seizure. That was the first time.

Once I am dressed I will either get to return to my bed or stay in the wheelchair, and because I am a super-efficient mass of broken body, breakfast as an occasion, a meal, can be skipped. My trusty machines do all those inconvenient time consuming things for me. Breathing, eating, swallowing, these are things I no longer have to worry myself with, and so there is no break-up of the day once I am dressed other than the nurses visiting to check I am still alive, and when I get my almost daily visit from my grandparents.

Sometimes they will stay for hours, reading to me, and with the help of my computer we also have stunted conversations.

My granddad always tries to hide it but I can see the heartbreak in his eyes, the tears only just held back. My grandma is more positive and practical for me compared to granddad's sorrow and regret, a true fighter who, if I'm honest, has been the one to instil that tiny glimmer of hope inside me. She talks about specialist doctors she is in contact with and a few have even visited the hospital to run tests. Each doctor has come to the same conclusion, that there is a very specific part of my brainstem which is damaged, the connection point between brain and body, thought and physical.

Time and time again these doctors have given us the same prognosis, that Cerebromedollospinal disconnection is an affliction which there is no known cure for. They tell me I should be thankful I do not have total locked in syndrome where by my eyes would be paralysed like the rest of my body, making communication of any kind impossible but I don't feel like being thankful.

'Unfortunately it is extremely rare for a patient to have significant motor function return to them,' each doctor would end with.

My Grandma would scoff each time this life sentence is handed to me from all of the different doctors, the eternal optimist.

'But there have been recoveries?' she would ask each time, already well aware of how many people in the world have recovered totally from LIS and having even met one of them to try better to understand the hell I go through with every waking moment.

'Well yes but…' the doctors try but there is no telling my grandma that I won't recover from this terrible affliction. After two years and twice as many specialists grandma has now focused her energy on getting me home.

From what I have learned over the years, my granddad made a fortune through amassing a large property portfolio back in the sixties and seventies. This meant he was able to retire early and live a very comfortable life from the income those properties made. It also meant when grandma told him they were going to transform their ten-bedroomed estate Chesterfield Manor, into a 'Sophie friendly environment' he set forth, bank card in hand.

The first thing they bought was my computer, next they hired a full time nurse for when I am released from the hospital (Nurse Bradshaw, or Pips 'Pippa' as she keeps telling me to call her when we talk, will be a welcome addition to the household) and sought her council over how the house must be modified to enable a comfortable 'life' for me.

During my grandparent's visits my grandma will always disappear to find a doctor to harass about my release, it has been nine months now and still a parole date has not been set. While grandma is out fighting the world on my behalf my granddad sits with me and we talk. One side of the conversation is crackled and ageing and the other side sounding robotic with no sense of tone, words with no illumination which often bothers me. My computer will translate my thoughts into spoken words but it cannot express the feeling I wish to convey.

We talk about a lot of things but my favourite theme is when granddad tells me about my dad, about what kind of a man he was, although the stories he tells me are never of when dad was a child and granddad often gets dates mixed up and I'm sure people too. Like the time he and dad drank a case of beer each the night of the moon landing (my dad was born in 1968 so would have been a year old at the time). Or how at grandma and granddad's wedding in 1958 my dad delivered a knock out best man's speech which had everyone in stitches...I suppose granddad is getting old bless him.

Mostly he will talk about how much my dad loved me. He will tell me about when I was a toddler and my dad taking me to the park at the weekends with a friend of his, but he will never mention my mum and the horrors surrounding her disappearance.

Eventually and reluctantly my grandparents leave. They promise they will return in the next few days and as I watch my company vacate my cell and the door clicks shut I am once again alone. I will then silently sob, my cries deafening inside my head but even at the height of my emotional state my sorrow and frustration remain confined. An outside observer would only see the statue before them.

The similarities between my life here in room 203 and that of a prison inmates are not lost on me. The only real difference being there is no parole for a victim of Locked-in Syndrome, my sentence is indefinite.

I have a secret though; I have found a doorway out of my cell. I cannot explain it, nor do I try to think too much about how it came to be because rationalization would surely send my mind the way of my body. My 'day releases' are infrequent and rely upon good natured doctors and nurses, although as I have explained before in the case of Doctor West his intentions are more primal lust than compassion. Even so his touch, like the rest of them, opens up my secret doorway and freedom from my broken body. This is the only real thing which keeps me going from day to day, that glimmer of hope that my routine will be smashed into oblivion by the touch of another. In the case of my grandparents, who frequently hold my hand and kiss my forehead during their visits, I would not try to jump with them. This is a strange magic which I possess and I would never put anyone I love into harm's way of the unknown.

My days here consist of routine but very soon that routine will be broken. Tonight when Pips comes to me I will ask her to hold my hand and I will escape. Call it a birthday treat, to walk and talk and not have to rely upon machines to breathe for me.

Tonight I will have my freedom.

4

BILLY: DOWN THE PUB

It is raining outside now and in some strange way this seems to add weight to my hangover. I've got to wonder if I have that Seasonal Affective Disorder because as soon as the sun comes out my mood tends to brighten up. Living in the north west of England though this happens very rarely and I spend most of the year depressed for no reason. That, I suppose, is why I find myself in the pub more often than not. More than living a typical university student's life, I find I am depressed and then head off to the pub on a daily basis. Hell, I even have my own booth in my local, upstairs, pass the bar, and head into the corner and you will see me there most of the time when I am not in lectures. Sad isn't it? But hey, that's the name of my mood disorder. I've tried the happy pills but the only thing that brings me out of my depressive daze is the sun. I'd make a rubbish vampire.

I'm here now, sitting at my booth reading through the comments dad wrote on my essay when Paul walks upstairs and makes his way over.

'Alright pal?' he asks and sits down across from me, sliding over a pint and then hissing.

'What?'

He nods in front of me at the glass, 'don't you think it's a bit early for the whiskey?'

I shake my head in response, 'I blame the weather.'

'Oh yeah, right,' he laughs, 'the weather, the perfect excuse to drink hard spirits on your own in a badly lit booth in a pub in the middle of the day.'

He's just trying to get a reaction out of me but I'm not biting, not today, I'm too depressed. Did you know that this year there were just eighteen days of sunshine? Eighteen. What kind of a joke is that?

'I've just come from speaking to your dad,' Paul tells me and this time I do bite.

'My dad or Professor Johnson?' I ask, because there's a difference. My dad taught me how to swim and ride my bike; Professor Johnson simply teaches me that my essays aren't worth the paper they're written on.

'Urh...well both, kind of. Professor Johnson seemed a bit distant when I asked him a question about Charles Darwin but then your dad kind of took over, swinging our conversation around to you.'

'Me? Why, what was he saying?'

Paul shrugs, 'I don't know, he asked if I'd read your essay and I told him I had and I thought it was good, and then somehow we got onto your sleeping pattern.'

'My sleeping? You didn't tell him about my nightly falling sessions did you?'

A grimace on Paul's part followed by a slight nod and then, 'yeah I mentioned them, and he appeared concerned.'

'Of course he did. He's wants to know if I'm pissing all of Granddad Johnson's hard earned money I inherited last year up the wall.'

'Your Granddad died last year? Shit, I'm sorry, I didn't know, you didn't mention it at the time.'

I smile, 'I never met the guy, dad told me he died when he was young and left a load of money, some of which I inherited upon my twenty first birthday.'

Paul shakes his head, 'but how does your sleeping patterns tell him you're on the piss all of the time?'

'It doesn't, but he'll assume my interrupted sleep patterns are because of drinking. What exactly did you tell him?'

A shrug, a sip of his pint, and then, 'just that there was a point when you were jumping, or falling, a lot in your sleep and that it has calmed down recently. Anyway, have you got that sorted yet? You said you were going to go and see someone.'

I nod a yes to this but the truth is I haven't seen anyone. I don't know what causes my slip from almost sleeping back into real life and usually a heap on the floor. There was a point during what pitiful summer we had that it was happening every night, ten times a night. I hardly slept a wink for weeks but it didn't matter because there was sunshine, and those warm rays seemed to energize me.

'He also asked if you'd give him a call this weekend.'

I frown at this and Paul lifts his hands out in defence, muttering something about a gun and a messenger. Why the hell would he want me to ring him? We don't do phone conversations. Usually it's a voicemail asking me to give my mum a ring, that she hasn't spoken to me for a while and she'd like to hear my voice. What on earth would I have to talk about to dad? Genetics? Biology? Charles bloody Darwin?

'Anything else?' I ask a little too harshly. That's another thing about me when it rains, I can be a right twat with people.

'Well,' Paul says, reaching into his satchel, 'I was going to put something to you which I think you'd like, but if you're in your twatty mood then I'll ask someone else if they'd like to accompany me and my family to our Christmas retreat in Cape Town.'

I grin. Despite the rain Paul has managed to lift me out of my SAD depression and my comedown in one swoop. Christmas in Cape Town, South Africa, sun, ohh glorious sun.

'When?' I ask, now eager.

'Next Saturday. Straight after we break up for the Christmas holidays. One of Lisa's mates couldn't make it so there is a free ticket going if you fancy it?'

I laugh out loud, 'of course...Christmas in the sun and the prospect of seeing your sister in a bikini on the beach, what more could any red blooded male ask for?'

'Fuck off Billy, she's too young and innocent and you're trying to use the fact that you know she has a soft spot for you to piss me off.'

I laugh again, 'no mate, Lisa is madly in love with me and she's not too young at all. She's nineteen, and contrary to what you might think with those brotherly blinkers on she is not a virgin.'

'Don't,' he tells me with a smirk as I embark upon our age old argument.

'How old were you when you lost your virginity?'

'Fifteen,' he sighs, bored already because we have echoed this conversation a million times before.

'And how old was the girl you scarred for life with your tiny pickle?'

'The same,' he adds.

'And she probably wasn't half as fit as your...'

'Okay, I've heard it all before,' he interrupts, putting up his hands to stop me. 'Yes or no right now, are you coming?'

I nod.

'That's fantastic because now you can be my winger.'

I raise my eyebrow, 'winger?'

Paul nods. 'Lisa's mate is an absolute stunner and I reckon I can get in there.'

'That too is fantastic' I tell him, 'because then we can double date. You and this bird and me and...'

'You're not shagging my sister Billy. No way, no how, she's my baby sister, you're my best mate, and I don't want to have to choose sides when you eventually get bored and dump another one.'

'Ok, ok, I'll leave her alone; I won't speak to her, or look at her, ok?'

Paul nods, 'Good. You can have anyone else, the bikini clad world is your oyster, but if I find out you've shagged Lisa while we're away I'll burn your passport and return ticket on a barbecue and you'll have to figure out another way of flying home.'

Charming. We shake on it but I know for a fact Lisa will be disappointed though, especially since we have spent the past two months seeing each other in secret. Paul will come around eventually, I mean, it's not as if he'd really try to kill me if he caught me in bed with his little sister.

'Right, I'm off training, I'll see you later?'

'Later?' I ask, necking back my whiskey.

'Yes later Bill, I'm fighting tonight and you've a cage side seat remember?'

My mate Paul Fielding, the boy who would cry if you chased him around the playground with a slug on the end of a stick, now the big hard MMA champ and brutal at it too. I've seen many a guy end up floored, begging for him to stop as he pummels his opponent relentlessly.

'Yes I'll be there,' I tell him and he smiles, nodding goodbye and then leaving me to get another drink.

Watching my best mate leave I am only slightly aware of the woman in her mid-twenties as she approaches.

'Hi,' she says, sitting down in the seat opposite me and smiling.

'errr, hi,' I say.

'You're Willy, sorry, Billy Johnson aren't you?'

She's fit.

I smile and nod my head. Since when did the fit ones come over and introduce themselves.

'I am, and who might you be?'

She doesn't respond, just sits there staring into my eyes. She has nice eyes, deep mahogany which match her hair.

'Think Billy, look beyond my face, look into my soul.'

It's original, I'll give her that, but I can't help think this is some kind of wind up. Any minute a gaggle of girls will show themselves and mahogany girl will have won whatever bet was arranged prior to our encounter.

'I'm sorry,' I counter after trying to look into her soul and only getting as far as her chest, 'have we met before?'

She shakes her head reaching over and placing her hand over mine. 'I'm sorry, I'm too early.'

She then gets up and leaves and I watch her go, she glances back twice before jumping out of my life and I put the encounter down to something I will most probably forget with the next drink.

5

SOPHIE: BIRTHDAY WISHES

'Now we want you to look presentable for your grandparents on your birthday don't we dear?'

Nurse Beatrix, droning on as per. She hasn't bothered to make eye contact just yet but she has only been in the room twenty minutes so there's still time.

Nurse Bradshaw is on the late shift today so I'm stuck with Beatrix's dress sense and no way of communicating my distaste for the clothes she picks for me to wear. Earlier she mentioned putting me in a nice summer dress but now it's come to the crunch she selects on old tweed skirt, floral blouse, thick tights, and an old grey cardigan.

Ten minutes later I am wearing what a fifty year old spinster deems presentable and feel absolutely miserable. Pips would do my makeup and maybe plat my hair; Nurse Beatrix scrapes my greasy hair back into a greasy ponytail. Fortunately before she can do any more damage to what little constitutes as my self-esteem these days, my grandparents come bustling into the room.

'Happy birthday my darling,' grandma announces as she skips across the room to where I am sat in my wheelchair, and gives me a huge hug, plastering kisses all over my face. My inward smile levitates my mood, it has been two days since they last visited and it feels like it has been months.

Behind her, granddad sets down three bulging carrier bags and gives me a smile and a wink before setting himself down too.

'Ok now Nurse Beatrix, we will let you know if we need anything,' grandma tells this morning's 'carer' as she leads her out of the room. 'That woman,' grandma says as the door shuts, 'she would have hung around all afternoon if I hadn't shown her the door. Remember last month when she kept hovering around while we were here Alan?'

Granddad nods.

'Asking us about what our plans were for dinner later that evening? It's almost as if she was waiting for an invitation.'

Granddad rolls his eyes and winks at me again and I too roll my eyes, one of the last little tricks I am still able to accomplish.

'Ok Sheila, sit yourself down and let's get cracking with these prezzies.'

Granddad then stands and switches my computer monitor on, wheeling me besides my bed so I can see the screen. He then opens my bedside drawer and fishes out my glasses, placing them onto the end of my nose and touches the small sensor by the lens to switch them on.

The computer beeps, recognising the software and then the starter screen, my custom starter screen, appears on the monitor. The qwerty keyboard slides up from the bottom of the screen and I begin to key in the letters.

t h a n k y o u f o r c o m i n g t o d a y b e a t r i x w a s d o i n g m y h e a d i n a n d l o o k w h a t s h e d r e s s e d m e i n

I hit the speech button and the computer separates the letters into words and a robotic voice expresses my message.

'That woman,' grandma says, shaking her head. 'Is nurse Bradshaw working today?'

3

Grandma checks her watch and I consult the wall clock. And silence. There are often many silences on these visits. Despite grandma trying to talk none stop to ward off those silences even she has to pause for air now and again.

w h a t i s i n t h e b a g s

Granddad smiles, 'why don't we have a look?'

For the next half an hour they read birthday cards out to me from well-wishers who have never bothered to visit. There is a huge 30th birthday card signed by all my 'close friends' which granddad reads out.

'Get well soon Soph, You're one in a million, Miss ya lots chick, See you soon mate...' and lots more mindless drivel from the people in my former life who think writing a few words in a card somehow makes up for not once visiting me. I'd like to think if it had been one of them stuck like this I would have visited but then again having spent the majority of my adult life as a doctor for the Red Cross I was very rarely in this country. Granddad tells me not to harness bitterness towards these people. That these friends still have their busy lives to be getting on with and it might be difficult for them to see me like this. On some days I agree with him but on others I despise these people who were my friends, and I despise the carefree lives they continue to live.

Next we unwrap some presents.

A handful of new movies to watch on my computer, pairs of socks (of course), a beautiful lilac cashmere scarf, perfect for when the weather turns in this temperature controlled hospital room, or for those long walks in the wilderness no doubt, a huge makeup set for them all to spruce me up like a doll...I begin to grow bored of these gifts which are utterly useless to me and become eager for the bag from which they are pulled out of to empty.

There is one birthday card which my grandparents have not opened and read to me yet, the birthday card from my dad. Every year I would find a card from him, it would always be the last one I would open, and to this day I do not know if it was granddad writing as my father or if dad wrote out multiple cards, one for each year of my life. I have never asked my grandparents. In truth I have never wanted to know the reality of the annual card's origin. Some mysteries are better left unanswered.

At some point during the present opening I must have dozed off because when I wake silence greets me. I quickly scan the room and see my granddad asleep on the chair next to my bed. Grandma must have left to wreak havoc on the ward.

W a k e u p o l d m an

Granddad opens his eyes and smiles, reaching for my hand and giving it a squeeze, 'sorry angel, you're not the only one who tires of your grandma's constant prattling on.'

h a h a

He sits up and surveys the wrapper strewn room and shakes his head, 'I told her we shouldn't go over the top with these gifts. Most of which you are unable to use right now.'

g r a n d m a l i k e s t o t r y a n d a c t l i k e e v e r y t h i n g i s n o r m a l

'Amen to that,' he pauses for a moment, letting out a deep sigh, 'I'm guessing you've noticed your dad's card wasn't amongst the pile?'

y e s

'It's at home, and there is a parcel with it. I didn't bring it for a reason, because after this birthday card they stop and I want to talk to you about that and about your dad.'

There are so many questions I want to ask but not like this. There is one question which I need to ask now, a question which has haunted me for twenty one years.

h o w d i d d a d d i e

Granddad bows his head into his hands and when he looks back up into my eyes tears roll down from his. 'I'm sorry Soph but I can't tell you here. There are things about your father that you must know but not here and not now.'

He leans forward and kisses my forehead and for a moment I am tempted to jump, to take over his body and run all the way home, to find dad's letter and the parcel and rip them open, to try and make sense of this. As I look into those tired teary eyes though I know I don't have it in me. For one thing, to jump into an elderly man's body...I simply don't know what affects it would have on granddad. The stress could cause him to go into cardiac arrest and then which body would be privy to the heart attack? Would I find myself trapped in granddad's body while his life slowly ebbed away, all the while with him looking on in horror, frozen as Sophie? Or would the stress follow granddad into my useless cocoon where I would watch myself die and then spend the rest of my days living as an elderly gentleman?

I guess it would be granddad's body which would suffer the heart attack, physics being what it is, but then how am I able to do what I do under the laws of physics? Even so, neither of these scenarios are the reason I do not jump. It is because I love this man before me. From the age of nine granddad became the only father figure in my life and I will always love him as a father.

There are still questions which I need answers to, and the first inkling of a plan has begun to form as Pips opens my cell door to say hello.

6

BILLY: FALLING

I can't be sure what time I was finished drinking the last of my whiskeys. It was possibly moments before the barmaid refused to serve me another drink on the grounds I couldn't even stand up properly, never mind walk straight. It was kind of those two door supervisors to help me down the stairs, although they needn't have pushed me out of the doorway quite so hard so that I almost tripped and landed in the middle of the main road in rush hour traffic. How I got back to the house is beyond me, and I should really remember this as it was only a few minutes ago.

Did I get a taxi?

Yes, I must have done.

Was I sick on the way home in the taxi?

Using the garden gate as a means to turn back around and survey the way I have just walked/staggered/lunged, by leaning on it and swinging back and forth, I can make out that yes I did in fact get a taxi and yes I was in fact sick, on the road and a bit on the door of the black cab.

I wave to the taxi driver who is now wiping my vomit from his vehicle and I think he waves back. I can't really hear what he has just said but that doesn't matter, I'm pissed, nothing matters.

Using the garden hedge to steady myself I start my long and perilous journey to the front door. Key in my hand...no, wait, that's not my key that's a cigarette lighter...but I don't even smoke? Where the fuck is my key? No matter.

I land on the doorstep with my head and relax. It's comfy down here on the pebbledash pathway, and look, the clouds are parting and...and it's sunny. For the first time in over a month the sun's rays massage my aching winter ravaged body. I've missed you sun, but I'll be seeing a lot more of you soon when I arrive in Cape Africa in South Town for Christmas. And Lisa's going to be there too. I love Lisa, she's so fantastic and...

'For fuck sakes Billy, what the hell are you doing lying on the garden path,' Paul shouts at me as he opens the front door and almost trips over my head.

I smile up at him, what a great guy, and say, 'you my friend are my bestest friend.'

He rolls his eyes at me and I laugh at this, accepting his hand as he pulls me up to my feet.

'I only left you two hours ago, how the hell did you manage to get into this state in such a short time?'

I shrug, sensing with my acute sense of sensibleness that this is a rhetorical question.

'I think you need to go to bed mate,' Paul says as he lifts me into the house and we help each other up the stairs and into my room.

No sooner is the door open I stumble the few steps to my bed and fall on top of the mountain of pillows, a precaution for when I am falling a lot in my sleep. Paul leaves the room, closing my door, and I roll onto my back, reaching out to open my curtains so that I can feel the glorious sun on my face again. The curtains and pole come crashing down on top of me but that's fine. I shrug them to the floor and get undressed, lying naked above my covers so that the dwindling rays massage my whole body. I can feel a tingling sensation in my legs, it is moving across my torso and up my neck to my face. I turn over onto my front, feeling energised but at the same time quite drowsy. I need to sleep. I'm pissed and I need to sleep. I close my eyes and the sun is behind my eyelids, momentarily burnt into my retinas and shining bright into my soul. It is growing, engulfing my whole line of sight, the tingling now feeling as though it is moving my whole body, charging me up into a great explosion which does not come. Instead the sun dies out and I begin to fall aslee...begin to fall asl...begin to fall...I'm falling!

My bedroom door slams open to Candy, another one of my house mates, standing there, hands on hips and a bemused smirk across her pretty face. I open my eyes and notice that I am now at the other side of the room and on the floor.

'Bad dream?' she asks and I blink a couple of times before standing up, my feet still tingling from the sun. She throws me a pair of shorts from the pile of dirty washing by the door and I slip into them.

'No, not at all, I was just drifting off and then...' I stop as I glance out of the window. All traces of daylight have disappeared and it is now raining hard. Shaking my head I ask her what the time is, to which she smiles and tells me it is quarter past nine.

Quarter past nine. How did that happen?

'Paul,' I call out but there is no answer.

'He's out, his fight is tonight remember?'

'What time did I get home?'

She shrugs and then adds, 'it was before six because I got back then and you were sleeping like a little naked baby on top of your covers.'

Three hours. How can I have been sleeping for three hours? I have just closed my eyes this very second.

'Would you like a coffee? You still reek of whiskey.'

I nod, grabbing my towel which is sort of hanging up over the clothes rack that is my wardrobe, 'I'm going to grab a quick shower,' I tell her as I bolt past her and across the landing to the bathroom.

'You ok?' she asks through the bathroom door to which I groan a yes and jump into the sobering ice spikes which are better at waking you up than any cup of coffee.

Ten minutes later and I'm downstairs sitting at the kitchen table, Candy facing me, cups of coffee between us.

'Did you fall again?' she asks once she's rolled herself a spliff and lit it.

I nod, 'I guess so, but this time it was different. Usually I have been asleep for moments before I fall, this time it was over three hours.'

She shrugs because she does not have any insight to add into my strange sleeping patterns, and so I too shrug, smiling a little and accepting the spliff as she offers it to me.

I still feel as though I'm half asleep.

Am I, or is this just the hangover kicking in for the second time today?

'Do *you* ever fall?' I ask my fellow stoner.

'Sometimes. It has never ended with the crash your falls do though. I just jump and wake myself up, happy the bed cushioned my descent.'

I laugh at this. I wish I could have it that easy. I haven't woken up across the room for nearly four months, and usually the booze helps me avoid any unpleasantness at all. Usually I will get a decent night sleep when I'm pissed out of my head. Why not this time?

I pass the joint back to Candy and she gets up from her seat, coming around the table and giving me a hug, 'you're a strange one Mr. Johnson but I love you for it, now I'm off meeting everyone down the pub, fancy joining us? Paul's going to be pissed off you weren't there at his fight but a few drinks and you'll be bezzies once more.'

I shake my head, 'nah, I think I'll try a bout of sobriety for the rest of the evening and besides, I don't fancy like going out in this weather anyway. Paul will have to wait.'

Candy shakes her head, and as she picks up her coat and handbag mumbles, 'I don't know, you and the bloody rain. It's any wonder you didn't decide to go to university somewhere along the equator, then you'd have your precious sun almost all year around.'

She comes back around the table and gives me a quick kiss on the cheek, 'and before I forget, your phone has been going off like mad for the past hour.'

'Shit,' I say, getting up and heading off upstairs to try and find the stupid thing. I was supposed to be meeting Lisa before Paul's fight.

'No wanking in the living room,' Candy shouts up after me.

'Why would I when there's your crisp and clean double bed up here,' I shout back down but she's already gone and with her departure the front door slams shut.

I find my phone in my jeans pocket and check the screen. Shit. Eighteen missed calls from Lisa and three text messages which don't seem all too great either.

IF UR PISSED AGAIN U CAN 4GET RINGING ME L8ER!!!

That was the nice one.

Scrolling down the list I see dad has rung me too and I then remember Paul's message from dad to give him a ring. I select his name and press call. The phone rings nine consecutive times before I hear dad's voice, slightly out of breath. He has probably legged it from the kitchen to his office upstairs so that he can receive his telephone call in private. Is he even aware that it is Friday and mum'll be out at bingo so he's the whole house to himself? Probably not, that'll be the old age creeping in.

'Hello?' he answers and I can hear his leather armchair squeak as he sits down.

'Hiya dad it's Billy, Paul mentioned you'd asked me to ring you over the weekend...'

A pause. He'll be trying to recall this particular conversation which he shared with Paul just five short hours earlier. It's the old 'forgetful Professor' routine, fun at first but contrary to my previous remark about dad's memory, he's as sharp as a razor. Alarmingly so actually, he remembers everything.

'Oh, yeah, hi William, I just wanted to know if you were getting on alright. It seems like ages since we've had a chat outside of the lecture theatre, however brief that might be,.'

I smile, 'well you keep setting us a million essays with added reading material every week dad, I'm usually quite busy.'

There's a pause before, 'hmm, and are you still doing most of your work upstairs in the corner booth at that pub?'

'It's quieter than the house and a great place to observe our species taking a step back through the evolutionary process, first by degenerating the ability to speak and then losing the capacity to walk upright. It's great watching the fifth ape revert back to an image of its ancestors.'

'Indeed,' dad replies before the old deep sigh and then, 'you are alright aren't you Bill? It doesn't take a genius to work out you're drinking somewhat excessively. I've seen it a thousand times sitting in on my lectures, the bloodshot eyes, the inability to focus on anything coherent...'

'Dad I'm a university student,' I argue, cutting him off before this turns into another one of Professor Johnson's lectures, 'I'm living the uni life, I'm making the grades, and I'm enjoying a healthy social life. Look, it's a Friday night and I'm not out painting the town red am I? I'm talking to you instead.'

Another quick sigh to say he's satisfied and his worrying is over for the moment, 'Ok. Now what's this I hear about your bad dreams coming back?'

As a kid I could never seem to settle at night. Put me out in the garden on a beautiful summer day and I'd sleep forever, but come night time mum and dad used to say I was like a junkie turning my back on the gear. It was like a fever which never broke but which would constantly turn me out in hot and cold flushes. Eventually I'd knacker myself out enough so that I would fall asleep, only to be woken from 'bad dreams' which were in fact my old friend the sensation of falling and then waking up with a start. Sleep therapy was an expensive waste of time, the Doctor could find nothing wrong, and so I was drugged every night. This stopped the falling and the sweats for a decade, until I reached puberty and then it seemed my body had bigger problems to worry about. The falling has only really started again in the last year or so, since I've been living away from home and my night dose of night nurse. These days a belly full of beer and whiskey is my night nurse but it doesn't always work.

'Dad, they're not bad dreams, I'm not waking up in the middle of the night crying like a baby and wanting my mum, this is me drifting off to sleep and then suddenly being snapped back to reality so hard I manage to throw myself out of bed' and across the room (although I'm not going to mention that).

'And how often does this happen? When was the last time you fell?'

I check my watch, 'errr...thirty five minutes ago was the last time it happened and it occurs nighty, often several times a night. It's back to the same drill as when I was younger.'

'And they're more often when the weather's warmer?'

'Yep, as soon as the sun is out I'm like a jack in the box all night.'

I wait for the next question, is he going to ask me to name the Capital of Brazil for ten bonus points? I hope not, I'm crap at Geography.'

'This isn't affecting your studies is it William, because if it is I'll enquire about you seeing another specialist.'

'Dad, don't worry. I'm fine...well, I'm better than fine actually, Paul has invited me on his family Christmas holiday to Cape Town at the end of term, and for free as well.'

'That's, that's fantastic...' he stutters and then pauses, probably trying to muster a little more sincerity in his tone because we both know he would much rather have me at home for Christmas. Our family may not be a large one, just dad and uncle Eric on his side and my grandparents and my mum's sister on hers, but what we lack in size is made up for in prezzies. I'm a big kid at heart, '...we'll miss you on Christmas day.'

'Yeah, I know, but you'll still have uncle Eric to play Jenga with.'

'I'm concerned Billy,' dad continues, which is just what I need. Dad chill the fuck out for once in your life. Were you actually born with your stuffy Professor's jacket and half-moon specs on?

'I'll be fine. We're staying at their gated house with swimming pool and...'

'No, not about Christmas, I'm sure you'll have a great time and I wish I was going in your place, no, what I'm concerned about is your sleeping and I don't want you to think that you can't speak to me about anything that might be on your mind. No matter how silly it may sound.'

My phone beeps, call waiting, it's Lisa.

'I'm fine Dad, listen, I've got another call I need to take so I'll speak to you soon ok?'

We say our goodbyes and I laugh at dad's last words. I wonder how he'd respond if I told him I seem to be able to literally catapult myself across my room while I'm asleep? Or if when I told him about...shit, what am I doing going off on a tangent, Lisa's on the line waiting for me to speak.

'Hi there sexy,' I say as I put her call through.

'DON'T YOU HI THERE SEXY ME'

Women.

7

SOPHIE: JUMPING

'Hey there Sophie,' are Pip's first words as she pops her head around the door. She then smiles at my grandparents and tells me she will be back in a while once my visitors have left.

On cue grandma gets up and scurries after the nurse, probably to enquire once again about me leaving the hospital. Inwardly I smile. If only she knew that by tomorrow morning Grandma would have me back in her house and I'd be sitting at the kitchen table with granddad having a steaming cup of coffee.

There is no time to waste, with grandma out of the room I begin furiously typing out what I need to tell granddad.

i a m g o i n g t o a s k n u r s e p i p p a t o g o t o t h e h o u s e a n d c o l l e c t m y p a r c e l f r o m d a d

I watch for granddad's reaction as the computer turns the stream of letters into its robotic words. I see an uncomfortableness wash over him and he lifts himself out of the armchair next to me.

'errr...I was hoping I'd be able to talk with you about your dad before you receive the parcel,' he tells me, trying to show a smile, to regain his composure but it is too late. His initial facial response has raised more questions which I need answering.

l e t s t a l k t h e n

Granddad frowns, a rarity, especially around me, and sits back down, taking hold of my hand once again. I look down at our entwined fingers. The sensation of his touch there but me unable to reciprocate, give his hand a little squeeze maybe.

'Sophie please, this isn't the time. Your grandma will be back any second and I need time to organise my thoughts.'

w h a t i s i t

The old man shakes his head and begins to silently sob, lifting up my hand and kissing it hard, 'my darling there are things in this life you could not possibly understand. Even now over eighty years in I still do not understand...'

He trails off and I am left wondering what it is about dad and the parcel he left for me to receive over two decades ago on my thirtieth birthday.

I look back over at the only father I have ever really had, the only constant man who has ever been in my life. He looks tired, worried, worn down by a secret surrounding my dad which he has carried now for a long time.

He shakes his head and looks back up from my lifeless hand, a quick smile and the granddad I have always known and loved is back. He nods his head and says, 'when should I expect the nurse?'

i w i l l a s k h e r t o n i g h t i f s h e w i l l p i c k u p t h e p a r c e l

Just as the last metallic echo of my computer voice fades, grandma slips back into the room with a smile of her own, 'come on now old man, let us get ourselves off, we've Martha and Donald Jones coming for supper.'

Granddad rolls his eyes and then winks at me. I wink back and then too roll my eyes, the only aidless communication I have. Grandma then smothers me with a thousand wet kisses and promises they will be back on Sunday after church, and then they are gone.

Ordinarily the aftermath of visitors is a sad time for me as I sit or lie here in my room alone. The loneliness engulfs me and as much as I try not to let it in, self-pity will often veer its nasty little head and stay for a while. Not now though. I need to prepare myself, have all my actions worked out once I am on the other side of this body because everything must be fluid, my interactions with others must be pleasant but forgettable.

Pip is my favourite host and while I am 'with her' I always respect the life she lives.

I move the cursor across my computer screen and click on the alarm clock icon. I set it for five. Pip's nightshift ends at six o'clock in the morning and she always checks on me just before she is leaving. Next I type out the words PLEASE LEAVE ON across the computer screen and then close my eyes. Sleep always comes to me quickly, lifting me away from this room and taking me on a journey across time and space. I often find myself reliving long forgotten memories when I dream. I am nine years old and dad has taken me to the park with his friend, the giant of a man whose name I cannot remember but who spent a lot of time with us during my childhood. I know that I am nine because this is when the giant man introduces me to his young son. The toddler and I play on the swings while dad and the giant man sit on a bench and watch us as they talk. I wave across to them both and they smile and wave back. The sun's rays are hot today and the toddler runs around none stop, even when I tire.

I call out to my dad and ask what the little boy's name is. He shouts back something but the words are lost in the breeze. Later the four of us eat ice cream and walk around the lake. My little friend falls asleep in his pram when we get to feeding the ducks, tired out from all of that running. I remember him waking very suddenly, his pram violently rocking as he is slammed back into consciousness. He starts to cry and as both dad and the giant man try to sooth the boy, they talk.

'*He wakes up like this all the time,*' the giant man tells dad, '*I worry this is the start of something bigger trying to break free.*'

Dad grins, looking down at the child, '*you're worried the little man is a chip off the old block Doc?*'

Doc, dad just called the giant man Doc and now a little more comes back to me, the nickname doc and a childhood using this name for the giant man.

Doc smiles and shrugs his shoulders, '*do you ever worry Sophie might be one of us? It has yet to happen but maybe this generation...*'

'*I constantly worry. I worry because I am scared I won't be there for her if she is like us, to try and explain what it is we are.*'

'Don't be worried daddy,' I tell him, latching onto his leg and squeezing. I look into the eyes of both adults and receive a look of adoration back from both of them. Dad picks me up and starts tickling me and I scream like anyone would when being attacked with the tickly fingers. I grab hold of his neck and scream for him to stop. Eventually he does and we are all laughing.

'What's the matter Soph,' the giant man doc says, *'don't you like being tickled.'*

I shake my head and as we walk on I hear a distant humming in the air. Dad looks down at me and tells me that he loves me and so does granddad and grandma.

'And what about Doc?' I ask. He smiles and before the humming gets too much I catch him telling me both he and little William also love me very much.

William.

His son's name.

Why had I forgotten that?

As my dream turns lucid I am aware that the humming sound is the alarm I set for five am and I know that any moment I will wake. I hold on tight to dad's neck and tell him that I miss him and don't want to wake.

With a kiss and a big hug, he then whispers something into my ear. I try to hold on, to keep the protective clutches of sleep all around me, but the alarm is now deafening and I can feel my grasp around daddy's neck loosening.

'But I don't want to go. I want to stay here with you.'

He repeats those words again and I open my eyes back in my hospital room.

Pip was good enough to leave my glasses on while I slept and so I click the alarm off. Those words buzz around my head, a message from my dad from beyond the grave.

Find the Doc.

I blink a few times which is my version of stretching my aching post-sleep body. I can feel the onset of cramp in my left calf and close my eyes, trying to focus my mind as far away as possible until the pain recedes.

One of the worst things about being stuck in this lifeless body is without a doubt when the cramps set in, torturing my limbs with a vengeance for not using them. Sometimes I can catch someone to massage the cramp away but this relies upon them paying attention to me, my computer being switched on, and them actually being in the room when the cramp visits. There is no buzzer to alert people of my distress. There is no way of me sounding the alarm. Instead I take my mind back into my memories and I journey back to that little village in Ghana where I spent almost two years.

Find the Doc.

Working for the Red Cross as a Doctor I was welcomed to the village and it didn't take long to fall in love with the people. My role was to treat the sick but I spent more time teaching English to the children who were all so eager for knowledge in a community which knew so little of the world outside their own. Far away in the distance I hear my door open but that is in another life, a life of oppression where my body is my cell. The children took to me a lot quicker than the adults. Viewed with suspicion, at first a lot of the community shunned the white woman who wanted to stick everyone with her needles, and it wasn't until an outbreak of smallpox in the community and their traditional doctor's failure to cure the disease, that my team and I were approached.

Find the Doc.

Through my living memories I hear Pip's voice calling to me in the haze which separates me now from the present.

I am aware that my eyes are still open but through them I cannot see. I am back in my classroom teaching about how the quick brown fox jumps over the lazy dog to the delight of twenty children.

In the distance a click of the fingers in front of my face.

None responsive.

The pain succeeds and as I leave my children I do so once again with regret.

Pip is now by my side checking my chart.

c r a m p i n m y l e f t c a l f

The nurse turns and smiles. Sitting down in the chair next to my bed she pulls up the leg of my pyjamas pants, exposing the muscle which twitches uncontrollably, and rubs her hands together to create some warmth.

Focus.

I watch as she slowly massages my leg.

Nausea.

My stomach starts to roll and a tingling sensation in my head begins to morph into waves before my eyes. I feel like I'm being pushed gently on a swing, my body moves forward and then back again without actually having moved at all. Pip is talking to me but now her words are mute. All I hear is the cracking of electricity, static surrounding my whole body. I focus on the nurse's hands working their fingers into my flesh. I feel her energy, like a hot slice of metal burning down into my leg. Within her actions I follow the kinetic connection we both share, the swinging towards those hands becomes faster as the crackling in my ears intensifies. I close my eyes and for a split second watch as I massage the leg in front of me. I open my eyes again and roll into the static which is alive in my head, my mind swings in continuous broad strokes towards the nurse; I take my first lung full of air in a month and cough. In front of me my host coughs, the knuckles on her fingers growing white as she squeezes the paralysed flesh beneath them. I close my eyes again and feel the flesh beneath my fingers, the cool rigidity. I look up into the ghost of a face I once knew so well and then blink and I am back looking at the Nurse, although her face has now sagged and is an expressionless void, a shell in which I am to inhabit.

I can smell the perfume on my host's neck, some flowery concoction which reminds me of long childhood summers. I blink and my own drawn out face is back before me, another breath of sterile, hospital room air, the crackling in my ears reaching its crescendo. I shut my eyes and concentrate on my breathing, my host's breathing, listening as the static subsides.

Breathe. Breathe. I open my eyes and let out a low primeval sigh, standing up on unsteady legs. I feel sick, the nausea has returned but it will soon pass. My host's heart races in her chest and I feel a little dizzy because of this. A wave of tiredness passes over me but I fight it off. To sleep would be to wake up back in my own body. I reach across to my face and take off the glasses which control my computer. Looking down on myself I feel an urge to sob but I push back the self-pity, there is no room in this body for that sort of thing. I then smile and kiss her forehead.

'I'll be back soon,' I whisper to the body which failed me and then leave the room, picking up my new cashmere scarf from the side on my way out. It is, after all, a chilly morning outside.

8

BILLY: MAN'S BIRTHPLACE

'Willie. Slow down, you're too fast, I can't catch you'
  'Come on, run faster, try and catch me,' I cry out as we race around the park's open green.
  The little girl chasing jumps out to me, tackling me to the ground and we roll about in the grass laughing.
  'Oh Willie,' she says, straightening her long dark hair, *'I wish you were my little brother and not just my cousin, then we would live together in the same house and have so much fun every day!'*
  She grabs me around my neck and squeezes, *'I love you Willie.'*

I jolt awake to the crash of my knees hitting the fold down table in front of me and I land back on my seat, dazed but feeling no confusion whatsoever. I had fallen and my body had propelled itself upwards, pulling tight my seatbelt and then forcing my knees up in front of me, knocking everything off the table.
  Paul slaps my arm a couple of times and laughs, 'Jesus Billy, I think you might have rocked the plane with that jerk.'
  I smile and apologise, to which he grins. On closing my eyes again I am met with the little girl from my dreams. She is, as always, smiling at me. Why does this scene at the park, with dad and uncle Eric and the little girl, keep coming back to me?
  And cousin?
  What the fuck?
  Trying to understand the significance of this dream or supressed memory, I attempt to work my way back through my life to when I was a kid but my memories fade the further back I go. I can remember going to the park, but uncle Eric was not

with dad and me, and I was old enough to talk in any memories I still keep hold of.

I look around and see Paul is back in the land of Zeds. I then peer across at Lisa who is watching a movie and will her to make eye contact so that I can tell her, telepathically of course, to come to the back of the plane so that I can kiss her. Because I am not an X-man, my non-existent telepathy doesn't work and so I resign to watching her watch her movie while Paul snores in my ear.

After what feels like a week, Lisa gets up to visit the little girl's room and I too am up in a flash, following her to the back of the plane, pinching her very fine derriere as we walk.

Once in the toilet I throw myself at her, kissing and groping, hungry for her, until there is a knock at the door.

We both stifle laughter and Lisa sighs, biting her lower lip, 'is this how it's going to be all Christmas, stealing kisses whenever Paul is out of the room?'

I open my mouth to tell her no, that I will tell him about us soon, but am interrupted again by another knock at the door.

'Come on you two,' our stewardess whispers good-naturedly and we open up, me grinning like an idiot and Lisa turning bright red with embarrassment. 'This is not the mile high club flight kids,' she continues with an *'I've seen it all before'* smile.

On the way back to our seats, after pinching Lisa's arse once more and her stifling a giggle, I lean over her shoulder and whisper 'I love you' into her ear.

She whispers back, 'I've always loved you,' and then sits down, smiling across towards me as I take my seat back beside Paul.

As I close my eyes once more to feign sleep, I feel the sun's rays move over my face from the small aircraft window. I rejoice in the big ball of fire finally showing itself over the early morning African sky.

As a child I was always sickly during the winter, always running up a fever which would come and go sporadically but never really break until spring time, and the months from

October 'til mid-Aprilish affect my health to this day. Dad used to make up stories about it when I was a kid. He'd tell me because I was born in the summer my body lived for the sunshine. He's say when there was no sun all the little people who worked as a great big team to keep my body running couldn't see what they were doing. This was the reason I would feel ill. He even incorporated my falling into his story. As my falling has always been much more frequent in the summer months he'd say it was the little people (who were all called Sammy the cell) working overtime to catch up on the work they missed in the winter because of the dark.

This story, even now, comforts me, and I mention it because all my little Sammys are going haywire right now. One day they are fumbling around in the dark, not sure where they left those important documents which need to be faxed to the brain ASAP, and then, as the plane touches down at Cape Town International Airport and I walk through into the forty degree heat of mid-summer, their shift leader (also called Sammy) announces out of the blue that it's overtime for the foreseeable future. This is how I feel as we walk through arrivals and outside into the baking heat, that my entire body has been jolted awake, every little Sammy given a sudden burst of energy and now working hell for leather.

Ian, Paul and Lisa's dad, heads off to find the hire car and their mum lights her first cigarette in twelve hours. Paul is busy watching all the bronzed bikini clad holiday makers returning to go back home and this is the moment which Lisa chooses to come up behind me and quickly kiss the nape of my neck.

I smile and reach behind me to find her hand and give it a squeeze .

In the beginning Lisa and I would flirt, but I think to begin with I was doing it more to wind Paul up. Lisa has always been an attractive girl and Paul has always been all too aware of the attention this has brought her from guys.

I began to take an interest in her after she came home from her year back packing across Europe with friends. She had always had a crush on me, from an early age, but when she returned to the UK she had changed. I'd like to say she left a girl and came back a woman but I know how clichéd that sounds…but when she did get back, and I chatted to her at her welcome home party I found I wanted to spend the entire night talking to her.

Later, when the party had finished and everyone else had gone to bed, we kissed and I had fallen for her. The next night we slept together and the day after that I told her I was going to one day marry her. She had laughed, hit me on the shoulder, and told me she had wanted to marry me since she was five years old. I guess that's why we work; we have known each other forever. I am almost like a part of the family and have been so since I started playing at Paul's house as a kid.

'Right then, I've found the car,' Ian says as he returns from the sea of vehicles parked in rows under whitewashed metal awnings, 'it's this way.'

We begin to steer our luggage trolleys in said direction and Paul approaches and slaps me on the back, 'not a bad flight hey? Just think this time yesterday we were back in the sleet and rain.'

I smile and nod at this, he's right, the journey over wasn't too bad at all.

When we arrived at the airport and had booked our baggage in I had received a phone call from dad. He asked where I was and when I answered Manchester Airport he told me to turn around. Instinctively I did as he asked and there he was smiling like he used to when I was a kid, a smile I have not seen for a number of years.

'What the f… what you doing here old man?' I said as we walked towards one another and he wrapped his arms around me, kissing my forehead which felt a bit strange.

'I've come to see you off haven't I? What, you think because you're off to the other side of the world to no doubt try and impregnate everything that moves around in a short skirt, that you're too old for an embarrassing send off from your old man?'

I tightened my arms around dad's back and whispered my thanks to him. Despite all my Billy-Bullshit-Bravado and the hard time I usually give dad, I was very happy to see him.

As we pulled away dad stepped back from me and wiped his eyes. Silly old man, I was only off on holiday and he was bibbing like my mum would whenever one of her favourite soap characters died.

'Alright dad, calm down on the emotion will you, people are looking.'

I caught Paul's eye and he pointed to the restaurant they were all going to wait and have a drink in, and I nodded as he disappeared with his family.

Through the tears dad laughed and said, 'I'm sorry Billy, come on, let's take a walk. What time is your flight?'

'In about an hour or so.'

Dad nodded and then reached into his jacket pocket, taking out a plastic shopping bag and handing it to me.

'What's this, a going away present?'

'Just some light reading for the plane. I thought you'd like it given your penchant for superpowers and red capes.'

I laughed and thanked him for the book he would read to me as a child, although the skinflint could have bought me a new copy. Glancing over *The Divine* it appeared quite weather worn and old. Obviously picking up on my distaste for the book's condition, dad told me it was now out of print and had been banned from publication for some time. This sparked an interest and I made a mental note to get reacquainted with the scribblings of Mr E.

We arrived at a bank of chairs outside a Mac Donald's and sat down, watching people come and go for a while, stuffing their faces with burgers and fries. Dad turned to me and asked how my falling was, to which I replied with a shrug, 'same old same old.

Those little Sammies are still banging around in the dark, but not for long. Once I'm out there in the sun it'll be overtime all day every day for them.'

'If anything happens Billy, if anything ever happens to you that you don't understand, you know you can come to me don't you?'

I frowned and shrugged at this as we stood, what was the old man going on about? Probably worrying as usual about me and the choices I make in my life.

Dad checked his watch and then held out his hand, I shook it, and moved in further for another hug.

'Thanks for coming dad, mum rang me earlier to wish me a safe trip but she never mentioned you coming here and seeing me off tonight.'

'I, errr…was just passing,' he said grimacing at his own words.

I nodded, 'course you were. Just happened to have this book with you too eh? No, cheers dad, it means a lot.'

He then gave me an embarrassing thumbs up and turned to walk away, 'have a good time Bill,' he said.

I mock saluted him, 'will do dad, see you later.'

And then he was gone, swallowed up by the throng of busy travellers.

The 'car' is actually a 4x4 truck with flatbed to the rear, and while Lisa and her friend Melissa get comfortable in the back of the vehicle, Ian driving and Linda next to him on the passenger seat, Paul and I climb in the back with the suitcases.

The drive to Fish Hook, or Vis hoek as the sign says on our way out of the car park, is an eye opener. Ten minutes into our journey to the coast and I witness the very real poverty which holds the majority in its grip. A fenced off shanty town runs parallel with the road for about a mile and a half. Thousands upon thousands of poorly built shacks with rusting corrugated iron roofs and crude holes in the walls for windows stretch out as far as the eye can see. And people really live in these shacks, often quite large families I am led to believe as Paul gives me a running commentary.

'Amazing,' I tell him and as we turn off the motorway I glance behind me into the car and catch Lisa's eye. She smiles and I watch as her and Melissa then start to giggle.

'What you smiling at?' Paul asks as I turn back to face the stretch of road our vehicle leaves in its wake.

'Nothing,' I am just happy to be here, away from it all, away from my life of pubs, drunken fights, and hangovers, I feel fantastic.

As the first specks of deep blue edge onto the horizon I marvel at the wonder of this land. Africa. This is where we all came from, where man evolved and then migrated outwards to end up dominating the planet. This place is our species' first home and it feels a real privilege now to be here.

Growing up, my dad would tell me stories about this place. Not so much Cape Town but more Africa as a whole. He had travelled extensively in his youth and it was our species' first home continent which he had always talked of the most fondly. He passed down stories of my great-grandfather who had fought alongside Churchill in the Boer war, and their capture and subsequent escape from Pretoria after being taken prisoner. He spoke of villages so remote that the inhabitants had absolutely no idea about the larger world outside their territory. As a child the tales of Africa would spark my imagination and I often spent hours in dad's study pouring over maps and picture books of this place. Dad would usually come over from his work at the desk and we'd go through the books together. I'd ask a tiresome amount of questions about every little thing and he would answer my musings with another tale of adventure in this far off land, promising one day to take me here. That day never came but here I am anyway, following in the footsteps of Johnsons who have lived before me, happy to be here and excited for the unfolding of my adventure I might one day tell to children of my own.

9

SOPHIE: THE IMPOSTER

Outside my hospital room I am filled with a sense of dread. This feeling has washed over me every time I have jumped, feeling I am going to be stopped and questioned over the nature of my business. Like getting pulled over in a stolen vehicle and being asked for my licence and registration. It is of course absurd, that anyone in their right mind would question Pip about her purpose in walking around in her own body, but still this feeling of being an impostor walking about in another's skin stays with me throughout my jumps.

I head down the hallway and pass the nurses station, smiling at anyone I might come into contact with. My feet and hands tingle but I know that will stop within the next ten minutes or so. I head towards the door marked STAFF and sweep the nurse's ID pass across the plastic pad. This is the sixth time I have made this journey so I am becoming quite familiar with my surroundings.

As a patient here I am restricted to where I might go. I am wheeled to the wash room for my showers and baths; I am taken to the far end of the corridor to the lift which on occasion takes me outside and into the grounds. Because of this I have had to think on my feet when in another's body.

The first time I jumped it had been a brief outing; unable to understand what was happening I thought I was having a stroke or a heart attack. The touch of the nurse had made my body or mind or both react and the next thing I knew I was staring at my own frozen face. Within the matter of a minute I think I must have fainted, and when I woke I was back frozen in my own body.

It had been my second outing, this time having just been sexually assaulted by Dr West that I decided to try and leave the hospital. With the Doctor as a host I was able to walk around unrestricted. Kind orderlies showed me how to operate the swipe machine on each door, probably concluding that I was either really tired or really drunk not knowing how to open the secure doors despite me (Dr West) having worked here for the past three years.

Once in the locker room I had a little bit of trouble finding the correct locker (another Doctor assisted Dr West in the tracking down of his locker and then asked me if I was ok). After assuring my colleague I was fine and just a bit tired I got changed and headed down to the staff car park, jumping in the Doctor's little two seater convertible and racing away.

As West I was able to leave without any questions being asked but now I am Pip and that is why I waited for the end of her shift before jumping. The nurse will have a rota and people watching her. I have witnessed nurse Beatrix reduce a member of staff to tears because they have been away from their post during shift and I would not want Pip getting into trouble at a later date by leaving early because of my anxiety to get out into the big wide world.

Jump number three was in the middle of the night. Pip had come in to check my vitals and leaned over me to brush my hair away from my face. I had been ready and I had jumped, but I knew I could not leave the hospital. The nurse was only half way through her shift and although I could have used the old 'I've taken ill, I need to go home' excuse, people would undoubtedly ask Pip at a later date when she came back to work if she was feeling alright. Having no memory of leaving half way through her shift this would cause her to ask herself questions I would rather not have asked.

And so on my third jump I spent the night as the ward's night nurse, I made the rounds (fortunately everyone was sleeping and no one was dying), I went down to the cafeteria, ate a tired ham salad sandwich that tasted absolutely sublime having not eaten anything for so long. I interacted with people, spoke, conversed, simple things which I had missed so much. I went through the nurse's locker and found her car keys and sat in her little Nissan for a while, letting the cool air from the air-con wash over me, trying to understand how any of this was possible or if it was even real. I fell asleep and when I woke I was back in my room, in my bed, in my body. Later on that night my host visited me and I watched for any sign that something might be amiss with her. There didn't appear to be but even so, I am cautious with what I do and where I go when I jump.

I make my way into the locker room and head straight to locker number six, fishing out the correct key from the bunch on my belt. I check my watch, 05:56, and pull out the clothes which are neatly folded in a pile. A pair of slim blue jeans, pink t-shirt with a print of a city skyline on it, a lovely soft tortoiseshell pullover which, when I pull it over my head infuses my senses with a soft lavender fragrance. I sit down and pull on Pip's Ugg boots and as I grab her jacket the locker room door opens. I freeze on the spot. The imposter. Another nurse walks in and smiles at me. I don't recognise her but that isn't to say Pip wouldn't. Returning the smile I quickly sling the small sports bag onto my shoulder and leave before any words might pass between us. I check my watch, 06:02. Two minute past freedom.

Nurse Beatrix will now be on the ward but I know from conversations with Pip that she routinely tries to avoid the women when their shifts collide, so it would not be out of the ordinary to leave the hospital without talking to her.

I reach the lift and as the doors shut I let out a huge sigh, catching a glimpse of my reflection in the mirror opposite me and then turning away from it. It is still an unnerving experience to look into a mirror and be greeted by another face.

I close my eyes. Another wave of tiredness hits. I need coffee or an energy drink to keep the body from fighting me and shutting down, expelling my intruding mind back to where it came. Something buzzes in my bag and my heart begins to race. I set it down on the floor and open the side pocket. Her phone. Someone is ringing her. Someone called Patrick if the caller ID is to be believed. I take a deep breath and answer.

'Hi there sexy nursey,' the alien voice announces. Why the hell did I answer? I could have ignored the buzzing. Fear.

That's why I answered, fear of acting out of the ordinary despite being alone in a lift.

'Hi,' I say back.

'Sooooo, what about it?'

This is my worst nightmare, being caught up in a conversation I have no way of manoeuvring around.

'What about what?' I ask the voice of Patrick noncommittally.

The voice laughs out loud, 'oooooh you are such a tease Miss Bradshaw, you know exactly what. You getting your sexy little arse around here this minute so that I can make you breakfast and then give you a night cap that is sure to make you sleep.'

I smile despite myself. Patrick is obviously the nurse's love interest. My first impulse is to make up some excuse that I can't come around but I stop myself. Something stirs deep in my stomach. A feeling I have been void of for as long as I can remember. Butterflies. This body is lusting after physical contact and if I'm honest, the thought of sex, of the intimacy, of the raw lust and physical gratification sends my head in a whirl.

'Nursey? Pippa?'

I clear my throat, feeling my cheeks flush as I think about a chance encounter with this total stranger.

'How about you come to mine? I'll let you make me breakfast in bed after my nightcap.' Oh my god I am actually flirting with this man.

'Tell me when beautiful and I am there,' my soon to be lover demands.

What the hell am I doing? My plan had been to go to granddad and grandma's house, pick up my parcel, head back to the hospital and deliver the parcel to my room and then head off home, or rather to Pip's home and get into bed.

'I've a couple of errands to run before I head home,' the voice of Pip says as I walk into the hospital foyer and head out towards the car park, scanning the half dozen cars for a small red one, 'give me a couple of hours and then I'll be all yours.'

There's a pause on the other end of the line. Have I said something, worded something wrong? Would Pip have said 'go home' instead of 'head home?'

'I'll see you then beautiful,' Patrick says and then hangs up.

Oh the joys of paranoia.

I put the phone away and stop in front of the nurse's little red Nissan.

I always have to give it a minute before I drive while inside a host. This is without a doubt the most dangerous of times. What if my concentration was to lapse and I jumped back while driving? Although this has never happened, the fear that it could is always there. And then what would become of my host, suddenly finding themselves speeding down the road with no clue how they got there? I always keep this in mind and my mind focused when entering a vehicle while jumping.

I get into the car and immediately open the driver's side window. Yes it might be the middle of winter and it might also be teetering on freezing at this time in the morning but the cold will keep me alert and fight off the tiredness.

The fourth time I jumped was into Nurse Beatrix and I simply couldn't stay awake. She ended up falling asleep in the hospital cafeteria and I woke up once more entombed in my own flesh, a journey wasted.

I start the engine and push the gear into drive, thankful as always the nurse drives an automatic. I then pull out and I am away, speeding along the road towards my grandparents wondering what the hell I am going to say to granddad when he opens the door to greet his granddaughter's favourite carer.

Forty-five minutes later, as I turn into the little cul-de-sac where I spent my teenage years playing out, I glance at the weak winter sun rising to meet the day and smile. I look up into the hills, following the stone wall which leads up to my grandparents' house, set in the surrounding fields with a little woodland area to the right of the building. I stop in front of the gates and get out of the car, making my way around to the intercom and after a couple of buzzes granddad answers, static crackling down the line or is it in my mind?

'Hi there Mr Chesterfield, it's Pippa Bradshaw, your granddaughter Sophie's nurse?'

A pause and more static before, 'yes of course, Sophie told me she was going to ask you to pop by.'

The gate begins to open inwards and I feel delighted at the safe familiarity welcoming me back. The rolling fields tarnished with a soft sprinkling of snow which leads up to my home. 'Straight to the top, my dear, I'll put the kettle on.'

As I drive I am reminded of a thousand happy childhood memories. To the left stands the great Oak, a primitive rope swing which I helped my dad put up for me when I was seven years old hangs still in the morning smog. I remember dad spending hours with me underneath that tree, pushing me on the swing or reading to me in the cool shade on hot summer afternoons. I park up in front of the house and granddad greets me at the door with a wave. I smile and wave back as I get out of the car.

'Come on in my dear and get yourself out of the cold. Would you like tea or coffee?'

'Coffee, strong please,' I tell him, forcing a little distance between us as we walk into the house. My initial response in this old man's presence is to grab hold of him and hug him tightly but that would not be what Pip would do and so when offered, a simple hand shake is all I receive.

'How is Sophie?' granddad asks as he leads us into the kitchen and shows me to a seat at the breakfast bar. I look around me, they've redecorated since I was last here. Gone are the worn wooden worktops and in their place are shiny dark granite slabs. The same battered kettle still stands by the oven though, looking somewhat out of place in this new modern monstrosity but defiant against the winds of change.

'She is doing okay. Frustrated to say the least but she is trying to remain optimistic.'

Granddad hands me a mug and sits down next to me at the bar, turning in his seat so that we are facing each other. His smile is forced and I can see the sadness in his eyes.

Without realizing what I am doing I reach for his hand and squeeze it tight. 'It's going to be alright.'

He breaks down, his body deflating and the tears burst from his eyes as he shakes his head and sobs into his free hand, 'I'm so sorry, it is just too much to bear. My little angel stuck in her body like a prisoner. You know as a child she used to be so active, forever running out into the woods and building forts and tree swings, making campfires and often coming back with all manner of cuts and scrapes on her. A regular tomboy she was….'

I nod and smile, it's true, dressing up and dolls were not something I involved myself with. If there was a tree then I always needed to climb it.

'What life is she ever going to be able to lead now?'

I shake my head. He is asking the wrong person. This is the one question I have asked myself over and over again in my deepest moments of despair, when all feels lost and I'd rather die than spend another day trapped in my body. What kind of life can I lead as a victim of Locked-in Syndrome?

I shake the nurse's head. There are no words to comfort my granddad. I want to reach out to him, to tell him that inside this body I am here, his Sophie, his princess, but that would be the quickest way of getting thrown out of my home.

'You know I have seen things in my life, things you wouldn't believe if I told you. There are people who can do amazing things that are simply inexplicable. My granddaughter is part of that legacy and she doesn't even know it. Her whole childhood has been surrounded by secrets and lies. Secrets and lies,' he repeats, only this time in a whisper.

'You know you can trust me Mr Chesterfield. I have only Sophie's best interests at heart. I have agreed to quit my post at the hospital when the time comes so that when Sophie comes back here I can give her the care she will need, and if there is anything you feel you need to tell Sophie but don't know how then I am…'

Granddad raises his hand to stop me, 'young lady I believe your intentions are good but my story is for Sophie's ears only, for family. I do not mean to appear rude in saying this; it's just the way it is.'

I smile and nod but inside I scream *'it's me granddad, Sophie. The inexplicable you talk about is staring you right in the face. You talk about amazing; I can jump into any person's body that makes contact with me. Top that old man!'*

'Sophie told me she receives a birthday card from her father every year despite his passing many years ago. Tell me about that.' I place my hand back on top of granddads. He looks so old and weak now, like all his energy has been sapped from his very soul.

He nods; taking a sip of his coffee and then carefully placing the mug back down in front of him. 'Sophie's father, Eric, was a great man. I really don't know where to begin, to tell you the truth, or how much I can trust you not to talk to Sophie about this. It must come from me.'

The nurse lifts up her arms and shows granddad her palms, 'anything you tell me to keep quiet will remain so sir.'

Granddad smiles and shakes his head, leaning back on the breakfast bar stool. He reaches behind him on the floor and picks up a battered leather briefcase and lifts it gently onto the worktop.

As he flicks the catch and the lock springs open he looks into my eyes and says, 'I'm sorry but this really is for Sophie to hear from me once she has received her present.'

He then reaches inside the briefcase and pulls out a mahogany coloured leather bound book and hands it to me. I turn it over in my hands.

'The Divine,' I hear myself saying out loud to which granddad nods and turns back to his coffee. Noticing the author's name I then ask him who Mr E might be.

Granddad cracks another smile, this time I can see it isn't forced and I watch as something inside him illuminates, making his eyes sparkle. 'That, my dear, has been one of the publishing world's best kept secrets since the book was first published in 1958. Mystery, or Mr E, is a pseudonym of the author because they had the foresight to realize controversy would plague the book. They were right.'

I frown. But what would a dusty old book published in 1958 have to do with dad? He wouldn't be born for another decade. Opening the cover the spine crackles and I'm met with that musty smell which only really old books possess.

'The Divine, first edition,' I read out loud and then look up at granddad who is still nursing his coffee. 'What is this book about to have caused such controversy?'

He shrugs, 'immortality, evolution, angels, and one self-proclaimed devil. Mr E's book has been banned in the UK since 1960 which made it all the more popular, and now because of the internet and social media, bloggers, online conspiracy theorists, and 'divinians' as the fanatics like to label themselves, there is a rumour this book will soon be re-released.'

I turn the first few pages over and read out loud the author's dedication.

For those of you out there, my brothers and sisters who live in the shadows.
I love you all

Mr E

Having never really had an interest in books outside the medical text books I studied through at university, I am now curious about this particular piece of work. Not least because my father had for some reason intended it for me.

'Was Sophie's dad a big reader?'

Granddad laughs out loud at this, 'Eric? No. He could speak and read in a dozen languages but not once did I ever see him pick up a book.'

'He could speak a dozen languages? Why? How, where did he learn…' I stop. These are not questions the nurse should be asking. These are my questions for granddad and they will come soon enough but from me not my host. She has no right to ask them. 'I'm sorry, Sophie has talked at great length about the things she remembers about her dad and I suppose to learn something new and exclusive…'

Granddad frowns at me with suspicion and I realize, as Pip, I have over stepped the mark. I close the book and shake my head, 'I'm sorry, you don't need me hammering you down with questions. You will obviously want to talk to Sophie about these things.'

He nods and then smiles again, reaching back into his briefcase and pulling out a small padded envelope which has yellowed with age. On the front in simple bold writing, my dad's writing, it says To Sophie.

'I was planning to bring the book and the envelope in for Sophie when we next visited but as you know she can be impatient at times.'

He then reaches into his pocket and pulls out a USB drive, handing it across to me with the envelope, 'the book has been scanned into a file on this drive so that Soph can read it at her own leisure. Please tell her that no matter what, her grandmother and I love her.

I nod and reach to give Granddad's hand another squeeze. Having now concluded our business he stands up and moves around to the kitchen sink. I quickly finish off my coffee and follow suit, thanking him for the hot drink and his hospitality. Upon showing me the way back to the car I turn and ask him, 'The Divine? Is it a work of fiction or non-fiction?'

Before closing the front door my granddad shakes his head and tells me, 'if that book was just a work of fiction then there wouldn't ever have been any problem.'

10

BILLY: HIDE AND SEEK

When I was younger I idolised my father. I'd follow him around everywhere and cry when he would leave the house to go to work. My mum would try to console me but it would do no good, my hero had gone, left me for a classroom full of students. I would resent that and I would resent how busy dad always was even when he was around in the evenings.

The hours I'd spend in his study playing with my toys while dad would be busy working behind his desk are some of my fondest childhood memories believe it or not. Eventually dad would stop his work and look over at me playing by myself, coming to join me on the floor in front of the fire. We would play trucks, or maybe hide and seek around the house, sometimes we would go down into the cellar and make a 'base' with old boxes and spare blankets. And when it was time for bed it was my dad who would hide with me from the evil tyranny of my mum.

Eventually though the tyrant would have her way and my dad and I were separated. I would be sent off to the POW camp which was also bed, and dad would, I believed at that young age, be *forced* back into his study to do more work.

On summer days and at the weekend dad would take me to the park with uncle Eric, and in my earliest memories of such occasions I think I can recall a girl playing with me. She was much older than me and I would follow her around everywhere. Her name now escapes me and I cannot remember if my memory of her is just one occasion which I have superimposed over all my other memories of the park and childhood summer days, or if this little girl was a childhood friend. I was very young, and memories are always open to corruption. The brightest memory might have actually been a dream from long ago which my mind has hung onto and over time those images have been reconstructed as very real memories. Sometimes I think about that girl from my childhood. I wonder who she was and if she actually existed at all and was not just some character from a dream long forgotten which has now come back to haunt me when I sleep.

I have never asked my dad about her and if she really existed, but even now when I shut my eyes I can see her vividly, the pretty yellow floral dress she wears, her long wavy chestnut brown hair and her bright green eyes. She still visits me in my dreams when I am back in the park from my childhood. She pushes me on the swings and we race around after each other. Dad and uncle Eric watch on and wave at us and this is the one true time when I feel content in my life. Sad isn't it, that only when I sleep do I feel happy with my lot? Then of course my consciousness will violently yank me away from my little friend and I wake up across the room with a crash and usually the last remnants of a hangover still pounding in my head.

I open my eyes and watch the red neon digits on my bedside alarm clock, which is now upside down and on the floor, change from 08:29 to 08:30.

Willy, come back, I can't catch you the little girl's voice echoes into reality

My landing has woken me up with a thud onto the pile of dirty washing besides the door and I groan, rubbing my eyes, and am greeted by the sun shining through the window and a naked Lisa asleep in my bed.

Shit. We were only supposed to cuddle for a few moments after our secret midnight liaison and yet here she still is, starkers and in my bed

'Lisa,' I hiss, army crawling back towards the bed. 'Lisa get the fuck up woman, your idea of a few minutes cuddling is completely fucked.'

Nothing, she doesn't even stir. Any moment Paul could...

There's a knock on the door.

'Come mate, wakey time. Let's get down to Boulders beach for a morning swim with the penguins.'

I must still be asleep. Swimming with penguins? We're not in the North Pole.

'Just give me a minute,' I call.

'You're not wanking are you?'

No mate that was hours ago and instead of using my hand, your sister gave me a help in hand so to speak.

'No, I'm just getting up.' I turn back to Lisa and through clenched teeth hiss as loud as humanely possible, 'Lisa get the fuck up now.'

'I'll see you on the terrace in ten then,' Paul tells me and I listen to his flip-flops flip-flopping down the hallway. When they have disappeared completely I spring up and jump onto the bed, trying my hardest not to admire the slim toned body of the girl I love and instead concentrating on getting her the fuck out of my room.

Quickly Willy, faster, faster.

Great, just what I need, remnants of my reoccurring dream getting involved. I shake Lisa to life and she jumps up with a well-placed 'Shit it's light,' jumping off my bed and throwing her dressing gown around her. She smiles before blowing me a kiss and pulling open the door, checking the coast is clear and then disappearing into the hallway.

I sigh and flop down onto the bed, shaking my head. That was a little too close for comfort. Paul would have gone mental if he'd have barged into the room. Four days into the holiday of a lifetime and I very nearly had myself hung drawn and quartered by an avenging older brother.

With the girl who spends her time constantly in my thoughts while I'm awake now dispatched back to her own room, I turn my thoughts to the girl who is becoming more of a regular occurrence in my sleep.

She was there again, playing with the toddler me, chasing me around the park, playing tag with me, playing hide and seek, not being able to catch me because I'm too fast. Why has this memory unearthed itself now? I need to know who she is. I need to find out if she is real and then…and then what? Go searching for her? Rock up at some lady's house with a smile and a 'remember me, it's Willy, we used to play together in the park when we were little?' This is stupid but I can't shake her from my head.

I reach for my phone and unlock it, take a deep breath and then press call.

'I'm sorry the person you are calling is not available, please try again later,' that stupid cheery woman on the other end announces and then hangs up on me. Bitch. I try dad again and get the same response which is strange because he is always available and even if he is using his phone it should direct me to his voicemail.

I try once more and am greeted in the same fashion. Dad has his phone switched off.

Let's play hide and seek Willy, you try and find me!

'I will,' I tell the ghost of the little girl barely remembered, and find another number which is stored in my contacts list.

'Hello?' that voice says after two rings.

'Uncle Eric?'

'Billy, how's it going boy?'

Instead of engaging in the small talk which would usually surround the opening of telephone conversations with my family, I jump right in, intrigued as to how Eric will react to my enquiry.

'Who is the little girl from my childhood Eric?'

Silence.

'Uncle Eric come on, speak to me. Lately I have been having vivid dreams of when I was a little kid with you and dad in the park and there is a little girl in these dreams too. Who is she?'

'Billy listen to me,' the only other man I have known my entire life and who I respect to no end says to me, 'you are not ready for this. Have a great time while you are out there in Cape Town, get drunk and eat too much and forget about this.'

'But Eric…'

'Billy do not pursue this. I'm sorry, you want to talk when you get back then we will…'

'No I don't want to talk when I get back Eric, I rang you now expecting you to laugh at me and tell me I've a little girl stalking my dreams, to get a grip but instead you haven't, which means the girl is real, was real...and we were once close.'

More fucking silence.

'Who is she Eric?' I ask him quietly and hear a heavy sigh on the other end of the phone.

'My daughter.'

'What do you mean your daughter?' I ask a little too quickly. 'Well where is she, what's her name?'

I listen to a defeated half laugh and then, 'Her name is Sophie,' he then hangs up.

Let's play hide and seek Willy, you try and find me!
If it is the last thing I do Sophie, I *will* find you.

11

SOPHIE: THE SECRET

I am back frozen again. This morning at around ten o'clock Pip slipped into my room and left me the leather bound hardback book with the unopened envelope on the side table and the USB drive slotted into my computer. I (Sophie) was sleeping at the time and didn't wake. She was then good enough to put my glasses upon my head and switch on the sensor, ready for when I woke up. With nothing else to do I then left in my host's body and headed off to the nurse's home, completely forgetting about the nurse's lover Patrick until the phone rang again. This time I didn't answer. As much as a chance encounter with a stranger would have been nice, I now had to get back to my own body before the nurse woke up and found herself still trapped in my room, bed, and skin.

It is a constant worry that my hosts talk about their encounters with me when I jump. I had jumped into the nurse's body early this morning and now, after four hours, it was time to jump back by falling asleep. That way the nurse would wake up in her bed, possibly a little disorientated and not remembering how she got home that morning but her memories of being stuck inside my body would be put down to a very strange bad dream. There would be no evidence to suggest anything other than that.

When I arrived at the house I let myself in and went straight to her bedroom. This was my porthole back into my body and almost immediately after my head hit the nurse's pillow I felt the static begin to buzz inside my head.

And here I am back in room 203. As I open my eyes my first thought is the book. I glance across the room at where I had left it on the side table. I wish now I had opened the envelope and read dad's letter but there hadn't been time, fatigue was pushing me out of the nurse's skin and I knew I had to move quickly, the four hours I'd spent within my host is my longest jump to date.

I blink at my computer screen and the monitor springs to life, I then open up the file on the USB drive and copy it onto my desktop, getting ready to settle down for a read. Before I manage to open the file marked divine.doc Nurse Beatrix flutters into my room. I follow her around my bed and to my monitors.

Good morning to you too, you rude bitch, I scream inside my head. Fuck this; I haven't time for her messing around, switching on my TV and settling down for an hour of mindless drivel.

p l e a s e l e a v e

Beatrix spins around on her heels to the sound of my computer voice, her smile slipping from her face.

'Excuse me young lady but there is no need to be rude. I am here to help you.'

h e l p m e b y l e a v i n g

As she makes eye contact with me I see that we are in a standoff situation. Beatrix doesn't have people tell her what to do. She runs the ward on her shifts, every member of staff is beneath her and us patients are so far down the food chain we don't even get a smile from this woman. The only time she puts on the fairy godmother act is when family and friends of patients are present, a regular nurse Ratchet that's for sure. So for a patient to make a stand like this, especially a patient who cannot even ask her to leave with her own voice, it must be grating on her.

n o w p l e a s e

Her expression hardens and I see a flash of something in her eyes. Having called her out I have forced her to make a decision, fight or flight. For a moment it appears as though she is going to swallow her pride when she walks towards the door and touches the handle. I never take my eyes off her. She pauses for a moment but then turns back to me, taking her hand off the door handle and walking back into the room.

'You know young lady I cannot tolerate this kind of insolence on my ward. We are here to help you.'

l e a v e m y r o o m I d o n t w a n t y o u h e r e

She smiles at this and moves closer, running her fingers along the chrome bed guard until she is close enough to me so that, was I able, I'd have no problem lashing out at her.

'How about we switch this off Sophie,' she says, reaching up to my monitor and flicking the button. The screen dies and I am now left without any means of communication. 'There,' she hisses through clenched teeth, 'that will keep the insolence to a minimum, won't it?'

Nurse Beatrix moves in closer, her nose just inches from mine.

Please touch me; please let your nose brush past mine, because that is all I need.

'I think you need to learn some manners young lady. This is not your room, you are a guest here and I am the one who decides how comfortable your stay might be.'

I close my eyes, showing that I am not listening to her, tempting her to lose control.

She slaps me hard across the face and my eyes shoot open.

Do it again you evil bitch, I promise this time you will not have a chance to recover.

'You silly little girl, do you think I got to this position in life by letting patients order me about like some hotel maid?'

She pivots again, raising her hand to strike and I focus. I focus in on that hand. It will be quick, barely a touch before contact is lost. I focus and as the hand flies towards my face time for me slows, the solitary bead of sweat crawls down the side of nurse Beatrix's face, her face contorts with sheer hate, not for me, she barely knows me, I am a mere insignificance. This hate I can feel is directed at my willingness to stand up against her. No one likes to be told to fuck off, especially not some highly strung middle aged spinster who was probably bullied as a child, powerless towards the torment her peers unleashed upon her and that is why now she holds onto her power in this hospital like her life depends on it. That is also why she lashed out at me when I defied her but she won't do it again.

Focus.

Her hand moves downwards towards my left cheek and once again the pendulum swings towards that hand, the static in my ears deafening me. As our bodies make contact, hand to face, I open my eyes and immediately step backwards away from my body. I look into those eyes and see fear. She is in there somewhere, crying out, unable to comprehend what just happened.

I take a step forward and grab hold of my face, moving Beatrix's mouth close to my ear and saying, 'you venomous bitch. This is what you deserve. Stay away from me and my room or this will happen again.'

I then turn and grab The Divine and envelope which sits on top, walking out of room 203 for the second time today. I immediately make my way down to the cafeteria, checking my watch. It is ten past eleven in the morning. I spent only an hour in my own body before jumping again.

'Strong coffee please, and a bacon sandwich,' I ask the lady behind the counter and I turn to find a place to sit. As I pay for the coffee the cafeteria lady smiles at me and I walk over to the nearest table, setting out the book and envelope and then sitting down. The tingling in my hands and feet begins to subside and I sip my hot coffee, savouring its bitter taste.

I reach across to the envelope and pick it up, turning it over in my hands, watching as dad's unmistakable scribbled Sophie disappears and reappears.

'There you go,' the lady says as she places the bacon sandwich down in front of me.

'Thank you,' I reply and as she walks away I open the envelope.

Inside, as predicted, is my birthday card. On the front there is a picture of a white teddy bear holding a pink balloon with HAPPY BIRTHDAY written on it. I smile and open the card and another smaller envelope falls out onto the table. I ignore it for a moment and read the inscription in the card.

To my little angel Sophie,

As your grandparents will have told you, this is to be the last birthday card you receive from me. I wish I could have been there for each of the passing years to give those cards to you myself on your birthday but this is how it has had to be.

I love you Sophie, and I always will. You are the light of my life and now, on your Thirtieth birthday, I hope that you are happy in your life. I miss you and I always will.

*Dad
xxx*

This is the first year I have read one of dad's birthday cards through another person's eyes but even still I can feel the tears welling up. I close the card and kiss the white teddy bear, whispering under my breath, 'I love you daddy' and then placing the card underneath The Divine. I next turn my attention to the bacon sandwich. I need to keep this body fuelled to keep the tiredness at bay. I devour it in seconds, marvelling in the meat's saltiness.

God I miss food so much.

I rip open the second smaller envelope and tip out its contents, two photographs and a folded sheet of paper. The first photograph is of dad holding a tiny baby in his arms and smiling at the camera. He is wearing a white shirt and jeans and he stands in front of granddad and grandma's house leaning on the bonnet of a car. He is how I always remember him, the deep brown eyes and almost black tousled hair, giving way to an easy smile. I flick the photo over and written on the back it says Eric and baby Sophie Feb 1985. I am two months old in that picture.

Placing the photograph down I pick up the second one, this much older, the edges frayed with time. I read the faded inscription on the back, proud Godfather Eric and baby Alan, 3rd September 1934.

Something stirs deep inside me, adrenaline.

The baby in the picture is my granddad. I know this before even flicking the photo over and taking a look because

Granddad's birthday is 3rd of September, he was born in 1934 and his Christian name is Alan. I take a deep breath to try and steady the tremors in my hands and turn the picture over. The photograph is black and white or sepia as I believe the correct term for the colouring is, and standing there in much the same pose as before, baby cradled in his arms, is my dad. He smiles out at the camera, the same easy going smile showing anyone who might pick this picture up and look that he is the proud Godfather of this new arrival. He is stood inside a nondescript doorway wearing an old fashioned double breasted suit. The baby is wrapped up in a light coloured blanket and appears to be sleeping.

How is this even possible? Is it a hoax? I study the older picture. It appears legitimate but how is my dad there holding his new born father in his arms? What does this mean?

I place the photographs down side by side onto the table, pick up the piece of paper, unfold it, and read.

Dearest Sophie,

This is the hardest letter I have had to write in my entire life. By now you will no doubt have looked at the two photographs and you will have so many questions racing around your head and clouding your judgement. As with any family ours has secrets, skeletons locked in closets.

Please read the book that comes with this letter, The Divine, and read it with an open mind because you will need that if nothing else.

I love you my baby.
Now and for eternity

Dad xxx

I look up from the letter towards the book. My host's heart is racing in her chest and with each thud I feel another wave of tiredness overcome me. I pick up both of the photographs again and study them, each time dad smiles back at me, telling me to read on and discover the truth behind his ability to pose for photographs fifty-one years apart without aging a single day.

With another sip of my coffee I pick up the book and open the front cover. *THE DIVINE by Mr E.* I turn a couple of pages further and rest upon the first chapter entitled *A New Dawn*. My tiredness is beginning to tunnel my vision, a sure fire indicator that soon I will be battling to stay awake but stay awake I must. I cannot afford to jump back right now. I start to read.

A NEW DAWN

It is widely accepted these days that man evolved from apes, and that if we traced our ancestry back through the ages all of man and today's apes would arrive at one being, the common ancestor. Slowly through time our mother ape's offspring branched out into many different species, but it was the evolution of man which would shape the world in which we now live. Indeed it was man who conquered the earth.

Although hard to imagine the early days, through thousands and then millions of years, mankind's path spewed off from that of the apes creating new species. Man evolved from Homo-habilis to Homo-erectus, and then finally to the Homo-sapien. At each point along this journey man changed, his brain growing larger and with it he learned new tricks to hedge his chances of survival on the earth. From fashioning tools to help him hunt, the discovery of fire, creating shelter and then communities, agriculture, religion, war, construction, industry, and technology, man's destiny as the planet's dominate species has spiralled him to the top of the food chain where he has remained indefinitely. The survival of their species was down to their larger brains which, in turn, have guaranteed them their mantel.

Let us go back for a moment, back to our mother ape. While we moved on through the ages she and her species died out, but we were not alone on this journey. Our cousins, whose ancestors and ours is the same, are today's Orang-utans, Gorillas, and Chimpanzees.

Over millions of years we all divided and went our separate ways, and then our particular species split again, creating a sub-species. It is believed that around three hundred and fifty thousand years ago five separate species of human lived on the earth at the same time and for about seventy thousand years. It is believed also that these five 'brothers', Homo-erectus, Homo-ergaster, Homo-neanderthalensis, Homo-heidelbergensis, and Homo-rhodesienis lived in different parts of the world, although whether they fought, lived separately in their own communities, or even cross bred with one another is unknown.

Now a new dawn is upon us.

Although I can tell you that evolution's new dawn has been rising for eight hundred years, I cannot begin to estimate when my kind and mankind split.

Am I an ambassador for the next step in mankind's journey?

Is my kind a sub-species of the Homo-sapien?

Is the Homo-sapien's time coming to a close?

These are questions I cannot answer, and I know by writing this memoir I will be putting not only myself, but my entire species under threat.

History has shown me time and time again that Man exterminates what he does not understand and so fears. It would be nice to say through time Man has evolved in himself and learned the true nature of his namesake humanity, but this would be untrue. He has simply modified his methods through technology of culling that which he does not understand.

Man will fear us and a new war will be fought, not for religion or politics, land or wealth, but for fear of us, the unknown, the Divine. And I fear we still number so few that we will be slaughtered instead of embraced.

A new dawn is upon us all, we are the Divine and we are amongst you..

12

BILLY: RUNNING

Walking out onto the terrace I am greeted with a cheer by the whole Fielding clan. Despite learning moments earlier of my cousin Sophie's actual existence I know there is nothing I can do while I am here. As soon as I get back to the UK though I am going to go find dad and giving him the biggest bollocking ever. All this time she has been out there somewhere.

'Glad you could join us,' Lisa says with a smile and I catch Paul's eyes. He is busying himself with a piece of toast and chocolate spread.

Pushing the little girl in the park to the back of my mind I return Lisa's smile and say, 'couldn't seem to sleep last night, something kept me up,' to which Lisa raises her eyebrows and giggles.

Paul then passes me an orange juice and I sit down, happy to kick back and watch the family go about their holiday breakfast.

Crickets buzz around the pristine gardens which look out over Fish Hook bay. The morning sun is bearing down on us with the promise of more of the same as the day progresses and I grin like an idiot as I listen to Jan and Ian (Parents) talk of their plans to go to the Waterfront, a quayside shopping centre with bars and restaurants overlooking Table Mountain, for a spot of lunch later.

'Any takers?' Ian asks the table which nudges me out of daze.

Lisa and Melissa opt in for the excursion and Ian then turns his attention to the boys, me and Paul. Paul shakes his head as he swallows the last of his toast and says, 'nah, Bill and me are off for a wander down the beach and then maybe into Simons Town to Boulders.'

Jan and Ian smile at this and Jan says, 'oh Billy you will absolutely love Boulders. It is where a colony of Jackass Penguins nest, there is a little lagoon to swim in with them and plenty of boulders, obviously, to jump off into the water from. You'll have a blast.'

I turn to Paul who, although is aware I am staring at him, doesn't meet my gaze.

Ian claps his hands together and stands up from his seat, 'right then, I'm off for a shower, girls, make sure you are ready to leave in forty-five minutes, lads, have a great time bumming around the beach. We'll see you this afternoon.'

He and Jan disappear back into the house and Paul perks up, slapping me on the arm saying, 'right Billy boy, first port of call is the beach to checkout any hot bronzed beauties who might be out for a swim.'

Although he is talking to me, I watch him watching Lisa for a reaction.

He knows.

Fuck.

Or is he just testing the water, playing the game and trying to get Lisa to reveal all by her reaction to his comments.

Lisa, as cool as ever, laughs at this, 'at this time in the morning the only bronzed beauties down on the beach will be the retired expats. I didn't know geriatrics were what you guys went for these days.'

Melissa too joins in with the giggling and I smile, 'yeah mate, not really my thing eyeing up the wrinkled inhabitants of the bay.'

I wait for Paul to crack a grin but he doesn't, instead he simply shrugs and stands up, 'suit yourself mate, I'm heading down there anyway.'

'Wait, Paul, where you off?'

'To get into some swimming shorts,' he says without turning back as he heads into the house.

Lisa motions with her eyes for me to go after him and like a good little boyfriend I do as she silently suggests.

I catch up with Paul just as he is about to enter his room and spin him around to face me, 'what's up mate, you seem well off today?'

Paul frowns for a second, I can see the betrayal there in his eyes, the vulnerability and upset, a moment later though it is gone and he wears the mask, with his grin and cocky self-assurance, well, 'sorry mate, nothing, just a bit grouchy this morning. I didn't sleep well either, kept up half the night by creaking beds.'

He definitely knows. The creaking bed was mine because his baby sister and I were creaking the hell out of it. Bloody creaks, why the hell doesn't anyone oil those damn things?

'Look Paul…'

Paul holds up his hands, 'come on, I'll meet you out the front in five.'

I am there and waiting moments later, apprehensive about the conversation which will now ensue between us. I imagine he will swing for me and I suppose I deserve the punch. I have been fucking his sister for the past nine months and haven't bothered to let him know. What kind of a mate does that make me?

George, the gardener, approaches me and nods, 'howzit boss.'

'Not too bad mate,' I tell him as he offers his hand and I shake it.

'Going to be another lekker day today, plenty of braais and beers later I hope?'

'Well this *is* a holiday George, it'd be rude not to,' I say, not really sure what lekker or braai is.

'Miss Lisa is growing up into a beautiful young lady yes?'

Fuck, why would he say this? Does the fucking gardener know I'm fucking '*Miss Lisa*' too?

'Yes.'

'But mister Paul always a jealous and possessive big brother?'

'Don't I know it pal.'

'Be more careful boss, if I see you so does mister Paul.'

He then walks off, picking up a rake which leans by the wall and attacking a small lawn at the side of the house. As I turn I find Paul by my side and grin, 'we all set for playing on the beach matey?'

Paul smiles, 'of course,' clicking the fob for the driveway's electric gates, and we make our way down the road, side by side.

I now find myself in something of a predicament, I mean although I am sure from Paul's body language at the breakfast table and the comments he made that he knows about me and Lisa, he doesn't know that I know he knows and so I need to carry on as usual. This is going to be tough. Paul will play the part of not knowing, and that Paul will wonder why I'm not flirting with the natives. As much as I'd love to explain to him the reason I'm not looking is because I am in love with his sister, this is now a game of pretence and I will not be the one to crack. On the other hand, if I play along, umming and ahhing at the talent on the beach then Paul could easily voice my gazing's to the whole family later, landing me in hot water with Lisa.

So it's pretend to be on the pull, to act the way Billy acts with the unsuspecting Paul because that is how he would expect me to act, and then have Lisa at my throat later, or appear nonchalant around any young bikini clad ladies and Paul will question my reluctance to flirt, even though I am now sure he knows why.

This is all my fault, you see as cover for sneaking off for liaisons with Lisa I have developed a web of lies for Paul which paint me as a serial shagger on a rampage to stick my bits into every female on the planet. When asked where I was last night, or where I disappeared to so early at the party I will spin off a name and then a brief description about the lucky 'fake' lady I was with last night. Not only is this exhausting but it has also meant I've had to remember specific details about my made up life and the ladies which inhabit it.

I hope you're happy Lisa because all this has been for you and now I'm going to have to try and double bluff my way through today.

As we walk Paul plays tour guide, pointing out places of interest in the bay and I listen to him, watching for any sign that he might just lash out but it does not come. The paranoia is my own doing and after a while I begin to relax, convinced he is not going to kill me just yet.

It is beginning to get hot, ridiculously hot, with not much of a breeze considering we are now spitting distance from the sea. Paul slaps me on the back and heads off sprinting away from me.

'Come on Billy, I'll race you along the catwalk to the beach,' he calls back, leaving me in his wake.

Paul is fast, a sprinter who used to always win the 100m, 200m and 800m dashes back in high school. I on the other hand would usually be behind the proverbial bike shed during P.E, smoking or snogging whatever I could get my hands on. Right here and now though, with the sun beating down on my bare back and no bike shed in sight, I feel ready to burst with energy, my whole body is tingling and before I know it my walk has quickened into a stride, stride into a jog, jog into a sprint of my own and I'm running, flip-flops kicked off, my bare feet barely touching the hot stone pathway as I leg it after him.

I feel exhilarated, I feel free, and I feel myself speeding up more. I am running fast now and the ground between us is closing up. Paul glances back at me and I catch the twinkle of fear in his eye. He has always been immensely competitive and even this silly 'race you to the beach' will be taken seriously by him. He wants to win and now I want to beat him, now I will beat him, the conditions are perfect; the sun is my ally, powering me forward.

I catch up with him and laugh. His pace is beginning to slacken but still he pushes forward, taking to the rocks to the right of us, jumping across two and then landing back onto the catwalk, shortening the distance for him to the finish line, the beach. I too take to the rocks and we hop, skip and jump our way across, both still neck and neck. Up ahead I can see a great big boulder strutting out of the sea, it's a fair distance to jump to it and Paul sees it too.

'You'll never make it,' he pants, laughing as I lose my footing for a moment and he races ahead.

I spring back up, completely focused on that rock, trying to work out the best angle in which to jump and make the jump. Leaping back onto the catwalk I speed up, watching Paul in the corner of my eye as he continues to leap across the boulders. I can't believe I'm still going. Where is my stitch? Why am I not keeled over at the side of the path trying to catch my breath?

'You'll hurt yourself,' Paul calls to me but I'm not listening, all that matters is making this jump and landing on that boulder because then, for the first time ever, I will have beaten Paul in a race and maybe then I will be worthy in his eyes to see his sister. Maybe.

'I've tried jumping it a hundred times and have always landed in the sea.'

That's because you didn't have the sun powering you on my old friend, but I do. The rock juts out of the water about a hundred yards ahead of me, a solitary guardian of Fish Hook beach, and I power my legs faster than ever, anticipating the jump and following the straightest path that will lead to my lift off and victory.

Fifty yards to go and my whole body is tingling with the sun's rays, a billion Sammies going hell for leather. At the water's edge lies a single rock which will be my springboard over the water and onto my crowning glory. I concentrate on this rock now, adjusting my strides slightly so that my left foot lands on the very edge of the rock to give me more propulsion into the air. I bend my knees a little and as I jump know already that I have misjudged something, I am not going to make it. As I flay through the air I have a strange sensation something is amiss, the air feels thicker, like it is carrying me forward and higher than possible. The sun sparkles up at me in the sea's reflection and I hear rushing in my ears, a spike of pins and needles travels through my limbs and with this my concentration wains and I fall, splashing down into the cool waters of the bay. I hold my breath, not beaten yet as Paul will have stopped to search the water's edge for me, and swim under water, around the boulder and reach the beach, defeated but not beaten.

I almost had it, I could feel myself making the jump but then gravity got in the way. Stupid gravity. I watch Paul from the beach entrance still searching the water and call across to him. He turns and smiles, giving me a round of applause as he jogs towards me.

'Jesus Billy you almost made it.'

'I did?' I ask, looking back over his shoulder at the jagged guardian of Fish Hook beach.

Paul nods, 'another couple of feet and you'd have been the first person I've ever seen to land on that rock from the catwalk.'

I smile but it is only for his benefit. I could have made it. Something happened during my jump, almost as though I was willing myself across, the thickness of the air, the rushing in my ears. For a split second I felt as though I was in complete control of my jump and had been willing myself across. As stupid as it sounds that's how it felt.

Paul slaps my back and heads on past me, 'come on mate, there's a café over there. Let's grab ourselves a drink and then go for a swim. Unlike you, I haven't sampled the water yet.

PART TWO

BAPTISM OF LIFE

13

WILLIAM: *BAPTISM OF LIFE*

From what I am led to believe, and certainly what modern day historians have conjured up, I was born circa 1270. The second son of three, my father named me William. Tradition dictated a father names his first born son after himself, and keeping to such traditions the name William has followed me throughout my life.

In the year 1295 I was thrown in a Warders Prison an outlaw and a murderer where, after several months of being fed just crumbs of bread and rotting Herring, I slowly starved and, again as the history books say, fell into a coma. I'm sure these days some of my memories of this time in my life are false memories, made up from what I have read, but one such memory I do know to be very real is my awakening from the dead.

News of my death had travelled fast and then news of my subsequent return from the grave caused the soothsayer Thomas the Rhymer to declare:
For sooth, ere he decease,
Shall many thousands in the field make end.
From Scotland he shall forth the Southron send,
And Scotland thrice he shall bring to peace.
So good of hand again shall ne'er be kenned.
Whether or not the man actually did speak these words is irrelevant really. News of my great awakening led storytellers to begin their embellishments until my name became legend, and I suppose, at the age of twenty three years old this new found celebrity, in a time when there was no concept of fame, went to my head a little. I had stared death in the face and won, and now fearless, I knew where my destiny lay.

My legend grew, and with it support from my countrymen. We were to fight the oppression our country found itself under, and it was I, the second son of a mediocre Scottish landowner, who would lead the way. It wasn't until the battle of Stirling Bridge though when I found any wounds inflicted upon me would heal instantly.

My name now is unimportant, as I will be publishing this memoir either anonymously or simply by the pseudonym William, my name back then was Wallace and this is my story.

Others who pen their memoirs do so when their lives are coming to a close to try and find some sense to this crazy journey called life, but as I don't appear to suffer from the same affliction as those authors who have gone before me, I think that now I have waited for long enough. Still I search for others like me and I hope these pages reach them well.

It can be a lonely road to infinity if walked alone. This is my story, the story of my immortality, this...

'Sorry Sir,' says the voice behind me after a brief knock on my office door. I stop reading and turn in my chair, smiling at the student in front of me.

'Nay bother,' I tell him, a quick nod to a life I once lived. I clear my throat as I register the pupil's expression on hearing his stuffy Professor's Queen's English being momentarily replaced by a thick Celtic brogue. 'Sorry about that,' I tell the lad, motioning him to a chair, 'frog in my throat.'

The boy smiles and sits, rifling through his ring binder and I wait, trying to recall if he is a student from my Medieval History or Genetics class. He answers my musing with a question about Darwin, a man whom I would have like to have gotten to know during his lifetime as I have spent the past century catching up with his theories of evolution. Unfortunately we never met because during the nineteenth century I was across the pond in the frontier towns, a place people now call the Wild West. I still sometimes have nightmares now about the atrocious savagery we showed the natives during our constant push towards the Pacific, and also how...

'Sir?' my student says, bringing back to the present for a second time in as many minutes.

'Sorry son,' I tell him, shaking my head to try and clear my thoughts and before he can utter another word I ask him, 'were you in class this morning?'

He nods.

'And William...sorry, Billy Johnson, do you know him?'

Another nod and then a smile, 'yeah Billy's a mate of mine, we share a student house with three others and...' a little hesitation and then, '...as it happens I'm meeting him for a drink when I finish here.'

'And his essay paper which I so publically awarded an F grade, have you read it?'

'Yes I have read it and I thought it was fun.'

I smile. If only he knew how close Billy had come to hitting the proverbial nail right on the head.

I lean across my desk and begin explaining what direction the lad should take when answering the essay question I set this morning but my mind is wandering.

It's true there are internet websites dotted about with theories mirroring Billy's red cape and invisible man essay. These are silly pages packed with grave inaccuracies. Some believe there are people who have evolved into a new species and this is where their different 'powers' come from (survival of the fittest). Others believe it is God bestowing God like powers on the few to guard the many from danger (angels). Creation Vs Evolution, a debate which has been fought for many years. I can't answer where my ability to regenerate at an alarming rate comes from, nor can I explain why I have not yet died, and throughout my life I have supported both sides of the debate, gaining much and nothing from each.

There are others out there, the Divine, they are scared and I understand why.

The history of mankind is littered with examples of how the many exterminate the few. Indeed, that was King Edward longshanks' view when we fought his armies and then took the fight to him, and like longshanks, if the human race were to find there were a more powerful being than themselves walking amongst them, they too would try to exterminate us all. I have seen it a hundred times. Mankind does not change, and at the turn of the twentieth century I almost paid dearly when another one of God's supposed angels tried to kill me.

Now, I am not sure what would happen to an immortal man if he was tied to an anchor and thrown into the depths of the Atlantic, but I know I am no fish. The ability to survive underwater eludes me and it is for this reason that when faced with the gang of men wanting to silence my musings of where it is people like us came from, I literally jumped ship. Hypothermia, however unpleasant, I knew I could survive.

I turn back to my son's friend and smile, 'Billy's alright isn't he...I mean, he's doing ok, he's not unhappy in his life?'

He shrugs, 'yeah, Billy's cool. He's having trouble sleeping at the moment but I think the falling has stopped now. It got really bad at one point...'

'Falling?' I interrupt.

'Yeah, you know when you're almost asleep and then you jump, waking yourself up back into consciousness? Billy went through a good six months of that happening ten, twenty times a night. In fact it got so bad at one point he was keeping the whole house up with his leaping out of his bed and landing on the floor."

'But that has now stopped?'

He nods, 'Almost, certainly in its regularity. It's only now and again we are woken up to a crash and then a groan and curse in the middle of the night.'

A smile from the housemate, and I wonder if Billy's sleeping pattern is a house joke, Billy is always ready to laugh at his own expense. I really need to make more of an effort to spend some father-son time with him. I can't remember the last time we sat down and simply chatted about anything and nothing.

'When you see him later could you ask him to give me a ring over the weekend?'

The housemate appears slightly taken aback by my request but then nods as he packs up his notes and thanks me for my time. As the office door clicks shut I turn back to the book and sigh. Having been interrupted I have now lost my flow and the memories feel stale. I read through the rest of the chapter and then close the book. I think back to a time when I thought the world was ready for The Divine. How wrong I was.

14

ERIC: THE HUNGER

It is dark again, but then that is not really any change for me. I am a man who lives his life within the cloak of darkness. The wind and rain sweeps mercilessly through the isolated graveyard and somewhere in the distance the flicker of a lightning bolt illuminates the evil sky. It is, after all, an evil night.

As I kneel before the crumbling gravestones of those long since passed, I weep. So many having lived full and happy lives and then, as nature intended, passed away to make room for their offspring to do the same.

I am one of the exceptions to the rule.

Somewhere along the line I slipped off Mother Nature's table and disappeared into the abandoned shadows of existence.

I can feel it inside me now, the hunger mounting like sulphuric acid on the tongue, and unless the doctor arrives soon I will once again be a slave to that hunger and look to seek my fill.

Kissing the granite which now represents an old man I once watched grow from a boy, I stand, pulling up the hood on my trench coat and disappearing into the night.

'Eric, you have enormous power, and if you will just work with me I believe we can cure the terrible afflictions which you suffer as part as your gift,' the Doctor's words echo through the night to me. Those words always filled with such urgency.

What on earth is there to be urgent about Doctor? Neither of us is going anywhere any time soon. Where you get to live your lives and bask in the glory of civilisation, I spend my eternity trapped to the darkness, labelled a monster by society and shunned out into the cold. Yes I have killed in cold blood but so have you Doctor. We are the same person only we live on opposite sides of the fence.

Walking on through the graveyard I can see houses past the stone all's perimeter. Everybody is indoors and out of the wind and the rain with their loved ones, watching television, surfing the web, eating dinner, settling in for the night, cosy in front of the fire. I can remember when there were real fires, not the new gas and electric gadgets civilisation warm themselves in front of nowadays, but wide open fire places. Those fires would fill all of the rooms in the house with smoke and cause you to cough the next morning but they didn't half keep the chill from you bones. Before that I remember fires set in the middle of camps, a focal point for whole communities and children running around them naked, their mothers chasing after them.

It is sad reminiscing over the lives I once lived but at the same time that sadness fills me with joy, or at least maybe a satisfaction of knowing I still have my emotions and the hunger has not raped me of them yet.

Not yet.

The church clock chimes eleven times and I make my way from the yard, keeping to the undergrowth for my own protection as much as anyone else's. As the wind downsizes towards a breeze I catch the scent of an animal, possibly canine, and the distinct foulness of rotting meat on the animal's breath almost turns my stomach. I read somewhere once that in Korea they eat dog meat as a dish, out of choice. Even the thought of it revolts me; I mean their blood is dreadful enough, even when the hunger is in full swing, but to digest the meat...

Using the shadowed silhouette of a cluster of conifer trees I float upwards, my hunger now subdued from the concentration it takes for me to levitate myself. The initial floating had come to me quite quickly after the change; it was learning to control direction and speed that has taken time.
As I soar high enough into the sky so I don't catch the eye of the local man walking his dog, I sigh heavily into the storm and will myself over to the church roof. Sitting down next to

the frozen gargoyles that surrounded me I pat the closest spiritual scarecrow on the head and smile at the irony. These demons were posted on top of churches and cathedrals throughout the world to keep the mythical likes of me away:

> Evil spirits do not come near
> We are Gargoyles, you can see us clear
> Surrounding our homestead to provoke much fear
> Move on sons of Satan, you're not welcome here.

The thing is though, history and the myth makers have got it all wrong. I am no son of Satan.

At my grandson's funeral in the nineteenth century I had been exiled from society. How was it a man did not age and yet all around him everyone else did? Over the years prior to my grandson's death he would come and visit me, and I him. We were very close and I was close also to his family, I adored his wife and children. Of course Benjamin knew about my refusal to age, and always he played along, introducing me as a distant nephew to his family. The problem came in the shape of an elderly minister who had put two and two together and come up with six six six.

'*You sir are the nephew of the late Benjamin Woodley?*' the minister asked me after Ben's funeral.

'*Yes father I am,*' I had told him.

There had then been hushed words between the minister and a few of the local men and women, the occasional glance in my direction and finger pointed my way, and then the minister approached me again.

'*What do you have to say to the allegations that you sir are in fact the grandfather of the deceased?*'

What could I have possibly told the man?

'*Yes father it is true, this family is not my first and nor do I imagine it will be my last. It is a lonely path that my life journeys down and I spend my time traveling from place to place, changing my name, starting families when I fall in love and then eventually having to move on and leave them because men like you will not leave me in peace.*'

I would have been hanged to no avail right there and then.

'Who father, would suggest such a preposterous remark?' I had asked, and then came forward an elderly gentleman I remember as a neighbour of my son's household some thirty years previous.

'You sir are Richard Woodley,' the gentleman said, 'and I have watched all my life as your family grew older and yet you stayed youthful... The devil,' he spat.

It wasn't the first time I had been called such and there was a time when I kind of liked the idea of a persona, but in another time and place it is sometimes easy to at first live up to and then turn into that what people expect of you. I talk now of my first life.

After the elderly neighbour's remark there was a riot and the whole town turned on me. I was branded an imposter, the walking dead, the devil himself, and I'm sure if a kind stranger had not stepped in right there and then I would have been buried alive.

That kind stranger, a new face to the town Dr William Steel, did step in and held the lynch mob back while I made my way out of my local church, the very same church in which I am sat upon now. I didn't see Dr Steel for a great number of years. It was 1916 and already I had spent two months in a trench watching my friends and country men die all around me. It was early September when Dr Steel, or rather Captain Johnson joined us at the Somme and up until then I was unaware of there being anyone else like me.

Looking up at the night sky the clouds part momentarily and I am basked in moonlight. The hunger, the beast, the sickness my condition endures, stirs restlessly, letting out a roar from within.

It is almost time.

Soon I will lose control of my senses, soon the veil of blood will fall down upon me and I will be powerless, soon the beast, the infection will have taken over my senses. It needs its feed and is relentless in its quest. The beast within, the hunger, has gripped me like a vice every night, lusting for blood and needing the blood of the living to take the pangs away, at least for a while. Then the beast will sleep and so too can I.

I can feel the thirst, and looking up at the church clock tower I whisper, 'Where is he,' to the gargoyles.

The mist is beginning to move in over my eyes. How long before I am at the hunger's mercy? Already I am beginning to fantasise about the taste of the red, how my lips would quiver as I lean my head down towards my victim's neck. That soft flesh beneath which lay my desired...

'STOP IT,' I scream out into the night, shaking my head violently from side to side.

I need to concentrate on something, anything, as long as it keeps me from turning. That is the hunger's great ally, the power of suggestion. It will leak those soft images into my head so I can almost smell the fear of my victim as I imagine draining them of their life.

I set off upwards, higher and higher up into the night sky, trying to outrun the plague that is burrowed deep into my psyche. My skin begins to tighten, another sign I am now delaying the inevitable. Higher and higher, searching the ever receding graveyard for the Doctor but he is not there. Thunder cracks and with it a bolt of lightning scorches the earth, lifting silhouettes from the surrounding streets into the night sky.

A scuffle.

Four figures, one of them fighting off the rest.

It appears the good Doctor may need my help as much as I do his.

15

WILLIAM: *BATTLE SCARS*

I have loved many women in my time, taken many wives, and given life to many sons and daughters. I do not feel my prolonged life has been a curse, indeed for almost two hundred years I have been on a quest to try and understand why it is my cells regenerate at such an alarming rate, and why only the very few have been granted such gifts.

I remember the first time I was shot, within minutes I was up and about as though nothing had happened. If it had been anyone else witnessing my radical recovery I believe things may not have turned out quite the same for me, but as it was, it was my Corporal who watched in amazement as my organs repaired themselves and then my chest cavity closed.

The year was 1916 and I had joined the 1st battalion of the York & Lancaster regiment two months into their campaign on the Somme. Having seen so much bloodshed already in my life when the Great War (the war to end all wars) broke I was happy staying out of this one. At the time I was passing myself off as a forty year old Professor of English at Cambridge University and was exempt from fighting in the war. It was only when I started to see more and more young men leaving the town to go and fight that I too signed up. I couldn't sit back and watch the mortal give their lives while I knew I could perhaps make a difference.

After passing basic fitness training we were shipped off to the Somme where I was awarded the rank of Captain. It was only a few days later while enjoying a quite cigarette on night watch when I was introduced to Corporal Chesterfield.

'Captain Johnson sir,' said a voice in the dark. I turned and saw no one but then into the moonlight moved Eric. 'I have been posted onto night watch with you sir.'

I smiled. It had been over a century and a half since I had saved Richard Woodley from his villagers questioning his mortality.

At first I believe he may not have recognised me, and if he did he certainly did not show it.

The first night on watch together was uneventful and we scarcely spoke. In the trenches there is much silence and contemplation, we are alone in this world and we hope to get back home to see our families.

'Who are you back home sir?' Eric asked me on the second night of our posting together. The sky was clear and the moon shone down upon no man's land like a search spotlight, looking to depict the enemy to both sides.

'I am a professor at Cambridge University, and you?'

My words hung on the cool night air for a very long time, so long in fact that I had almost forgotten returning his question back to him. Eventually he answered, his voice hoarse like the cries of the wounded we could hear further down the line, the day's casualties from no man's land.

'I am a student back home, studying to join the priesthood.'

'A very noble profession my good man, but why then, might I ask, do you find yourself on the Western Front? Surely you might find yourself exempt from enlisting if your path was for something greater?'

Eric then took his time to turn and face me before saying, quite clearly, 'the very same reason you find yourself watching over the tides of death night after night.'

I nodded at this. I had been wrong, the man had recognised me from his grandson's funeral and I would not shame myself to try and deny that Dr Steel had not been yet another alias. Instead I stood up from my perch and held out my hand. Eric grasped it with a firm grip and stood to meet my gaze.

'Why did you intervene that day three life times ago? How did you know?'

I shrugged my shoulders and told him, 'I have spent almost my entire life searching for men like myself, the divine who possess a further step in the evolutionary chain.'

Eric held out his hand, 'let me stop you right there because if not we will be a loggerheads with one another all night. I am a follower of the Lord, I respect your opinion but let us not discuss the point of origin of our gifts because you will think me naive just as I will see you as a blasphemer.'

Although I wanted him to listen, although I felt I needed to sit him down and talk to him about natural selection, explain how the myth of a God was in fact instilled upon civilisations long before either of us as a form of control, and that the first worshiping civilisations in fact worshiped the earth, making them naturists and, in a sense, none believers also, I felt to follow this course might alienate my new found comrade.

Instead I simply nodded and said, 'understood,' and then we spoke at length of our experiences. While I imagined us the same many years ago when I came by the quiet Mr Woodley living in the rural Cumbrian dales, throughout our discussions I found subtle differences in our evolutions which made me question my theories of how the divine came to live amongst man.

Back then I had yet to discover the likes of rapid cell regeneration, and DNA mapping was light years away, but I imagined us the next step. For the fittest to survive they had to adapt themselves to the ever changing world, and the most perfect form of survival would be to regenerate tissue mass quicker than it might diminish. In Eric I became aware of more startling feats of divinity, but first it seemed I would show my hand.

The day I was shot was the day almost our whole platoon was wiped out. We were ordered over the top and into no man's land to make a push for the German lines. Upon our briefing we were led to believe the enemy had all but vacated the trenches we were soon hoping to call our own. Throughout the morning heavy artillery bombarded our destination with the most awesome fire power no mortal man *could ever hope to survive, and with Corporal Chesterfield by my side we led the attack. No sooner had we made it out of our trenches we were annihilated with heavy machine gun fire, mortars, and the crack aim of German sharp shooters. Further forward we pushed, zigzagging across the barren landscape, through swampy foxholes and the cries of our dying comrades. And then I felt the wind being taken out of me not twenty yards from the enemy line, but still further I pushed forward, deafened by the constant stream of fire, blinded by mud kicked up from the ground, unaware all this time I was in fact the last man still upright and still pushing forward. Another shot, this time catching me in the arm and I was spun around with the sheer force. As I fell to my knees, my back now to the enemy, I surveyed the ground I had crossed, littered with the debris of the men who had followed me to their deaths. I was completely alone, and then, appearing from out of thin air Eric picked me up and lunged us both into a watery foxhole.*

'My God you're hit,' he cried out, his arm around my neck to keep my head from falling under the murky swamp, maroon with the blood of men lost underneath our feet.

I laughed at this comment for some reason. Maybe it was the shock and adrenaline battling through my system, I don't know, but when I peered down at my torso I watched with Eric as my fatal wounds healed. A few moments later I was as fit and as healthy as the day William Wallace was hung drawn and quartered for the baying crowd at Smithfield in London. I stood in the crowds that day and watched as my doppelganger was tortured before being beheaded, but that is another story.

'Are you ready for that final push sir?' Eric shouted into my ringing ears as I knelt forward, heaving at the stench of the rotting bodies which shared our hole.

Later Eric told me I had grinned wildly at this suggestion and charged with a feral like fury spurring me on. As we reached the enemy's line Eric appeared to jump the barbed webbing which was there to keep us out, landing upon two German soldiers and as he gutted one with his bayonet he sunk his teeth into the neck of the second, ripping out his jugular and then gutting this man also.

It was a massacre. Two invincible English knights against the frightened army of the Hun. We were both awarded medals for our courageous valour, but unfortunately both Eric Chesterfield and Captain William Johnson were killed in action upon their next skirmish in no man's land. Neither of their bodies were recovered and given a proper Army burial, but hey, that's life.

I had found a contemporary with whom I shared a bond which most of humanity would not understand. We were the same but different, and as the Great War ended Eric and I travelled across the Atlantic to America. In order to understand our gifts we would need to employ only the brightest teams of scientists to help us figure out what exactly are gifts were and how they worked. This would need money, and in 1919 prohibition in the United States enabled us to earn more money than we would ever need. It was also in the year 1919 that I found out to what extent Eric's gifts had hold over him as well as he over them.

I often enjoy finding myself transported back to a much simpler time, when the grey areas in society were few. Man knew right from wrong, man policed his own life, and if man was wronged then he would seek to put that wrong doing right. Things change, friends, family, and loved ones die, and I move on. It seems it is just Eric and I who are destined to walk hand in hand upon this earth for all of eternity. I have found few others with the ability to live beyond their years and this worries me somewhat. It means, for one, that Darwin was inaccurate in his theory of evolution. Maybe I still have a long search ahead, or maybe I am not looking hard enough. I know there are people out there who can do some amazing things, and I wish they would help me help us all to understand our purpose on this earth. Darwin's theory of evolution through natural selection states the purpose in life is to reproduce, to pass on life so that future generations can do the same, and slowly throughout time all species will either adapt to their ever changing world or die out. If this is true then why have I watched my sons and daughters live and die so many times over?

    With all of them long dead and buried I am beginning to feel like maybe time is running out for me. There are people in this world who know about me, although only one or two a century has always been my rule. When too many discover the impossible they begin to wonder if there is any personal gain in this knowledge. I have, in the past, trusted too many a man at once with my secret so that they could help me discover more like me quickly, for their lives are short. This has always ended badly and resulted in me having to disappear, assume a new identity, and often slay the betrayers. Despite this my search must continue. It is what drives my very existence. To figure out the big why am I here is all that really matters in the end.

16

ERIC: FEEDING FRENZY

The beast stirs deep within me. It is both physical and psychological, controlling my impulses, controlling my thoughts. When the beast's hunger takes hold I am powerless to stop the onslaught and yet my physical power increases tenfold, my senses sharpen to an alarming clarity, I can hear the beating of a small rodent's heart from two hundred paces, smell the rot on the breath of a distant pack of wolves, and see with startling clarity on a moonless night.

My body changes, it is in hunting mode and it hunts efficiently for what it craves. The blood. The warm merlot causing through every living being's system, their life-force, their life. The beast yearns for that life force so that I too can live. Without the blood I am crippled in an incredible agony. The hunger screams for its fill.

I am a prisoner of my condition, I am a merciless predator. The beast is the incarnation of my first life. He still stirs deep down inside me no matter how much I might try to change my ways. Through my time I have massacred hundreds of thousands of men, fields of dying soldiers impaled on spears and crying out in agony lie in my wake. Back then I was a monster and my curse for my actions is the hunger.

At first I develop a thirst which no amount of water seems able to quench, then over the space of a day or two, as my senses begin to hone and the beast stirs, my mind can think of nothing else but blood until it is time to take a life and be rewarded.

But since the end of The Great War I have cheated the beast. To stop the senseless massacre triggered by my hunger the Doc stepped in and, apart from a few relapses, has become my own personal blood bank. On a weekly basis he donates a litre of his own blood to keep the beast at bay.

In my first life the blood and my insatiable appetite for it *became* my life. I am the original Vampire, cursed with this hunger which, if left to fester turns me into no more than a prowling animal. The Doc's blood sedates this part of me and for that I am eternally grateful. We have spoken at great length about the beast, about its origin, the doc has run tests, tried to understand why my body craves the blood and why I need it to function. Like a lot of the big questions about our lives though, the jury is still out on that one and so we just keep on keeping on.

The storm rages.

Thunder and lightning battle the torrents of rain for control over the sky, and in the midst of this battle for supremacy I move effortlessly through the wind, the hunger now prowling for a kill. A shock of lightening illuminates the sky and the silhouettes of four men bounce into the clouds. I turn and the beast watches with interest as three men approach a fourth. There are raised voices, muffled in the wind and rain.

The Doc.

We meet in this graveyard whenever I call upon a donation and now three mortals are standing in the way of that. I follow the wind's path through the sky, passing over a small row of houses, up high and cloaked in the darkness.

'We want your money.'

A flash of steel in one of the assailant's hands, and another produces a gun.

I watch the Doc and smile when he does. The threat of extreme violence lost its worth a long time ago and these days when one is made it almost appears comical. You shoot me and it will hurt, you stab me I will cry out in agony, you take a hammer to my head and beat me into a bloody pulp and I will suffer, but I *will* survive, I *will* rise up again and I *will* make sure me taking your blood is the last thing you see on this Earth.

'I am not here to cause any trouble guys,' the Doc says, ever the diplomat.

'Hand over your wallet and car keys and we will be on our way,' one of the delightful ambassadors of twenty first century youth says.

The Doc shakes his head, the smile turning into a grin, and I can almost feel the warrior inside him rising to the surface. There was a time when this man would think nothing of slaughtering all three of them where they stand. But as he has told me on many occasions, it is important for us to change with the times, to live in the moment, and to blend in, live in plain sight.

I silently lower down behind the livestock. They have their backs to me and are approaching the Doc. Over the shoulder of the one with the gun I nod to the Doc and he rolls his eyes at the inconvenience.

'What is it you are really here for gentlemen?' he asks, giving them one last chance at the rest of their lives.

I can feel their heart's beating in unity, the adrenaline soaring through their veins. My whole body is alive with the hunger, my heart beats with theirs, connecting to their life source. The beast stirs and he is famished. I hear my breathing getting heavier and beyond my razor sharp tunnelled vision one of the walking blood bags turns.

'Get the fuck out of here prick,' he shouts to me, pulling out a small axe and swiping through the air with it.

'What do you boy's want?' the Doc asks, opening his arms and inviting them to attack.

'We have a message for you,' one of the group growls, pulling an envelope from the inside of his jacket. 'But before you get this we want your wallet and keys to your car.'

I hear something to my right and turn. A young girl, perhaps sixteen years old, waves to me as she walks from the shadows of the underbrush and into the glare of the street light. I sense no fear from her and watch as she sits down on the sloping garden lawn beneath her bare feet. She smiles and beckons me over. My movements are quick and I am in front of her in seconds.

'Leave,' the beast growls as I use all of my will power not to attack.

She smiles and lies back on the grass, shaking her head and reaching her arms out above her, trailing the sodden grass and earth in her fingers, 'no, you should leave,' she says, a Caribbean lilt to her words.

Turning back to the Doc's assailants I watch as they attack. Axe man screams out as he swings wildly, pushing forward and sinking his weapon into the Doc's collarbone. Instantly the air turns red and all that I see now is the Doc's blood spurting from his body. The girl is forgotten as I fly up high into the night and roar with delight, descending upon my prey.

The youth with the knife runs towards the Doc and I drop down directly in his path, gripping him by the neck and then taking off again into the air. He screams in terror, looking down over the road on which moments ago he was stood.

'What the fuck man,' he yells and I move my mouth in over his neck, digging my teeth deep into his jugular. He cries out for only a moment before the shock takes away his breath and I drink deeper, his life force causing down my throat. I watch the street from over my victim's shoulder. Below I see knife man charge the Doc and watch as the Doc is stabbed in his abdomen. He cries out into the night and then snaps the man's neck with one swift movement. Three shots sound out and this brings me back from my blood lust.

The thirst now quenched, the beast sedated, I discard axe man and watch as his lifeless body falls back to earth, slowly head over feet, landing with a crash through a nearby residential house's roof. I follow the body back down and as I reach the ground watch the Doc take a fourth bullet, this time in the side of his head. His body too drops to the ground and there is blood everywhere, glistening like a pool of black tar seeping into the wet road.

The Doc will survive as he always does but his attacker…

I am in front of him now and I reveal myself, head lowered, breathing steady. Although he doesn't show it outwardly I can feel his fear, smell it like a bad stench.

'How…how did you do that? You just appeared from out of nowhere.'

I raise my head and look the man square in the eyes. He is young, perhaps twenty, possibly younger.'

Behind him, on the front lawn of a house the young black girl still lies there only now her body is motionless. I hardly notice the youth discharge his firearm into my chest two times but the force of impact knocks me back, away from my intended victim. For a few seconds I double over trying to catch my breath as the gun continues to click over empty chambers.

I cough, feeling the hot spike of pain subside, and look back up with a smile, 'you should have brought more bullets,' I tell him and then we are in the air, twisting and turning upwards as he fights to be released. I of course oblige and watch as he falls back to earth with a deathly shriek.

'Doc,' I call out when he stands back up from the pool of his own blood and walks over to the youth whose neck he snapped, reaching down into the man's pocket to take out a piece of paper. He looks up into the sky at me but as I move towards him he then takes off in the opposite direction at a speed unmatched by any mortal man. From the sky I follow him, up the lane he sprints, gaining speed with each footfall, through the graveyard and around the church toward the car park. Beyond there stands a rocky quarry with a gruesome hundred foot fall to the bottom.

What is he doing?

'Will?' I call out to him but there is no response as he leaps over the side of the quarry edge. I lower myself to the ground and peer into the quarry basin. The Doc lies in a second pool of his own blood, still, motionless, and if he were mortal he would undoubtedly be dead.

Lowering myself down towards him I call out again, 'quite the theatrical conclusion don't you think Will?'

He sits up and looks around, 'what the fuck just happened? One second I am teaching that young man the error of his ways, the next…'

He holds his hands out, searching and then looks up at me, 'what the hell just happened Eric?'

'You ran, you leant down over that boy's body, took a note from his jacket pocket and then you ran.'

The Doc pats himself down for the note he took and finds it crumpled up in his trouser pocket. Taking it out he glances up at me and I see fear in my friend's eyes. 'My blood, Eric, it is now all over the scene of a triple murder.'

I shrug, it is not the first time we have left bodies in our wake and I doubt it will be the last. As he starts to read the note I tell him there was a young girl too and how surreal her even being there in the middle of a stormy night in the company of three…She may still be there.

I shoot up into the sky and speed back to the scene, leaving the Doc to read his note. In the distance I hear sirens and as the flicker of neon blue arrives below me I see that the young girl who had walked from the shadows into the storm, barefoot and wearing only nightwear, and had lay herself down on the wet grass and told me I needed to leave, is gone.

When I get back to the quarry basin the Doc is sat on a rock with a strange smirk on his face.

'The police, ambulance service and fire service have arrived. I think it's time we disappear.'

The Doc nods but doesn't move, his eyes transfixed on the piece of paper he holds in front of him.

'Doc,' I shout.

He looks up at me and then nods, 'in less than an hour the police forensics will arrive at the scene of three very bizarre murders. One of the victims had his vertebrae snapped, another fell through the roof of a nearby house and the third?'

'Also had a bit of a fall,' I tell him with a shrug.

'The Crime Scene Investigators will take the victim's blood samples and fingerprints. They will also contain the scene and search for anything which might shed light on how their deaths came about. That includes the pool of my blood from when I was shot. One of the bullets pierced the blood bag I was bringing for you.'

I sigh and nod. I know that this means for the second time in the Doc's life the police will have his DNA, linking him to those murders and the ensuing investigation.

'So it's time to leave?'

The Doc shakes his head, 'no, not yet,' he says, holding up the note in his hand, 'I have been called out Eric. A voice from the past has now issued me with an invitation to meet.'

A voice from the past? Considering the extensive pasts we possess the enormity of this is not lost on me. Another Divine wanting to get the Doc's attention and doing so by isolating him from the life he is currently leading.

'Who wrote the note?' I whisper.

He offers me the note to read and then says, 'my sister.'

17

WILLIAM: *THE DIVINE*

There have been many times during my life when I have questioned my existence. In the thirteen hundreds, once William Wallace was, to all intent and purposes dead, I felt a great burden lift from my shoulders. The man I was brought into this life as was dead and now I had the freedom to forge a new path of my own.

Back then I was an educated man for the times but there were questions I sought answers to and still do. Over the ages I have met very few like me and apart from Eric none were keen to join me on my voyage of discovery.

The question of what we are, as a species, is the big one.

Do I have it wrong and are we really 'Gods' or 'Angels' put here to protect mankind? Being a man of science I prefer to shy away from this notion. I do not possess a halo, my savagery in past lives would not do well in earning me one either, and if my feathered wings were ever going to sprout out of my back I would have thought after eight hundred years they would have made an appearance.

As a scientist I rely upon evidence to draw my conclusions from but so far there has been none. Indeed, before Eric came along there had been just two others I had come across over the years who I believed to be Divine.

I met the charismatic Count de Saint-Germain, a man who courted the limelight in society circles all over Europe, in the eighteenth century. I had the pleasure of dining with him in 1760 while working in Paris as a science professor. Before then I had heard the rumours, that there was a man whose skin does not age. The man was well read, well-travelled, charming, easy going and had a great scientific mind. We spoke for hours about the art of alchemy, a subject which the

Count was enthusiastic about, but when I pressed more about immortality the man clammed up.

There is of course many myths surrounding this man and there have been many sightings of the Saint-Germain up and down the ages. The Count spoke many languages and we conversed in several over dinner. After our meal we had agreed to meet for a nightcap at his room to talk some more. I wanted to persuade him that we may help each other in one another's work but he had left Paris quickly during our interlude.

Had I spooked him, having almost confessed to him that he was not the only immortal man walking the Earth? Maybe, I'll never know as I never met him again.

A few months later, while dining with the high society set I had managed to embroil myself within I bore witness to a fantastic tale told by an elderly Countess, Madame de Pompadour, the then aging mistress of Louis XV. She said she had known Count de Saint-Germain in Venice in the early 1700s and upon meeting him this time around she had been curious how it appeared he hadn't seemed to age a day in the fifty years since their first meeting. When she asked the man if it had in fact been his father she had known all those years ago the Count replied, 'No Madame, I myself was living in Venice at the end of the last and beginning of this century and I had the honour to pay you court then.'

'Forgive me but that is impossible,' the Countess had responded, 'the Count Saint-Germain I knew all that time ago was at least forty-five years old, and you at the outside are that age at present.'

The Countess told us he had then smiled and replied, 'Madame I am very old.'

When she questioned him further, stating that he must be nearly one hundred years old the Count had told her that such things were impossible and then proceeded to convince her that he was in fact the same man that she knew fifty years previous in Venice.

In this day and age living to the age of one hundred, for a mortal man, is possible. I add a year upon my own age *every summer. Maybe the Count does not. I might understand why this is when we do not age and I only wish I had met with him some more on my travels, but as my journeying took me across to the Americas to learn the native tongues, hoping to learn also of men or women like myself, St-Germain stayed in Europe and continued to court the Parisian high society. The man popped up throughout the rest of the eighteenth century and in writer Albert Vandam's memoir 'An Englishman in Paris 1843-1903' Vandam claimed to have met a man who bore a striking resemblance to Count de Saint-Germain but who went by the name of Major Fraser.*

He wrote: he called himself Major Fraser, lived alone and never alluded to his family. Moreover he was lavish with money, though the source of his fortune remained a mystery to everyone. He possessed marvellous knowledge of all countries in Europe at all periods. His memory was absolutely incredible and, curiously enough, he often gave his hearers to understand that he had acquired his learning elsewhere than from books. Many is the time he told me, with a strange smile, that he was certain he had known Nero, had spoken with Dante and so on.'

Now, if these claims were true and St-Germain had known the Roman Emperor Nero then that would mean he would be closing in on two thousand years old. I could speculate forever about this man I met just once and tie him in with a whole manner of 'miracles' and magnificents which are now quite frankly considered Gospel. I only wonder why though, when I questioned him on immortality he was so reserved where in other documented instances the man has seemingly gushed about his secrets?

Perhaps one day I will have the pleasure in meeting with this intriguing gentleman again and asking him this.

Another who I found was the same as me came as quite a shock because I had loved and cared for this person centuries earlier. There had been a point where we had been inseparable but as our lives steered us in different directions we lost contact. I had no idea they were Divine and in hindsight, I probably should have.

This person, who I will not name, repaid the love and care I gave to them by accusing me of betraying them and then burying me inside an iron tomb for forty years until I managed to escape. I believe they were hoping I would remain there for eternity.

It was a nightmarish time those four decades of solitary but it taught me something new about my cell's regeneration, being that if starved of food and water my body will slowdown and hibernate. I was able to conduct a medical examination on myself periodically and found my heart was beating at a steady two beats a day thus delivering oxygen to my organs much slower than usual. Days, weeks, months might have passed during those dark times and will have felt like minutes as the connections in my brain also slowed to a near standstill. I was conscious but my mind was sluggish. This time of confinement became a time of reflection, to try and understand more what kept my body going and my body's limits.

It took me forty solid years to scratch my way out of my tomb which was in fact a cast iron coffin of sorts. Then I found myself buried deep in a forest in Scotland. By the time I reached civilisation again instead of embarking on a trail of vengeance I made the decision to simply continue on my quest to find more of the Divine.

I imagine my path will one day cross with my captor, and in writing this they will undoubtedly learn of my escape from the prison they entombed me inside. Let me just say that when our paths do again cross I will not be as kind as to bury their head still attached to their body.

Eric Chesterfield, my brother, my companion for the past hundred years, I met simply by chance. It appears for all my searching it is chance which leads me to my quarry and in finding Eric there was no exception.

Having studied science and medicine in several lives, I have been accustomed to being able to settle into any community when I grow weary of my travels. Dr William Steel was one such incarnation in which I felt like a rest.

I had spent the best part of a century traveling around the globe and decided it was time to relax for twenty or thirty years, to stop obsessing and searching for my kind, to forget about the meaning of the Divine's existence and simply live my life.

I chose a small Cumbrian town on the cusp of the Pennines to set up shop as the town's Doctor. My credentials were good, I had studied medicine ten years earlier at King's college and so in this life I was not required to forge my qualifications as I have previously had to.

Roaming through this life with infinite year ahead of me I have found education a fantastic stimulant and I have often excelled in many subjects. I am a professor of biology and natural history; I am fluent in twenty languages and can manage to hold conversations in another fifteen. Periodic history I have lived through and so have an eyewitness account which makes teaching about it simply a trip down memory lane. The subjects which interest have generally been the ones which might aid me on my search. Medicine was a given. To understand my own physiology I needed to understand that of my closest ancestor which is the Homo-sapian.

When the post of village Doctor arose in the small town of Kendal I was happy to fill it and so I set up shop as the village doctor. Not only am I fluent in many languages but my dialects, accents, in and around Britain are reasonably accurate. The broad northern gait I slipped into with ease won over the locals and I soon became one of them.

Small town gossip usually runs rife anywhere in the world and Kendal was no exception. Again, it was simply by chance one day that I overheard a couple of the old boys chatting in my surgery's reception area.

'You can't trust that family, keeping themselves to themselves like they do, living all the way out in the sticks on that farm and only coming into town for supplies and for church on Sundays.'

'Yep. That nephew of theirs I haven't seen for ten years although his uncle, old Benjamin, assured me last week that Richard still stays with them.'

If it hadn't been for the next remark I most probably would not have stopped dead in my tracks.

'Old lady Vera said she can remember the family when she was a girl, and even then she said she remembers Richard Woodley around, toiling the land and breaking in horses.'

'As a boy? I'd have not thought him over thirty-five now.'

'Well that's the thing, and old George Hillsop the town elder will confirm it, Richard hasn't appeared to age a day in three decades. He still appears in his mid-thirties now.'

This sent my adrenaline bouncing around in my veins. It was a similar story to that told by the Parisian countess a century earlier. The recluse Richard Woodley was one of the Divine.

In the following months I tried to get close to the man but found it impossible. He did not leave the Woodley farm and they seldom received visits. It wasn't until old Benjamin Woodley died that Richard ventured off the family farm to attend his grandson's funeral.

At the funeral Richard was called out, branded first an imposter and then the devil and I believe had I not intervened, knowing what I now know about my friend, there would have been many mortal deaths that day.

Richard fled the town he had called home with the family he had reared for one hundred and fifty years and soon after so too did Dr William Steel. Having once again stumbled upon one of my own I knew I would have to start again, to assume a fresh identity and continue my search for more people like me.

And so my search continued, but being a member of such an obscure and hidden ethnic group has been like looking for the proverbial needle…physically we appear just like man. It is only on the cellular level where there are differences. We once were you, before our 'awakening' as I like to call the moment our cells begin to regenerate rapidly.

Upon writing I am around seven hundred and forty years old, and in that time I have discovered only three others like me. Although it stands to reason there must be more, we hide well in plain sight and this leads me to the second big question I have no way of finding the answer to.

How many do the Divine number?

We are not mythical creatures created by God to roam the earth. And even if we were, which God would have created us? From vast experience on my travels I have learned that the Christian God is just one of thousands of Gods worshiped the world over.

The scientist and evolutionist inside me shuns this very notion and concentrates on the facts. We are born to mortal parents and at some point in our lives the rapid cell regeneration process kicks in which stops us aging and heals us whenever we are hurt. But, as fantastic as it is, is it only cell regeneration where our powers lie?

My thoughts return to my old acquaintance Count Saint-Germain who could quite possibly have been around at the time of Christ and also be able to pull off Christ's crucifixion and subsequent resurrection. Stories passed down through the ages have always had a habit of becoming legend and even 'gospel'. Eric has also had people write stories based upon him throughout history, indeed there is a certain Irish novelist who Eric befriended in the small town of Whitby in the late nineteenth century who has a lot to answer for. But that, as they say, is another story.

18

ERIC: THE KEEPER

I went back to the crime scene after the Doc left the other night. Remaining cloaked to the world I was able to wander amongst the investigating officers and crime scene specialists without any reproach.

I watched as samples of all spilt blood were taken, three victims and the Doc's. Of the blood, only three would match the victims while the fourth pool would be taken back to the police labs and run through their computer databases and DNA analysis machines so that they may get a positive match and identify its owner. It would then only be a matter of time before they found the Doc's blood sample has turned up once before on their network.

It was a few years ago and William had been out for a meal with his wife Anne in the city centre. Before returning home they had ventured forth for a night cap in one of the busy pubs. There had been a ruckus at the bar, someone had pushed in and gotten served out if turn and things had escalated. A fight broke out, William stepped in to try and calm things, a bottle was thrown and Anne was hurt and the one time saviour of Scotland retaliated with savage force which landed him in the police cells for the night and his DNA taken and stored on the police database.

Such a silly incident which wouldn't have merited mention if not for the fact that now the police will come looking for the Doc. The blood match will create the first lead, which they will pursue, tracking down the Doc and either inviting him in for questioning or arresting him on suspicion of murder. While the Doc is holed up in a police cell his blood would be analysed some more and there is always the chance the specialists find something in our DNA which distinguishes us from man. This is the reason the Doc feels he must disappear. Like a caged animal he looks for escape and our way has always been to flee. The most powerful species on the planet and at the first sign of trouble we run and hide to ensure our species' survival.

What the good Doctor has forgotten is he has an ally on this journey through life. Me. And although I am plagued with my insatiable hunger which at times controls my very being, I am also blessed with abilities neither of us understands.

There was a lot of head scratching at the scene, investigators throwing out theories left, right and centre.

How did one of the deceased fall through the roof of that house? Was there a plane? Who were the three murdered man fighting, themselves?

The theories continued into the early hours of the morning back at the police station where I accompanied the boys in blue, albeit an uninvited guest and cloaked to their world.

There was once a time when I would use my invisibility in order to acquire sensitive documents and state secrets from whichever enemy I was pointed in the direction of. As a once assassin for the highest bidder, my ability to cloak myself from view also came in handy. Needless to say, stealing the Doc's blood sample from the police lab wasn't very difficult at all. Things go missing in evidence all the time. I guess the three murders will just be another unanswered case.

There is a knock at my door and I call for the Doc to let himself in. He rang me earlier to arrange this meet and I'm guessing it is to say his goodbyes.

I take the bottle of scotch from the sideboard with two Waterford crystal glasses and begin pouring as the big man enters the room. He is wearing jeans and a thick pullover underneath his three quarter length coat and he smiles as our eyes meet.

'Drink?' I ask, holding out a glass.

He nods, 'It would certainly be rude not to on such an awful night.'

We head over to the fire and sit in companionable silence for a while. When you have spent so much time with another through the ages sometimes there isn't any need for words. We know each other too well to have to bother with the bullshit chit-chat the mortals feel compelled to enter into. There is no bravado between us, no one-upmanship, and to tell each other about our day grew tiresome in the early fifties.

I reach for the bottle for top ups and only when I have placed it back down by the side of my chair does William speak.

'How are you after last night Eric?'

'Hungry Will,' I shrug, turning in my chair to him and automatically searching his body for a bulge to indicate he has brought some blood.

He nods at this and smiles, catching my eyes dart over him, 'I didn't have time to make up a bag so it'll have to be fresh.'

He begins to roll up his right sleeve, exposing the flesh of his arm and asks me, 'what was it like, after all this time, to take a life again?'

I frown at this. For a man who questions everything he has never before questioned my hunger. In truth there was no sensation attached to the killing of those men last night. The hunger sought blood and theirs was at hand, it is as simple as that.

'I felt nothing. The hunger was all that drove my actions.'

He nods at this response, turning back towards the fire as I kneel down in front of him and feed. When I have finished and he has cleaned up the blood which has run down his arm, I sit back down and he says, 'you know my blood I was carrying for you last night is still at the crime scene?'

I nod.

'And the police will find it and then hunt me?'

Another nod.

'So that is why I must leave. Once a DNA analysis has been performed and matched my blood, the scientists will see that there are some irregularities. It is written in our genetic code Eric, our DNA sequence has altered slightly from that of man and this discovery will frighten them. They will hunt me and after that they will hunt my family, and so tomorrow I must leave.'

I shake my head, 'but why haven't they discovered these irregularities in your blood already, they have had a sample for years?'

'It will be stored on a database for safe keeping. It is only when a crime is committed and evidence has been collected that they run a check through that database.'

I reach into my pocket and pull out the sealed test tube with swab of blood contained inside it.

The Doc laughs, 'I should have known. Was it much trouble acquiring that?'

I shake my head 'much less so than acquiring the scalps of various SS officers once upon a time.'

The Doc reaches over and slaps me on the arm, thanking me. 'This means my family is safe but I still have to go.'

'Go where? You are walking out on your family when you need not,' I tell him.

'I was set up last night. Those thugs were there by design not chance, to deliver a letter and to spill my blood so that I would be backed out of the safety net of the life I have built. And then there was the blackout and me waking at the bottom of that quarry, you say you saw a young girl who had no reason to be there and when you returned to the crime scene she had gone. After thinking about this all night I believe that girl is like us but has an untold ability to control people. The girl, those thugs, they were all there for me and this is all down to Nessie.'

'Your sister.'

William nods, 'she wants to meet, says she represents others like us and it is time I am put to work.'

I stand up, the growling of the beast veering his head from within, 'I'm coming with you. She buried you in a metal coffin for forty years; you cannot trust anything she says.'

'That, my friend, is very true but I must go alone. I can't have you exposed to them, although I am in no doubt they are aware you are around still. Plus I have something to ask of you.'

Sitting back down the Doc takes my hand in his and kisses it, 'my dear boy we have been through more together than anyone could ever imagine. You are a wonder of this world with the feats you can display and the one person on this earth who I trust above any other.'

'Right back at you Doc, what do you need?'

'I need you to watch over Billy. There is something with the boy I am not sure about. His falling when he sleeps I think is the beginning of something more. I am going to see him off at the airport tomorrow evening, embarrass him no doubt because his stuffy professor father has come to wish him farewell for his holidays. Then I am going to leave this life and find Nessie.'

The boy?

In this life I have masqueraded as Will's brother and so I am known to Billy as Uncle Eric, and over the years have myself grown close to him. In the past William and I have both searched our linage for others like us, I spent two hundred years in touch with my Chesterfield legacy in the hope, because it stands to reason I would pass down my regeneration through my DNA, but this has never been so. Whether the genes which somehow turn off our aging and speed our regeneration are killed off with the merging of our DNA with another's to create life, I do not know, but as far as either of us is aware we have not fathered any of the Divine.

'It would of course be a pleasure to watch over Billy.'

The Doc squeezes my hand in thanks.

'What do you think your sister really wants?'

The Doc shakes his head, 'I have no clue. It could be that like us, she is simply searching for more of the Divine and seeks my help.'

'And how do you get in touch with me when you undoubtedly find yourself in trouble and need old Eric to swoop in and rescue you?'

He laughs at this and I too smile.

'I believe there is an elderly gentleman who lives not so far away from here in a house you helped build?'

'Ok,' I tell him, reading the underlining message in his words.

'You knew this day was coming Eric. You left because you couldn't control your beast and you were afraid with the red mist descended, you might hurt her, but you always knew in the future you would have to go back.'

I nod and lower my head, feeling the hot tears splash into my lap, 'you know she turned thirty years old a few days ago? And as instructed I left her a copy of the book.'

The Doc stands and I follow him up. He wraps his bear like arms around me and whispers, 'you cannot change the past.'

We straighten ourselves out and the Doc holds out his hand which I shake, 'watch over my son, Eric, and see that he comes to no harm.' As he moves past me and opens the living room door he turns back, adding, 'I love you my boy, stay safe.'

And then he is gone.

19

WILLIAM: PAST LIVES & IMMORTALITY

In previous lives down the ages I have found it quite easy to disappear without a trace and pop up in another town in another country thousands of miles away from my previous incarnation. Indeed, for centuries this is how I travelled and this is how I went unnoticed. I found thirty years was the maximum amount of years I could ever stay in one place due to the people who would populate my life aging and me not.

Now though it is becoming increasingly difficult to overcome the problem of identification. National insurance numbers, Social security, Birth Certificates, Passports, drivers licence, ID books, without these things it is impossible to live a normal life in plain sight and blend in with the crowds. There have been occasions where we have collected identifications from the victims of Eric's hunger but these paper lives have always been there as safeguards in case we have to leave a place very quickly and quietly.

Between the years of 1952 and 1958 Eric was working freelance for the US government, disappearing marks upon his employer's request. He lived on the east coast of Mexico under the assumed identity of Jose Garcia. The money was good, he was able to relax on the beach, a place he has always been fond of, and live as normal an existence as any freelance assassin is able to.

His private villa was right down on the beach and Eric had a small boat he would take out onto the Mexican gulf to fish and scuba dive. He kept several girlfriends, and I believe he was content while he lived out there. His line of work fed his hunger and he was able to live out in the sun instead of stalk the shadows to feed his urges.

The Divine had just been released to an unsuspecting public and, until the religious nuts got hold of it, it was a success, selling by the bucket load. But fear is an emotion which drives many a man, and it was the fear we might actually exist which caused my book to be banned and removed from bookshops indefinitely. My literary agent, one of the few people who knew the identity of the mysterious Mr E, delivered the bad news to me and I was delighted. My intentions in writing the book in the first place had been to shout out to others like me, the Divine, and I had struck a nerve with someone somewhere. I waited for something big to happen and when Eric was abducted in 1958 this was finally proof there were more of us. Someone was out there running scared because I had announced to the world the truth of our existence.

Eric doesn't like to talk about his abduction and I believe he suffered more than he had ever physically known possible. Someone out there was after me, a nameless and faceless entity, and the boy did not give me up.

After slaying his torturers Eric escaped and began a yearlong killing spree to find those who had ordered his abduction. The Diageo crime family who assisted in taking him were completely wiped off the face of the earth. Wives, children, parents, grandparents were all slain in his search for the person responsible, but he eventually reached a dead-end and left Mexico to come back to England.

A week or so after him arriving back here Jose Garcia's small boat was found drifting five miles off the coast of Mexico. On closer inspection the coastguard found scuba equipment missing and this tied up all loose ends with Eric's life in Mexico. With Jose Garcia dead in South America, he returned to England, assuming the two hundred year old identity of Eric Chesterfield.

The Swiss and their numbered bank accounts make it possible to pass fortunes from one identity to another, one life to the next. Since the turn of the twentieth century I have adopted the surname Johnson as my own. My son Billy is fourth generation Johnson, his great grandfather was a Cambridge Professor who signed up to fight the Hun at the Somme and lost his life a few months later. The first Johnson left behind a fictional son who popped up in the States, and William Johnson II moved to England to fight the Nazis when war broke out for a second time. Billy's 'grandfather', who died before the boy was born, saw his demise by getting hit by a bus of all things. William Johnson II had been highly decorated by Churchill during the war and like his father before him had in later life taught History as a Professor at Cambridge University. His death had been a shock to all and although there had been rumours of a wayward son, none turned up at the funeral. That was because by the time I stood in front of that bus and braced myself, I had already enrolled at Manchester University to study Biology and Psychology as the Johnson whose life I am living now.

I met my wife in the stacks at the university library and for the first time in my existence, I fell madly in love.

It is true there have been several wives and ensuing children down the centuries with Anne I fell head over heels, and for no reason other than wanting to share my entire being with this person, I told her everything. I didn't want any distance between us, I wanted my girl to know every aspect of me and there to never be any secrets. I wanted to spend the rest of her life with her, not just the usual thirty years, and we spent over a decade with each other before we decided to have Billy, and the fourth generation of the Johnson clan was born.

One day I imagine I will return to my son, possibly claiming to be a long lost cousin, adopting a different accent and then continuing the Johnson linage, but soon now I must leave.

I am careful to open the front door, and as I enter what has been my home for over three decades I walk through to my study at the back of the house next to the dining room. Anne will be asleep upstairs now. I left her a note saying I was going to meet Eric so she knew not to wait up. Our meetings usually end with a bottle of whiskey and a night reminiscing into the early hours of the morning. This one ended in the deaths of three men, so it goes to show that even after a century, a night out with Eric can still be unpredictable.

I start a fire in the small fireplace by my desk, stacking the logs up high, and strip until I am standing naked in front of the flames. I then toss my blood stained clothes onto the fire and watch as they burn. Lastly I toss my shoes on top and sit down in my reading chair, savouring the warmth and light the fire brings to my naked body. In my hand I hold the note, stained with both my blood and that of the young man I killed tonight. I could argue I took his life in self-defence but that would be nonsense. I had no need to defend myself; he was just a kid following orders, Nessie's orders.

I read the handwritten note again, and when I am finished find that I am weeping. Little Nessie, from my first life, was the bastard child of my mother and a forceful English soldier. Born eighteen years after me, I saw her on only three occasions during that life and have seen her once since, the day she condemned my body to the ground for forty years. By then she was an old woman bitter with rage. She thinks I betrayed her when I went off to fight the English. She was only five years old at the time and after my death her life and that of all Scotsmen deteriorated. I had been a folk hero and I had chosen my own selfish life instead of rising up and fighting again. I want to reach out to the old lady now, to try and explain that the brother she once knew died a long time ago. I want to explain to her that as the Divine we have to try and forge some sort of path through this life which will bring it meaning. Most of all I just want to embrace little Nessie as the sister I always held dear.

To my brother William,

You hide yourself well. It has been fifty seven years in an ever shrinking world since you wrote that book, and it has taken much longer to find you again.

You have had your life ten times over and now it is time to put some of that knowledge you have worked so hard for to use.

I represent a committee of likeminded individuals who would be honoured to make your acquaintance. You will accept because, I am sure you understand, although you might want to run as William Johnson your time has now come to a close. You have just three days in which to post a comment on the williamwallace.com message board. You will simply write our Mother's name together with a time and a place for a car to pick you up.

I look forward to seeing you again brother,

Nessie
x

I smile to the ghost of a little girl who once sat on my knee and I told bedtime tales to. She is long gone now and only the memory remains.

But what of the lady who she grew up to become?

What is Nessie's motive in all of this, burying me for forty years and now this note? This isn't revenge because if it had been I may well have found myself buried once again. What is it my sister wants from me?

I stand up and reach for my dressing gown which hangs on the back of the chair. Shrugging the garment onto my shoulders I crumple Nessie's note up into a ball and throw it into the flames with my clothes. I then cover the fire with the metal grate and switch off the light to my study, walking back through the dining room and heading on upstairs to my love.

Anne is asleep, her soft breathing inviting me to her and I carefully sit myself down on the edge of the bed. I turn and look down at my sleeping beauty and then gently kiss her forehead. The lines around her eyes and mouth are softened by the light coming from the bathroom, and for a moment she looks as she did before old age began to creep in.

I feel for this woman I really do. Where once was the attractive youth and innocence with her whole life ahead of her now lays a cynical aging shell. She tries not to show it but I think the further through life man goes the more cynical they get. Their mortality begins to bare down on them and as their bodies age and begin to break down they realize they will not live forever and death begins to loom in front of them, the great nothingness.

Back when we first met Anne wanted to travel the world, to take in all that life had to offer in the short space of time she was a guest. Now though she has given up. Her attempts of remaining youthful have long since passed and where once I was looked upon in awe for having caught myself such a young and lustrous lady to be my wife, now she is the one who appears to be keeping a younger man.

Anne is fifty-three years old and the oldest I could ever hope to pass for is forty. We both knew this day would come and now it has, now that brief window of time we have been together is closing, Anne knows I must soon leave and that she will never see me again. You see for all of my power's advantages there is one disadvantage which always outweighs the good. All of the people you ever love will one day die and you will not.

For me it is much harder because I cannot wait until that day. If Anne was to live to one hundred I would still be wandering around wearing the mask of a forty year old. Questions would be asked and the answers to those questions Man would not understand, hell, I don't understand it.

One day very soon I must leave. Leave my love who promised to share her life with me, I feel like such a cheat. Anne chose to share her life with me and because that life is so short it is all the more special. She cannot up and leave, becoming someone else in some place new, she is a woman who in a couple of years will be approaching old age and I am ashamed to say she will be tackling her twilight years alone.

She does not know I will leave, none of my wives ever had. A simple note, the coward's way out you might say, is the only comfort I have to give to her. Oh how I love her, and always will. It takes a special woman for me, and Anne has been that woman. She gave me Billy my son and for that I will be eternally grateful.

Darwin teaches us how we are put here to reproduce, to pass on the genetic information stored in our DNA to our offspring so that they might do the same, and their children, and their children's children. It's a beautiful thing life, miraculous, and the most enchanting part is not conserving a part of you for future generations, it is simply living the life you have been given because the odds of any of us even being here in the first place are billions to one. It is the greatest lottery on earth being the fastest swimmer to fertilise the egg in our mother's womb, but before we could take that swim to life our parents before us had to make the same journey, and their parents before them. The staggering odds against any of us being here at all always amazes me when I think about it. Life really is precious.

Now though the life of William Johnson must cease, and it is for the preservation of my own species why I will soon leave.

'What's the matter sweetie,' Anne asks as she rolls over in bed and drapes a tired arm around my waist, smiling. Her smile is more pronounced, her laughter lines deeper than ever but her face still sparkles.

I want to speak, to tell her nothing, that everything is just fine but I fear to make even a single sound would cause me to breakdown in tears. Instead I kiss her once more on the forehead and stroke her hair, a single tear escapes and rolls down my cheek but she does not see it, she is already asleep again.

20

ERIC: SOFT EARTH

To fly, to levitate and control direction, has always been a difficult trick for me to master. There was no guide book and there was no guide to talk me through the procedure. My first instances of levitation came quite unexpectedly. I was running through the woods, trying to evade capture by a group of sixteenth century demon hunters who, unluckily for me, thought me the demon, when I tripped and fell down a ditch landing in a shallow stream. I was up again to my feet instantly, this was a time before I found I could cloak myself in both light and darkness, invisibility had yet to be added to my repertoire of abilities and so made hiding near most impossible with the demon hunters' dogs closing in on my trail.

I followed the stream, hoping the water would mask my scent and throw the dogs off track and even when I could hear the animals behind me, barking and yapping, I still powered on. It was dark so I couldn't really tell when the stream turned into river but still I ran on top of the shallows until I reached an opening, the moon lit my way across the soft earth and into the trees beyond where I stopped to catch my breath and look back on the beasts which hunted me.

I could hear them still barking and growling but peering back across the opening which I had just crossed I could not see them. That was until I heard the splash and watched in horror as half a dozen canines' heads bobbed up and down as they swam across the lake I had thought soft earth. Admittedly this was not flight, I had not taken off into the sky like the bats which flapped above my head, hunting for their own prey, but at that very instant, when my foot had touched down on the water and the air had held me when it should have released me into the lake's murky depths, I knew there were powers my kind possessed greater than longevity.

Even still, four hundred years later, I find flying mentally exhausting and I lack the focus to travel any great distance. Keeping the beast and its nasty little head at bay, does not help in my endeavours and this is why when I need to travel any great distance I do so the same as anybody else, I use the modes of transport available to me for that time.

As great as it would be to take off into the sky and zip around the globe on a whim, around fifty miles is the farthest I have travelled flying of my own accord, and as great as it would be to soar miles and miles above the earth, the severe cold saps my concentration, which means I cannot travel far. I am by no means complaining about one of man's chief desires, to take off and soar like the proverbial eagle, simply explaining the realisms, and this is why I travelled by plane to Cape Town to keep an eye on Billy. If the doc feels the boy's sleeping problems might be an indication of something more then who am I to argue?

Having spent the past century predominantly north of the equator and not having visited Cape Town since the first of the Portuguese settled here, I have a little catching up to do. I briefly considered moving over here during the seventies to help fight apartheid but then changed my mind knowing that having some form of control over the hunger in the blood the doc provided me with superseded the troubles of man ten thousand miles away. It may seem like a selfish stance to take but it is what it is. I had no affiliation with either side and if I'm honest, when the beast stirs it has no racial preference either. Blood is blood.

The house I have rented in Fish Hook bay overlooks that where Billy is staying, in fact as I lazed around in the sun by the pool yesterday I spotted the boy sitting on the terrace talking to a young lady. He looks well, growing tall and strong like his father but I do hope for his sake he is not like us. He deserves to live his life to the full and not be stunted by our immortality, to find someone he loves and grow old with them, to watch his children and grandchildren grow up and then be laid to rest and have his love ones mourn his passing. This is something the Divine are not privy to. I have outlived so many sons and grandsons down the ages and now there are not many left alive.

Unlocking the French windows, I walk through into the garden and inhale the cool morning air before gently lifting myself through it towards the pool, letting gravity take hold of me as I dive down into the chilly waters. I have often wondered what would happen if I did not come back up for air. I do not possess gills so if I inhaled the water it would fill my lungs and it would drown me, but would it kill me? In another life maybe I will experiment with pushing my mind and body to its limits to see how far our regeneration might go.

Above the water I hear my phone ring and so leap out and back onto the terrace, reaching first for first a towel and then the handset. It's Billy.

'Hello?' I answer as I dry my face, sitting down by the poolside, legs dangling in the water.

'Uncle Eric?'

'Billy, how's it going boy?'

Expecting Billy to talk about how nice the weather is, how cheap the booze is, and how horny he is surrounded by barely naked beach babes, what he says next knocks me for six.

'Who is the little girl from my childhood Eric?'

My heart starts racing, the adrenaline souring through my veins and turning my stomach. His words make a deep hidden pain which I had buried so long ago burst out to the surface. Sophie, my little angel, the light in a darkness that had been my life for so long. I see her now, jumping up to me, hear her call 'daddy' as she wraps her arms around my neck and kisses my lips, her love unconditional, the love a nine year old girl has for her daddy.

'Uncle Eric come on, speak to me. Lately I have been having vivid dreams of when I was a little kid with you and dad in the park and there is a little girl in these dreams too. Who is she?'

My face feels hot and wet and when I open my eyes I watch as a tear drop falls between my legs and into the pool, ripples of sorrow and regret swelling outwards. 'Billy, listen to me, you are not ready for this.' A lie, in truth it is me who is not ready for this because once the truth comes out about Sophie, the truth will surface about everything. 'Have a great time while you are out there in Cape Town, get drunk and eat too much and forget about this.'

'But Eric...' the boy tries but I cut him off.

'Billy do not pursue this. I'm sorry, you want to talk when you get back then we will...'

'No I don't want to talk when I get back Eric, I rang you now expecting you to laugh at me and tell me I've a little girl stalking my dreams, to get a grip but instead you haven't, which means the girl is real, was real...and as children we were once close.'

I can see them now, running after each other in the park, Sophie picking Billy up whenever he falls, dusting him off and with a hug sending him on his way towards the slide or swings.

'Daddy I wish little Willy could be my little brother, I love him so much,' she calls to me now.

'Who is she Eric?' Billy asks and I sigh. With the Doc now on his way towards God knows what I guess confiding in Billy won't hurt. He will figure it out on his own soon enough anyway.

'My daughter,' I tell him, a chill creeping down my spine as I think back to the last time I saw her, sound asleep in her bed at the house I built for a family long dead and buried.

'What do you mean your daughter? Well where is she? What's her name?'

For some reason I laugh, maybe it is because there are no more tears, 'Her name is Sophie,' I tell him, hanging up before he can ask any more questions.

I toss the phone to the side of me and let out a guttural groan. My little girl has just turned thirty years old. I have stayed away to protect her, to protect them all from my hunger and now she has come back to me. If I hadn't left when I did, hadn't walked out orphaning my own child, she would surely have met her demise in the hands of the beast, as would my God and great-great-grandson Alan, and his wife Sheila.

Instead I walked away to protect the people I could not protect from myself.

The phone buzzes and I answer without looking at the display, it wouldn't be anyone else but Billy.

'What the fuck do you mean your daughter uncle Eric? I have a cousin and you never thought to mention it?'

'Billy,' I try but he won't listen

'No no no, don't "Billy" me Eric. For over a month I have had this little girl visit me every night in my sleep, waking up childhood memories long forgotten and you tell me now that her name is Sophie and she is your daughter? Never think to mention it before, around the table at Christmas, on a day out to the zoo with you and dad, or on any single occasion through my whole life?'

'Billy,' I snap back at him and he quietens, 'I know this may come as a shock but do you not think for one second that there may be reasons behind me not mentioning my daughter? Do you not think for one fucking minute there is something bigger than you losing a playmate when you were a toddler that I have had to contend with?'

'I…uh,'

'Yeah, you uhhh, didn't think. I have been there for you your whole fucking life, you are like a son to me Bill, you know you are, so do you not for a single second think that maybe there is a pretty big reason why I have never mentioned my only daughter's existence to you?'

I am shouting now, the anger in my words are not for the boy, they are for me.

'Where is she Eric?'

'Safe Bill, and that's all that matters.'

'Safe?' he says with a half laugh, 'safe from what?'

'From me.' I cry out, my words carrying in the morning air and echoing off the mountain I stand before. 'Billy, leave this alone ok. Call me when you get back and we can meet up and talk.'

The line goes dead and I let out a roar, taking off into the air and speeding up along the mountain's vertical cliff face, concentrating, focusing, my anger having woken the beast inside me who I must calm before he takes control, battling for my wits against the angel of death. I mask myself in the morning sun and continue upwards, passing the mountain summit. I can feel the hunger receding and I keep hold of my senses, focusing on my flight path upwards until I can take it no longer and let go of the air, falling back down to earth, the mountain top moving in quick to meet my limp body as I fall from the sky. It will hurt when I hit the ground, hurt like hell, but it is nothing I do not deserve.

I land with a sickening thud onto the jagged rocks and open my eyes. I taste blood in my mouth and my left eyeball hangs from its socket but I do not feel any pain, my body is in shock, my chest cavity has collapsed, my ribs are broken and are impaling my lungs making it impossible to breathe, I cannot move because my spine has shattered and as I look up into the sky for a moment I am at peace. This single instant is the closest I will ever come to death, to serenity, when the entire world is still and my brain cannot function enough to torture me with my regrets.

Screaming out in horror as the pain comes I seek a place in its white hot fingers. This is where I belong for the thousands of lives I have ruined in my existence. Right here, before my cells begin to regroup and work furiously to put my broken body back together, this is where I should spend an eternity. It is what I deserve.

I cough out and with the movement feel my spine snap back into place, dead nerve endings reigniting and electrifying my body. The ringing in my ears begins to subside and I hear shouting in the distance, from over the edge of the summit and down along the beach. I crawl on broken limbs and peer down upon the bay, watching as two toy figurines race each other along the catwalk, hopping from rock to rock and then back onto the path which hugs the water's edge. Even from this distance I recognise Billy, bare backed and wearing only a pair of turquoise shorts as he runs faster than I have ever seen anyone go in my life. His companion calls out to him but it is lost while my eardrums repair themselves. With a broken and twisted arm I lift my eyeball back into the socket and close that eye, giving it chance to reconnect all the dots. With my right eye, although awash with congealing blood, I watch as Billy powers towards the sea and jumps, aiming for a great big chunk of rock close to the beach. The jump is good, he had his footing right, and then as I expect gravity to catch up with him and pull him down into the sea, for a moment it doesn't. There, for one split second, he moves higher still through the air, as though some invisible man has just given him a leg up. No one else would have seen it and I doubt even if Billy had felt it himself, but in that splinter of a second the boy was walking across soft earth.

    I roll over onto my back and start to laugh.

    What do you know, the boy can fly.

21

WILLIAM: *VLAD*

Theories are all I really have. As a man of science it is infuriating to know that although the data must be out there somewhere, it has been almost impossible to collect. To discover more about my kind I need test subjects and as I mentioned before, I have met only three other members of my species in my life. Out of the three, my dear friend Eric has been a constant in my life for the majority of this century, and I have learned so much from him. It is Eric and the amazing abilities he rather reluctantly possesses I would now like to talk about.

Eric was born Vlad III, Prince of Wallachia in 1431 in Eastern Europe. In the winter of 1476 Vlad, or Eric as he is known these days, was beheaded by the Turks and his head was sent back to Constantinople and put on display to the public impaled in a stake. Quite the grizzly ending for a man who, during his life, was rumoured to have slain 100,000 people, but as with the demise of Sir William Wallace a century earlier, it is possible to survive a beheading if in fact it is not you losing your head.

Eric first discovered his ability to heal in battle. On many occasions he has recounted the blow of the sabre to his left collarbone and him collapsing at the feet of his men only to rise again and fight on, and it is my belief that our first 'deaths' is what hold the key to our eternity.

Man's body heals. Cut him and he will bleed but given time wounds close and he will live to fight another day. When presented with that fatal blow our body's cells change, or rather something kick starts inside us, speeding up our rate of healing (rapid cell regeneration) and with this destroying the aging gene which leads to our inevitable immortality.

When Man's cells die they do so having copied themselves over and over again, but each copy is inferior to the last. In time the generations of cells begin to break down and this is how aging occurs. The blood thins, the immune system weakens, making man more susceptible to disease, hair pigment is lost, sight weakens, and these are but a few symptoms of old age, of the cells breaking down.

With our cells, they do not produce inferior copies. Our bodies are, in effect, frozen in time. After that initial trigger point when the body begins its rapid cell regeneration, we become much stronger. I can bench press 900lb and while this does not make me a record breaker, I am a scientist not a professional bodybuilder. Once the Divine cells have woken up I believe their density greatens. We are stronger, faster and heal at an alarming rate, and until I met Eric I believed that was the extent of my kind's abilities.

My thoughts go back to no man's land and Eric appearing from nowhere, out of thin air. He has the ability to bend light around his body, something I cannot even begin to fathom. And invisibility is not Eric's only trick. The first time he showed me how he could 'will' himself into the air I was astounded. When I questioned how he was able to do this, Eric explained that it had something to do with the sun, like plants photosynthesising, his body collects energy from the sun's rays and when harnessed and dispersed he is able to move through the air.

'The air feels heavy against me and with this I am able to manipulate my direction.'

I did not understand it then and I do not now but although so far I have not discovered the answers, there still must be reason behind these feats. As mystical as it appears when watching man take off into the air, there is science behind it, hiding, bending its own light around the answers which I search for.

Far Eastern cultures believe in Karma, ying and yang, that every action has an equal and opposite reaction and with Eric's power lurks a much darker side, the hunger. Eric himself calls his thirst for blood and the onslaught of symptoms beforehand, the beast. I, as always, am a little more sceptical. I do not imagine a beast lurks within my friend but I have seen how Eric turns when he does not quench his thirst. Instead of listing the theories I have regarding 'the beast' I will instead tell you a story.

In 1890 on the Yorkshire coast in the seaside town of Whitby, Eric's beast once more rose and made its way out into the night to seek its fill. Having prowled the dark night's streets, the beast found it's victim and pounced, taking the man by the throat, stifling his screams, and carrying them both up into the air, landing in the graveyard of Whitby castle which overlooks the town.

The man the beast chose for that night's fill was an Irish writer called Abraham and strangely enough he did not appear frightened in this ordeal. After feeding from the man Eric did not flee. He was curious as to why there was no fear.

Abraham has answered 'this has been the most deadly and enchanting experience, and although of course I feared for my life, my inquisitive nature overrode any fear I might have had.'

Eric saw something in Abraham that night. He had spent his life either embracing the beast which led to the massacre of thousands in his first life, or supressing it, which led to a life of constant craving, but one thing he had never done was talk about his need for the blood, until that night.

In his would be victim he found he was able to tell his story, and Abraham listened. Eric told him everything, from his time many lives ago as the Wallachia prince, to present day lurking in the shadows trying to survive. When they parted they shook hands and Abraham thanked Eric for his story. Seven years later, after what I imagine was a lot of research into Eric's origins, the Irish writer who had come so close to death, released a novel which romanticised everything about the beast Eric still fights to this day. That novel is now part of literary history, its primary character one of popular culture's best loved villains.

In 1476 Vlad III, Prince of Walachia died. He was posthumously dubbed Vlad the Impaler, because of his *penchant of impaling his enemies and drinking their blood to instil fear in his enemies. During his life he was a member of the House of Draculseti and had also been known by his patronymic name, Dracula.*

Thinking about all the others out there who may have special abilities of their own, I pull up to the gates of Chesterfield manor and stop the car, waiting a moment before pressing the intercom buzzer. It is possible that I possess other powers but, giving the relatively quiet lives I lead, have not discovered them yet. Invisibility, flight, great strength, invincibility, immortality, and then there was the young black girl who took my body for a run over the edge of a quarry and caused me to black out while this was going on. What other amazing feats might be out there for me to discover?

I press the buzzer and wait. It is quite late in the evening but I know Alan will still be up.

'Hello?' the voice of Eric's great-great grandson crackles down the line.

'Alan, its William.'

There is silence, followed by the creaking of the old gates opening.

After some consideration it feels meeting with Nessie and hearing what she has to say may unlock the secrets to our existence and that is the reason I made the decision to leave and join her. Eric is sceptical, of course, the boy fears for my safety and does not want any harm to come to me, but without risks, without that shot in the dark when all my instincts are telling me to run as hard and as fast as I can in the opposite direction, I feel I will be no closer to discovering anything new about my kind. The risk of walking into the lion's den defenceless is justified by the untold truths I may learn about the Divine.

I reach the house and get out of my car with my briefcase, inside of which is ten full blood bags for the boy. A parting gift one might say.

The old man stands in the doorway Eric built a century before he was born, and greets me with a reluctant shake of the hand.

'How are you William, how is Eric?'

I nod my head, 'in good health,' I tell him to which he snorts.

'Good health is something you and Eric can be relied upon for. Come in, I'll put the kettle on, I fear this may be a very long night.'

We sit down at the breakfast bar and Alan talks while he busies himself with the kettle. 'It has been close to twenty years William, to what do I owe the pleasure?'

'I need to ask something of you Alan. After all this time and the burden of truth we left you with…'

'Not once have I ever considered my granddaughter a burden,' the old man cuts in with venom.

'No, that is not what I meant. You have lived your whole life with our secret and when Eric left it must have been hard.'

'Hard? Have you any idea William? My earliest memories are of bouncing up and down on Eric's knee. He was the man I went to with my problems through adolescence, he was the first member of my family I introduced my Sheila to when we were courting, and he was best man at my wedding. Eric has been my uncle, my best friend, my nephew and when he left I was devastated. I understand William, why he left, why he felt he had no other choice but to leave, but because of him leaving a little girl grew up fatherless, orphaned, and I was left to pick up the pieces.'

'How is Sophie?'

Alan shakes his head, 'you don't have the right to ask that. Neither of you do. Like a good little mere mortal I have passed on your book and photographs so she can discover for herself her father is not dead. What is it you want William, and why did Eric not come? Why you?'

I shake my head. I have never really considered the people we leave behind and I am speechless now I have been confronted with the stark reality of our actions. When Eric made the decision to leave he did so to protect Sophie.

'I'm sorry Alan.'

The old man curses, 'why are you here William? What is it now you wish for me to do for you?'

'Nothing,' I tell him as I rise from my seat. 'It's not fair to ask anything more of you.'

Alan is to his feet and pushes me up against the sideboard, taking my throat in his hand, 'I swear William if you don't tell me why you came tonight I will die trying to kill you. A pointless task you might think but then you would never understand the concept of honour. You are a nomad, roaming the earth conscienceless, leaving in your wake heartbreak and sorrow through your actions.'

'I came because there is nobody else in the world I would ask. You see I am leaving again, embracing my nomadic instincts you might say, and I ask that you act as a medium between Eric and me.'

The old man loosens his grip on my throat and frowns, 'what's happened William? Twenty years you have stayed away and now you come telling me you are leaving and you need me to be a point of contact for you both, why?'

'Because I have no one else to ask,' I say, hearing the defeat in my own voice.

He sits back down and sighs, 'for Eric I would do anything. You know that, but you, I believe you are that which stands in the way of Eric ever finding peace. He was happy you know, through my life time he was happy, and when Sophie came along he finally found a reason once again to live a normal life.'

'But we are not normal Alan, we are searching…'

'*You* search William. Eric has always followed. This life he leads fighting his demons will eventually destroy him. I was there with him when Sophie was born; she became his reason for living. We would have found a way to deal with Eric's demons if you hadn't have been there in the shadows, whispering into his ear. Of course I will act as your go between, I will embrace Eric back into my life instantly, but you William, you I do not want to see again. There is a piece of paper and a pen on the side on your way out. Jot down the means I am to communicate any messages and leave and do not come back.'

I nod and hold out my hand which Alan ignores, moving around me and out of the room. I nod to the case and say, 'the content of that case is for Eric, you need to…'

'You're welcome,' he interrupts, continuing down the hall towards the front door, 'has been outstayed. Close the door on your way out William.'

I nod and then leave.

Back in my car I take out my phone and click onto the internet. There is nothing left for me to do here in this life. Despite what the old man thinks I do not feel I have ever manipulated Eric. He is his own man. I click onto williamwallace.com and scroll down to the message board.

'Margaret Crauford, tomorrow 2pm, Manchester Piccadilly train station. Come and get me'

PART THREE

THE SIXTH APE

22

SOPHIE: *AN EVOLUTION OF A SPECIES*

I feel my choice of title for this book was maybe a wrong one. The word Divine signifies Godlikeness, and although as a younger man I did follow God, as a scientist I cannot afford to be so short sighted. As a man of God I believed I had been put here to protect, an angel, one of His foot soldiers down here on earth. I believed this for the majority of my life until Darwin set us all straight on the matter. As a man with the luxury of time I have devoted myself to knowledge, I have studied far greater than the ten thousand hours people say you must surpass to be an expert on any given subject, and still I am at a loss.

My friend in time once spoke of his theory of why we are here, that we were fallen angels cast down from the heavens and forced to spend an eternity walking the earth in Man's image. I do not think he believes this anymore, he is no fool, and where mortal man can spend his life shutting reason out from his mind, Eric has been on this earth too long not to see the emerging pattern.
Man is a savage beast.

He seeks divinity in the way he lives his life, taking at will, killing those in his path to achieve great wealth and then fighting for more. Man is always striving to achieve more. More money, more land, more wives or mistresses, this selfish beast knows no bounds when it comes to living its life.

Every other living organism on the planet has its place and they seek to reproduce to ensure the survival of their species. For man this has become second to power, and religion plays a big part in this. Before religion man lived in small communities, hunted, fished, farmed, made love, had children, taught those children the way of the land so they too could feed their families when they grew. This was the circle of all life.

Man then stopped worshipping the earth that fed and sheltered him and looked up to the sky. He started worshipping the heavens above and the 'divine' being which resided up there. Stories were constructed around this fallacy until the earth, which had provided for man and man's children, was lost to an all knowing, all seeing deity. Stories turned into legend and books were written, books which held the answers to all of life's questions. Still the earth provided man's nourishment and shelter but now man, convinced he would find eternal happiness after death, abused his provider. For the centuries that followed wars were fought in God's name. And still, to this day, if you look for the reason for the fighting across the globe, it is either in the name of whichever deity is being followed, or for wealth of some sort.

The fifth ape certainly has come a long way.

Maybe it is up to the sixth ape to bring peace and order back to the earth before it is too late. This, of course, would mean there was a plan in motion, and if so some sort of 'divine' being would have had to create this plan. I don't know, perhaps I have it all wrong. Perhaps we really are angels sent from the heavens to keep the human race in check. Some days I wish this was so. I would have a purpose, a calling, a reason for my immortality. Instead I continue to absorb as much knowledge as I can about everything, I learn different languages, I study genetics, and in a previous life I studied theology, once upon a time being a man of the cloth. I try and learn from a history I experienced first-hand to prepare for a future I sometimes fear.

Man is becoming more and more powerful. His wars are not fought with the sword anymore. I fear the future because I fear one day one man will press one button and that will be the end of us all.

I close down the programme with a blink of my eyes and stare into darkness. I have to speak to granddad tonight, not when he next visits with grandma. These pictures, dad holding me as a baby and then the other which could have been taken the very next day if not for the current age of my father's 'Godson'.

All those stories granddad would tell me of dad, and how there were never any from his childhood. It is clear now why, because for as long as granddad can remember my father, Eric Chesterfield, has been a constant in his life.

The photographs, this book *The Divine*, they are now painting a picture and the next stroke of the brush will be for me to talk to granddad. Reading this book, I have tried to approach the content with an open mind, to forget all that I know of physics and the way the world works, life and death, black and white, so that I can digest the Author Mr E's story as fact. I have also asked myself countless times since I first picked the book up a week ago, if I too am one of the Divine.

My father does not age, but what of my mother? If Eric has been around my grandfather's life as often as granddad has told me in the past then granddad must have known the woman who gave birth to me.

So many questions, and with each chapter of this book more questions open themselves up. My ability to jump into the bodies of others also strikes me as a fantastic coincidence given I am trapped inside my own. I need to speak to granddad, but this time I cannot hide behind the mask of my host. This time granddad must understand it is me who is speaking to him so he can see I too am different and I am in fact very much my father's daughter.

It is Doctor West on duty tonight and I am grateful of it. He will visit and he will touch, the dirty pervert won't be able to help himself. I can hear him long before he approaches my door, who would have thought that behind those comforting deep baritones and sympathetic smile lurks a monster?

He is in the next room, his voice carrying through the wall and, although muffled, I get the sense he is speeding through his time with the patient in room 201, an elderly lady called Rita who broke her back five months ago. He wants to finish up with her, now anticipating his next call with his 'beautiful lady' as he likes to call me moments before his hand disappears beneath my sheets.

The door clicks shut next door and echoes down the hallway. I check the clock, 6pm.

'Here she is,' Doctor West announces with his easy going smile and I watch as he enters, followed by a nurse who hasn't long started working on this ward. 'And how are we this evening Miss Chesterfield?' he continues, catching my eye and winking.

I open my speech software and answer.

f i n e t h a n k y o u

I have begun building a box with the words I use most often and keep their tabs at the bottom of my computer screen. It makes conversations move a little swifter.

West tenses up when he hears my robotic voice answer him. The fear of what I might have my machine say is written all over his face.

I grin internally, rejoicing in his uncomfortableness.

'Glad to hear it,' he continues, frowning as he checks my life support machines and explains to the nurse what does what by my side.

c o u l d y o u s t a y f o r a f e w m i n u t e s d o c t o r w e s t

West turns from my ventilator and smiles. The stupid prick probably believes I enjoy being sexually assaulted by him.

'Certainly Miss Chesterfield,' he responds, nodding to the nurse to get started on room 205. He is over by my side before the door is even shut, that look on his face, eyes glazed over and pants throbbing with perverted desire.

'What is it Sophie?' he asks, brushing my fringe away from my eyes.

I make no effort with eye contact. Instead I am fiercely pairing together words on my computer.

c o u l d y o u h o l d m y h a n d p l e a s e i a m f e e l i n g v e r y l o n e l y t o d a y a n d w o u l d b e t h a n k f u l f o r a l i t t l e a f f e c t i o n

I had chosen these particular words earlier because I knew West wouldn't be able to resist.

'I can do better than that,' West grins, holding out his index finger and then putting it into his mouth, sucking it hard and lubricating the digit with saliva so it does not cause any discomfort on the way in. What a considerate man he is.

It is happening quicker now, as if my jumping is a muscle which, having being exercised, is getting stronger. Two days ago I managed to jump into an orderly in seconds whilst she bathed me, enjoying a pleasant lunchtime walk around the grounds. I am getting stronger. I have now jumped eleven times and I am beginning to battle through the onslaught of tiredness which I feel constantly while 'with host'.

West's hand moves down the seam of my bedspread and I watch his eyes, gazing emotionless into mine. I feel his touch, aware of pressure on my ankle as he slowly parts my lifeless legs with his hand. I watch as the tented bulge of his hand beneath my bed sheets begins to move towards my knee and then beyond. West's breathing shallows and his face quivers as his fingers rest upon the warmth of my underwear.

'You like this?' he whispers, sighing as he lifts he side of my knicker elastic and moves in.

The crackle of static fills my ears and West suddenly jerks away.

'What was that?' he asks me.

Did he hear the static too?

He stands up, breaking our connection but still I feel myself swinging towards him. Looking around the room he is confused now, he sits back down and smiles again. The roaring of the waves crashing down on my psyche fills my head and my vision tunnels, the opening far closer than ever before.

'Now,' West says, 'where…'

'Were we,' I complete, jumping back onto West's feet and away from the hospital bed and my body. I just jumped and he wasn't touching me.

'What the f...' I cry out, remembering at the last moment despite the magic being performed in room 203, this is still a hospital.

The pins and needles in my borrowed limbs have already gone and instead of feeling drowsy I am alert. I look down at Doctor West trapped inside my body and smile. My eyes appear wide and full of fear. He is scared and confused and doesn't understand what the fuck just happened. *I* don't understand either, the bastard wasn't touching me and still I managed to jump.

I sit down on the chair next to my bed and smile into my Doctor's eyes, 'you know Doctor West, I would feel sorry for you, being stuck in there, all alone, with nothing but your thoughts slowly driving you insane. I would sympathise and think I must return home soon so that my little outing doesn't raise any suspicion when you leave the hospital in a few moments. I would respect your position and not abuse mine. I would have done all of these things if you hadn't, time after time, abused a defenceless patient unable to cry out for help. I wonder how many other patients there have been, vulnerable and alone, in need of a friend. How many?'

Silence as West stares up at me from my hollow, gaunt face.

Reaching into my pocket I pull out West's keys, 'do we still use locker nine?' I then wink at him and turn, heading for the door.

23

ERIC: UNEARTHED LEGENDS

I am hungry today.

It has been four days and although my hunger was sedated by the homeless African family it devoured, now their blood is gone and I can feel the first symptoms of the beast stir again, the insatiable thirst, in this heat, is unbearable. That is my real relationship with the sun. If it is out then it is hot, if it is hot I am thirsty, and if I am thirsty when my hunger grows, I have in the past gone on such frightening killing sprees that even now centuries later I hear the dying victim's cries.

There are certain stories surrounding me I feel I should put to rest, the sun, for instance, does not burn my skin, in fact quite the opposite. My regenerating cells repair my skin pigment before any damage can be done by UV rays. These legends, like the garlic…in the middle-ages people would hang garlic on their doors and around their necks to ward off evil spirits. Personally I like garlic, although I prefer it fried and with pasta as opposed to wearing it as a necklace.

Wooden stakes hurt when driven through your body, believe me I know, it has happened in the past, but so does being shot through the torso twenty times with little metal stakes (bullets). The wooden stake legend comes from folk law passed down through generations, each version changing until the original message was lost.

I cannot turn into a bat, a rat, a dog, a snake or any other animal the fictional Dracula has embodied himself within, and even the word *Dracula* has been misquoted somewhere down the line, it does not mean son of the devil and nor am I. Dracula in fact means son of the dragon. My father, Vlad II Dracul was vested into the Order of the Dragon and at the age of five I too joined the clan, becoming Vlad III Dracula.

Although in recent times this word has come to mean evil, the origin is not so.

There was a savage time in history when I acted accordingly with the times. Man's life could be taken for as little as a crossed word, and for centuries I took advantage of this and let my hunger control me. I drank the blood of the dead and dying, and I did this publicly to instil fear into my enemies. For the first two hundred years of my existence the hunger, the beast, embodied me completely. It gave me great power which I abused for self-gratification but it also destroyed everything I once loved, my country, my wife, my children, none could escape from the shadow of Vlad Tepes the impaler. Even now, so many years later, my hunger is a constant reminder of the man I once was.

There have been times when my control of this hunger has waned and bad things have happened. People I have loved have lost their lives and other lives have been ruined. I do not dwell upon these things too much, for to do so would send one insane with regret and remorse, but leaving my little Sophie, abandoning her when she was just a child after so many happy years in her life, I will never forgive myself for. It is weak to rationalise my actions and say I was protecting her from the hunger. This is the truth but it is still weak. The truth is I am in constant turmoil and it eats away at me far worse than the hunger I carry around inside me.

I open my phone up and key in a number which has not changed since before my daughter was born.

It rings twice and Alan then answers, his voice cracking with age. A blink of an eye ago I had him sat upon my knee and I was telling him bedtime stories. He was five.

'Hello, Chesterfield residence. Hello?'

My mouth is dry but this time it is neither the hunger nor the heat of the day.

'Alan,' I say simply, and wait while my son, my brother, my father and my friend composes himself.

'Eric,' he says in a hoarse sigh, I can almost see his tears mirroring my own, 'oh Eric,' he repeats but that is okay. 'You need to come back to us Eric. Things have changed, I can't explain it but please, I miss my friend, Sophie needs her father.'

'I know,' I tell him. 'Is Soph…' I pause to let out a silent sob, 'is Sophie okay, I mean, she is okay isn't she?'

'Eric you need to come home. Where are you?'

I smile, *looking after someone else's kid when I should be looking out for my own*, I feel like telling him but that is not fair. Billy is my family, blood or no blood.

'I will be home in a couple of days, I promise. What will you tell Sophie?'

'Me? Nothing. It is you who must do this. You left, but Eric I need to speak to you before I let you see Sophie. Things have happened and…'

'Before you *let* me see my daughter? What is that supposed to mean Alan?'

There is a pause down the line, I shouldn't have snapped, 'you left. For twenty years Sophie has been my responsibility. I will not let you skip back into her life and turn it upside down again.'

He is right of course. Who am I to question my friend, it was he who raised Sophie, was there for her through adolescence and watched her grow into the woman she is today. Sophie could pass me on the street and I would not know it was her. Even now I still see her as the nine year old princess I abandoned. I have no photographs of her, only happy memories which would have continued if not for the decision I made.

'I'm sorry, I know,' is all I manage before hanging up and sliding my phone to the side. I need to eat before I continue with the covert babysitting of Billy.

Billy, oh Billy, of all the children the Doc has produced through all the points in history, how is it possible that the theoretical gene which makes us more than man chose you dear Billy? And more to the point how on earth am I ever going to be able to explain to the cocky, comic book loving child in a man's body all that being a member of the divine entails. Two more days and the boy flies home to find his father has disappeared. More questions will be asked and he will turn to me. What the hell was I thinking saying yes to watching over him while the Doc headed off into the wilderness to confront his sister? I have a family I need to get back to myself. Sophie will have seen the photographs and read The Divine now. I need to get back to her. I need to see my baby again.

24

SOPHIE: WEST

I punch in the gate code and move back behind the wheel of West's convertible, making my way up the driveway to the house which keeps all of my most treasured childhood memories. Chesterfield manor, as advertised in stone on the gate arch I pass underneath, was built two hundred years ago, back when the majority of the surrounding neighbourhood was fields owned by the lord of the manor. When I was younger my dad would tell me tales of the manor's history. At the time I imagined they were made up stories for a little girl's bedtime. Now...I mean, was he there? These stories of the Lord of the manor building the house himself, was that dad?

    I shake my head and take a couple of deep breaths, pushing my father to the back of my mind because first I have to contend with his God son, my grandfather.

    I knock on the door and wait. It is dark now. Another dreary winter's evening with the sky threatening rain. Above my head two spot lights illuminate the courtyard and cast shadows beyond their reach. I wonder how many ghosts from the past are out there. A past now brought closer to me because of my discovery.

    Granddad pulls open the great oak door and stands there, cast iron security gate between us. He is frowning and I notice he holds in his hand the walking stick I bought him when I was thirteen years old as a joke birthday present. Back then he said it'll be good for whacking intruders if they ever dare come to the door, and that will be the exact reason he has it with him now.

    'Who are you? How did you get through the gate?'

    For a moment I am speechless. What do I say, *it's me granddad, it's Soph*? Yeah right, that'll be the quickest way for granddad to sample his walking stick out on my head.

'My name is Doctor West, and I need to speak to you about your granddaughter.'

The old man drops the walking stick, 'Sophie, why what's wrong, she's ok isn't she?'

'She's fine Mr Chesterfield,' I tell him as he fumbles with the key to the security gate, opening it up and standing to the side to let me enter.

'What is it?' he asks again as he directs me through to the kitchen. He then shows me to a chair around the breakfast bar and offers me a coffee.

'Strong, black and very sweet,' I tell the old man. I might not be feeling any drowsiness yet but it wouldn't hurt to load up the body with caffeine and sugar.

As granddad busies himself with the drinks he asks me why I hadn't rung first.

I smile, ready to unleash my opening gambit, 'there wasn't time, I needed to see you face to face, to ask you about the photographs.'

Granddad pauses and I watch his body language carefully. A lifetime of lies surrounding him, my father's secret has made his poker face infallible.

'Photographs?' he asks, bringing across two mugs of coffee and sitting down next to me.

'Yes the photographs, The Divine, Eric Chesterfield, Sophie's dad...'

Granddad returns the smile, 'I'm sorry but Sophie's father, my son, died a number of years ago. What is it you would like to discuss? Sophie, she is alright isn't she?'

I want to take hold of him and shake him, screaming out *it's me granddad, I know it's hard to believe but trust me, it's your little Soph inside this body.*

'To save time I am going to tell you a story Mr Chesterfield. There was once a young lady trapped in a prison of which there was no escape. She had no contact with the outside world and slowly, over the space of two years began to question her very sanity having been left alone with just her thoughts as company. Then one day something magical happened, she found a way out, a tunnel which would open up for her and enable the prisoner to spend a little time out of her cell. Each time she escaped though, the cell would always pull her back to where she belonged. She was able to leave but she would never be released. The prisoner took every opportunity to use the tunnel to freedom when it appeared and though her day releases were brief, she knew the more she was outside of those cell walls, the stronger she would be to resist the pull back to captivity.'

Granddad shakes his head, 'I haven't the slightest idea what you are talking about.'

'Our prisoner learned of a book which documented the trials of other men able to escape their own confines, like vulnerability, gravity, even death, and she swore she would find the author so that he may help break her out of her prison for good.'

'Ah,' he says smiling, 'sir may I ask you a question?'

'Certainly,' I tell granddad.

'You are a doctor, you help heal people yes?'

Thoughts of the kind of healing this particular Doctor must do make me shudder inwardly. The Doctor with the magic fingers, as long as the patient has no way of crying out for help.

'That is what Doctors are trained to do,' I reply.

'And medicine is constructed scientifically, the use of science, reason, trial and error forms at the very roots of the diagnostics and medicines you use?'

'Of course.'

'Then why don't you tell me why you are here instead of telling me stories about magic tunnels and their prisoners?'

I sigh and shake my head. 'I'm sorry, Mr Chesterfield. What would you say if I told you Sophie was able to jump into the body of those who touched her?'

Granddad looks up from his coffee, right into my eyes and for a moment I see recognition in his.

'I'd say you need a much stronger coffee and possibly a chat with the hospital's psychiatrist Doctor.'

'Your gate code is 051285, Sophie's date of birth. Half way up the driveway on the left is a great big oak tree with a swing attached to one of the branches. Sophie helped her dad build that swing when she was nine years old. A little over a week ago Pip sat where I am sitting now and drank coffee with you just as I am doing now. She left with a book, *The Divine*, which was bequeathed to Sophie by her father Eric Chesterfield, the same Eric Chesterfield who is mentioned more than once in said book. An Eric Chesterfield who, if you believe the scribbling's of the author Mr E, is in fact over eight hundred years old, is able to make himself invisible, sore through the sky, and feeds on blood...'

'Now listen here,' Granddad cries out and is to his feet in an instant, his hand reaches out for my throat but I veer away as he grabs hold of the walking stick to use to strike me.

'Granddad stop...that walking stick, I bought it for you for your birthday when I was thirteen years old and on that very afternoon we had walked around the grounds. You had brought with you the stick and pretended you needed it. You told me next year I should buy you a flat cap and slippers to go with it. Please, it is me. I don't know how this is possible, but its Sophie. I found a magic tunnel granddad and now I can leave my body...please just put the stick down. You knock me unconscious and I'm gone, back to the hospital and back inside my body, it'll be the Doctor who wakes up here with a bump on his head.'

Granddad freezes and I watch as tears silently fill his eyes and begin rolling down his cheeks.

'Please, let's just sit back down'.

'Sophie?' he asks, 'but how is this possible?'

I shrug my shoulders, 'How is it possible for your godfather to be my father?'

He drops the stick and sits back down.

'We worked it out once, Eric and I. He is actually my great, great, great grandfather you know. Ha, I guess if you were to draw out the Chesterfield family tree that would make you my great, great aunt.'

He smiles and looks up at me.

'Don't, there is already too much for me to take in and I don't know how long I have.'

'What do you mean?'

'My host, his body will start trying to push me out and doing so by shutting down consciousness, sending me off to sleep.'

Granddad shakes his head, 'I'm sorry but this is a little too eerie to be able to take in. What happens to the person whose body you inhabit? Do they go…'

I nod, 'they are looking out through my eyes back at the hospital.'

'And they have to touch you?'

'I thought so but this time West wasn't making contact when I jumped, it's like this ability is getting stronger.'

'Or you are learning how to use it. Many years ago Eric told me of how he first discovered flight and it wasn't from zero to hero, he had to work at it to realize the ability's full potential.'

'I read that yes. The illusive Mr E does paint quite a picture in his book.'

'You know when that book was first published it changed everything. Conspiracy theories started popping up and I dare say some were right. It also led to the death of many innocent men and women believed to be divine.'

'Why was it written in the first place? This is what I do not understand. If you had lived for so long you would know to go public would result in bloodshed. People in their masses cannot be trusted, they follow the crowd, sheep, and the realisation that a new species of man had been walking around for hundreds of years would rightly provoke fear.'

'You got it kid. But the author thought he knew best, thought it might reach out to others like him, maybe start a club, I don't know what he was thinking. All I know is that after the book's release Eric arrived back here after living abroad for a number of years and he was scared, scared for both his own safety and the safety of his family, the safety of me and my brother, the safety of my own father who was still alive at the time.'

'What happened?'

'Eric moved back in here at the house and not long after *the Divine's* release the religious nuts petitioned for it to be banned and it was.'

'And the author, Mr E?'

I watch as the old man's nostril's flair and a guttural sound escapes in a growl. He knows the man personally.

'Who is he?'

He shakes his head, 'no, I'm sorry Sophie but I will not talk about him. I have spent twenty years protecting you from that man. You are my granddaughter and that man is dangerous.'

'What about dad? Is he dangerous, because from what I have read my father has quite a colourful history himself? I need some direction here granddad. In the past week I have learned that my father who died two decades ago is not only still alive but has resided in that state longer than humanly possible. This man, Mr E, he is a scientist and he wants people to come forward to help him understand. Maybe I need that too. I mean what is the alternative, to lay back in my bed frozen for the rest of my life?'

The phone rings, startling us both and granddad picks it up, speaks for a few moments and then replaces it back onto its base, 'that was your grandmother,' he bursts out laughing, 'I'm sorry speaking to you like this and then looking at the young man in front of me, a stranger who I am trying to treat as the granddaughter I have loved since the moment you were born…it's going to take some getting used to.'

I smile and reach for his hand, bringing it up to my mouth and kissing it, 'it's me granddad and you're not the only one, whenever I am inside a host and I pass a mirror I panic, my brain doesn't recognise the person in front of me as a reflection which then messes up my equilibrium.'

'I can't imagine,' granddad tells me and then takes back his hand, 'come with me, your grandma will be home soon and I'd like to show you something on the computer in my study.'

We walk through into the hallway and then through the drawing room to granddad's study. Once in there granddad shuts the door and switches on the computer, logging on to the internet instantly.

'I understand why you feel you need to talk to Mr E,' he spits out.

'What is it?'

He waves me away, 'it's nothing, we don't get on that's all.'

'Tell me about it please.'

'No, really, it doesn't matter.'

'Granddad!'

He looks up from the monitor and then holds up his hands in submission.

'Ok. Mr E and your father have been friends for a long time. Mr E is an uncompromising sort of man, fixated on finding more of his kind and in my experience, which is of course completely biased as I love Eric, has led your dad down a dark path on a number of occasions. Your father has demons which I have spent a life time trying to help him with, but whenever this man has called on Eric he has followed obediently. Eric is a family man, but the past lives he has led are very much still with him and he can find it hard to deal with the things he has done in the past.'

'Where is he granddad? My dad, where is he now?'

'I honestly don't know Soph.'

'Why did he leave me? He was everything to me. With mum leaving when I was just a baby he was both my dad and my mum, my best friend and the one person in the world I thought would always be there for me. Why did he leave?'

Granddad shakes his head, 'I...I can't tell you Sophie, it's not my place.'

I nod and smile, 'I understand,' watching as granddad moves his cursor over the browser and types in *the divine*, clicking the first link at the top of the search page.

Controversial 50's novel The Divine is to hit the shelves after being out of print for over 55 years. The Novel which depicts the journey of an immortal man throughout history was banned in 1959 after concern from

the Church of England about the novel's content and blasphemous connotations. The novel's author Mr E was unavailable for comment. It is understood The Divine will top the charts given the book's former status. The internet is alive with anticipation for the novel's rerelease and one New York lecturer has even included the book on next semester's syllabus saying 'it will be great to deconstruct this novel made infamous in the fifties by it's notoriety'.

The Divine is to be released next Monday.

I gasp.
Looking back up at granddad he smiles. 'It will happen again, you mark my word. That book should never have been written. It puts everyone in danger. When you go back check out the fan websites and forums, fanatics, the lot of them. No good will come of this.'
'The lecturer in New York, who is he?' I ask
'Who knows. Probably just another fan of the idea of The Divine.'
'Can you find out?'
'Why Sophie, what are you going to do, travel over to America in someone else's body?'
'Thought I might,' I tell him.
'Oh really?' he laughs.
I nod, 'yeah, I was there last month and...' I stop. I wasn't there last month at all. I've never been to the states in my life. I feel dizzy and so quickly sit down, closing my eyes.
'Sophie,' I hear granddad call in the muffled background, 'I open my eyes and I am looking down on Manhattan from the top of the Empire State building, a young woman with curly blonde hair wearing a bright red sweater moves in for a kiss...
'Sophie,' a distant voice echoes in the chilly air.
I am back at a boarding school I never attended. It is gym class and I am being pummelled in the changing rooms. I cry out for my mummy. I am at home and it is Christmas time and my mother, a small portly woman with an easy smile on

her face and glass of wine forever in her hand greets me at the door. I am introducing my latest girlfriend to the family. Lucy?

'Sophie?' granddad's voice comes back into focus and I open my eyes.

'His memories,' I whisper, 'I can access his memories.'

'What?'

'Granddad I was there. A moment ago I was sitting with an old girlfriend of Doctor West's speaking to his mother about plans for the forthcoming holidays. It's getting stronger. My ability is evolving.'

25

WILLIAM: TRANSITION

The last time I saw my sister Nessie she accused me of trying to kill her and locked me in a metal box until my escape forty years later. She was very much mistaken in her accusations as I had no knowledge of her prolonged existence, and until she introduced herself to me as an old lady I knew my sister only as the mischievous little girl who I had adored in my first life.

'You speak of the future as though you have the slightest idea of what it holds dear brother; you try to murder me, speaking of the fate of many resting upon my death.'

Those were the last words Nessie spoke to me before imprisoning me and to this day I haven't a clue what they mean. She had forced me into my iron cell and buried me deep in the south-western forests surrounding Loch Trool in Galloway, Scotland.

Time passes slow when imprisoned and so I had plenty of it to consider my sister's words; *you speak of the future* and *the fate of many resting upon my death*.

My memory is good, practically infallible, and I never spoke those words. It simply was not me who attempted to murder Nessie, and I have asked the question countless times, if it was not I then who? I have often fantasised of confronting Nessie about these words, to find out exactly what happened and after I had escaped the confinements of my metal coffin I scoured the globe for her but it seemed she was always one step ahead. I thought if I was to ever run into my sister I would take off her head, ending her life in the only way I imagine would work, but now, knowing I soon will see her again, I am more curious about the circumstances surrounding my incarceration than angry about spending four decades in forced hibernation.

The aircraft lands and I look out of the window at the grazing cattle beyond the runway enclosure. I have no clue where in the world we are. Having been approached by three men all wearing dark suits at Manchester Piccadilly train station I was escorted to a waiting van, asked politely to get in the back and then driven for two hours to an airfield in the middle of nowhere. I was then asked ever so politely again, to climb into the waiting Lear jet and within ten minutes we were in the air. Flanked by two of the three men who met me at the train station, I attempted to initiate conversation but none was forthcoming and so I dozed for a while.

The jet taxis across to a solitary hanger and we stop with a jerk.

'We're here,' the one on my left says, unbuckling his seat belt and moving out into the aisle, 'please follow me Mr Johnson,' he continues and I do as asked, following him down towards the front of the plane and then down the steps out into the empty hanger.

My man stops and reaches into his jacket pocket, turning to me with the first smile I have seen this side of wherever it is we are.

'Welcome to America,' he says and passes me a thick brown envelope. 'From now on it would do you good to practise the New York twang you adopted while living over here in the fifties.'

'What? How on Earth do you...'

He holds up his hand to halt me and shakes his head, 'William your eyes are about to be opened to the extent we do know, also it may do you good to get into the habit of Americanising your words. Z's instead of S's, parking lots in place of car parks.'

'Elevators instead of lifts?' I ask.

He grins, 'exactly,' and moves his hand out for me. I shake it and thank him for a pleasant trip.

'Miss Crawford has a car waiting for you out front sir. Enjoy your stay.'

He then turns and walks back to the jet, leaving me standing alone in the middle of the hanger. I notice the door with a sign over the top advertising the exit, head for it, and as I step through into a foyer area a young lady sitting behind her desk looks up with a smile.

'Mr Crawford,' she says, standing up and approaching me with her hand out. 'Your sister has arranged for a car,' she points through the floor to ceiling windows out onto the deserted parking lot save for the stretch limousine parked up against the curb. I step out into the sun and wait as the driver of the vehicle gets out and opens the door for me.

'Welcome back Mr Crawford,' he says tipping his hat and then shuts the door as I climb into the back. Once my driver is back behind the wheel he calls over his shoulder, 'you going straight to the office sir or would you like to go home to freshen up first?'

Home? What on earth is he talking about? My home is in England not wherever in America we are right now.

'Urgh, take me to the office please,' I say and then reach into the small refrigerator by my side, helping myself to a bottle of water. What the hell am I doing here? What is Nessie up to?

I rip open the envelope my chaperone had handed me in the hanger and let the contents spill out onto the seat next to me, an American passport, small tan wallet, smartphone, a bunch of keys and a further smaller envelope. I flick through the passport and am not surprised to see my face staring back up at me. I check the name next to the photo, William Crawford. Next I check the contents of the wallet. New York drivers licence, Bank of America checking card and an American express card, all under the name of William Crawford. I check for any cash and find ten crisp $100 bills in the note compartment of the wallet. Placing the wallet down on top of the passport I then reach for the envelope and open it up.

Dearest Brother,

Welcome to sunny Texas, I hope you had a pleasant flight. I have made all of the arrangements for your stay, identification, bank account with some money in, and a beautiful apartment overlooking the Gulf. Written on the back of this letter is your new residence which I have taken the liberty to furnish, you will need clothes and toiletries of course and I will give you chance to settle in before we meet.

I must admit, despite the circumstances I adopted getting you over here, we are all very excited about your forthcoming arrival, and on a personal note I hope us working together will draw a line in the sand for past unpleasantries on both sides.

Get settled in William and I'll send a car for you at nine o'clock tomorrow morning.

Nessie

I flip the letter over and clear my throat, 'Driver?'

My driver catches my eye in the rear view mirror and says, 'yes Mr Crawford, and its George.'

'George, change of plan, could you take me home please?'

'Anything you like Mr Crawford.'

'I'm at...'

'Yes sir, suite 8 Cladstine apartments on the coast.'

I check the address and it is as he says, 'errr, yes,' I chuckle and then sit back, relaxing into the soft leather seat.

We drive in silence and after a while watching the sparse Texan countryside pass us by, my mind wanders as I consider the life I have left. The woman I love, Anne my wife, will have been wondering why I hadn't called as I had set off in the rented yacht two days ago. The authorities will have now found the capsized boat and a search and rescue operation will be underway. Anne will have been notified of my disappearance and she will know that time we had spoken about over the years, when I would have to leave the life of William Johnson, is now here. She will play her part. She will play the grieving widow and arrange the memorial service for an empty casket. The two million pounds life insurance policy will be paid out and she will retire to relative comfort but she will do this alone.

I wish I could reach out to her now, hold her in my arms and tell her that everything will be ok but it won't. Anne will break the news to Billy of his father's death and Eric will be there for them both. This is the way it has always had to be and the transition between lives has always been hard when I have raised families and fallen in love. Time *is* a great healer but right now I only feel the guilt associated with deserting my family. I switch on my mobile phone, although I guess it is now a *cell* phone given my current location, and consider logging on to William Johnson's email account, writing a short and simple message and addressing it to my love, Anne. What words would help ease the pain and loss she must now be suffering? I could tell her how much I love her and I am sorry I had to leave, but these clichéd utterings would provide no comfort. I think about my son, the boy just turning into a man who, every day, grows more into the mirror image of me. How will he take my disappearance? What consequences will my leaving have on shaping the boy's life?

'We will be arriving home in ten minutes Mr Crawford.'

I thank George and then look down at my phone, clicking onto the internet and typing my name into the browser. Sure enough an article chronicling my disappearance pops up. I shut down my phone and close my eyes, traveling back into my memories to the time my sister and I met at the beginning of the 16th century. Had William Wallace not found an untimely death in 1305 he would have been one hundred and two years old when that bizarre meeting took place…

26

BILLY: MARATHON MAN

Two days to go and it is home time. Back to the winter chill and ridiculously early nightfall, and back to wearing more than shorts and the occasional t-shirt. Winter is not a good time for me, as I've mentioned before, and I am grateful to have been given the opportunity to skip some of it and bask in the sun with my best mate and his sister, my girlfriend. And love, it seems, is not just in *my* air. I have a sneaky suspicion Paul has been shagging Lisa's mate Melissa for the past couple of nights. They have seemed to be getting on pretty well, ever since we went clubbing in Cape Town centre last Friday, and I'm happy for them both. This has, of course, meant me and Lisa have been able to get away together more often so we have all been happy little rampant sex bunnies, doing what (I imagine) rampant sex bunnies do best.

Yes, two days and the dream is over and we will be back where meat cooked over flames is not every night's staple diet, and five gallons of beer to help the meat down is not a staple drink. In two days' time I will also be back home and able to question both dad and Eric over the little girl from my recurring dream and ask the both of them what the fuck happened? I am determined to find this girl, although she will be a woman now. Being an only child, having a cousin to call my own would be brilliant.

'You ready?' Paul asks me as he skips down the driveway to where I am waiting, rucksack slung over his shoulder and obligatory sunglasses perched on his nose. It's windy today and across Fish Hoek bay the sea swells against the coastal rocks.

'You guys are mental, you can't swim in this,' Lisa calls back from the house as we wave our farewells.

'She does have a point,' I tell Paul, 'I can't see much of anything out there in the water today. Everyone has stayed on land and probably for good reason.'

We start making our way down to Sunny Cove train stop, planning to hop on the train to Simon's Town and then spend the day at Boulder's beach amongst our little penguin friends, when a rogue wave crashes into the protecting rocks and sends spray across the train track, soaking us through.

'What the fuck?' I laugh, nudging Paul, 'you still fancy like a dip? Those waves would batter us against the rocks.'

Paul shrugs, 'we'll be fine at Boulders, it has a lagoon.'

'That's your argument, it has a lagoon? Paul when we were there a few days ago I went snorkelling in that *lagoon* if you remember and it's fucking deep. Not only that but even on the calmest of days the current started carrying me through the bordering forests of kelp and out to sea.'

'Well don't fucking swim then,' he replies with annoyance and I stop.

'What's up with you getting all periody? Did you forget to pack your Tampons?'

'You, winging, that's what's up with me. Don't swim if you're scared of the water, I just thought it would be a laugh. I've packed a six pack of beers and I thought we could just chill on the rocks and talk shit all afternoon. We have spent all Christmas doing family shit and now we have just a few days left before it's back to normality.'

I nod. The guy's got a point. As great as it has been out here it has been a family holiday with me and Melissa as honorary members of the Fielding clan. Paul and I haven't had much chance to just dick around and be a couple of boys in their early twenties on holiday. Christmas was great but coming from a more temperate climate and expecting snow on the day like any excited five year old, I was sourly disappointed, although I never thought I'd be able to say this but, I spent most of Christmas day on the beach sunbathing.

The train choo-choos to a halt and we climb on board the first class compartment. Despite apartheid's abolishment in the nineties the five African men who are also waiting for the train get on the compartment at the very end, third class, as this ticket is a lot cheaper. When I ask Paul why we don't get into the third class carriage he lets out an uneasy laugh.

'No thanks, don't fancy being robbed at knife point. Last year an elderly white lady got into the third class carriage by mistake and was thrown off the moving train minus her handbag and shoes.'

'Shoes?' I ask and Paul shrugs.

We find seats in the near deserted carriage and sit, closing the open window which is blowing a gale through the compartment.

'So,' I say with a grin, slapping Paul on the knee, 'you and Melissa hey, what happened there?'

Paul shrugs again, 'a shag's a shag, isn't that right?'

'Right,' I tell him a little unconvincingly. His tone isn't one of jovial laughter, it is serious.

He reaches into his rucksack and takes out a can, opening it and sipping a little of the beer. I frown, realising I am the helpless fly now stuck in a web of pretence and Paul's spider will soon pounce.

'Listen Paul I need to tell you...'

'Save it,' he smiles his spider smile, not once dropping his eye contact.

Shit.

The ten minute train ride into Simon's Town passes with an uncomfortable silence between us. I concentrate on the sea to my left, wishing it would come and swallow me up. A couple of times I glance at Paul and he continues to stare at me from the opposite seat. As the train stops and we get up to leave he moves in, his mouth close to my ear, and says, 'did you think I wouldn't find out?'

I am at a loss for words and as I try and force my brain to think quickly of something to say, Paul turns on his heel and steps down onto Simon's Town station's platform.

'Come on Billy,' he calls as though nothing is wrong and the train journey from hell had not just taken place, 'you were lucky the day we arrived here; let's have another race, this time to Boulders Beach.'

His request sounds more like a threat but I nod regardless.

'Good,' Paul continues, his pace quickening. I can feel my nerves begin to tingle in anticipation of the forthcoming race, 'first one to the top of that massive rock we were jumping off last time we were there, is the winner.'

He then takes off across a car park in the general direction of boulders beach, obviously planning to stick with the coastline. I sit down and sigh, watching as my best friend in the whole world disappears around the coast. How did it get to this? Why hadn't I told him about me and Lisa at the beginning? Now Paul feels I've betrayed him and he's angry.

I wait a couple more minutes and then stand back up, I can hear the crackling of static in my ears, drowning out the noise from the road to my right. I take a single deep breath and then start to run, my legs setting off at an alarming speed.

Something has happened to me since I came out here, I can run and run and run, there is no awkward stitch five paces into my sprints like I remember from school, there is no cramp in my calf half way into a stride which sends me tumbling to the ground and ending my race prematurely, there is only clarity, the static subsides when I start to run and everything goes away, I feel at peace with the world.

After my first win along the catwalk at Fish Hoek I started going for a jog each morning, along the coast, past Sunny Cove, Glencairn, and into Simon's Town and then on inland, following the sign posts, running faster and faster, my speed increasing more each following morning. I would arrive at Cape Point, the end of the line, where the sea from the west coast meets False Bay. I would then buy a bottle of water from the Cape Point gift shop and run back. This morning run would take about two hours, an hour there and an hour back. This morning I looked up the actual distance I have been running to keep my boundless energy in check. It is 20 miles from Fish Hoek to Cape Point which means I have been covering a distance of 40 miles every morning before breakfast which is impossible. I know for a fact the world record holder for running the marathon did this in a couple of minutes over two hours, and that is a 26 mile trip. I don't know how I am doing this, my falling has stopped and in its place I have this speed and stamina which, it would seem, no man can match. How am I able to run fourteen extra miles on the world record marathon holder in the same time it takes them to run 26? These athletes spend months and years training for the races which distance I am covering every morning without breaking a sweat.

When I realized this change in my body I rang my dad, the scientist, knowing that if anyone could, he would be able to find an explanation but once again his phone was off.

Two days and we head home, and I have changes I must make to my life, I know that now. I can't spend my days drinking myself into depression because it's fucking raining outside, I've a new found ability to try and understand and a cousin to track down, but first I must tackle a more immediate issue in my life, Paul.

Instead of taking the route Paul has headed off in I opt for the road, realising that when I arrive at Boulders I will need to double back on myself to get from the road down to the beach but that won't be a problem. Despite Paul's head start it means nothing now. I could have waited another five minutes and still I will be waiting for him at the finish line.

I hit the pavement and speed up, aware that I can't push it as I do along the deserted roads every morning for fear of running a little *too* fast in the presence of tourists and commuters alike. I concentrate on the traffic, making sure I am not overtaking any vehicles and head up the road, the sun beating down on my shoulders and wind cool in my face. It has occurred to me that with this ability I could start entering marathons back home, racing top athletes and leaving them all in my wake. Don't they usually knight great sportsmen? Sir William Johnson has a great ring to it, Sir Bill.

Just up ahead in the distance stands the sign post for Boulders Beach with a picture of a penguin next to it. I turn left and speed across the empty gravel car park, a huge trail of dust rising in my wake. I toss the attendant some coins for entry and head down the slope to the beach.

Stopping at the water's edge, a small wave crashes over my knees and I step back. The whole lagoon looks like it is swaying with the bobbing ocean. Another wave crashes into the huge rock I am about to climb and I notice that where usually there is water level lines on all the rocks, today there are none. Today the ocean is not our friend.

I look up at the monster in front of me and I begin to climb, careful not to slip on the gradual slope of the first rock which is both wet and covered with slime. I then move around to the back of the rock face and slowly lift myself up onto the small ledge which acts as a springboard to jump across to the much higher boulder. I am about 30 feet up now and am very aware that one misstep and I'd tumble through the crack in front of me, not only battering my body along the sharp surfaces in between the giant stones, but probably getting stuck in the bargain too.

I leap forward, looking for something to hold onto when I land to stop myself from sliding back down the sloping cliff top. There isn't much, the surface is smooth and with the wet running shoes on my feet this may very well be a deadly combination. I attempt to thrust myself forward and feel the wind against my back, pushing me a little more than possible so that as I land I am able to grab a small indentation in the rock's surface.

Shit.

Why didn't I consider waiting on the beach for Paul to arrive because now there is another daunting thought whizzing around my head as I reach the rock's summit and look out over the beach, I have to get down and the only way in these conditions is to jump over the edge into the sea and hope for the best.

27

ERIC: FIGHT OR FLIGHT

To say I am well-travelled could be seen as an understatement given my age. I have lived in many places and experienced many different and exciting cultures in my time, but Cape Town has always been a favourite. Boulders Beach, the majesty of the lagoon on a calm morning, the gentle lapping of the water against the rocks which rise up and out of the sea while small penguins gather in groups or splash about in the reeds. It is simply beautiful. This morning, however, there is no gentleness in the water's movement. The sea rolls violently to the shore, crashing against the beach's sentries and from the rock on which I now sit I watch Billy climb the small cliff face of the largest of the boulders in the lagoon.

 I remain shielded from view, the light wrapped around me, air thick and the strong winds shimmering around my unseen mass. Watching the boy work his way up the rock I marvel at his speed and confidence of the climb. The only time he hesitates is on a jump across to the second, much higher rock and although he will not realize it, he used his flight, or the infancy of that ability, to push himself further onto the summit. I recognize this because I am looking for it, the stunted push mid-air as gravity works against the boy's ability to defy it. Once upon a time I was that boy, running across soft earth which should have pulled me through its watery fingers to the bottom of the lake in which I sped across to evade my captors, not realizing my body was displaying its new capacity to stick two fingers up at the laws of physics.

 I hear foot falls behind me and turn. It is Paul, Billy's friend, sprinting as fast as he can towards the beach. As he notices the boy sitting upon their rendezvous, legs dangling over the side and waving, Paul stops to catch his breath, muttering something to himself as he jogs down to meet his friend. I watch as he climbs the same rock face Billy had a few minutes earlier, slipping twice but eventually arriving at the top with a help in hand from the boy for that final jump.

Almost immediately their muffled voices begin to echo across to me, getting louder and louder as an argument ensues. I rise up into the wind and gently move high across the water, succeeding with some difficulty in remaining invisible to the boys while flying above their heads.

'Why, out of all the girls in the world did you have to go and fuck my sister? Why?' Paul shouts into Billy's face. 'You must have known how I'd react, Billy. You go about your days fucking anything that moves. Every weekend a new girl's name and a new notch on the bedpost and that is fine but not with Lisa.'

Billy steps back, veering out of the way perhaps a little too quickly as Paul lunges for him and slips on the sodden rock.

'Come on Paul, it hasn't been like that mate. We love each other.'

'Love each other? How long has this been going on? How long have you been fucking my sister, tricking her into thinking you actually give a shit about her?'

'Fuck you Paul. You don't have a clue. All those girls, they were all lies, weekly alibis so I could spend time with Lisa and avoid this happening. I knew you would blow your top and so while we were seeing if what we had would go anywhere we decided to put off telling you. Lisa knew you would go insane because you have hated every one of her previous boyfriends, scaring most of them off, and I have spent years listening to you bad mouth anyone who so much as looks at your baby sister.'

'Exactly,' Paul cries out again, moving in with his fists raised and ready to strike. Again Billy is far too quick for the lazy punch and retaliates this time by pushing Paul across the rock.

'Stop it. Let's get down from here and talk about this on the beach before one of us slips and falls.'

'Fuck off. What did I tell you before we left to come here? I said don't shag my sister. That's all I asked of you and the one thing you wouldn't deliver.'

'But Paul, we have been together for months now, I don't think you realize, everyone knows. I've had dinner at your parent's house with Lisa, as a couple, we have made plans, we love each other and want to spend our lives together.'

'You've betrayed me in the worst way possible and now only one of us will make it down off this rock. You want my sister you fight me for her.'

With interest I watch as Billy's eyes narrow, he is sizing up the threat, working out who would come out of a violent encounter on top. I too can feel that adrenaline begin to evoke a reaction inside my own body. Fight or flight they call it, although chemical reactions such as this always ruse that part of me which I try to keep under control because flight is not an option for the divine. We fight. It is the only way.

28

BILLY: THE END

'You've betrayed me in the worst way possible and now only one of us will make it down off this rock. You want my sister you fight me for her.'

I've never seen him like this, face contorted with rage and fists shaking with the same adrenaline which has begun to course through my own body. I take a step back and relax into some sort of fighting stance. I am no fighter. In fact the most I have ever fought has been when there is a queue to the bar on a busy Saturday night. Paul on the other hand does fight, he has even won fights in Mixed Martial Art tournaments and although I am taller than him and probably have a larger reach with any punch I could throw, Paul has the skill and knowledge to deflect said punch and descend upon me with animal like ferocity.

He moves in again and swings for my head but this punch is slow and I am fast. I pivot my body to the right and push him away with his body's own momentum.

'Come on mate, stop it,' I cry out, moving again as he attempts another haymaker.

'Fight me you piece of shit.'

Another near miss and as I move behind Paul's position he turns, almost in slow motion, as though severely fatigued.

'Stop…your…moving…and…fight…me,' he says, his words matching the speed of his actions.

I look around me, the wind rustling the greenery down near the beach, a solitary penguin jumping off a rock and floating down to the water like a butterfly landing on a nectar filled flower. The world around me has slowed down, the wind through my hair even feels sluggish, massaging my head, whispering in my ears. As I turn back to Paul I am confronted with a fist inches from my face and before I can move out of the way everything speeds back up with the slam of knuckles against my cheekbone.

I drop to the ground and Paul starts kicking me in my head hard, any rationality that may have been in my friend's mind before has been lost to this blind rage over his sister. Another well placed foot connects with my nose and all that I can see is tainted red with my own blood as it fills my eyes and chokes me, and still he continues to lash out. Everything is happening so quickly now as he turns me around onto my back and straddles me, delivering blow after blow to my face, each punch slamming my head hard into the rock on which I lie.

As Paul stands up again, bearing over me, fists clenched, waiting to see what *my* next move is, I see something behind him, a shimmer in the wind. I close my eyes, waiting for the next blow, rolling into the foetal position to try and save my body from some of the battering.

'You should have left her alone,' I hear him cry out through the wind and as I open my eyes I watch him running up to me.

Again the shimmer behind him but this time I see a face emerge from the wind, before disappearing again and as Paul kicks me with deafening force over the side of the rock I feel the wind catch my breath. Through my blood stained vision I watch as the rock's summit shoots upwards away from me, the rock face to my right speeding by. I am falling only this time there will be no waking up from sleep across the room. Is this what my body has been trying to tell me my entire life, mimicking the very way I will see my end? I turn in the air, clipping the top of my head on the rock and feeling the intense sear of white pain as I hear the crack in my skull. Down I fall towards the evil ocean, its arms out wide, welcoming me into its murky bosom.

This is it.

This is the end.

No life flashes before my eyes, no montage of childhood memories, moving on to adolescence. Instead, in the end, all I have waiting for me is the ocean and the sharp rocks which lurk beneath, eager to take hold and claim me as its own.

29

SOPHIE: *THE SURVIVAL GAME*

Survival is what all living organisms on this planet strive for, both individually and for their species. It is written in our DNA, is part of our genetic code, and I have tried to develop a theory using the premise of survival to understand where my own species' abilities come from. I can only use personal experience to illustrate my musings, I wish I had come into contact with more like me so that my theories could be either confirmed or disproved but so far there have been very few of the Divine to cross my path.

I believe the rapid cell regeneration is the underlining trigger to our bodies changing. Something happens and this gene is woken up, changing us from mortal to immortal, our body's invincibility making our longevity possible. In my first life I was a warrior and in the physicality of war man needs speed and strength. After my first death, when I fell into a coma, my dormant Divine gene was woken up. Sensing my body's decline it kick-started my rapid cell regeneration, all broken connections in my body were repaired, my body healed, and I woke up.

Back then people rarely woke from comas. Physicians of the time had almost no knowledge of anatomy and the function of the brain. In fact my doctor was also my priest which I find a contradictory in terms. Prayers were offered and then answered when I rose unscathed, a God was thanked for sparing my life and on I went to fight for my country.

Almost immediately after people's 'prayers were answered' I found I was stronger and I could lift twice that of any other man. Again God was given the credit, giving me the tools to defeat the English in battle, and although I question the origins of my strength knowing there was no divine intervention, it appeared my strength and then my speed were direct attributes of my reawakening. At the time I was not aware I could heal almost instantly and it was not until in battle, when I fell to man's sword, did I find wounds would heal instantly.

I wonder if my strength and speed was manifested from my need for it, my body evolving to the world around it. When I compare this to Eric's ability to become invisible, and how when in the midst of his darker urges this ability would be a fine attribute to unleash, I find my theory sound. Once the Divine gene has kicked in the body can evolve to the mind's conscious needs.

This is, as always, just a theory which I have based my studies upon and I welcome being proved wrong. As a scientist I seek only the truth in anything I study.

I am talking now to you, my reader. Are you able to shed more light on our abilities or where they come from? I know you are out there dear Divine reader and this book is written for you.

I wait for you through time. Maybe one day we will meet and we will help each other find the truth.

I am here Mr E and your theory is half wrong. I agree with the body evolving with the mind's conscious need, this explains my ability to jump while my own body refuses to move, but this 'Divine gene' does not kick in once rapid cell regeneration had begun, I am living testament to that. I will find you Mr E, you are out there somewhere and I will find you.

I blink and the book closes down on my computer.

Today I am hoping to test myself to see if I am able to jump from one host to another. My own theory is that it may be possible and if this is so I may be able to get across to New York to meet with this professor who is studying the book The Divine. He is my only lead and despite trying to get granddad to somehow contact Eric, my father, he is reluctant to do so, telling me he does not know where he is. I don't believe him but I am not going to push this, granddad's loyalty is understandably towards Eric before anyone, he spent the majority of his life with the man. Dad can wait for now, it's not as if he is going anywhere. I have missed him for every day of my life ever since that day when he left. I was made to believe he had died and I understand granddad thought this was best for me, so that I didn't go through my life always wondering why he had left. Even now I do not know why, although from within the pages of this book a picture is beginning to form of the man my father really was, a man desperate for a release from his inner demon.

There is a gentle knock on the door and granddad enters without the hustle and bustle of grandma.

'Hi beautiful,' he says, moving across the room and sitting down in the seat next to my bed. 'It's nice to see you back in your own body.'

He lifts up my lifeless hand and kisses it, smiling.

i a m g l a d y o u c a m e

Granddad nods and then lets out a huge breath of air, 'are you sure you want to do this? There is no telling the affect it might have on either your body or mind.'

The email I had sent granddad lay out my plan in detail of the journey I was going to embark upon. Almost immediately he had emailed me back telling me to hang fire, that he was on his way to the hospital, and now here he is.

m y b o d y i s b r o k e n b u t m a y b e t h e r e i s a w a y t o f i x i t i f t h i s l e c t u r e r c a n h e l p m e t h e n i t i s w o r t h a s h o t

The old man nods and then says, 'you are going to need an accomplice Soph, someone who can help you on your way. A test subject who understands what it is you are trying to do.'

n o i w i l l n o t j u m p i n t o y o u

Granddad nods, 'yes Sophie, you will. I will reside in your body, have a nap, watch tv, browse the internet with your glasses, pass the time while you catch the first plane to New York and attend this lecturer's class. Use me my dear, if it can help to break you from your prison then it must be done and if you do manage a jump from my body to another then I am guessing I will wake up as you do, unharmed and in the big apple.'

I understand his logic, but there is still much to risk.

idontknowwhatwillhappenifidojumpfromonehosttoanother

Granddad shrugs an smiles, 'well then let's find out.'

Before I have made the conscious decision to jump into granddad's body I feel the rolling motion, as though it's no decision of my own. Instead of feeling the momentum of our bodies and minds merging so that I might pass across into granddad's mind, I feel a push. My subconscious has already made the decision to jump and I am powerless to stop it.

'Granddad,' I cry out in the old man's voice and slump down on the bedside, granddad's heart beats fast in my chest and when I sit up and gaze out of the old man's eyes everything appears blurred. I reach for his glasses and my world is sharp again. I lift the hand which granddad had kissed moments earlier and kiss it again.

'Are you ok?'

I watch as my eyes dart across the computer screen and then the robotic voice which has been my own for so long now speaks out to me.

iamoksophiegoandexperiment

Kissing my own forehead I notice how much weight I have lost in the recent weeks. My body is deteriorating.

'I love you,' I tell him and then stand up onto aching legs. A thought then enters my mind and I sit back down.

gosoph

'No,' I smile, 'there is someone I need to speak to first.'

I close my eyes and think back to the journey to the hospital this morning, a memory fresh in granddad's mind. I feel the gentle lolling of granddad's Mercedes, the cool air on my face from the open driver-side window and then I am driving, I am here, following Chesterfield manor's driveway down to the electric gates. I slam on the brakes and the car stops with a skid, jolting me back into the hospital room.

'Granddad what happened this morning when you set off to come here and as you were driving down towards the entrance gates?'

My eyes dart across the computer screen furiously and I marvel at how quickly the old man can put together sentences using my software with only his eyes.

h o w d o y o u k n o w a b o u t t h a t

'I was there, moments ago I was driving your car and as I hit the brakes I was jolted from your memory and back to this hospital room.'

y o u s t o p p e d m y c a r

I nod.

y o u r e a l i z e w h a t t h i s m e a n s d o n t y o u

Another nod. Yes I do realize what this means, far from being able to simply observe a host's memories, I relive them, controlling my host just as I am now.

'What happened this morning?'

i b l a c k e d o u t f o r a m o m e n t

'And I stopped your car.'

s o p h i e j u s t s t o p t h i s c o u l d b e d a n g e r o u s

I close my eyes, ignoring granddad's protests. I have a life time of his memories to…to what? Time travel to? There is only one person I need to see now. Granddad may be reluctant to give me my dad's whereabouts but he cannot stop what has already happened, alter a life time of memories of my father.

Thinking about my home, Chesterfield Manor, I see the tree halfway up the drive to the house, the huge Oak which dad and I built a swing in during one hot summer day in my childhood. I see that tree manifest in front of me only now the swing is not there and I stand leaning against the cool bark. There is frost on the ground and the sun is still rising in the sky. I put my hands out in front of me, child's hands. I have travelled back to granddad's childhood.

'Daddy…' I cry out and then stop. Turning and running to the house, aware that all the occupants save for one will be strangers to me, a little boy's family that I will not recognize. I wonder if granddad knows of Eric's immortality now or if that information is still to come.

I open the front door and a dog barks…Timothy, the grey Alsatian. I recall stories from granddad of this fiercely loyal family pet but as he bounds through the kitchen towards me, he stops, head tilting to the side and ears raised. He begins a low guttural growl. The dog knows something is wrong, he can sense it, smell it. The growl is spat out into a bark before a voice booms from another room.

'Timmy!'

The dog yelps at his owner's warning, and hides under the kitchen table, growling once more as he watches me pass further on into the house.

I walk through into the hallway, the home I know so well now dressed up with 1940's memorabilia. Lace curtains frame each window and where thick cream carpets will one day cover the stairs and hallway, now they are adorned with lots of small colourful rugs, testament I imagine, to my father's travels.

I make my way through to the living room where there is no fifty inch flat screen television above the fireplace or granddad's prized landscape watercolours which he entitled Four seasons of home, instead paintings of families I do not recognize (apart from the ever present Eric Chesterfield) adjourn the walls.

I hear a cough from the study, granddad's study, and slowly walk towards the door. I knock. Dad is sat at the desk with his back to me writing on thick cream paper. To his side a fire cracks and hisses in the fire place, throwing out shadows against the walls, dancing flames celebrating the warmth it has created in the room.

He turns in his seat and smiles that same old crooked smile which, one day he will show me and I will love him for it.

'Well hello there little man, you're up early this morning. Now was it you teasing old Timothy which caused him to bark?' he asks, still smiling.

I nod, not daring to speak for to do so could give the game away. Instead I run to him, arms outstretched, and jump into his lap, hugging him tight around the neck.

'I've missed you,' I cry through tears of sadness and joy. All these years without my dad and now here I am holding him as much as I can, knowing that I must go back and he will be gone from my life once more.

'Well,' daddy laughs, 'Alan as long as it has been since I read you your favourite story at bed time last night, this certainly is a welcome greeting. He kisses my hair as I tuck my head into his shoulder.

I am now at a crossroad and know not how I should proceed. I want to tell him everything, to explain that I am his daughter inside my grandfather's child body. I want him to understand that things will not be happy families in eighty years' time and this peace I see in his expression will disappear and the demons will return. I want to cry out to him but I know I cannot say these things. Everything must remain as it is because it has already happened. You can't change the past because I know trying to change anything will do no good. When granddad was a child he blacked out and his future granddaughter found her way into her father's study to be held by him once again. This memory I have accessed is not real, it is a ghost from the past, everything happened so long ago.

'Uncle Eric?' I venture forth, careful with my words.

'Alan I have told you before, less of the Uncle, you make me feel so old.'

I smile at this and then decide fuck it, and throw caution to the wind, 'how old are you?'

Dad pauses, a smirk remaining on his face, 'how old do you think I am?'

'Older than you look,' I tell him, holding his giant hand with the child's I possess. 'I remember my grandmother talking about when she was a girl and she also had an Uncle called Eric.'

Granddad has told me this story a hundred times. His grandmother had been second generation Chesterfield and so is as close to the family origins as I am able to get. A few days ago Granddad updated this story explaining Eric had arrived to the north west of England some five years before the birth of his 'niece'. He had arrived with his own son, a man who would be my brother, and when that man had his first child they masqueraded Eric as the doting uncle instead of a thirty year old looking grandfather. Two hundred years on 'uncle' Eric's last 'nephew' is now an eighty four year old man whose mind is trapped inside the body of his adopted granddaughter.

'That is correct little man. The first Eric Chesterfield came here with his brother David to find work, and together they built this very house we live in now.'

'Why don't you have children Uncle Eric?'

I catch the frown flicker on Dad's brow before disappearing, 'well you know Mr Questions, maybe I just haven't met the right special lady who can cook better than your mummy.'

'You will find a lady some day and you will have a little girl and she will be like you but you will leave.'

Dad unlatches himself from me and puts me down on to my feet in front of him, 'Alan buddy, what are you talking about?'

'Just remember my words Uncle Eric because I will not. She is like you.'

I then jump up into his arms for one final hug and tear myself away, running back outside to the tree where granddad stood at the beginning of this memory. He will have blacked out but will not realize this if he is in the same position, leaning against the old oak tree, the one my father and my brother long dead planted during Queen Victoria's reign.

Behind me I see dad running after me and I turn and wave.

'Go easy on him, he won't remember any of it,' I call out and then close my eyes, the tears escaping and running down my cheeks, the same tears I feel as I reopen my eyes and see my own face staring back at me, eyes wide.

w h e r e w e r e y o u

I smile, 'with dad.'

30

WILLIAM: *1607*

It had been three hundred and two years since one of history's greatest escapes, and to this day I sometimes think about the man who took my place at my execution. His name was Donnchadh Mór, which translated from Gaelic meant Big Duncan, a man who like me, towered over his peers, a farmer and a father who fought many battles against the English by my side. Men would often comment of our likeness and when we wore beards the resemblance was uncanny. After our betrayal and defeat by the Scottish nobles at Falkirk I was branded an outlaw and so went into hiding. Traveling to France to rally support from the French king. Knowing my days were numbered, that someone would betray me soon, I then travelled back to Scotland and the council of my men.

Big Duncan attended this meeting and put a plan to me which could very well have toppled the English crown. We would swap places; he would become William Wallace while I would travel back to France in a bid for support from King Philip IV. Upon my return with the forces of France behind me, Scotland could then invade England once again, only this time we would have the power to be able to crush King Edward I's forces.

Acting as my body double Big Duncan was captured by the English and tried at Westminster Abbey where he was sentenced to death. On August 23rd 1305 I watched from the crowds as my doppelganger was tortured and beheaded. His body was hacked up, his head was boiled and set on London Bridge and his quartered body was sent to Newcastle, Berwick, Sterling and Perth as a warning to anyone who dared defy the English King.

With William Wallace dead I had a decision to make. Would I reprise my role as Scottish warrior and continue to fight, to inspire my countrymen into fighting for Scotland by returning from the dead, or would I walk away. Over the years I believe I made the right decision, with Sir William Wallace dead he became more than a single man, he became a folk hero, a legend, an identity for my home country, he became the embodiment of the Scottish people, much more than I could have ever been.

And so I left, heading South through France, onto Spain and then down to Morocco, always searching for others like me, others able to survive the sword. For three centuries I travelled the known world, following local myths and legends to try and find their origins, to try and find others. This search found me back in Scotland on the trail of an old woman born before any other could remember. It was rumoured the Crawford Witch lived out in the forests surrounding Loch Trool in Galloway. I can recall as clear as this morning's breakfast my encounter with the witch who had lived longer than any other.

It was a bright morning in spring. I had made camp for the night with my horse and cart and planned journeying into the forest that very morning to find the fabled immortal witch. I had been awake for perhaps half an hour when my horse stirred, pulling at his reigns which secured him to the cart. As I moved around the cart to see what the trouble was she appeared from the trees, hair shining silver in the morning light and in her hand she held a what I now know to be a Japanese samurai sword.

I lifted up my hand in greeting and she returned the courtesy with a flick of the katana blade.

'You are not welcome here,' she told me, speeding up her movement as we approached each other, 'leave now.'

I held up my hands, 'I mean you know harm,' I told her as her face became clearer. She then stopped and gasped, the sword falling to the earth and her to her knees.

'William? No, it cannot be. William?'

I stopped, now wary of the name I had not used in over a century. I reached for my own sword, the heavy metal in my hand reassuring.

'You are the witch Crawford are you not? I come to speak to you of things of a magical essence.'

The old lady was slumped over onto her elbows and was sobbing uncontrollably. This hadn't been the start to the meeting I had envisioned.

'You come to speak to me of magic,' she said, sitting up onto her knees, her skin although aged, still had a colour of youth about it, making the old lady appear as though she was a much younger woman dressing up as an old one. 'Tell me Sir William Wallace, in the one hundred and two years since your execution is it magic which brings you to me now?'

I gazed into her pale blue eyes, and the glimpse of recognition stirred something inside me.

'Who are you? How is it you know of me?'

'I was just a young girl when you left to fight and you never came back for me. You left without sparing me a second thought.'

'Nessie?'

My little sister smiled and then stood up off the ground, and it was at that moment, as she walked towards me with her arms held out for me that I could see the little girl whom I had promised I would not desert. In our embrace I dropped to my knees and kissed the wrinkled hand which belonged to my little sister.

'I don't understand, how is it you did not die many years ago?'

Picking myself back up we walked back towards my cart and Nessie said, 'I did die, in my fifty second year I fell ill with a great cough. I then fell into a deep sleep and when I woke my family had me laid out in my best dress ready for burial. I had returned from the dead and the town in which I had lived for thirty years turned against me. I was captured and tortured, burned at the stake and then my charred body was dumped into a casket and thrown into a swamp. My body healed and I made my way to the surface, realising there was no point in going back and so, like you, I moved away.'

I nodded to her sword, 'that is an interesting shaped sword.'

'It's Japanese, dear brother, the Katana sword. I moved far enough away so that the stories of my rising from the dead did not follow.'

'Why did you come back?'

Nessie shrugged at this, 'Scotland is my home, and after sixty years my story is now third generation. Any woman old enough to remember my face is now long dead and buried. These days any old lady past the age of sixty is witch Crawford,' she smiled.

We stopped at my cart and I took Nessie's hand in mine, 'I am so happy to see you. I have felt so alone for all these years, not knowing if I was the only one with this amazing gift, and now I find you.'

Nessie smiled again, the little girl I remembered so well shining through in that smile.

'Oh William, you must stay with me, there is so much we have to talk about.'

I nodded at this, 'of course, first let me make the trip into the next town so that I might buy provisions for my stay. I will spare no expense. Tonight we will dine on roasted Pheasant and potatoes and wash it down with the finest mead I can purchase. Tell me dear Nessie, where is your home so that I might find it upon my return?'

Nessie pointed at the trees, 'a ten minute walk up that ridge lays Loch Trool. On the far side of the loch there is a path which winds into the forest. Follow that path and you will eventually arrive at the wicked witch Crawford's evil cabin.'

'Sounds enchanting,' I told her as I saddled my horse, 'I will see you in a few hours.'

She waved me off down the road and when I returned that evening she would ambush me, locking me in the Iron box I called home for forty years. The year was 1607 and Nessie was the first of my kind I ever came into contact with.

As the limousine pulls up outside a chrome and glass monstrosity of a sky scraper in downtown Houston I thank George and get out onto the sidewalk. All last night I was practising my American twang and believe it is at least passable now. Pushing aside thoughts of my family back in England I walk through the revolving doors and head across to the reception desk.

'Hi there, my name is Mr…'

'Mr Crawford,' the young lady on the reception desk says with her Barbie girl smile, 'please head for floor eighty where someone will meet you.'

I thank the girl and head across to the lift…elevators.

Behind me I hear the receptionist calling me back, 'sir, you will need this key to access the top five floors. It is your personal key so please don't lose it.'

I smile and thank the lady again, resuming my journey towards the elevators. As I press the button one of the elevator doors slides open in front of me and I step inside. I then read the touchscreen display, scrolling upwards past law practises, financial consultants, and corporate institutions until I reach the top, floors 80 – 85 The Phoenix Committee. I press for the 80th floor and am greeted with a buzzing sound. The floor list disappears and the words **Please Insert Key** appears on screen. Slotting my key into the designated slot beside the touch screen panel, I brace my body as I hurtle upwards, more roller-coaster than any elevator I have travelled in before. Twenty seconds and eighty floors later I step out into The Phoenix Committee's lobby area.

Like downstairs, there is another Barbie clone behind a desk, only instead of glass and chrome, this theme is more height of the Roman Empire with cream marble surfaces and dark polished wood everywhere.

Set in the marble of the front desk is the company's emblem in sunburnt orange, a phoenix with its wings held back mid-flight. Approaching the desk I hear a voice to my right and turn to see Nessie standing there. She is wearing a smart charcoal grey suit with white blouse underneath and her silver hair is tied up into a bun on top of her head. Her makeup is flawless and if I didn't know that her age of death, the age in which she will always appear to look, was fifty two, I would have guessed ten years younger.

'Hi there stranger,' she says in her own Americanised accent and like her attire, the voice is flawless.

I smile tight lipped and nod, 'Hi Nessie,' and we shake hands very formally. So much has changed since our first encounter as immortals.

'You look well William.'

'And you,' I tell her.

She shrugs, 'good genes I guess.'

'Touché.'

She smiles, 'I'm sorry for the way in which I got you to come over here but as you will soon see, I was left with little choice.'

'What do you mean?' I ask her, following her through a door to the right and down a corridor, 'what is this place?'

'This place is a sanctuary for your Divine William. Your book reached out as you intended it to and we were here to welcome our brothers and sisters into a family which would not fear them, which would not hunt them for being different and burn them at the stake, cast out of society as demons. You called out to us all with your book, dear brother, and the Phoenix Committee was here to receive those lost souls. You will not know this but the man who was once William Wallace, the author Mr E, is a living legend in the Divine circles.'

'Divine circles?'

'Yes Divine, you changed everything with that book, coined an identity for our species. We are your Divine William.'

We reach the end of the corridor and Nessie knocks on the door once, opening it and standing to the side, 'after you Mr E.'

I enter the office to be greeted with the magnificent view of the city skyline. Huge floor to ceiling windows cover one side of the spacious room. The furniture is modern and expensive looking, swish tan easy chairs face each other in the centre of the room and standing in between them a glass coffee table with a handful of books on seventeenth century architecture lying on top of it.

At the end of the room stands a desk and behind it sits a man who rises from his seat as I enter, smiling and walking around to greet me.

'Here he is, the legendary William Wallace, the elusive Mr E, and the brilliant William Johnson,' the man says with a huge grin, a man I recall meeting for dinner one time in 1760 while working in Paris as a Professor of science, a man fabled as immortal but when I had questioned him he had disappeared. I shake the man's hand and smile.

'I should have known one day we would meet again,' I say good naturedly.

The Count de Saint-Germain grins and slaps me on the back, introducing himself as Victor Morris and invites me to sit on the couch facing that magnificent skyline. He sits down opposite me and to my right Nessie closes the office door, moving over to us and standing behind me. I turn to her and she smiles, nodding towards Mr Morris who was once Saint-Germain. The man's attire has changed somewhat since our last encounter but his face remains exactly the same. He has cut his hair but so have I. In a world where only hippies and rockers wear their hair long, flowing locks don't seem appropriate these days.

'But of course dear William, you, or rather your pseudonym Mr E has become quite the celebrity in our circles for the past fifty eight years and the notoriety of the book has helped join our brothers and sisters together and give them direction.'

'Direction?' I ask.

Victor nods and winks, 'make yourself comfortable William, we have much to discuss.'

31

ERIC: R.I.P

The sea turns pink as Billy's body bounces off the rocks and lands, lifeless amidst the swelling water, disappearing into its depths.

I turn to his friend, Paul, the man whose penchant for childish violence has brought destruction to the boy I watched grow up, the child of my greatest friend. He stands by the rock edge, looking over the side and into the crimson waters.

'Oh fuck,' I hear escape his breath in a whisper on the wind.

Paul steps backwards from the rock edge, tripping and landing on his knees.

'Oh no no no no,' he cries out as he puts his head in his hands, 'what the fuck have I done?'

'You have killed your friend,' I whisper and he jumps up, looking about the deserted rock summit.

I then step out from my veil of light, showing myself to the grief stricken boy and he gasps.

'You…you're, you're, you're.'

'Eric,' I tell him with a smile, 'we met last Christmas at Billy's house.'

'But how did you…'

I silence him with the wave of a hand and move towards him with a speed he would not understand, taking him by the collar and forcing him over the edge.

'Be quiet and listen young man,' I see terror in his eyes as his feet struggle to find something solid to connect with, flaying about in panic, his arms mimicking this action. He cries out and I switch my grip to his neck, pulling him back in towards me, 'do you think Billy survived that fall, given the amount of blood which stains the sea?'

Paul begins to cry, 'please, I didn't mean to.'

'Yes you did, I watched you, the violence in your eyes, the red mist descending upon you so that nothing else but the kill mattered.'

'Please,' he pleads, sobbing uncontrollably, 'he could be ok. We need to get down there and find him.'

I shake my head, 'no, I will do this. What you need to do is return home, pack Billy's belongings into his holdall and leave this at the end of your driveway concealed in the bushes. When your family ask where Billy is you will tell them he decided to do some traveling and left. Tell them he said he needed to do this alone, that he had come to a crossroads in his life and was searching for direction, tell them whatever you like because my boy, if they do not believe you it will be you who must explain it to the police.'

With tears streaming down the boy's face he nods his head and I throw him back onto the rock in a heap.

'Compose yourself Paul and then do as I say,' I tell him as I step backwards off the rock's edge and feel the soft earth under my feet. Paul watches as my body remains still in the thickness of the air around me.

'This isn't possible,' he gasps and I wink at him before falling from his sight, descending with gravity and closing my eyes as the water jumps up to greet me. Through the blood stained sea Billy's body floats close to the water's surface. His eyes are closed and no air comes from his mouth or nose. I reach out for his lifeless body and pull it down to the sea bed, holding him in a bear hug as my feet make contact with the sand and I bend my knees, throwing my invisibility around both of our bodies. For a moment we both hang there in the water, suspended in this alien underworld. I then push upwards hard with my legs and as the momentum of my actions begins to send us upwards we speed up and head skywards, passing the huge boulder from which we arrived into the sea's murky depths.

Billy's body is heavy in my arms as we fly through the clouds as fast as I can manage, making it back to my rented villa in good time. Immediately I set the boy down on the ground and unlock the terrace doors, opening them up to the dining area. I reach for my phone and dial Chesterfield manor. The connection rings out.

'Shit,' I curse, sprinting back out to Billy's body and picking him up and bringing him into the house. I lie him down on the bed in the spare room and then try my phone again for Alan. Again no one answers.

I sit down on the floor in the corner of the room, watching the boy for any movement. From where I sit I can see where the rock face has torn away at Billy's scalp, and beneath the bloody matt of hair and flesh his cracked skull lies exposed to the air.

I close my eyes, hoping beyond all hope that a lifetime of William's theories comes true. I wait.

Time stands still in this room where I sit in the corner on the floor. Memories which haunt my dreams unearth themselves in my wandering mind while I wait for the impossible. So many dead at my hands and now I wait with a dwindling faith for those ghosts from the past to tell me that what goes around comes around. Now it is their turn to wreak their revenge by taking a life from me as I did theirs.

The sky darkening goes unnoticed as I sit with Billy and wait. Periodically I try Chesterfield Manor but no one answers. I think back to my own first death, so long ago, in a time when there was so much death in the world. It was in battle where I met my end and it was in battle where I woke immortal.

I move to Billy's side and stroke his head. The blood has now congealed and looks like black tar against his pale face. Hot tears sting my eyes and drop onto the boy's lifeless body. I got it wrong. The doc got it wrong. He is not one of us. Billy really is dead.

32

WILLIAM: THE PHOENIX COMMITTEE

I nod, 'so I have created a cult. Fantastic. You know when I wrote that book I did so out of frustration. For centuries I travelled the globe and searched for the Divine and it was only chance circumstance and following myths which led me to finding the both of you. And what did I have to show for it on both occasions? Nessie locked me in a box for forty years and you disappeared into the night. All this did was frustrate me even more, knowing that there *were* others out there like me but none willing to help me so that we could help our kind.'

'Until you found Eric that is,' Nessie says behind me and I turn again, nodding.

'Absolutely until I found Eric,' I tell her, 'how you even know about Eric escapes me but I am sure you and Mr Morris are about to reveal all.'

Victor begins to clap, applauding what exactly I don't know but doing so anyway, 'William calm down, you'll give yourself a heart attack.'

'Tried one once but it didn't suit so never bothered again,' I tell him smiling sarcastically.

'Such fire,' he cries out, 'I love it. I knew now was the right time to recruit you.'

I stop and recompose myself, simmering that temper which would only serve to end this meeting abruptly.

'Tell me William, why are you here?'

'To find more like us.'

'That is done. I can introduce you to seven hundred and twenty three people like us, now what? You have spent your life searching for us and now that you have found enough of your Divine to fill a football field with, what are your intentions, say hello, shake hands and be on your way?'

Seven hundred? How is it possible that so many have come forward to these people?

'Perhaps we should back up for a moment,' Victor continues, 'Nessie, would you mind bringing us some drinks please my dear?'

I hear her head back to the office door and the handle turning before the door clicks shut again and my host leans forward in his place.

'Back when we met in the seventeen hundreds I had just started up the Phoenix Committee, and like you was searching for others to join me. I created Count de Saint-Germain as the face of the Phoenix committee, a cocky aristocratic Lothario whose stories would span the centuries. This man, Saint-Germain, would pop up throughout the ages after searching for people like us and try and recruit them into the committee, that is why I was in Paris, to meet with you, and recruit you.'

'But you left, that night after our dinner I came to find you to speak some more and you had disappeared into the night, why if your intention was to recruit me?'

Victor's expression changes from light hearted giddiness to one of confusion and he frowns, 'William what do you recall as our last meeting?'

'The dinner.'

'So you do not have any recollection of ambushing me in my bedchamber and dragging me across the town by my hair before breaking into a blacksmiths workshop and placing my head in a vice?'

What?

'Are you serious? What are talking about?' I ask him, mirroring his frown.

'That night William, you broke into my bedchambers, hit me hard enough to snap two vertebrae in my neck, and dragged me through the streets of Paris before breaking into a blacksmith's workshop and placing my head in a vice.'

I shoot up to my feet, fists clenched, searching the room for weapons, imagining at what speed and force I would have to run if I was able to smash through one of those windows as an escape.

'What is this?' I ask.

'Sit down William; I have not brought you all the way over here for a fight. First you need to accept this is what happened and the reason behind my leaving in 1760.'

I sit back down and my body tenses up when I hear the door open again. Nessie enters with a tray of assorted coffee cups, bottles of water and cans of pop (soda). Her smile drops from her face as she places the tray in the middle of the coffee table and she says to Victor, 'so you told him?'

I watch as Victor nods and then leans over to pour coffee.

'Can I interest you in any refreshments?'

I take a bottle of still water and twist the cap, sipping the cool liquid.

Victor hands Nessie a cup and saucer and she moves back behind me with her drink.

As he pours his own drink he looks up and nods, 'perhaps I should be wreaking revenge for my attempted murder yes? The reason I am not is because I know it was not you, or rather not your mind trying to end my life, just as it was not you who attempted to end your sister's life.'

I shake my head, 'I don't understand any of this Victor. You say I tried to kill you but then you say it was not my mind?'

'Indeed. Have you ever come into contact with a jumper William?'

'Jumper?'

'Yes, there are those of us who have the ability to jump into the mind of others. We call them jumpers. Do you recall the night you received Nessie's letter?'

'Of course,' I reply, thinking back to the night my life changed and I was forced to leave my family.

'You ended up at the bottom of a ravine I am told, but yet you were unaware of how you got there?'

'The girl, Eric said he saw a teenaged girl appear from nowhere and lie down on the wet grass close to where we were being attacked. She spoke to him when he told her to leave.'

'Yes, that was Delores, and she is a jumper. She has the ability to manifest a ghost like image of herself close to her intended victim and then get inside their head. That image of herself she projected was not real. In fact she resides in a hospital in Jamaica in a coma. She is a very special young lady who we have used from time to time when the need has occurred. In return the Phoenix committee pays all of her medical bills and continues to throw millions of dollars a year into medical research.'

'So you think someone jumped into my mind and tried to kill you through me in 1760?' I ask him. 'It seems a little farfetched given there wouldn't have been that many of the Divine discovered back then.'

'There wasn't. You were to be my first recruit William. Back then I knew very little of other abilities men and women like us might possess and so when you tried to kill me, twisting that vice handle so that my skull began to crack inside my head, I didn't for one second think it was anyone but you attempting to end me. It was only when your sister told me of you trying to kill her did I begin to think outside of the box. I now know for certain who it was trying to kill the both of us and I know why…but enough of that for now, let's talk business, the reason we have recruited you.'

Another sip of my water, my mind racing with the possibilities seven hundred test subjects would bring, 'Ok, what would be my role in this committee, were I to accept your invitation of course?'

Nessie moves forward, placing her cup down on the table and says, 'we would give you access to our research, introduce you to men and women like yourself, with great scientific minds who strive to understand how we are capable of our rapid regeneration and longevity.'

'For the past century,' Victor continues, 'you have always taught at universities. We can place you in any university in the world where you can continue to teach if that is what you desire.'

'And what is it you want from me? I was quite happy with my post at Manchester University until you forced me to leave.'

Victor shakes his head, a wave of annoyance passing over his face, 'you see that is your problem William, you need to stop obsessing over a single moment in time. You act like them, the mortals, and you should really start thinking more long term.'

'Thirty years I spent...'

'Thirty years, fifty years, a century, it is immaterial. Our bodies do not age, the dying cells regenerate perfectly while the mortal man's time on this earth is limited because their cells breakdown until they are no more, you know this. In fact this is *your* theory. I myself walk the earth in the body of a forty three year old, Nessie was fifty two when she stopped aging, and William Wallace?'

'Thirty three years old,' I tell him and decide to change the subject. There will be time later to talk about the semantics of time and the aging process. 'Why now? And don't tell me because it has taken this long to find me. In 1958 you were behind the abduction of my friend Eric and the reason he was taken was to find me. That emblem you have on your front desk, of the phoenix in flight, Eric described and then drew that very logo after he returned to England having slaughtered all of your men. That logo was on every uniform of every guard he destroyed.'

I watch as Nessie turns away shaking her head.

'Oh you doubt my words? Then perhaps we might resume this conversation after I have invited Eric to join us.' Their faces change, fearful of the thought, and I laugh, 'You fear him don't you? You fear him because of who he once was and what he can become if roused.'

'No, you don't understand William, 1958 wasn't us.'

'Really?' I ask, standing up once more from my place.

'Yes, William,' Victor continues again, 'really. Young man I have been around since before the birth of Christ. I fought the Persians alongside Alexander the Great, fought Gladiators at the Colosseum in Rome, I do not want to fight you. The publication of your book brought our kind together but it also unearthed a threat to our kind. An invisible group of hunters emerged, scouring the earth and capturing the Divine, experimenting on us and then slaying us. Eric was lucky in 1958, the team employed to abduct him did not understand our power but their employers do. They have been slaying us for centuries, originally believed to be a religious sect tasked with protecting the word of their Christian Lord from the non-believers, they evolved into something more, an army of religious nuts hell bent on seeing us 'demons' sent straight back to hell.'

'That is fucking crazy. So we have this sect of the Christian church running around abducting innocent people because they believe we are demons?'

Nessie nods, 'they believe we mock their lord because as He rose from the dead so too do we, impervious to harm once we are reborn.'

'Well I am an atheist dear sister, in my time I have studied most religions, tried believing in a few too but reason always won to any faith.'

'We're not talking about you and what you believe, we are talking about a dangerous and highly motivated army of men and women across the globe, sleeper cells who go about their daily lives but are trained when the need arises to track, abduct and slay us.'

'Eric isn't the only one to have escaped their grasp. During the second world war I too was captured,' Victor says, 'their scientists were torturous, picking at my body for months, trying to understand how it is I could heal from the cuts from their scalpels and my broken bones would fix. They test us to try and find our weaknesses and as of yet I have not met a single of our kind to survive a beheading.'

'Sounds like you guys have got your hands full, but this still does not answer where I fit in. If what you tell me is correct and there is a group of crazed religious nuts running around killing our kind because we mock Christ, then why would I want anything to do with you?

'Because we are planning on fighting back, and when our armies rise we need warriors like you once were,' Victor growls. 'What the Phoenix committee requires from you is for you to prove your theories. We have hundreds of men and women willing to be your test subjects. They will be paid handsomely by us but ultimately any lab you set up to work out of will be your own. Next week The Divine is going to be republished and released to the public again. The book's notoriety will land it at the top of the charts and we will reach out to more of our kind than ever before possible. With the book's release we also require an 'expert' on the book to teach classes.'

'Ah, now I get it. The penny has finally dropped. You will offer me all of your resources, set me up in a lab and give me access to as many of our kind that I require and in return I will in essence set up a recruiting station for others like us to join your army and fight the men who are hunting and killing us?'

Victor nods, 'that's the deal. You may choose anywhere in the world to set up your lab and with it a post at the local university will open where you can set up your recruitment desk so to speak.'

I finish my bottle of water, leaning over the table to shake Victor's hand and then turn to Nessie, nodding to the door. She in turn nods back and I follow her as she opens it for me.

'Just one thing Victor, before I leave to consider your proposal, how are you able to republish *The Divine*? My publishers in London hold the rights to that work and I doubt they would have sold without notifying me.'

'You're absolutely right they wouldn't, and so I bought the publishers yesterday afternoon and had one of my men stationed in London, a very prominent MP you will have heard of, draft a proposal for the ban on your book to be lifted. He took it straight to the Prime Minister who signed it off immediately. You see William, when you have sat at the table of kings and been an advisor to emperors, convincing a modern day failing politician anything requires just one thing, a fat enough wallet.'

I leave, adrenaline buzzing around my body. A shadow organisation on the lose hunting, torturing and then killing the divine, a new dawn certainly is here and man has already started fighting back, crushing that what they do not understand and fear.

33

BILLY: AWAKENING

Darkness.

In the back of my mind I can hear the waves crashing against the rocks as I make my descent towards nothingness. The cool water spikes my senses and I close my eyes, ready to meet my oblivion. And then nothing. Static fills my body and deafening silence fills my head. There are no thoughts, just peace.

A high pitch ringing in my ears begins to sound, ever so faint at first, and then from the darkness I see a twinkle of light. My head begins to burn uncontrollably and my whole body cries out in pain. I am frozen, paralysed in this moment, the ringing in my ears and the light in front of me slowly growing together, coming closer to greet my bodiless being.

As I try and open my eyes they too burn but I persevere. A shadow passes across my fazed line of sight and then a crash in my chest, forcing me forward and into the light. Another crash, which seizes my body upwards with its force and the shadow passes over me once again.

Inside my head I am screaming for release as my chest is hit with another great boom, steadying itself into a rhythmic beat. My heart beat.

I open my eyes and see only blurred shapes all around me. The shadow moves again, this time close to my face and the word 'Billy' is whispered in the distance. I don't recognise this word but now it is filling my head, becoming louder and louder each time it appears from the shadow.

My eyes close again involuntarily and from the darkness I am falling, twisting around in the air, my head banging on the hard rock edge as I descend, the sea beneath me swirling black and desolate.

'Billy,' the wind whispers as I fall for an eternity.

'Billy,' I hear again, and then a faint twinge of recognition.

'Billy, open your eyes,' the shadow by my side tells me and I obey, the crackle of moonlight seeping into this room from behind me, throwing its shadows across the pale walls.

I cough and then take in a huge lungful of air, coughing again.

Turning my head to where the phantom talks to me, the vail of darkness lifts and I see Uncle Eric kneeling by my side, face wet with tears which dance in the soft light.

As I attempt to move I hear my back crack with such force and I cry out, grabbing for the arm Eric extends to aid me.

'Carefully Billy,' he says as together we move me into a sitting position.

Eric puts a glass with a drinking straw by my mouth and I drink gratefully, coughing again when I finish the glass and vomiting into my lap.

'Sea water,' he says and I nod at this.

'Uncle Eric,' I manage to croak out.

'Don't talk yet, try and stand. It'll hurt. It'll feel like your whole body is collapsing in on itself but let me assure you quite the opposite is happening.'

He pulls me forward and I cry out again with the most incredible pain, every nerve ending on fire with searing heat, engulfing my whole being.

'No, no. no,' I whisper through the heat, trying to lie back where the pain cannot find me.

Eric ignores my screams for mercy and lifts me up off the bed. I feel my feet hit the floor, heavy and weak.

'Listen mate, you need to stand.'

I cry out again, trying to ignore the grating from my femur into my pelvis.

'I can't Eric, I can't.'

Eric's hold on me does not waver as he lets me find my feet, gently releasing his grip until I am standing beside him.

'There we go,' he says and begins to undress me, the blood stained clothes dropping to the floor and I am completely naked in front of him, 'come on, I'll help you to the shower.'

Arm in arm we baby step towards the door, each step my confidence in my own strength growing.

'Your body is in shock. It hasn't a clue what is going on.'

'That makes two of us,' I say as we take to a small corridor and then through to a bathroom. Speckles of blood trail behind us but they do not concern me.

'What happened Eric, why are you here, where is *here*?' I ask, my questions coming in union. Eric switches on the shower and hands me a bar of soap.

'Shower first Billy, you have questions and there will be many more, but first you must get clean. I will go and put the coffee on and pour you a large brandy to accompany it.'

I shower slowly and deliberately. Inside my head the decent into the sea by Paul's hand plays on a loop, each time another piece of the puzzle revealing itself, another memory unearthed. With my head under the shower I watch by my feet as the water runs red with my blood but then when I search for any sign of a wound there is none. I wash my hair and with the final rinse all of the blood is gone.

Eric shouts to me through the bathroom door that my belongings are in the room where I woke, and I walk through, towel wrapped around my waist to find the small suitcase I brought with me on holiday. I open the case and find my passport sitting on top of the hastily folded clothes. Getting dressed quickly into a pair of jeans and a t-shirt I call out to Eric as I walk bare foot down the hallway which opens up into a lounge/dining room. Beyond the dining area stands Eric with his back to me on the terrace overlooking first the swimming pool and then Fish Hoek bay.

I approach with a cough to get my uncle's attention but he does not turn, instead he holds out a brandy goblet to his side for me.

'Get that down you Bill, you may want a refill before we talk.'

I swallow down the amber liquid, savouring the warmth it brings to my belly and I move forward to stand beside him.

When we are shoulder to shoulder Eric turns to me and smiles, 'you look well.'

I shrug, 'what happened Eric. Why did I wake up here and why are you here in the first place?'

Eric nods his head into the house and I follow him to the lounge where coffee is waiting. We sit and he pours the drinks, frequently looking up at me while performing this task.

'I really don't know where to start son.'

'How about the beginning?' I ask softly to which he sighs, shaking his head.

'The beginning has many faces. Perhaps it would be best to start with a book, the one I noticed in your bag.'

'*The Divine*? Dad gave it to me for something to read on the plane.'

Eric shakes his head, 'no, your dad gave it to you to read, to study, to understand, to immerse yourself in the world that book creates like you used to your comics. Have you read it?'

'Dad used to read it to me when I was a kid, I had a flick through on the plane here. To be honest it seemed like a bit of a rip off of the X-men comics.'

Eric smiles, 'did it now. First published in 1958 and you say this book stole its ideas from X-men?

'Yeah, a new species living amongst us, have done for centuries, with the ability to heal and the inability to die.'

Eric nods at this and gets up from his seat, walking out of the room for a moment. I hear a drawer open and the rattle of metal, and then he is back, standing in the doorway holding a small steak knife. He tosses it in the air, the steel blade spinning around before he catches it. In the other hand he holds two more of the knives by their blade.

I frown, watching, transfixed by the way the light catches the blade as it spins in the air. He then approaches and without warning and quicker than I have ever known anything to move, throws one of the knives towards me. I watch, the glint of the blade lost in its passage. There is a popping in my ears and the knife slows down mid-air. As I move from the chair I notice the chair's cushion I disturb rolling off the edge in slow motion but despite this when Eric moves he moves with speed towards me, teeth clenched with a knife now in each hand. He throws the second blade, this one overtaking the first and narrowly missing my shoulder. I turn to run as fast as I am able to, knowing that with my new found speed I could easily outrun my uncle. As I pivot my body, getting set to let rip through the terrace doors and out into the safety of the night, Uncle Eric appears in front of me and plunges his third knife deep into my chest. The world around me speeds up again, the cushion lands on the floor and so too does the first steak knife Eric threw.

I cry out and fall backwards to the floor but before I reach the ground Eric is there again to catch me.

'You stabbed me,' I scream out at him with both anger and fear of what his next move might be.

'Shh, shh, shh,' Eric tells me as he gently lays my body down onto the soft rug in the centre of the room, 'you'll forgive me,' he continues before grabbing hold of the knife handle protruding from my chest and yanking out the blade.

'Just watch,' he whispers, tearing my t-shirt from my body.

I look down at my chest, a mass of flowing blood, my arms, fingers and toes' tingling as my blood is forced out of my body instead of circulating around it.

'I'm dying, Eric, you stabbed me,' I cry out, following the deep red trickles. The blood congeals right in front of my eyes and I watch as it hardens, scabbing over within seconds and then flaking away to reveal fresh skin.

I look up at Eric and he looks back at me, a smirk forming on his face, 'do you understand now?' he asks me, lifting me onto my feet.

'What?' I whisper, 'what the fuck just happened?'

'Sit down and I'll explain everything now that I have your attention.'

I do as commanded and sit back down, taking the fresh goblet of brandy Eric offers me and thanking him.

'You stabbed me, I was dying.'

Eric nods his head and then sits himself, 'yep, I *did* stab you and you *were* dying, but only for a moment. Welcome to the divine my boy, and…errr…sorry about your t-shirt, I know you liked that one.'

34

SOPHIE: A WALK IN THE PARK

Walking slowly through Central Park I smile as three children run past me, throwing snowballs at each other and skipping gleefully on, ignoring the protests of their mother behind me. One of the kids knocks into me and calls out an apology as he throws another snowball at his friend. Immediately the young mother appears by my side pushing a pram.

She takes hold of my arm and says, 'I'm so sorry about Alex, he should know better than to push past you.'

I turn to the lady, 'it's fine, really, no harm done.'

The young lady returns my smile and offers to escort me to a nearby park bench to which I accept graciously.

'You're English right?'

I nod, 'yes that is correct, I am on holiday and meeting with my granddaughter very soon. She must be running late.'

'Oh my, I've never met an English gentleman before sir, it really is an honour.'

I bow my head in thanks as we approach the bench but as I raise my head back up from the bow my balance waivers, knocking me into the pram. The young mother takes my arm to help me sit and I thank her, my vision blurring for a moment. I close my eyes and concentrate on the hand which holds my arm, and when I open my eyes again I find myself standing over granddad who gasps.

'It worked,' he says. 'Sophie that was quite the most eerie experience of my life, one moment I was watching television in your room, an old western starring John Wayne, then next I felt my body being propelled forward and here I am, sitting on a park bench...' he pauses to take in his surroundings, 'in Central Park.'

I smile, helping the old man to his feet, 'beats traveling eight hours by plane right?'

He laughs, 'absolutely.'

'Something's wrong though. A moment ago I lost my balance and my vision was distorted. I think I have spent too long out of my own body, my mind needs to rest.'

A look of horror moves over granddad's face, 'what are you going to do?

I shake my head, I'll be fine, 'come on, I need to find another host, this one has this little one,' I say, nodding at the pram as I push it along the path, 'and three children running around the park. I don't fancy like babysitting all afternoon.'

As we walk, granddad watches the baby sleep and smiles, 'did you ever think about children Soph?'

I too look down at the sleeping child and then shrug, 'before the accident I was always away in the less desirable places of the world, helping the sick and needy. There was never any time to meet a man and get to know him well enough to even think about starting a life with him.'

Granddad nods, 'my little girl, always trying to save the lives of others without stopping and thinking about your own life and what it is *you* want.'

'I thought about children from time to time. My friends from University were all getting married and having babies, of course I thought about it.'

'But?' granddad asks.

'But, I guess the children in the African communities I would be sent to became my adopted children. I cried every time I left to be sent somewhere else, cried because I would not see these young ones grow into the next generation of their tribes and communities, but I also cried because every time I left it would be a stark reminder of how I did not belong there with them, that I was only ever a guest, always an outsider no matter how close I believed I was to them.'

'You were lonely.'

I nod. 'Yes, I always felt so lonely when I left, and then I would think about maybe meeting a man, settling down and having babies of my own.'

Granddad pats my hand, 'you will one day my dear.'

'Yeah right,' I snort, 'I'm going to meet my prince charming while I'm frozen in my bed in the hospital. I accept that children and a family won't be for me and its fine. For now I have all the family I need in you.'

A wave of nausea suddenly hits me and I stop, dry retching, a tingling in my ears getting louder and louder so that it drowns out everything else. I fall into the pram, closing my eyes and when I open them I am back in my hospital room. I blink again and find myself on my knees clutching the handle of my host's pram, granddad over me, his arm on my shoulder.

'Sophie are you alright?'

I shake my head, 'I've pushed it too far. Come on,' I say, standing up.

'What just happened?

'For a second I was back in my own body, I'm fine,' I say leaning over and kissing granddad's cheek just as the little boy who barged past me before comes skidding around the corner.

'Mom can I have two dollars for a go on the winter wonderland ride?' he asks, looking at me and then granddad.

'I'm coming,' I tell my host's son and then to granddad, 'I need to find a more suitable host.'

'Agreed,' granddad says, stopping at the next park bench and seating himself, 'I'll wait here while you change. Are you sure you are alright?'

'Mom, quicker!'

Granddad starts chuckling to himself, 'go on, quickly, that young man isn't going to hang about.'

'Two minutes,' I tell granddad and then follow the kid around the corner to be confronted by a brass band playing a tune to two or three hundred people. To the side of the small stage where the music booms out from is a fun fair with an assortment of children's games and rides.

I look around for my next host, someone here alone who may walk off without being questioned by friends, lovers or children. My eyes fog over again and when I blink I am back in my body and then back here and then back in my body. The connection is severing. My body want's my mind back or my mind's hold on my host is weakening.

I spot her stood by the trees talking on her mobile phone, she is in her mid-twenties, long dark hair flowing down her back with a green scarf wrapped around her neck, laughing at something her caller had said. As I approach she sees me and smiles, telling her caller she has to go.

'Hello,' I say, 'I was wondering if you have seen three young boys?'

She instinctively lifts her arm and points to the child shouting 'mom, mom,' behind me, and I reach for the hand, pushing myself into her body.

I watch as a look of fear appears on the face of my previous host, the young mother, and cut in before she can say anything.

'The kids are behind you,' I smile and she turns.

'Come on mom, I want a go on the winter wonderland ride…please?'

She then looks back to me, smiling uneasily and thanks me before pushing the pram away towards the throng of people.

'You're welcome,' I whisper and then smile, reaching into my pocket and answering the ringing phone.

'Why hang up like that Claudia?' a woman's voice asks.

'Sorry, listen, I think I'm going to head off home. It's cold out and I fancy like a night in on my own.'

'But the party, we were su…'

'There'll be other parties. Listen, I've got to go. I'll ring you tomorrow,' I hang up the phone and head back towards granddad, switching the phone off to stop any more unwanted calls.

I sit down next to the old man on the park bench and sigh, 'you know soon I will need to sleep. My mind has been active for almost two days now.'

Granddad nods, 'so you are planning on leaving me thousands of miles from home my dear?'

I smile at his tone, 'I'm sorry, I didn't think this through. It's impossible. My body wants its mind back.'

Taking my hand in his granddad says, 'what were you going to ask this professor?'

I shrug, 'I was hoping he would be able to reveal all, have that inside knowledge which I crave, be able to answer the whys and hows of my being able to jump into others bodies and memories.'

'That's quite an introduction.'

I nod, feeling the weight of everything heavy on my shoulders. My bottom lip begins to wobble and the heat of my tears sting my eyes.

'I'm sorry granddad. It's just all too much for me.'

Granddad puts his arms around me and kisses my host's head, 'I'll hear less of that my girl. The things you have discovered you can do are amazing but your abilities are only in their infancy. Push too hard and you wear yourself out.'

I close my eyes, stifling the tears, 'you know before I discovered this I was on my way out, the Locked in Syndrome was slowly sending me insane, and then this magic was offered up to me and I grabbed hold of it with everything I had because it is hope, and without hope…'

The static crackles in my mind and I daren't open my eyes again, knowing granddad is now gone, still sat on a park bench next to the lady who had a party planned tonight while I am back in Sophie Chesterfield's tomb of a body.

To my side the monitors beep quietly and the ventilator pushes and then dispels air from my broken lungs. The silence is sometimes quite terrifying, lying here on your own, not able to do anything but think.

I keep my eyes closed. Soon the seizures will come, carry me off to a world where I needn't latch onto others to accomplish my goals, where I am able to roam free in my own body. For all the magnificence of my ability I would trade it in a heartbeat for the use of my own body back. That is my hope and that is the reason I have been doing any of this, to be able to live my life again and not through another's eyes.

I listen as the heart rate monitor begins to quicken its pace, the aftermath of cheating physics, of cheating my body by getting out for a bit. I try and concentrate on my ventilator's hissing and sucking as my spine cramps up and my back arches with the intensity. I try and envision that day two years ago, when a relatively carefree Doctor walked home after lunch with a few old friends. I want to shout out to her, tell her to go back, turn around, get the fuck out of the way of the oncoming vehicle. As I feel myself slipping into the darkness I feel the warmth of the breeze on my face, can hear the traffic and bustle of lunch time commuters. As I open my eyes I see that I am back, walking across the square towards the road which will change the direction of my life forever.

35

BILLY: SINK OR SWIM

'Willy run faster,' the little girl laughs as I speed around the unmanned bowling green after her. She wears the same bright yellow floral dress as always and giggles her all familiar giggle as my little legs power on.

She stops quite abruptly and turns to greet me but I am running too fast to slow so that when our bodies collide we hit the ground in a jumble of limbs, both laughing as we sit up across from each other.

'Willy I want to tell you a secret.'

I smile. I love secrets.

'One day we will be all grown up and you must come and find me. Like hide and seek. You like playing hide and seek don't you?'

I nod. I do love to play hide and seek. Especially with my best friend in the whole wide world who now sits in front of me.

'We will be all grown up and I will be sick and you must find me because I think we are somehow connected and when you are older you will be able to help me get better.'

'Will you need a plaster?' I ask my bestest friend in the whole wide world.

The little girl laughs, reaching for my face and caressing my cheek, 'in a sense yes, but more importantly I will need you. Come to me Willy, let's play hide and seek and you have to find me.'

'But how will I know where to look when we are older? You could be hiding anywhere.'

She smiles and then leans forward onto her knees, whispering into me ear. The words are distant and distorted apart from the last three…in room 203.

I open my eyes and stare up at the ceiling. I remember this. Even now, outside of the dream I recall this happening as clear as if it was yesterday. How is that? These dreams, past memories, have always left me whenever I have woken, leaving just traces of their meaning with my conscious mind. This time it is different but I suppose so am I. If *The Divine* is to be taken literally, all of my cells now reproduce exact copies of themselves and any broken links have been repaired. Eric and I spoke at length about this when I had finished the book and although this is all only theory, the evidence of my rapid cell regeneration suggests the theory is sound.

Why are you calling to me Sophie? What is in room 203? Where is room 203?

I was very young when we sat across from each other that day in the park and she too was just a child. How could she have known we would not be in contact later in our lives?

I jump up out of bed and throw a pair of shorts on, heading down the hallway where I see Eric has opened the terrace doors.

'Eric?' I call as I walk through into the midday heat and see him lying down on a sunbed by the poolside reading a book, a fat cigar burning away in an ashtray by his side.

I walk over and sit myself down on the sunbed next to his.

'When did you start smoking?' I ask, smiling.

'The turn of the century,' he tells me, flicking over a page in his book.

'Why? By then the evidence between tobacco smoke and cancer had been out for decades.'

Eric turns to me and shakes his head, 'not that century Bill, the turn of the twentieth century when it was deemed 'cool'.

'Yeah, right, sorry.'

'You'll get used to it,' he then sits up on the sunbed and pivots his body so that we are facing each other, knees almost touching. 'I went to the airport as you requested and watched Paul and his family leave.'

'And Lisa, how did she look?' I ask, understanding why we cannot be together but loving her still just as strongly, perhaps more in this forced absence from her.

'Devastated Billy, of course, she thinks you just left. Without even giving her a moment's thought you packed your bags and disappeared. Paul is likely to take what really happened to the grave, and so here we are, a new chapter of your life has begun. Like I told you last night, don't dwell on the past too much. If you went back not only would you have to talk your way out of a fall that should have killed you, did kill you, but in the years that follow you will not age while everyone around you does.'

'Yes I know, the thirty year rule, I've been swotting up, but forgetting Lisa for a moment, what about mum? You say dad faked his death so he could go chasing ghosts from his past, is it really fair on her to lose her son in the same week as well?'

'She hasn't lost her son Billy. Paul will tell her the story and she too will believe you went for a walk about. You will see your mother again, but not yet. There is so much I need to show you first.'

I nod, 'What is room 203 Eric?'

He frowns, shaking his head, 'what are you talking about?'

'Sophie.'

Eric stands up, holding out his arm to stop me, 'I don't want to go there with you just yet because it will lead to me showing you something I doubt you are ready for.'

I too jump to my feet, 'I *do* want to go there. Since I died and came back able to heal, lost memories have been coming back clearer in my dreams and this reoccurring dream with your daughter has changed. That little girl is trying to tell me something. She wants me to find her.'

An arm goes out, grip solid around my neck and as my feet leave the ground so too do Eric's. For a moment we hover in mid-air, Eric holding me out from his body.

'You want to know about Sophie then fine. First though you must stay there when I release my grip.'

'I told you Eric, I ca…'

'Listen to yourself. You carry on still as if the laws of physics still apply to you. Those are their laws, not ours. Feel the air around you, not the wind against your skin, but the actual atmosphere, the gravity fighting to keep you grounded. You could dodge a bullet if I fired a gun at you son, you could run on water if you let yourself go and was willing to listen to your body. I've told you, stop trying to work out the whys of your abilities before discovering their potential. You can fly, I don't know how I can make you do this, I can only guide you. You want to talk about Sophie, you want me to let you into my world then first earn it little boy.'

'Eric,' I gasp, 'you're choking me.'

'Stop me then,' he tells me, moving us up higher into the sky. 'You want me to stop choking you then stop me. You are fast, faster than I will ever be but this doesn't help when we are hovering twenty meters above the ground.'

I punch his chest as hard as I can and he shakes his head, laughing.

'I don't have the words Billy, perhaps you would have been better off with your dad mentoring you but shit happens, daddy left and in his place you have me, and as much as I will discuss anything you would like to discuss, I am more of a sink or swim kind of teacher when it comes to the practicalities of your ability.'

I hit out at him again but this does nothing despite my reach being longer than his.

'Stop hitting me Billy and concentrate. Feel the air against your skin, that rush you had all of those years when you used to fall in your sleep, waking up on the other side of the room. That was your ability trying to burst out of you. I fly because my body stores energy from the sun, like photosynthesis. You would always be depressed through the winter months; you found a new lease of life when you came out to sunny old Cape Town. Think. That tingling sensation in your fingers and toes, that is your ability, you need to redirect it into your core.'

Eric releases his grip on my neck and I begin to fall but then I realise he is right because although the ground is coming up to meet me I am not hurtling downwards like I should be. I can feel the air thick against my skin but I have no way of knowing what to do with this. I need to practise, to be taught how to harness this energy. I tense my body, ready to receive the ground, closing my eyes and then nothing. My whole body is buzzing, my heart beating so fast that I cannot tell when one beat ends and another starts. Opening my eyes I stare down at my reflection in the swimming pool, suspended in the air, unable to think.

I hear myself laughing hysterically and then Eric is by my side.

'Whatever it is, hold on to it. Keep it deep inside you, store it away this feeling. It is part of you, you just need to know how to access it.'

'Eric I'm fucking flying,' I cry out.

'No,' he laughs, 'you are levitating, flying is adding direction. See if you can move across the water to the edge of the pool.'

'How?'

'Good question,' Eric says, 'think of the air as that water beneath us, gravity pulls us down through the water but we can fight it by swimming, by making ourselves buoyant, fighting gravity. I suppose in a way this is similar.'

'But there is nothing to fight against Eric,' I say, watching my refection telling his the same thing.

Beyond my refection I notice the tile mosaic at the bottom of the pool, a dolphin jumping from the water. I want to touch it, feel the soft porcelain beneath my fingers. Thinking about this my body moves me towards it, following gravity's pull but still resisting its advances. I am flying, be it downwards and into the water but still I am controlling this. Eric has it all wrong, what works for him won't for me, I have to find my own way and now, as I touch the dolphin, stroking it's cool hard surface I think I understand how I am able to move myself through the air. I bend my knees when my feet touch the bottom of the pool and power upwards, the water forming no resistance as I am released from gravity's grasp and into the air before landing upright by the side of the pool.

Eric skims the water until he too is back on solid ground, 'you've got it.'

I nod, 'it's nothing like you said Uncle Eric, I need to have a focal point, to clear my mind of everything else.'

He smiles and slaps me on the back, 'see I told you I was no good with words.'

I shake my head, 'you did right, sink or swim is the way to go and I swam.'

'Well actually, you sank,' he says with a smile.

'But on my own terms, not gravity's.'

I sit down on the sunbed and lie back, the grin impossible to keep from my face. Eric joins me, slapping my knee in encouragement, 'good lad,' he says.

'You do realize what's coming next don't you?' I ask him.

Eric then turns to me and says, 'I don't think *you* do my boy, because I will tell you about Sophie, but in telling that story first I need to tell you about myself.'

36

ERIC: CONFESSIONAL

'I was born in 1431 into the house of Draculesti in Wallachia, a region of the Ottoman empire which is now modern day Romania. My name back then was Vladamir Tepes, but I was known by many names through my first life, Vlad Tepes, Vlad III, Vlad the impaler…'

The boy sits up on his sunbed, the colour draining from his face.

'Fuck off,' he says, I think surprising himself as much as me with the escaping. He back tracks, holding up his hands in apology and then continues, 'you were Vlad the impaler?'

I smile, 'so you've heard of him?'

'Uncle Eric, I grew up a comic book nerd and part of that is following the myths and legends surrounding characters depicted in comics. Vlad the impaler is the original vampire. You're a vampire? But how are you sitting out in the sun? And Garlic, I saw you chop up two cloves and put them in our meal as you were preparing it last night.'

I nod, rolling my eyes, 'I know, I also have a reflection and I cannot turn into a bat, it's a travesty you and the rest of the world have been kept in the dark. Let's just say the legend of the house of Draculesti and its most famous member has been open to some creative embellishments by story tellers down the ages. Vampires do not exist, an Irishman whom I entrusted with my story at a time when I was in turmoil, however, does exist.'

'You're talking about Bram Stoker aren't you?'

'Of course I am. Sensationalising my life and creating a figure who to this day keeps the masses buying books and watching films and television shows on the subject of vampires. Before he wrote that book there were whisperings down the ages but nothing more. Now you have troubled teenagers who class Vampire as their religion and post pictures on their social network pages proudly. Trust me Billy there is no pride in the atrocities I have committed in the past. It is not 'cool' to be me.'

Billy leans forward, a grin spreading on his face and says, 'yes it is. It is so cool Uncle Eric, you just don't see it.'

'No Billy, you see for all the fallacies surrounding this real life Dracula there is one rule of the vampire which I am powerless to control. The blood. There is a hunger inside me, the beast, the other side, the slaughterer of tens of thousands down the ages, which try as I might to subdue, always surfaces to feed. That is the great trade off you see. I am able to live forever, I am impervious to harm, I can fly and I can make myself invisible but with these abilities I must hunt for blood when the hunger stirs, it takes over and in doing so I become the beast. Vlad the impaler was that beast's embodiment, a savage animal who slaughtered many for his search for blood. In my first life I allowed my hunger to take over my life and to this day I still hear the screams of the dying, every single one of them.'

'What changed?' Billy asks me and I have to think about this. What did change? What was the defining moment when I made the decision to step out from the veil of blood my other side had created? Her face comes back to the forefront of my mind and I smile.

'Love. Despite all his ruthlessness Vlad Tepes had one great love. Her name was Eliza, a simple Transylvanian woman who I fell madly in love with. History is quite accurate in so much as reporting I had two wives, but neither were my great love. I met Eliza when I was between wives and she showed me that I could be something more than the savage beast. Eliza believed in me and trusted me and in doing so sealed her fate. The beast turned on her and...' I shrug, and attempt a light hearted smile, 'I suppose she would be long gone now anyway.'

Billy stares at me silently. He then moves forward and wraps his arms around my neck, 'I'm sorry Uncle Eric, for the loss your life has endured.'

I sniff back the memories and shrug again, 'a long time ago my boy, needless to say, I continued on this crazy journey called life, traveling the globe and meeting your father in the trenches of the Somme where we discovered in each other a kinship which has endured much hardship in the past century, but has also given us both a sense of purpose. For a hundred years previous to our finding each other I had been the lord of Chesterfield Manor, a place I built with my family. It was my sanctuary from the outside world who at the time, would have happily labelled me an immortal demon and tried burning me at the stake. At the manor I took on the role of brother to the head of the family, my son David. When he had children I became the doting uncle and when my descendants died as they all did, the next line would take their place as head of the household and adopt me again as their brother and uncle.'

'So your family have always known of your immortality?'

'Yes. I have never tried to conceal my inability to age from those closest to me and the Chesterfield clan have known about it from such a young age that it has always seemed the norm until they grow old enough to understand I am different from the rest of them.'

'And has anyone ever tried to sell you out?'

I nod, 'once. In the late nineteenth century three brothers, my grandsons plus a couple of generations, lived in my manor and the youngest went to the authorities to tell them of his uncle who did not age.'

'What happened to him?'

'Jacob was thrown into an asylum by his brothers, two good boys who were fiercely loyal to their Uncle Eric. He died of pneumonia at the turn of the twentieth century, strapped to a bed having sent himself crazy with the thoughts of a man who would live until the end of time.'

Billy lets out a long sigh and grimaces, 'tell me about Sophie Uncle Eric. Tell me why I would keep having these dreams and why she is calling out to me, urging for me to find her. Are they just dreams?'

I shake my head, 'they're not dreams they are forgotten memories. More will come, but I'll get to that in a moment. With the last of my descendants at Chesterfield manor growing up and neither producing children, Alan's wife was unable to have children and his brother Peter joined the Navy at eighteen and that was the last any of us ever saw of him.'

'Right.'

'Well anyway, with no more children on the horizon for the first time in two hundred and fifty years the Chesterfield line looked as though it might fade out.'

'But why not start again, uproot and find somewhere else to begin a new family?'

'Because of your father. For a number of years I had managed to control the hunger through regular donations from your father. With his blood I was for the first time in my life able to live a normal life, able to love my family and quietly live my life with that love around me. The predator had been subdued with your father's blood and I was happy. Like an addict dependant on his dealer I was dependant on your father to supply me with blood so that the savagery would be kept at bay and this arrangement worked for a time.

In 1959 I returned from overseas and being back amongst my family at the manor and close to your father for the blood, I was content, happy even. Then Sophie's Mother came into my life a few years later and I decided I wanted a child of my own again. A year later Sophie was born and I loved her completely, my first daughter in four hundred years who lit up my life and made it all the more worth living. With the new arrival came a bout of depression from Sophie's mother though. The baby blues hit her hard and she was often quite violent towards me in her depression. She refused to nurse Sophie or even acknowledge our little girl as her own child. Then she cut herself. A cry for help maybe but all the help she would ever need was simply a request away.

One night, after I had put Sophie to bed I went upstairs to find Sophie's mother waiting for me in the bedroom with a knife. She attacked me with it, screaming that I had turned our four month old baby against her, stabbing me repeatedly in the chest. With this violence the beast stirred inside me and attacked, ending her life in the most bloody of ways possible. It then fed from her body until there was no blood left. My godson Alan told me later that when he arrived to the room I was gone and so was the body. I had disappeared into the night and slaughtered five others that evening. The local and national newspapers reported heavily on the slayings in the following weeks. The police investigated but the killer was never caught. The body of Sophie's mother was never found either. That night she had disappeared from the manor and had never returned.

This is the story I told the police at the time of their investigation and this is what Sophie still believes. As a young girl she decided she was going to track down her mother, and it wasn't long before she stumbled across the slayings which plagued our town that one night thirty years ago. She believed her mother might have been both the victim and slayer, trying to investigate further into the police's cold case but in the end she gave up.

That night was a stark reminder of the power which lurks within me always. I of course confided in your father about this and he was of the belief that if I continued to take his blood then the control I had shown to keep the beast at bay would continue.

Years passed and I brought up my daughter to the best of my abilities. She was my world and I was hers.'

'And then you left.'

I nod and immediately the tears of grief burst from my eyes and I sob, 'I knew one day the beast would regain control and Sophie would be in danger. Me leaving was the only way to ensure her safety.'

'I remember the trips to the park when I was very young. How old would Sophie have been then?' Billy asks me.

'Nine years old. That Summer was the last I spent with my baby girl. You were just a toddler, maybe two years old if that.'

'So you stayed away but you didn't go far?'

'I couldn't. Your dad's blood has kept my demons from unearthing. The modern world does not want to see Vlad the Impaler reborn. It would get messy and it would put all of you in danger.'

'But don't you think you should see her now, Sophie is crying out to me and telling me to find her. I don't know why and I don't know how but I know I must.'

I nod, 'perhaps.'

'Do you think she is one of the Divine Uncle Eric?'

I smile, remembering back to that cold winter morning when my Alsatian Timothy started barking at Alan when he was just a young boy, and then the things he said to me, things later he did not remember saying. That I would have a daughter one day and how tight he clung onto my neck upon seeing me. I realize now, having lived through the premonitions, the words spoken were not young Alan's that morning.

'I know she is Billy, I have known long before she was even born.'

37

WILLIAM: *GOD OR MONSTER*

Anonymity is our friend.
    When I climbed out of my metal tomb in 1647 I made the decision to shun my anonymity and go public, tell the world who I was and what I was capable of in the hope of reaching out to more like me. I was under the illusion I could meet with men of power and explain my predicament and they would listen. They did not.
    I travelled the world in the hope of being granted an audience with kings and emperors. My time in solitary had taught me patience but now I was becoming more and more impatient. People would not listen to me and if I showed my audiences what my body could survive I was either looked upon as a God or feared as a monster. Little there, I imagine, has changed if I was to reveal myself again now, in the twenty-first century.
    The human condition, I have come to believe, is fear. I have already written within these pages that man fears what he does not understand. He does not search for enlightenment, and in the masses man acts like a swarm of ants might, following the one in front of them, like sheep with their herd mentality.
    Perhaps one day we will number enough to be able to walk out into the sun and show the world that we understand, that we know they are scared, but we do not have the answers, we are like them, asking the same basic question, what is our purpose?
    Of course to ask that very question 'what is our purpose' is to go against everything I have come to believe. It begins hinting towards a belief in a grand design and if so there would be a designer. The universe is completely random, my

scientific mind understands this. Chaos produced our world and every living thing in it, I know this, but even still I search for others to understand why when really there is no answer. We are because the world in which we live holds the perfect conditions to host life. Through time that life evolves or dies out, and again chaos dictates this. Perhaps I should abandon my search for others and in turn stop chasing our purpose in this ever changing always fluid world. From the moment we are born life is merely a fight for survival.

Those who follow whichever God they choose argue that there is a plan, that our time on this earth is a trial run or test for greater things to come once we die and float up to heaven on fluffy white clouds. The afterlife is our true calling provided we are good according to a set of rules written by men centuries ago blinded by their own faith in the almighty. If there was a God and we were welcomed into heaven once we die, what then? Do our souls spend their days sunbathing in the gardens sipping margaritas and being eternally happy? To me that sounds dull, and I would become bored of the eternal happiness and eternal peace. Without pain there is no peace, without anguish there is no happiness. If being welcomed into the kingdom of heaven is our purpose then what then? Personally I feel sitting atop a cloud with the angels would become tedious, but what do I know?

My purpose in writing this memoir and scrapbook of ideas was always to try to reach out to those who might feel lost and need to know that there are others like them out there, but who am I kidding, I am just as lost as they are. I live my life as a man when I am something more, the great pretender lying his way through this very long and mostly eventless life. I need my brothers and sisters who are out there just as much as they might need me, more so even because I am the one attempting to contact them. I am a being lost in the dark and this book is a signal fire I am lighting so that others may find me. Perhaps there are communities of my kind already built, men and women from across history who are still here to this day sharing information and experiences and doing their utmost to protect our emerging species. I'd like to think so, I'd *like to think that I will one day be welcomed into the bosom of a community of my kind and then maybe I will feel at peace, then maybe I will have found a place to call home, no longer a reject of time.*

Mr E, July 18th 1958

I think back over the ages I have seen come and go, passing me by in an instant. I also think about something which Victor Morris, the once St Germain, said to me, that fifty years is immaterial. If what he says is true and he fought alongside Alexander the great, that makes him over two thousand years old, and although I can understand where his comment arrives from I cannot condone it. Listening to the way Victor had spoken, disregarding half a century as a mere insignificance, makes me believe the man has completely lost touch with our closest kin, man, and he has nothing in common with our homo-sapien brother anymore. Fifty years is a very significant amount of time, the majority of man's life, of our closest relative's being, and to be able to disregard that would be to disregard Man.

There are still a lot of questions left unanswered, for instance who the hell 'jumped' into my body and tried murdering both Victor and Nessie centuries ago? What was their motive? How did they know who Victor and Nessie were? How did they know who I was?

I roll across my bed and land on my feet, opening the curtains to be greeted with a clear January New York skyline. I smile and marvel at the view of downtown Manhattan, the Empire States Building greeting me on this fine winter morning.

New York City is a place I have visited many times but never lived in, and so when given the choice of anywhere in the world, the Big Apple it was. As promised I was awarded a position teaching at New York University. I begin the semester today, teaching post graduate History and also under graduate creative writing, a strange combination of subjects one faculty member commented during my tour of the University but they suit my needs. History is an obvious choice for the man who has lived through it, and with my book re-entering the world after a five and a half decade hibernation, creative writing will give me a chance to publicly deconstruct the theme, creating debates from students, this in turn may in itself cause a little controversy and then reach out to those who need a focal point for their own divinity.

No doubt I will be inundated with students wanting to learn more about the book because they think it would be 'cool' to live forever, but maybe in the middle of the fans there will be one person scared and alone with no one to talk to for fear of being branded a freak. I will answer their questions and I will assure them they are alone no longer.

Whether I will then point them in the direction of the Phoenix Committee I cannot be certain. Something is not right there, Victor talks of secret societies hunting the divine but I don't believe him, and because of this I do not trust the man. I need to talk to Eric, to get him over here so that we can approach this Committee as we have approached everything, together. He will arrive in the UK tomorrow if he is following Billy back off his holidays. I will contact Alan and ask him to send a message.

Thoughts of Alan Chesterfield and the last time we met come back to me and I feel a cold shudder down my spine. Alan has never been my biggest fan and I understand why, he thinks I lead Eric down a path which results in Eric's other side being close to the surface. Until I passed on the briefcase of blood to him he didn't know about my blood and how much I wish for my friend to find peace. We both Love Eric but for very different reasons, Eric is my brother in arms, my friend, my confident, to Alan though, Eric is the embodiment of family and love. Alan thinks family will cure Eric of his demons but there is no curing someone from themselves

Our last meeting had been heated but it was afterwards, once Alan had told me to close the door on my way out of Chesterfield manor, and moments before I contacted Nessie with the post on the William Wallace website, something happened which made me understand that there is one 'jumper' out there who is capable of so much more than I would ever have imagined.

The scene plays over and over in my mind as I enter the bathroom and turn on the shower, and as the water begins to heat up I close my eyes and enter the warm stream...

'But we are not normal Alan, we are searching...'
'*You* search William. Eric has always followed. This life he leads fighting his demons will eventually destroy him. I was there with him when Sophie was born; she became his reason for living. We would have found a way to deal with Eric's demons if you hadn't have been there in the shadows, whispering into his ear. Of course I will act as your go between, I will embrace Eric back into my life instantly, but you William, you I do not want to see again. There is a piece of paper and a pen on the side on your way out. Jot down the means I am to communicate any messages and leave and do not come back.'

I nodded and held out my hand which Alan ignored, moving around me and out of the room.

'Close the door on your way out William,' is the last thing he said as I left, and I did as he asked.

Outside I began walking back towards my car, thinking about the old man's words when the door opened. As I turned I saw Alan walk out onto the driveway, I lifted my hand up to wave, and he called out for me, hurrying along to greet me between my car and the house.

'What is it Alan?' I asked rather wearily, I was in no mood for another outburst from the old man, he made his point clear with his hands around my neck in the kitchen.

'Please,' he said in a faint whisper, 'please answer the questions I ask.'

I frowned, nodding for him to continue.

'You are the one my father calls the Doc?'

'Alan, what is thi...'

'Please, just for now, please humour me. Alan Chesterfield is not here. Eric Chesterfield calls or called you Doc, I am right aren't I?'

I nodded, 'what…'

The old man's hand shot up to stop me and I discontinued my words.

'Do you know where Eric, my father, is now?'

I nodded again.

'You need to get to him, to tell him that you spoke to me and that we are all in very real danger. They tried killing me once and left me trapped in my broken body but now they are after us all. You need to tell him and you need to make him listen to you. In a few weeks I will come to you at your University in New York, I will be wearing a navy beret and tight denim jeans, my host's hair will be long and dark. They will ask you to do something and you must do it. The others will not understand but I will. Please, William, get hold of my dad as soon as he arrives back from Cape Town with Willy.'

'What is this Alan, what are you saying?'

The old man shook his head and began to walk backwards towards the house, 'we will speak in a few weeks' time. I will not recall this meeting because it won't have happened yet for me but please William, trust me, they are coming.'

'They? Who is they?' I asked the slowly retreating figure.

'The Phoenix committee, you cannot trust them. Remember, call my dad as soon as he gets back, they're coming.'

Alan moved back inside the house and shut the door and I turned back to the car. Once I was sat behind the wheel I took out my phone and clicked onto the internet, onto williamwallace.com and scrolled down to the message board, my decisions seemingly already made, my life now mapped out before me.

…I jump out of the shower and dry myself with a towel. We had always wondered, Eric and I, if our children would ever share our genetic makeup. Sophie. That little girl who used to chase Billy around the park, so full of life, so full of innocence…

Today I begin my first day as a Professor William Crawford of New York University and I wonder when she will come to me again. I will watch out for the lady with the navy beret and long dark hair and I'll watch out for the little girl we all loved so much who grew up to travel through time.

New York City. I had no choice in the matter really, she led me here and now I wait for my first recruit.

PART FOUR

THIEF OF TIME

38

SOPHIE: PIP

Is this real? I look down at my hands, clench and unclench my fists, watch the whites of my knuckles return to pink. I know that somewhere beyond what I am seeing and feeling I now lie in my hospital bed in a coma. The Doctors and nurses will be flapping around my bed, twiddling dials, jotting scribbles on charts, someone will notify my grandparents and they will come and sit by my side, hold my hand, shed tears.

In the distance I can see where I was heading to that day, back to my apartment on the tenth floor of Chesterfield Oaks Luxury Apartments. If I search now I could pin point my apartment windows, the small corner balcony I liked to step out onto in the evenings with a glass of wine, watching the world go by as day would turn to night and the city would wake up with its neon glow.

The warm breeze runs its finger through my hair and I close my eyes. I am really here; it is too real not to be so. Last time I didn't see him coming but this time I see the man with the leaflets approach. He does not smile but gives me a nod as I reach out for the bright pink declaration.

I jump.

And then I watch as Sophie walks on towards her doom. The rules appear to change here in this place. I am unconscious in my hospital bed so there is nowhere for the leaflet distributor's mind to go. His mind cannot occupy my past self's mind because she is not the one jumping, I am, an entity without its own body who has come here to try and save her, save us.

I drop the batch of leaflets I am carrying into a nearby bin and hurry around to cross the very road Sophie is approaching. A young man stands beside me, a kid really, he looks up at me and...I am looking up at him now as he wonders where all his leaflets have gone. Sorry pal, they were heavy and I'm in a hurry.

I cross the road, reaching into my pocket for some money and purchasing a can of Coke from the pop up news kiosk.

Watching Sophie, our eyes connect as she crosses the street towards me. I take a sip of my can and then follow her as she continues towards the apartment. I remember waiting for the kid with the can of coke to wolf whistle, remember it like it was, well happening right now. I now understand why he didn't, because he is me, and we are here to save her from…

Up ahead she walks towards the road when the white van speeds around the corner. Inside I see two people, a man in his mid to late thirties driving and a woman in her fifties sitting in the passenger seat. As they careen towards us she lashes out at the driver and up ahead Sophie turns and notices I have gone when really I am still here just moving quick now back across the road.

'Move!' I call out as the van passes me and swerves into the curb, in towards Sophie, but she is frozen to the spot and will continue to be frozen for the next two years.

The van smashes into her body and she is thrown through the air, landing with a sickening thud on the road.

Car horns blare; pedestrians cry out in horror, some reaching into their pockets for their phones to film or snap a picture of the hit and run.

Fighting my way through the bystanders surrounding my broken body, none of them with any clue of what to do, I kneel down next to Sophie's head and stroke her hair, my face is battered and bleeding, hair tainted red from all of the blood. As I stroke her head I feel the prick of tears rolling down the teenage boy's cheeks.

'I tried to warn you but it never changes, I'm sorry Sophie,' I whisper.

Her eyes open and in the distance sirens begin to wail. Soon I will start on the journey which has led me back here to this moment.

I can feel myself slipping away, not back to my hospital room but to that other place, my limbo, where my mind goes when my body starts to shut down. I see the little boy in front of me, turn and there is my father and the doc. I am nine years old and soon my father will leave. Leave because he believes it is the only way to protect me but it isn't.

'*Catch me Sophie,*' Willy laughs and I smile, taking off after him, shielding my eyes from the sun on this perfect day…

I open my eyes and Pip is sat by my side holding my hand. I blink a couple of times which tells her to put my glasses on my face.

h o w l o n g w a s i o u t

She smiles, squeezing my fingers, 'eighteen hours. Where do you go, when you leave us, who do you visit?'

t o d a d m o s t l y b a c k t o m y c h i l d h o o d

Pip nods, 'you miss him don't you?'

e v e r y d a y s i n c e i w a s n i n e y e a r s o l d

'So you visit him when you fall into your comas, back into your memories.'

I blink.

Pip nods, turning and picking up my copy of *The Divine* from beside her and showing it to me. 'I've been reading your book. It's certainly interesting to say the least.

i t h o u g h t s o

'But completely unbelievable.'

c o m p l e t e l y

My last word hangs in the air as Pip stares into my eyes, searching for something from me. What do you want? What are you looking for?

'The blackouts started about six months ago,' she tells me. 'I would find myself losing time, waking up in my bed and not being able to recall half of the previous night's shift. It was always when I was working and your room always my last memory, every single time. I would wake up in my bed at home having had the strangest dream, that I was stuck in your bed, in your body, in your head, looking up at the ceiling, your ceiling.'

Beeping next to my head, my heart rate monitor begins to speed up. I can hide nothing from her, my body tells no lies.

I have jumped using Pip a dozen times now, of course this was inevitable and she would start to wonder where this missing time was going.

Looking back up at her now I believe I can trust her with my secret but it isn't that simple. To reveal all would change everything for her, what she thought she knew about the world around her, time, physics, and also what is written in the pages of the book she holds.

h o l d m y h a n d p i p

For a second she hesitates, sensing rightly so that this is not an act for comfort, I want to show her, share with her my secret. I know she thinks this because I can feel her thoughts even without a physical connection.

c l o s e y o u r e y e s

I open mine and let go of Sophie's hand. Pip stares up from beneath my skeletal complexion and I take a step back, sitting down. She follows me with her eyes and then, realizing she is wearing my glasses, stares up at my computer screen.

I wait, flicking through *The Divine*, reading a paragraph about my dad during the second world war.

h o w d i d y o u d o t h a t, the robotic drone sounds out.

I place the book down and shrug, 'I really don't know. It's like a rolling sensation, being carried over to you on a cloud of electric charge, me feeling your psyche and then entering it, discarding your own mind in the process.'

i m p o s s i b l e

'I'd say more improbable than impossible. I don't know how. From reading that book I have learnt it may have something to do with my cells but the author doesn't mention any instances of jumping, I just don't have any answers. All I know is my body reacted to overcome an obstacle, it evolved, I evolved.

e v o l v e d

I nod, listening to the sound of approaching footsteps, 'There is a professor in New York…'

The door handle creaks and a head appears around the side of the door.

'Good morning ladies,' West sneers as he enters the room. I stand back from the bed, my eyes locking with Pip's for a long second before breaking away. We both watch him as he walks towards us and before I can reach back over to the patient, to jump back into my own body, West speaks up.

'Could you check on Arthur Rogers in room 208 please Nurse Bradshaw, he has been asking after you.'

And just like that poor Pip's fate is sealed. I have no doubt what the doctor will do as soon as the door is shut. I wish I had warned Pip about him but I guess there are some things you just don't know how to put into words.

The mask goes on, all repulsion and disgust hidden behind the kindness of my friend's smile.

'Certainly Doctor,' and glancing back once more at the patient, I make my way out mouthing sorry to her as I go.

As the door closes I catch West making his way over to my bed, his words muffled but the eagerness in his walk apparent. I'm so sorry Pip, sorry you will now have to go through this ordeal at the hands of our friendly ward doctor.

Ignoring room 208 and a patient who is apparently fond of nurse Bradshaw, I head downstairs to the cafeteria and buy myself a coffee. Sitting down at the same table where only a few short weeks ago Nurse Beatrix ate a bacon sandwich and my life changed forever with the discovery of the photographs and the letters which came with *The Divine*, I let out a deep sigh. Something has to be done about Doctor West.

His visits are becoming more and more frequent, his touch more brutal. I close my eyes and his face comes into view, I am lying back in my bed and he is at the side of me, hand hidden beneath my sheet and mouth inches from my face, stale cigarettes and peppermint in the air. Blinking a few times I am back at my table in the cafeteria, mug of coffee in my hands.

'I'm sorry Pip,' I whisper with my alien voice, 'so sorry.'

39

BILLY: LEARNING TO FALL

Although I'm not officially dead, and the only witness to my 'death' having left Cape Town after telling everyone I went walk about, Eric has insisted I refrain from using my passport to get back to the UK.

'Air liner passenger lists are recorded. No matter how in the clear you think you are, trust me you are not.'

'So what next then? How do we get back home if I'm unable to jump on a plane, because it's a hell of a long walk and there is no way I'm going to fly it. I can barely make the length of the swimming pool. Athletes have jumped further.'

Flying is not all it's cracked up to be. The amount of concentration and focus it takes is killing me. Eric tells me I have to train my body to respond to the act of flight, that I am an infant teaching himself to take his first steps and like that infant it takes practise before the act becomes second nature.

'Have you ever skydived?' he asks smiling.

'No, not until a week ago when you let go of me while we were in the air.'

'It's easy, as long as there is gravity you'll be great at it.'

'Falling, Eric, I'll be great at falling? I can't imagine it takes much in the way of training to do this. Why, what do you have in mind?'

'Two flights, the first a chartered jet from Johannesburg to Paris, we spend the night in the French Capital and then the next morning I will have arranged a flight back home.'

'And the skydiving? Where does that come in?'

Eric grins as he heads back inside the house, chuckling to himself as if to a private joke, no doubt a joke where the punchline is 'and Billy shits himself'.

40

ERIC: TERMINAL VELOCITY

'Are you ready my boy?' I shout out over the drone of the twin engine Cessna which I hired from Paris to give us a ride over the water and back home to the UK.

'Don't you fucking 'my boy' me Eric, you want me to jump out of this plane, in the dark, with no training whatsoever, in the dark.'

'You said in the dark already,' I let him know and supress my laughter as Billy's face looks as though he is about to explode.

'Well maybe it is important Eric, maybe jumping through that door and into nothingness, pitch black nothingness at that, is not an everyday occurrence for me and don't you dare start laughing, immortal or not I'm going to kill you when we get down from here.'

I straighten my face, 'listen, the reason we are going this way is so you might benefit from a little flying lesson once we hit the air and start falling, we are high enough for you to be able to try and hone your abilities.'

'No no no, you're not going to try and justify this as like the first time you let go of the back of a child's bike when teaching them to ride. There is no terminal velocity peddling at three miles an hour.'

'Ready?' the pilot hollers over the engines and I turn and give him a thumbs up.

'Listen Billy we need to jump now if we are going to land anywhere near Chesterfield manor. I've an old man waiting for me. In ten minutes time you will be out of your jump suit and sat in front of a roaring log fire sipping a hot toddy, but first…'

Billy puts up his hand for me to stop and I do.

'Ok, just give me a moment,' he says, checking the digital altimeter strapped to his wrist, 'so when this starts glowing red I need to pull my ripcord?'

'Well yes but I am hoping you won't need it...'

'Yeah, yeah, yeah, because I will have found my feet blah blah blah, but let's just pretend for a second I am an ordinary bloke doing an ordinary jump. When it flashes red I need to pull?'

I nod and watch as his eyes widen and he gasps and splutters to get his words out, pointing at me continually.

'You...you're not, not, fucking wearing a parachute!'

I raise my eyebrows and shake my head, 'why on earth would I Billy?'

'But won't the pilot wonder why only one chute has left with the two of us?'

I shake my head, for the price this flight has cost me the pilot would only see it as a bonus that he has to replace just one parachute instead of two.

'Twenty seconds,' the very man calls to us and I lift Billy to his feet.

'The initial jumping out of the aircraft is the most unnerving bit, stepping out into nothingness.'

Billy groans, 'you're not helping Eric.'

I move him towards the open door, the rush of air greeting us as the pilot shouts out 'ten seconds'.

'Just focus Billy,' I say and then grab him around the waist, powering us both out of the open hatch before he realizes what's happened.

Out into the dark void of space the wind is deafening as we fall through the black sky, I steady myself and ignoring Billy's screams and limbs flaying all over the place, I steady him too. Once I have my bearings I take hold of his arm and slow us down to a stop, the air is cool against my face and at this altitude the road lights beneath us look like small orange cracks in an otherwise pure black canvass. I turn us so that we are facing northwards and the city lights come into view.

Billy gasps, taking in the extraordinary view, 'my god it's beautiful,' he says with a laugh.

I point out the tiny illuminated square which is Chesterfield Manor's court yard and then tell him I am going to let go of him now and that he should focus on that light if it is the focal point which enables him to use his ability. He nods and cries out, 'this is so fucking awesome.'

I chuckle to myself, and then let go of the boy, I guess it *is* kind of awesome.

Billy disappears from view with a cry and I allow gravity to take hold, pushing me down towards my home. From the moon's reflection I catch Billy twisting and rolling and watch, curious. The boy is finding his feet so to speak, experimenting with the freedom of his freefall. I watch from above as he turns to the right and then flips over and I catch an excited laugh as he then speeds up, arms to his side and legs straight as an arrow, he might not realize it, he might think gravity is still dictating his decent, but I can see he has fought off his terminal velocity and it is he who now controls his speed and direction.

I dive past him and then turn so that my back is to the ever growing ground, 'try slow Billy, change direction, move upwards.'

Billy nods and grins like an idiot, double summersaulting and then powering up through the air, whooping and cheering as he then dives again, speeding past me and yanking my leg.

I turn back over into the wind and laugh, he's doing it, he's flying, twisting and turning in and out of gravity's hold. His altimeter begins to flash red and I shout out to him but my voice is lost in the air. The ground is coming up rapidly now and I dive faster to try and catch up with him, the boy is too fast though, dipping and twisting, not paying attention to the ground which smiles up at us, a grin which can be one of kindness or menace.

'Billy,' I scream, we are about half a mile out from Chesterfield manor, heading for a collision with the woodland area where I have built forts in the trees for five generations of my decedents when they were children.

Billy spins over and faces me up above him, I tap my wrist and he then understands, looking at the red neon light flashing on the end of his arm. I watch as he turns, slowing some but not enough as he crashes into the canopy, taking out a couple of trees as he goes. The thump that indicates the boy's arrival back to earth is deafening. I slow to a hover and make my way through the broken branches and snapped tree trunks, following the carnage until I see Billy's body slumped, head down in a ditch his impact with the earth has created.

'Billy?' I call out, dropping onto the ground myself and running across to where he is lay. There is no sound from him, his body completely mangled. I turn him onto his back and look down at the broken face, deep lacerations from his broken jaw all the way up to his protruding eye. His limbs are twisted at unnatural angles and when I lift his head I hear his spine snap beneath my fingers.

'Billy Billy,' I whisper and then stand back up away from the boy's lifeless body and wait.

He is not dead, we die only once before eternity takes hold. His body is in shock and struggles to work out what the hell just happened.

I hear that first great lung full of air being gulped at and smile as the boy screams out in horror.

'Calm down Bill,' I try through his screech but my words are lost. He cannot hear me, cannot see me. His cells are kicking the shit out of his body in order to repair it. It is excruciating but thankfully doesn't last too long.

'Eric, Eric,' Billy calls out and I kneel besides him.

'I'm here,' I say, stroking his hair and feeling a huge crack in his skull. 'Just relax, your body is repairing itself but you really fucked it up. Hitting the ground at that speed is going to turn you into a bag of goo and now your defences are sifting through that goo to try and make out what it is they're fixing.'

'Uncle Eric,' Billy whispers.

'Yes?'

He then cracks a smile and says, 'that is perhaps the most disgusting thing I've ever heard,' he sits up and coughs hard, spitting out an unwanted mouthful of blood, 'was that your attempt of keeping me calm? Talking about my insides being a bag of goo, because not very comforting is what I took from it.'

I smile despite myself, 'well it's a shame your smart arse mouth wasn't shattered into a thousand pieces.'

'It was, that's how strongly I feel about your little comfort sermon having the piss taken out of it. Broken face or no broken face you need to take it easy with comforting, I'll be having nightmares for weeks.'

'Come on mouth,' I tell him as I help him to his feet, 'let's get to the house so that you can meet my Godson and bore him with your complaints.'

Billy stands and nods his head, 'I did it Eric,' he says and I watch as he then starts to slowly rise up into the air. He turns on the spot, facing in the direction of the house beyond the trees, 'come on old man, first one to the house is the winner,' he says, disappearing up into the sky.

'Kids,' I whisper and laugh to myself, 'he thinks he's bloody Superman,' I then bend my knees, summoning up all the energy I can muster and take off skywards, clipping Billy on the ear as I pass him and laughing out loud, saying to him, 'less of the old man.'

41

SOPHIE: LIVING MEMORIES

As beings we are always evolving, and so too is my ability. This time when I go back I will achieve the impossible, I will change everything so that when I am pulled back to the present this hospital room is gone and so am I, living a different life. I will have changed the course of my history and in doing so will be able to live my life instead of merely existing in this room. Things don't have to be as they are.

 I close my eyes and think back to that fateful day. The last day I was able to take a breath for myself. Back from Ghana after a stint over there inoculating a community's young, I wait for my next posting. During my short stays in the UK home is a small comfortable apartment in the city centre which granddad leases out to me in exchange for my company every Sunday for lunch. With rates like that who am I to refuse? I have been home a month and am growing restless now, I have caught up with friends and family and now I need to ship out again. I have not made a life for myself here and I crave the African children's smiles and laughter again. When I am here I am simply going through the motions, out there I feel alive. Helping those children, integrating myself into their communities, this is my calling, the reason I was put here on this earth.

 It is a clear spring evening, and as I turn the corner and stop at the edge of the pavement to cross the road, heading back to my apartment after an early dinner with a friend from University, a white van careens out of a side street. I am aware of what happens next, the boy across the road shouts for me to move, the van swerves into the curb and hits me and I fall and knock my head on the ground, somehow severing my brainstem which results in my current predicament. I know this happens because it has already happened. The first time I was obviously unaware of what was to come, but having travelled back to this moment I know that if I step back from the edge of the pavement now, turn and walk away, then the van will not hit me, I will not hit my head, and I will not live through the next two years in a torturous nightmare.

Traveling back through my own memories as opposed to when I jump and journey into the past through others, is different. I have been here before, these experiences are not new and this gives the world in which I inhabit a dream like quality, everything is faded, softened. Is this even real?

My vision begins to tunnel as the van moves towards me and I can hear the static charge building in my ears, as I step out into the road I watch as the white van swerves in towards me and I glance up, catching a brief glimpse of the driver, our eyes meet and I watch, powerless as he smirks at me before I hear the engine's revs power up and he speeds towards me. The driver wears a navy blue shirt and peaked cap and on that cap is an orange bird in flight and sitting in the passenger seat an older lady with thick silver hair strikes the driver but it is too late.

I try and step backwards out of the gutter but this moment passed two years ago and I am able to alter its course as much as I am able to alter what I had for breakfast last year. I close my eyes, feel the tear roll down my cheek and then let my mind travel back to my present, the driver's eyes, his smirk, the silver haired woman hitting him, and that bird motif seared into my consciousness and my whole understanding of time and space transformed.

I want my granddad, I want to talk to him about time travel, I want to listen to his opinions and take in any advice he might give, but he is probably still in New York, and I am stuck here, my quest to curing my Locked in syndrome no closer than the day I arrived at this hospital.

The pent up anger engulfs me and I yearn to cry out, hear my frustration echo through the hallways.

I have travelled back through my own memories over a dozen times now and although it feels real, although I believe I am jumping back in time into the body of my younger self, there is always that doubt in the back of my mind. Is it really just my over active imagination bursting out and filling the void left behind by my broken body, or is it as it seems, am I truly back in time and in control of my former self's faculties, because although I may have control over my body I cannot change anything. There is no way to truly know unless I reveal myself to those in the past. The young boy Willy inhabits my dreams with our childish games and carefree lives, and I have since visited him at the park, spoken to him and told him to find me in real time. The problem is that memory is a fickle thing and he may not recall our conversation, as he is very young.

  I want to go to my dad, to tell him everything so that he will not leave and when I come back to the present everything is different, I am happy and he is with me. It doesn't work like that though. There is no butterfly effect, if I kill a butterfly in the past there is no great disaster in the present. Why couldn't I step back away from the road just then? Why am I destined to get hit by that van? Time is linear, I cannot alter anything in my past because it was not altered, it has already happened. I have the opportunity to observe and interact but there is no changing anything. Our lives are governed by the decisions we make and this cannot be undone. What will happen has already happened.

  I hear footsteps along the corridor on the other side of my door. It will be Doctor West on his rounds. I have no desire to be here and listen to him flirt with me, convincing himself time and time again that what I really desire and need is a good ole finger fucking from him to snap me out of my terrible affliction

  I once again close my eyes, hoping beyond hope that these excursions are not overactive daydreams, that they are in fact real. I feel the heat on my face, smell the sweet aroma of summer in the breeze, muffled voices begin to come into focus and when I open my eyes I squint from the sun. Perhaps twenty yards ahead of me Willy is running away, screaming with childish glee. I am nine years old and back in the park, I turn and see my dad and Willy's dad sitting and talking on the park bench. I wave and they both wave back and then I run after little Willy, the toddler I have entrusted my secret to in the past so that he may find me in the present.

'Willy, Willy stop,' I cry out and he does so, turning and running back to me, arms open for me to lift him up.

We hug and he gives me a big wet kiss on the mouth. He is teething and sports a bib of dribble on his t-shirt. We sit down on the grass and I ask him if he likes birds.

'Birdy, tweet tweet,' he tells me with a huge grin.

What am I doing? He is too young, but I know this summer is the last time I will see this little boy. Dad will leave in a couple of months and when he goes so too does Willy and his dad.

'You have to remember this Willy, the orange birdy hurt Sophie. Can you say that?'

'Onginge birdy hurt Sophie,' he repeats back to me.

'Yes, orange birdy hurt Sophie,' I tell him once more. Do you remember the hospital room?

The little boy frowns for a moment and then says, 'room 203, room 203, room 203,' jumping up onto his feet and running to my dad and his.

'Daddy, daddy, onginge birdy hurt Sophie in room 203.'

Dad smiles and says to the giant man, 'you're the Doc, Doc, do you think she needs a check-up? Those orange birdies can be lethal.'

Both grownups laugh at this and I get a hair ruffle from the Doc.

I have been so blind. All this time he has been here, locked away in my memories, the Doc, a man of science, a giant man who towers above everyone else. A giant man like William Wallace. The man in front of me is the man who I search for in the present.

'Why does daddy call you Doc?' I ask, ever the inquisitive nine year old.

Doc looks down at me and smiles, 'because long ago I used to be a Doctor, now I just teach people.'

'each feeple,' Willy repeats and the Doc laughs at this, picking up his son and bouncing him on his lap.

Careful to watch for the Doc's reaction I say, 'we learned about William Wallace in school last week, he was very tall like you Doc,' his eyes dart towards me and although he smiles there is something else there, an uncomfortableness. I look at dad, his own smile is frozen on his face, unchanging. I've got them, I'm calling them out because they need to help me. The smirking driver with the navy blue cap and orange bird motif was aiming for me. It wasn't an accident, it was attempted murder, but why?

'Come on Soph,' dad says, standing up and taking my hand, 'how about we go and feed the ducks?'

'Yay' I manage, although feeding the ducks is the last thing on my mind, 'is Willy and Doc coming?'

Mr E, William Wallace, Doc, shakes his head, 'no, not this time Soph, we have to be getting home, next Saturday though, definitely.'

I smile and give Willy a huge hug, whispering in his ear, 'room 203 Willy, you need to come.'

Willy laughs and kisses me on the cheek and with our dads we part company.

Dad and I walk in silence along the path which leads down to the duck pond. I look up at him and he catches me doing so, winking back at me.

'You never told me you were learning about William Wallace,' he says, squeezing my hand a little and stopping when we arrive at the water's edge. We have no bread to feed the ducks but a dozen or so quack their way towards us expecting their prize. From out of the reeds a gaggle of Canadian geese also flap their way across to us too, squawking and hissing at each other as they try and get in the best position for a feed.

'There is a lot I've learned recently daddy.'

We sit down on the low stone wall which contains the pond and dad turns to me, a frown forming on his brow, 'what's the matter my little girl, you're not your usual talkative self?'

I sigh and reach for dad's hand, squeezing it tight in mine, 'do you feel that? Because I'm struggling to figure out whether it is real or not, whether I am really here or if this is a dream, my mind working overtime.'

'What are you talking about Soph?'

'Time travel dad, do you believe in it?'

Dad cocks his head to the side and stares at me for a long while before answering, 'once upon a time I would have said no, don't be ridiculous, but these days I try to keep an open mind. I have spent a long time wondering if it is possible, why do you ask?'

'Because I know something bad is going to happen and you will leave because of it.'

Dad's eyes widen and I watch as a sudden realization moves across his face. When he speaks my name it comes out as a faint, coarse whisper which I barely hear. He then reaches over and lifts me up onto his lap, holding me tight.

'It was you that morning at Chesterfield manor, when your grandfather was five years old.'

'Yes,' I tell him, my bottom lip beginning to wobble and my voice cracking.

'But how? Why?'

Tears begin to prickle my eyes, 'I needed to see you, it had been so long, I needed to feel your arms around me, to know that everything was going to be ok. I wait for you in my time, alone and with no one but granddad to confide in. I feel like I am getting closer and closer to you but time is running out. My body keeps pulling me back and each time I jump I fear when I return it will be my last. I have seizures which end with me in a coma.'

'Sophie I don't understand,' he says.

Of course he doesn't, how could he possibly? I am drawn to this day in my dreams as well as traveling back, if that is in fact what I am doing. If not then this is just another dream and means nothing other than a reminder of what once was.

'I don't have the answers daddy, I am trying to work them out but I don't know.'

'Then tell me when you come from my little girl and I will find you.'

I shake my head, 'it doesn't work like that, you haven't found me and that means I don't tell you when I am. It means I can't tell you. I have tried changing things in my past but nothing can be changed. This conversation we are having always happened, when I came to you that winter morning back when granddad was a child, there was never a version of events when I wasn't there looking through the eyes of a five year old boy.'

'Well, how old are you? Are you happy? What do you do for a living? Are you married? Do you have children of your own?' Dad asks frantically.

I smile and touch his cheek, 'like the Doc, or Mr E as he is known to many, I was a Doctor for a time…'

'Mr E?' dad laughs, 'so you know about his book?'

'Of course, you left it to me…' I stop, having just revealed my knowledge about *The Divine* means dad will leave the book to me for my thirtieth birthday. He now knows I have read the book and figured out its Author. He also knows that I will still have to read the book to figure this out. This has convinced me that I am not dreaming that this is in fact time travel despite the fuzzy outlines.

'So you can travel through time, entering the bodies of others to get here?' he smiles.

I nod, 'and you can fly and are immortal. It was a nice touch with the photographs by the way, it helped me understand as much as I ever could the secrets you have kept for centuries.'

'Photographs?' he asks shrugging his shoulders, 'sorry Soph, it must be on my to do list.'

I nod, 'it is. I can't tell you what happens but you leave me that book *The Divine* at a time when I needed it the most.'

The static begins to crack and as I look down at the pond Doctor West's face appears in the water, I close my eyes and again his face jumps out at me. I can hear him grunting, smell his breath, peppermint and cigarettes and the stench of whiskey, on the breeze.

'I'm slipping back,' I whisper and jump back into my dad's arms. 'When I go, your nine year old daughter won't remember this.'

'I know,' dad says, kissing me hard on the head as we hug, 'I remember what my five year old godson told me nearly eighty years ago. Sophie please come and visit me again.'

I shake my head, 'I can't daddy, soon there will be no more memories to use, you need to find me in my time. Please come to me…please.'

I close my eyes and the grunting from Doctor West comes into sharp focus. As I open my eyes I see him on top of me, my nightgown hitched up above my waist while his pants are down by his ankles. He's…he's raping me.

42

BILLY: ALAN CHESTERFIELD

We land together where the tree line ends. Up ahead the security lights swath the vast gardens, encasing the manor in a cocoon of brilliant bright light. Behind us the darkness of the night chills my bones as we make our way towards the house.

'I'll tell you Billy, I'm more than a little apprehensive about seeing Alan after so long. I don't know if he will want to hug me or throttle me.'

I smile, 'so this man, Alan, your godson, he was raised here at this estate by you over eighty years ago? You helped mould him into the man he is today?'

Eric shrugs, 'I have been there with Alan through every stage of his life from toddler to grandfather, and now my boy will be well into old age. After his father died in the second war I made family my priority. Both Alan and his older brother Peter became my life. Their mother was widowed at such a very young age and needed the help, and I'd had my fill of the front line, of the bloodshed.'

'*The* Vampire, the inspiration for Bram Stoker, growing tired of the bloodshed? Come on now Eric.'

We stop by the side of the house in the shadows for a moment and Eric says, 'your dad and I were summoned to Downing street by an old acquaintance of your fathers and we were asked to work with the Ministry Of Defence as spies, putting some of my more covert abilities to good use for the allies.'

'Downing street?' I half laugh.

Eric nods, 'Old Churchill and your father had been friendly back when Churchill was but a lowly war correspondent for The Morning Post. They were imprisoned together in Pretoria during the Boer War, escaped from the POW camp together, and so when the time came for the great man to help an old friend out Winston Churchill extended an Olive branch and your father and I became his own private hitmen.'

'Did Churchill know about you two?'

'Of course. He was amazed by our abilities, most especially the flying.'

'Well, I gotta admit I'm a little bit amazed by it all too, and this is coming from a guy who flew down here like superman.'

'I've never seen superman crash land like you did,' Eric laughs.

'Well you haven't been looking,' I tell him and he smiles.

As we walk into the courtyard the security lights flick on and moments later I catch a twitch at one of the curtains upstairs.

'He's seen us,' Eric whispers and we stop a couple of steps away from the main doors.

'So how did it pan out, working for Churchill as a spy and having had your fill of all the bloodshed?'

'By 1943 Hitler was close to announcing a state of emergency within the ranks of the SS. Eighteen of his captains had wound up dead, their bodies mutilated beyond all recognition. There were rumours of a beast stalking the Nazis, and in a sense that was correct, an allied beast working his way through the higher echelons of the Führer's powerhouse. I was an assassin, killing to order, destroying each name on my hit list and all the while I was able to spend the majority of my time back at Chesterfield manor with the boys and their mother. You see Billy I have found myself at odds with this strange old world for the majority of my time here and the only time I feel content, feel 'normal' is when I play the family man.'

I want to reach out to him, pat him on the back, put my arms around his shoulders and tell him how sorry I am for all he has been forced to endure. My uncle, true to form the family man, who has always been there for me, treated me like a son while having given up his daughter.

'I love you uncle Eric,' I tell him and he looks across at me and smiles, a sad sort of smile. He reaches over to me and squeezes my arm as we walk under a sensor and the courtyard lights flick on, illuminating us against the shadowy backdrop.

The metallic creak of a key being twisted sounds out into the night air and then the front doors open with a groan. For a moment I struggle to make out the long cylinder shape which appears through the crack in the door but it all becomes clear as the old man follows it out into the night, his burgundy dressing gown a couple of sizes too big for him and upturns the gravel as he walks.

'Now listen here men…' he begins, squinting at us, struggling to identify us without the aid of the glasses which hang on a chain around his neck, and repeatedly swinging the shotgun barrel between Eric and I. '…I want you off my land this instant.'

'Al it's me,' Eric says moving forward and I hear the gasp escape from the old man's lungs. The shotgun clatters as it hits the ground and then Alan Chesterfield follows it, falling to his knees.

'Eric?' he whispers, holding out his arms like a toddler would to their parent.

Eric then kneels down, helping the man to his feet and I watch as they hug each other, both of them now crying in each other's arms.

'Oh Eric,' he says again and as I look closer I see tears escape Eric's eyes as he kisses the old man's forehead, a gesture I imagine he has been doing since Alan was first brought into this world.

A few moments pass before they break apart and Alan clears his throat, 'come on then, lets get you two out of the cold. And who might you be young man?' he asks me.

I move closer and hold out my hand, 'I'm Billy Johnson Mr Chesterfield and thank you for welcoming us into your home.'

Alan takes my hand and shakes, then frowns as he looks me over, 'Johnson you say? I once knew a Johnson, arrogant son of a bitch, we never did see eye to eye on things. I hope you might better yourself from your father's failings.'

'How…' I begin but he has already turned to lead us into the house.

Eric slaps me on the back, 'don't worry about that, your dad and Al have never gotten on.'

'Because of you?' I ask.

Eric mulls this over for a moment and then replies, 'because they fight from two very different corners.'

'Come now gentlemen, I'll build a fire in the study and pour some brandy to stomp out the cold in your bones.'

We follow Alan though into the hallway where on the wall a portrait painting hangs, dominating all other pictures surrounding it.

I stop to admire the work and feel Eric by my side, 'sir Godfrey Kneller painted that in 1679, a year before his knighthood. Damn fool insisted I wear a wig but back then having or being seen to possess a great flush of hair meant something.'

I look up into the eyes of Eric's portrait and shudder. It could have been painted last week for the change in Eric, minus the wig of course, is non-existent. Following the paintings along the wall slowly they turn to old style photographs of people I do not recognize, families of Eric's now long gone.

The old man stops at a black and white framed 6" x 9" and smiles, turning back to me and winking, 'handsome devil wasn't I?' before moving on. In the photo a small child of about five or six years old is sat on a lawn, legs open as he catches a ball. He smiles in the photo, smiles at the doting Eric who is on his knees in front of him. So much history, lifetimes of memories encapsulated inside these walls.

Eric grins when he turns his attention to the photo, '1940, that summer was a scorcher, I remember us all spending our time down by the lake at the back of the manor where we could swim the heat of the days off.'

'Some of my first memories,' Alan adds.

As we move further on down the photographs become a little more up to date, wisps of colour enter the frames, two teenage boys riding their bicycles in front of the house, a proud Eric watching on, a wedding day, both groom and best man pose for a snap, they appear around the same age. As we move on Alan slowly begins to age but Eric always remains. Gradually we arrive at Eric holding a small baby in his arms, Alan is all grins standing next to him, the proud father and grandfather.

'Sophie,' I say softly and both men stop, frozen in time. They turn and look at the photograph and then the next, the baby now a young girl being pushed on a swing by Eric and then in the next snap by Alan.

'A nice day,' Alan says, tapping the glass protecting both photographs.

The next photograph causes me to freeze on the spot, powerless to move. It is another one of Sophie, the little girl grinning at the camera, only this time she is my little girl, the girl who chases me in my dreams, the girl with the emerald eyes who wears the little yellow summers dress and calls me Willy. I find myself pointing at the photograph like an idiot, no words able to escape my lips.

Eric clasps his hand on my shoulder and whispers into my ear, 'it's ok Bill.'

'But this...' I manage, but then nothing.

'You will have been mulling around somewhere out of shot, tearing up the bowling green to the dismay of the old timers no doubt.'

'No, you don't understand, this moment, this day, it is the day Sophie talks to me in my dreams. Warns me of the birdy hurting Sophie.'

I look closer into the eyes of a little girl frozen in time. I wish she could speak to me now, tell me what I need to do, tell me where she is. I turn to Alan and ask, 'where is she Mr Chesterfield? She speaks to me in my dreams, tells me I must remember things but I don't understand why.'

The old man smiles, nodding his head and as he turns, gesturing with his arm for us to follow he begins to cough, a shallow watery rasp, the pain on his face evident as he bows over, trying to get it up. Eric gives him a couple of slaps on the back to aid his recovery but Alan pushes him away, shaking his head, 'it won't do any good,' he manages to croak through his chokes and I watch powerless as he spits a great lump of blood into a handkerchief.

I glance at Eric who reels back from the sight. For a man who has spent his life in the company of blood, this reaction is a surprise, but then when I look into his face I see it is not the blood, more what it represents and where it came from.

Alan recovers and smiles an apology, squeezing Eric's arm as he too notes the heartbreak on his face.

'Are you ok?' I ask, moving forward with my hand out to steady the man.

Alan bats my hand away and I turn to Eric who is frowning.

'How long has it been back?'

Alan shrugs and then smirks, 'it never really went away, sure I was in remission for the best part of forty years but that damn cancer has lived with me for every single day between then and now.'

'How long do you have?'

Alan nods and then winces, a twinge in his mouth and then lets out a shallow gasp. 'A couple of days before the doctors want to make me comfortable, damn doctor speak for drugging me up and letting me die in a funky head haze.'

'There must be something.'

'There's not, and it's ok, I've made peace with this Eric. Old people die kiddo, that's our distinctive character trait and that is ok with me. It is my time, that's all, and that is partly the reason why you needed to return. The cancer won't hold off forever and I need to be strong enough still to be able to tell you about Sophie before it *is* too late.'

'Oh Al', Eric cries out grabbing hold of the old man and squeezing him tight in his arms. 'I should have come home sooner. Sophie, does she know? Where is she?'

'She needs you now Eric, she is in a place in her life where it is your guidance and yours alone which will see her through. Come now, we have much to discuss.'

We follow the old man into the study and immediately Alan busies himself at the fireplace, piling logs in a crisscross formation and stuffing kindling in the gaps. He then takes a barbecue fire lighter and slots it underneath his creation, taking out a small gold pipe lighter from his dressing gown pocket and lighting the fire. For a couple of moments he stays by his creation, making sure the flames take to the kindling, and then moves back, sitting himself down in the armchair just behind him.

When he speaks next he does so quietly, rising from his chair and making his way over to the sideboard adjacent to the now roaring fire, 'tell me men, have either of you ever heard of the medical term Locked-In Syndrome?'

Eric and I glance at each other and then back at the old man with shakes of our heads.

When Alan turns back around he is holding a photograph faced towards him.

'What is that?' Eric growls.

The old man sits back down and passes the photograph across to him, 'that, my dear boy, is a photograph of Sophie we would never frame and put up on the wall in the hallway. That is Locked-In Syndrome. That is Sophie. That is why you needed to come home.'

43

SOPHIE: JUST DESSERTS

As I am pulled back from my nine year old self's body the smell of whiskey hits me, engulfing my failed sinuses. West has moved my legs apart, my nightgown hitched up to just above my waist and he lies on top of me. I can feel him inside me, the searing pain spreading through me as he rapes my lifeless body.

He buries his face into the side of my neck, his breath heavy in my ear. He groans out and begins to laugh.

'You've been wanting this little miss prim and proper, haven't you?' he slurs, pushing deeper inside me.

Get the fuck off me! I scream inside my head as he ploughs away uninvited and unwanted.

'No more hard to get you little tease. You love it don't you?'

My head knocks into the chrome bars at the top of my bed, again and again as West fucks me harder and harder, gasping and groaning in my ear.

Stop, please stop I cry out but no words form.

The first time he slaps my face, sneering over me and then licking my lips, shocks me. The second slap, much harder this time, knocks my head to the side, pulling at the frozen muscles in my neck and those burning muscles begin to cramp up. The shock morphs into fear and then into something else, something much stronger, something I can use. Anger.

I jump into West's body and roll from the bed, catching my breath from the good doctor's excursions. I can hear the heavy breaths from West's lungs and as I open my eyes I watch the sweat drip down from my host's forehead and onto the floor.

My host's heart races inside his chest and I struggle to my feet, using the bottom of my hospital bed to help me up. I cry out as I stand and look down at myself, my legs battered and bruised, positioned askew, one hanging off the far side of the bed while the other is turned outwards, exposing my swollen vagina. Blood seeps from the opening, staining the creased and ruffled linen below my arse. My hand goes up to my mouth and I gasp, sobbing for a few moments while the enormity of what has happed sinks in.

I move closer to my body, lifting the night gown so that it exposes my breasts. Red finger prints mark where he has squeezed the lifeless flesh and what can only be described as a love bite sits on top of the side of my right nipple.

I quickly rearrange the statue, grabbing toilet roll from the unused bathroom and dabbing at my genitals. Next I pull the nightie back down to my ankles and place the thin sheet on top of me, all tucked up.

I stare into my eyes and smile, 'you must feel powerful, raping a completely defenceless woman.'

West watches me, eyes following as I pace the room.

'This is not the first time we have done this Doctor West. I don't know why you keep coming back because you know what I can do. You have watched from behind my eyes, frozen, watched as I control your body, watched with horror as I have taken over your life and left you with mine. You will stay away for a few days, avoid my room, and then you come back.'

I move in close, our noses almost touching and I stay like this, our eyes locked. He is in there screaming out at me now, pleading with me to stop, but like him I will not.

'You will not come back again, that I can assure you.'

I then turn and walk across to the bathroom. Inside, opposite the toilet is a locked mirrored cabinet where the nurses keep some basic first aid paraphernalia as well as local anaesthetic. Every doctor on the ward has a key to these lock boxes and reaching into West's pocket it takes only a few moments to find the correct key from the keychain. I locate the local anaesthetic and a syringe to administer the numbing agent and walk back through to my audience. I ignore those eyes, wide with anticipation and fear. He is right to fear me, this rapist scum. A doctor, entrusted to care for the sick and vulnerable and instead he prays on his patients for his own sexual gratification. Not anymore.

I whistle tunelessly as I re-enter the room, placing the syringe and anaesthetic on the window ledge so that West can get a good look.

'In my former life I was a patron of the medical profession, I helped children all over the world, I loved my patients Doctor West, I treated them well and saved many of their lives. Something I don't believe you have ever understood judging by the way you have treated me'.

I move across to my little wardrobe and open the doors, kneeling down and lifting out a shoe box which granddad had brought with him the first week I arrived here. Inside are the letters and photographs dad sent with my copy of *The Divine* as well as a few other bits and pieces. A couple of holiday snaps from before the accident, postcards from friends 'wishing I was there', and beneath these artefacts from a life lost is a framed black and white photograph of me surrounded by all of the children of a small tribal village just north of the Congo. Thirty excited children pose for the shot, their dark skin almost black in contrast to their bright smiles. I stand in the middle of them all, laughing at something. I wear a loose linin shirt and khaki shorts while the children roam the earth naked. Attached to my belt is a tribal hunting knife which was given to me by the chief the day before I left to come back to the UK. I reach beneath the photograph and feel the knife's' weaved leather handle, pulling the weapon from the box.

Turning, I expose the blade, dropping the sheaf back from where it came. I then head back over to the bed and smile, taking the syringe from its packaging and screwing the needle to the plunger. Stopping and looking down at the pants my host is wearing I unbuckle the belt and the trousers fall to the floor.

'Perhaps I should explain what is going to happen next but you are an intelligent man, I think you can guess.' I watch as the heart monitor's beeping begins to speed up and smile, sitting down on the chair next to the bed and pulling down the doctor's boxer shorts. His semi-excited penis rests on his inner thigh and I look at it with interest for a few short moments before glancing back up at my prisoner.

Plunging the syringe into the base of the penis shaft I wince in pain, 'you may choose to look away good doctor, because this will get messy,' I tell him, his eyes bulging in terror.

I point the knife in his direction and then wink, 'I have never before really thought about karma and I don't know if I believe in it, but with that said in this case what goes around is coming around you evil man.'

Holding his dick in my hand I take a deep breath and using the knife slice into the skin, applying more pressure once I realize the anaesthetic has taken hold.

'You will bleed out quite quickly so I suggest you seek medical attention soon,' I tell him as I make another slice. Blood flows freely through my fingers and drips down onto the upholstery of the chair on which I am sat.

I then begin to scream out, not because there is any pain, but because I need witnesses. One final cut and Doctor West's shrivelled up manhood is free from his body. I stand up, ignoring the blood and move across to the window, opening it and tossing his former appendage out into the unknown. I imagine it will make a nice meal for one of the stray cats who roam the grounds at night.

Limping back across to the hospital bed I fall on top of my own body just as the door opens and there is a high pitched scream.

I stare into West's eyes and then smile, nodding as I feel an arm reach around my neck.

'So long West,' I cry out and then jump back.

Immediately West begins to screech with the shock of what he has witnessed. Now he has his vocal chords and most of his body back he slumps down, all the while two orderlies attempt to drag him away from my bed. I close my eyes and listen to the commotion and to West crying out, 'it was her, it was her,' but how could he blame me for anything? A patient with the debilitating Locked in Syndrome is not capable of doing anything other than dream of a release from the tomb in which they encapsulate.

43

WILLIAM: BROTHERS IN ARMS

Sophie. I try to imagine that little girl as a grown woman, so sure of herself in the way she spoke to me, and wonder why she has not attempted to contact either me or Eric in her present. Alan will no doubt have had a hand in her staying away but to his credit he stands only to protect the people he loves. Uncompromising and fiercely protective, the very reasons Eric left young Sophie in Alan's care in the first place

I wonder if it is today when she will come. Each day I study the faces in my lectures, waiting for the young lady with long dark hair who wears the navy beret, and each day I leave my class disappointed.

As usual I prepare my lecture at the front of the class, setting out the slides I plan to use as points of reference and shuffling through papers. It has been two weeks since semester began and each day I have received an unexpected guest in my theatre. Victor Morris sat in on my class the first morning, Nessie the second, checking up on me no doubt, making sure I am towing the line and being a good little recruitment agent. Always sat in the same seat right at the back of the packed room, a member of the Phoenix Committee has followed me as I talk about the book *The Divine*, it's mysterious author, and whether it belongs in the fiction or non-fiction section of bookstores and online. Not that it matters much for book placement as *The Divine* has remained at number one in all bestseller charts throughout the western world. The web is alive with speculation, the fanatic *divinians* with their forums and social media pages and blogs have come alive again since the book's re-release. I even caught a song on you tube a few nights back in which one lyric

'Wallace rules the day, the vampire rules the night, between these Godless angel's they sneer at Mankind's plight,' struck a chord.

Godless angels?

Laughing at man's mortality?

If anything I envy Man's short time here as it makes it all so special.

My students, for the most part, stick to themes raised in the book and I have enjoyed some lively debates with the class, listening and considering their perspective on the subjects of immortality, abilities, and our ever evolving genes.

As always, I arrive ten minutes before class and notice already the auditorium is half full. News of this class has travelled fast through the campus and now students who are not even studying this course (and faculty members too) have begun to find their seats.

As I set down my files I glance up, as always, to where the Phoenix Committee member sits, their face changing on a daily basis but their presence and position never wavering. Sitting in the hot seat today is a young man, perhaps in his mid-twenties, with fiery red hair pulled back into a ponytail and as our eyes meet he smiles, waving to me in greeting.

I turn back to my papers, a sense of de-ja-vu engulfing me, but when you have lived as long as I, these feelings are not uncommon, a familiar face in a crowd, a sentence spoken which you have heard before, the feeling that what has happened has happened before, our lives are governed by cycles and so de-ja-vu is bound to occur.

On this particular occasion though it is more than that, a name is coming to me, a young warrior from Ireland who once sought to fight alongside me, a fearless friend who stayed with me through to the execution of William Wallace. Niall of Ireland, a feisty and brutal right hand man who, back in Ireland, was rumoured to have fought off a group of twenty bandits on the road to Dublin, slaying the men who had tried to rob him and decapitating each one, leaving their heads for the birds to feast upon. A gifted solider who could end lives quicker and more effectively than any other man I had witnessed fight in battle. To see him move, so quick, his preferred short handled axe and razor sharp hunting knife flying in union through the air to hit whichever targets they were destined for. An angel of death that's for sure, Niall could kill quicker than the plague, end lives swifter than a firing squad, and once the battle had been won and enemy defeated Niall would always break out into song, praising God for our good fortune and asking that our fallen brothers rest in peace.

As I steal a glance back up at the man I do not see the smart grey suit and stylish silver framed spectacles, hair neatly combed and tied back, I see the leather and chainmail armour and war paint tainted with blood, his hair left wild and unruly, a head of uncontrollable flames. Niall is reading something on his phone and I smile at the absurdity, one of history's greatest forgotten warriors' texting on his smart phone.

I clear my throat and look around at another packed auditorium. I then reach for the microphone and switch it on, blowing on the receiver to test it is in fact working.

'Good morning,' I say with a smile. I watch as Niall puts away his phone and half bows, those cheeky Irish dimples showing themselves in his cheeky Irish smile. The rest of the lecture hall wishes me a good morning and I nod, switching on the overhead projector screen and dimming the lights.

'My name is Professor William Crawford and I welcome you to this lecture and debate on a book which, during its fifty-eight years out there,' I point to the side, indicating beyond these walls, 'has created much controversy. Rumour has it the pope himself ordered to have this book abolished because he had heard there would be no sequel,' laughter throughout the room and I begin to relax. There is nothing more daunting than public speaking and despite centuries of practise I still, even now, try to keep the possibility of light-heartedness alive in the room.

'If anyone has a question please feel free to shout it out and I'll try and answer all I can.'

'What makes you qualified to speak about this book?' a voice immediately jumps back at me from beyond the glare of the projector.

I smile, 'the second most asked question so far this semester, and to answer it I say my love of books, my love of science, my love of mysteries and my love of teaching the things I love.'

'Is it real? Do people like this really exist?' another voice from the darkness asks.

'And that is the *most* asked question so far this semester,' I reply, amidst a few more chuckles, flicking the remote so that the first slide, that of the re-released book *The Divine,* appears on screen, 'and that is why we are all here today, to talk about this book, fact or fiction, and why it has captured the public's imagination so much. We will talk about the science behind the book, the characters, and also the ever elusive author Mr E.'

'Sir, what do you believe?' a third student calls out and this time the question quietens the theatre down, all eyes on me, everyone eager to know if I believe in people hundreds of years old running around today.

'Ladies and Gentlemen, I believe a lot of things. There was a time I believed a book written centuries after the stories within it were set, by men blinded by a fallacy set up to control, could answer the questions which I asked throughout my life. Fortunately instead of relying upon faith in fairy tales I listened to the voice of reason every one of us possesses, and turned to science to answer my questions.'

'And has it answered your questions?'

I shrug, 'some. Unfortunately though, allowing reason into your life means we forfeit heaven,' laughter throughout again, 'but do not despair my friends because it means you also forfeit hell, now shall we start?' I ask as my congregation roll through a round of applause.

I shake my head and hold up my hands in defeat, 'please, no, there's no need for the clapping, I speak only the truths based upon evidence, and that is what I would like you all to keep in mind while we discuss this book, the evidence and not old wives tales found on google. So, Mr E, is he in fact an eight hundred year old former warrior who thought it time he wrote his memoirs, or is he in fact a very clever science fiction writer who used all of the tools available to him to guarantee a successful novel? Let's find out folks, and remember I want discussion, not amongst yourselves, that will come later, but with us all. Let's go on a journey back through time, back to a warrior screaming the words alba gu bràth, Scotland forever…'

'Éirinn go brách,' the voice calls out from the top of the empty auditorium. I had busied myself with my papers, packing away the projector to kill time while my student body left the lecture theatre, aware that Niall's seat was still filled as he too waited.

Éirinn go brách, Ireland forever, words spoken a dozen lifetimes ago by men willing to die for an ideal of freedom which gave them and their people a hope to hang on to while the strong oppressed the majority, slaying the disobedient. Oh my how disobedient we were.

'You speak the words of a dying language Niall. Perhaps it might be time to get with the times.'

I turn my head and watch as he stands, smirking and chuckling to himself as he makes his way towards me, 'my my William, who would have thought the great Wallace reduced to wearing tweed blazers and feigning interest in the views of know nothing children.'

I smile and shrug, 'for a man who died at the gallows five years after my own execution you certainly are opinionated.'

Niall shrugs his own shoulders as he takes the final three steps with a leap, 'I always was the mouthy one,' he says and we hug. 'It's good to see you William.'

'And it is surreal seeing you my friend. Eight hundred years and not once did you think it would be nice to drop me a line?'

Niall laughs at this and shakes his head, 'I'm sorry but I had no idea you were a survivor. I was there that day at Smithfields, your execution was pretty convincing.'

I nod, 'yes it was.'

'And plus I was in my infancy, enjoying the trappings of a warrior, the cold winter nights and warm mead in my belly, the young flesh of a woman or two, the glorious battlefield where the odds of survival were good for me…'

'And the Phoenix Committee, where did they fit in to your warrior lifestyle?'

He flashes me a look which, for a moment, reminds me how menacing my old friend could be. As soon as it arrives on his face it is replaced by another smile and Niall shakes his head, 'William I don't think you realize what the Phoenix committee is.'

'Sure I do friend, it's a club for the Divine, those of us who should be old and wise enough to know that the human race will fight back and destroy us out of fear as soon as they are aware we exist.'

'And writing a book and releasing it to the world is the way to keep us under the radar of man?'

'I was trying to…'

'I know what you were trying to do William, you were trying to reach out and you succeeded without even realizing it. The phoenix committee is not just some club, it is our chance to fix the world. I believe with our regeneration gene we can end disease, put a stop to famine and stop the world's suffering.'

I shrug, 'lately Niall I have begun to wonder what is the point. Why should we end mankind's suffering when they would happily end us? Maybe this is their destiny, to multiply and multiply until there is no more room, no more resources and then die out, leaving us here to build a better future for the planet.'

Niall's eyes widen, 'do you really believe that is the way forward?'

I shrug again, 'I said maybe. Recently I have hypothesized about a lot, and all these maybes amount to very little if I do not have access to others like us so that I might take a look into their DNA. Victor and Nessie promised me a laboratory but so far none has materialized, they promised me I would be put into contact with others like me......'

Niall spreads his arms out wide and grins, 'and here I am Dr Crawford.'

I smile, Niall's enthusiasm infecting me. 'So the powers that be have decided the best man for the job to handle me is a bumbling Irishman who didn't know his arse from his elbow before he found me and I taught him what it was to be a man?'

'Touché, my friend and no, there is another reason.'

'Layers to the story, do tell,' I say, perching myself on the corner of my desk.

'Once upon a time ago I married your sister. After your execution I kept my promise I made to you and stayed to look after Nessie. The years ran their course and it wasn't long before Nessie and I were around the same age. Back then you should have seen her William, she would turn any man's head but she only had eyes for that bumbling Irishman you mention. So I'm afraid, old chap, that makes us family.'

I begin to laugh, huge belly laughs, something which I have not done for so long I can't recall. In turn Niall joins in and together in the belly of the deserted auditorium we stand there laughing like idiots. I reach over and wrap my arm around his neck tight, 'god it's so good to see you,' I tell him when the funnies are all laughed out.

'Likewise Wallace, now tell me, are you ready to get down to work? Because Victor has a very special assignment for you.'

'Tell me Niall, Victor Morris, the once Count St-Germain, can I trust him?'

Niall looks at me as though the thought of *not* trusting this man had never once crossed his mind, and right there I know I do not have an ally in my once trusted solider. This man belongs to the Phoenix Committee, to Victor Morris and my sister.

'Of course you can trust him William, he has only all of our best interests at heart. With you here with us we are now more powerful than ever.'

'To do what, fight religious nuts, modern day witch hunters? Because this is the tale Morris has spun for me.'

'No my friend, to save the world.'

44

ERIC: LIS

I stare down at the photo, numbed with the shock. Amidst the tubes and wires, like spider legs, closing in tighter on their prey, lies the body of my daughter, face contorted, eyes open staring vacantly out at me. My little Sophie, reduced to this.

The fire crackles in the grate and I watch as Billy turns, savouring the warmth on his face. Alan gets up from his seat and moves around to the far side of the desk, opening the bottom drawer on the right. As predicted a bottle of brandy appears in his hand, three glass tumblers in the other.

'Let us toast to each other's health and then I shall see about setting you both up with a room and a hot shower, Eric your room is exactly as you left it. For a while during her teenage years Sophie would spend huge amounts of time in there, searching for clues about your sudden 'death' but slowly her expeditions became less frequent until your bedroom door remained shut.

'When was this taken?' I hear someone sounding like me ask.

Alan makes his way over to my side and rests his hand on my shoulder, 'about eighteen months ago. We took that picture when she woke from her first coma.'

'Coma?' Billy says and Alan nods.

'Two years ago Sophie was hit by a van when crossing the road. The impact completely shattered her skeleton. Both of her legs were broken, both arms, six ribs, her left lung was punctured, her back was broken and the stem of her spine which connects all the dots with the brain took a whack.

When she arrived at the hospital she had already fallen into the coma. Probably a good thing, as it kept Sophie from the worst of the pain.'

I shake my head, 'but she is awake in the photograph, she is okay now right?'

Alan takes a long drink from his beaker, 'she suffers from an affliction called Locked in Syndrome. Her body healed, the bones were reset, her bruises slowly disappeared, the body repaired itself but it took months. All the while Sophie's was in her coma oblivious and we waited by her side for her to wake. When she did wake we were ecstatic. When she opened her eyes after the accident and I looked into those beautiful emeralds I thought everything was going to be alright.'

Al shakes his head and tears appear at the side of his eyes, 'but she couldn't move. At first the doctors hadn't even realized she was awake. Sophie later told me that it had been a few hours before anyone noticed she had her eyes open. More tests were run and what they came back with was Locked in Syndrome. This is where the patient can think, see, hear and feel like normal but is unable to move at all other than their eyes. There is also the more severe total locked in syndrome where they cannot move their eyes either but thankfully Soph does not have that.'

'So she is frozen, stuck inside her own body?' Billy asks as I look back down at the photograph. My poor girl, she needed me and I was nowhere to be found.

'It is funny you should put it like that Billy because that is exactly how our girl expresses her predicament.'

'Expresses? How does she express anything?' I ask and Alan now smiles.

'I had a team of computer wizards design Sophie a programme whereby she can wear a pair of glasses which are sensitive to her blinking, enabling her to spell out words onto a computer. The computer then speaks for her.'

'And the cure, I mean surely there is a cure to this Locked in Syndrome?'

Alan shakes his head.

'Come on Al, the doctors must be working on a procedure...'

'Eric no, they have nothing. I have spent the past year pouring millions of my own money into medical research but the doctors have nothing. Some people wake up from this terrible state and others...'

'What?' I ask, 'others what Al?'

Alan nods and pours another drink for himself, 'Sophie has fits. These episodes then throw her back into the coma. Sometimes she wakes up a day or so later, but there have been times...'

'Times? Come on Alan, tell me,' I cry out. I can feel the beast responding to my aggression and curb it immediately. 'Sorry mate, just tell me straight, everything.'

Alan nods and then jumps up onto his feet, 'I think you know.'

'Know what?'

'About Sophie. In fact I know you do because she told me the last time she jumped she visited you...and you,' Alan says, turning and nodding to Billy.

'Me? What about me?'

'You say Sophie visits you in your dreams but you know really they are not dreams, they are memories resurfacing. She cries out to you, begging you to remember because soon she will need you.'

'But how is this possible?' I ask, scolding my five hundred and eighty four year old self for even asking and waiting for Alan to say...

'How is any of this possible? Eric you once told me you thought your abilities were born out of a need for them, that your gene's evolved to enable you to achieve your goals to preserve your longevity.'

I nod. I still believe this. My ability to defy gravity came when I was being chased. It could have manifested into speed like Billy has taken ownership of, but it didn't. Instead my body released energy, the same energy I believe my hunger manifests from, and I slowly learned to fly. Later down the years still my ability to turn invisible came along, borne of my body's need to disappear to enable my survival.

'So through these fits and comas Sophie is able to travel through time?'

Alan shakes his head, 'Eric it is so much more than that. Being stuck in a body which does not work Sophie's mind has been her only ally, and through the power of her mind she is able to project her consciousness into those close to her, effectively jumping into their bodies where she then has complete control of her host. I have experienced this first hand because she has jumped into my body before now.'

'And where did *you* go?' Billy asks.

'I was stuck inside her body, but there is more, because once inside her host she is able to trawl through their memories, jumping to that time and...'

'Effectively traveling through time, anywhere as anyone.'

The old man winks at this, 'her mind found a way out of the cocoon she is trapped inside.'

I turn to Billy, his face pale as he toys with the photograph of Sophie in the hospital bed. 'You okay there Bill?'

He shakes his head, 'Mahogany girl...before Christmas I was drinking in a pub in the city centre when a girl approached me, asking a whole manner of questions, strange questions, not coming on to me, more interrogating me, wanting me to look into her soul. She spoke to me like she knew me but I was so pissed I didn't get past her chest.'

'And you think it was Sophie?' Alan asks with a chuckle.

'Well yeah, now thinking about it. And it was the way she left me, her last words, *'I'm too early'*. At the time I put it down to it being an unconventional drinking time...could it have been her trying to reach out to me at a time when I was no use to anyone?'

'You could dissect every conversation you have ever had with a stranger, or indeed a five year old little boy one frosty winter morning back in the 30's,' I say nodding at Al, 'what matters now is getting to Sophie, here, in the present, and protecting her.'

'From what, herself?' Billy asks me. 'I have no idea when Sophie is coming from when she visits me, but always it is with the same message, *birdy hurt Sophie*. From what Alan has just said it would appear the biggest threat Sophie has to contend with is her own body and mind throwing her into fits and comas.'

'Where is she?' I ask.

Alan nods, 'I will take you to her tomorrow. It is getting late men, perhaps we should rest so that we are fresh for Sophie in the morning.'

Alan finishes off his drink and I help him up out of his chair. We hug and wish each other a good night. Billy then shakes Alan's hand and thanks him for welcoming us into his house.

'This is Eric's house, the rest of us are just passing through,' Alan replies, and then whispers something to Billy which I struggle to make out over the roar of the fire. He then bids us both a good night, disappearing through the doorway and into the dark.

'Don't go dying on me Alan,' I call down the hallway to him.

'How rude, I wouldn't dream of it,' comes back from the dark.

45

SOPHIE: A BLAST FROM THE PAST

It is a strange sensation using a child's body as my host. For one thing there is running around at three foot nothing, but there is also that child's sense of awe always trying to burst through into my own psyche. I watch as the old man talks to my host's mom as they walk with the pram. Watch as I speak words out of the lady's mouth to my granddad and as my 'mom' falls into the pram and granddad catches her.

'Sophie are you alright?' granddad asks and the host whose body I encapsulated at the time of this meeting shakes her head, 'I've pushed it too far. Come on,' she says, standing up.

'What just happened?'

'For a second I was back in my own body, I'm fine,' my former self says, leaning over and kissing granddad's cheek just as I run past them, almost knocking the pram flying again.

'Mom can I have two dollars for a go on the winter wonderland ride?' I ask, looking up at them both. I think back to when I was standing behind that pram where my host's mom is. It was only a week ago. I wonder why then I didn't let them know it was me. Would it have changed anything?

I didn't let on to them because I don't, that does not happen, cannot happen. The past is set. This isn't a science fiction movie with alternate realities ready to be played out at the change of something here in the past.

I race around the corner and jump into the first person I see, a young man jogging alone, the perfect host. As I run on, I glance back at the little boy, aware that in a moment neither mother nor son will recall the discussion about two dollars for the winter wonderland ride. I watch with that strange sense of de-ja-vu as mother approaches a young lady speaking on her phone and jumps into her by a simple touch of the arm.

I continue along my path, breathing in and out, powering up and down, a joy to be able to run along past the water edge, the cold blasts of air tasting wonderful as I speed up. Ahead of me I see the old man sat down staring out into the water, lost in his own thoughts. I stop, out of breath, revelling in the feeling of this cool air lining my lungs.

Granddad smiles at the weary jogger and gives him a polite nod and I sit down next to him.

'Granddad it's me.'

He smiles and shakes his head, 'I've just said goodbye to you, I thought you were being pulled back?'

I nod, 'that was a week ago in my time, I'm back now, didn't want to miss this meeting so shall we go and speak to Mr E?'

Grandad stands up 'after you my dear,' and then frowns, nodding to me. 'Would you not feel a little more comfortable in suitable clothes? Lycra, fluorescent running shoes, and a headband don't exactly scream out Uni student do they?'

I walk over to the water's edge and peer down at my refection, grinning at the young male jogger who smiles back up at me. As I search the walk way I notice a woman in her mid to late twenties. She walks towards us, her long dark hair shining in the winter sun from underneath the navy beret she wears on top of her head. Perfect.

The young lady smiles as she walks past us and we smile back. I hope she's not got plans. I stand up and call out to her. As she turns I hold out my hand. The rush of static propels me forward leaving the jogger behind. We complete our hand shake and the jogger, looking a little dazed and confused, nods to me when I thank him for his directions.

'A pleasure,' he adds, a little unsure and then goes about on his merry little way.

I turn back to the bench where granddad sits and shrug, smiling at him.

'You know for the briefest of moments dear, I noticed something which has escaped me before.'

'Oh?' I ask, helping the old man to his feet and linking arms with him.

'Yes. For less than a tenth of a second there is a point where neither you, nor your intended host, has any physical presence and are both lost in limbo, awaiting a body with which to find a home for your mind. Just be careful my dear, is all I ask.'

46

WILLIAM: THE HUNT

'Tell me Neiall, how old exactly is our friend Mr Morris?' I ask him. We are now sat facing each other in a dinar just off Campus. I said I'd treat Neiall to a choco-vanillia milkshake and he countered with a slice of cherry pie each too. As we eat we talk, like two old friends catching up on what they have been up to since they last saw each other at Thanksgiving.

Neiall shrugs, 'there are rumours within the committee, whisperings that he is the first of us, that he walked in the garden of Eden but wasn't particularly peckish the day mankind sealed their fate.'

'An interesting thought,' I smile, 'perhaps he was the snake who condemned mankind to their short lives?'

Neiall shrugs, 'Nessie believes Morris was once a humble Carpenter's son, and his rising from the dead would certainly keep him on the shortlist, although I have never witnessed him serve water and transform it into a full bodied Merlot.'

'Mores the pity,' I tell him with a smile and we clink milkshake glasses over our pies. 'So tell me more about his plan. Every leader has a plan, and while Morris wanted me to recruit others like us I can't believe this is all he seeks, to unite the Divine so we may bond together and defend ourselves against the 'witch hunters'.'

'You doubt him?'

'I don't know him Neiall. But I know you, convince me this man knows what he is doing. Show me the evidence that the witch hunters exist and have existed for centuries. Have you ever fought them?'

'Well no but...'

'Because as a scientist I rely upon evidence, data, reason, to form a conclusion to a problem and right now my problem is I am expected to bow down and take the tales spun by our Mr Morris as read. You see even that phrase, *taken as read* refers to taking scripture written hundreds and thousands of years ago, as it is read on the page, going against instinct and common sense and giving in to blind faith.'

Neiall holds out his hands, 'whoa William, let us just eat our pie, drink our shakes and not worry about Victor and what he has in store.'

I nod, poor Neiall. 'You don't know do you?'

He pauses for a moment and then shakes his head, 'no William, I don't. I trust Victor knows what he is doing, I help try and discover how it is we are here using the science and reason you talk about. In my time with the Phoenix Committee I have recruited others like us, hunted others like us too.'

'Hunted?'

Neiall nods, 'imagine the likes of Adolf Hitler discovering upon his suicide that he comes back. Imagine the impact that would have on the entire planet.'

'And those you have hunted, what happens to them?'

His eyes remain glued down at his pie. Is that guilt he is trying to conceal?

'What you need to understand William is that these people are not like you and I, they are monsters. We hunt them down to protect the masses.'

'But my dear friend isn't that what these so called witch hunters do too, hunt the Divine to protect the masses?'

Neiall smiles at this, 'the Phoenix committee are not a bunch of murderers William, we seek to discover more about ourselves.'

'A noble cause,' I tell him, 'but who is to say that the Divine you hunt are not trying to simply find their way in this world too? They will be feeling alone, desperate, isolated from the rest of society. If they have reawakened they will believe themselves truly Divine and think that the rules of modern society do not apply to them. Perhaps instead of hunting these people you should talk to them. A radical idea I know but it has worked in the past...since civilisation emerged. It is at the very core of being civilised, conversation.'

Nieall grins and reaches across the table, squeezing my arm, 'God I wish Morris had recruited you first. The way your mind puts things together, you're reasoning…you are brilliant.'

'Simple logic and common sense, everyone possesses these traits.'

Our waitress, a pretty Barbie doll named Chrissy swings by our table, removing our empty plates and glasses and asks if there will be anything else. I tell her no and give her twenty bucks, telling her to keep the change and Nieall and I leave, walking side by side back towards campus.

'Tell me William, what is it that you want out of your involvement with the Phoenix committee?'

I stop and take a moment. That is a very good question, what is it I want? For years I searched for people like me and that was my goal, to find others, my brothers and sisters. Now that I have others I can call upon what next?

'I want to understand how we are what we are.'

Nieall turns to me, 'you want to study us? Figure out how we tick?'

'That would be the obvious next step for me, to continue with my class but also get down to some real work in a lab.'

'I promise that *will* happen soon and you will have only the best of us to help with your work, but first we need to talk about something else.'

'Oh?'

'This is the reason I stayed after your lecture. Victor and Nessie have a request.'

I laugh, 'of course they do, send in the friendly face to deliver the news. What is it?'

'There is someone they are interested in finding. This person has the ability to travel through time. Imagine having someone like that on side, a single agent who could travel back and divert the course of history. Will you help us?'

Sophie.

'Of course,' I tell him, 'what is their name?'

'We don't know. This person is out there though. I believe Victor has spoken to you about them already?'

I nod, that night in 1760 when Count St Germain disappeared in the middle of the night after I allegedly beat him to a pulp and dragged him through to the blacksmiths, placing his head in a vice and twisting. It is all becoming clear, the reason Victor Morris and Nessie wanted me in the first place. Because it is me who is used as the jumper's host, it is me who can get close to this person whereas they have no clue where to find them, or rather, her. But why would Sophie want to kill Victor Morris? What did he do to her?

'They want you to hunt this person down. They tried to assassinate both Victor and Nessie centuries ago, a jumper who can travel through time, can be anyone anywhere. Others have already started looking but given your involvement in the attempted murders, playing host to our jumper, we thought that maybe you would want to try and find them.'

I shake my head and pat Nieall on the back, 'you know this isn't the first time I have heard of such a person.'

'And you know where you might find them?'

I smile, 'no not yet, but it won't be long.'

Sophie.

They will ask you to do something and you must do it. The others will not understand but I will.

Her message through Alan comes back to me now,

Centuries ago you used me to try and kill Morris and my sister. Why? What did they do to you little girl? You need to run and you need to hide because they will not stop. If not me they will have another one of us hunt you down. Run Sophie run!

'Listen carefully William, because what I am about to ask you to do may very well go against all you stand for, but is essential to the Phoenix Committee and the longevity of our species.'

47

SOPHIE: MR E

Looking up at the University of New York's main entrance I am filled with an imminent sense of dread. I do not know this man Professor Crawford. I have read and reread this book *The Divine* and Mr E's theories about those who do not die both excite me and fill me with fear. I can jump, I think I can travel through time, although it is entirely subjective and may all simply be vivid dreams. Will I wake up any second to the sound of my beeping monitors?

Dr West. He was real. His blood still stains the carpet at the foot of my bed. Was I really with my dad though before I came back? Maybe Crawford can help me or maybe he is just a crazed science fiction enthusiast. I suppose I have come this far there is only one way I can go now and that is forward, through those doors and into the Professor's theatre.

'Do you want me to come with you kiddo?' granddad asks and I shake my head.

'No, I'll be fine. You go and get yourself a steaming cup of Joe, as they say here, from that dinar around the corner and I'll meet you there when I'm finished.'

He kisses my cheek and then turns on his heel, 'just remember Soph, if you feel uncomfortable just jump back into your body. Don't forget you always have that ejector seat to keep you safe.'

I wave granddad away and then enter into the reception area. Students are bustling around in groups, chatting, laughing, living, and it reminds me of my years at Uni. The friendships you just *knew* would last a lifetime. Well I suppose that was all a lifetime ago and here now I stand, an impostor in someone else's body and possibly a member of the next link in man's evolution.

I linger by the reception desk, hesitant, until one of the receptionists looks up from her phone and smiles, 'can I help you?'

'err, yeah, I am looking for a Professor Crawford. I was hoping you might tell me where I can find him?'

A couple of clicks on the computer keyboard in front of her and she says, 'Professor Crawford had a lecture which finished two hours ago. His next one is in twenty minutes in the main auditorium, just follow the signs.'

'Thank you,' I say and start walking in the general direction of where she points.'

I find the auditorium easily enough and once I have knocked to no answer I open the door a crack, peering through. As the door shuts at my back I cough, announcing my arrival while scanning the rows upon rows of empty table/chair hybrids leading down to the belly of the beast where a solitary figure stands, sorting through papers on the table in front of him.

When he hears my cough he turns.

'Hello?' he says, searching for his company, and in that moment I almost give up and jump back to England, to room 203, to Sophie Chesterfield's body.

'H...Hi,' I call out, doing a little wave so that he can see where I am amidst the millions of chables. I begin to make my way down the steps towards him, and it is then that I hear him gasp, his hand shooting up towards his mouth.

'You're here,' he cries out, moving towards me at quite a speed and taking my hand. 'Thank God, thank God, you are finally here.'

I peer up at the professor, younger than I imagined and quite a bit taller too and then, right there a flash of something disrupts my train of thought. A vision, a memory, of the man my dad would call Doc, of Willy's own father.

'It's you,' I whisper and he stops, letting go of my hand, 'it was always you. William Wallace, the Doc, Mr E.' I reach into my pocket and take out the paperback version of The Divine I bought from a bookshop on the way over here. I then throw the book to the professor and he catches it, frowning down at the cover for quite some time.

'Who knows?' are his first words and I take a step back, 'just me and I really need to talk to you. What did you mean when you said *you're here*, like you were expecting me?'

Mr E, my father's closest friend, nods for us to sit down and I follow his lead to one of the chables, sitting myself next to him.

'For a month I have waited for you to arrive Sophie. It is you isn't it?'

'How do you...'

Professor Crawford laughs, reaching for my hand and patting it, 'I know everything my dear, I know of your gift, traveling through time, through people, I know because you came to me, you came to me through your grandfather to warn me you were coming, that you would be wearing that navy beret and beneath it would be your host's long dark hair.'

'What? I don't underst...'

'A future version of you came to me and told me of our meeting here, now, she told me to go easy on you, something I'm afraid I have not.'

He laughs and I try to smile but something is stopping me.

Distrust?

Possibly.

Although I have no reason to distrust this man. He is my father's closest friend and if The Divine tells an accurate tale, has been by my father's side for the best part of a century.

'I'm sorry this is a lot to take in. I have so many questions to ask you.'

'Please, Sophie, ask away.'

I flick through the pages of The Divine and then look up at the Doc, 'I need to trust you William. I need to be able to trust you like my dad trusts you.'

'Of course my dear.'

'I have read your book, memoir, and you say that the Divine must first die for the regeneration genes to kick in and you are then reborn invincible?'

The Doc nods, 'Sophie that book is merely the scribblings of theories I have. Unfortunately I have had a limited amount of test subjects to try my theories out against and so just theories they will remain until…'

'Until?'

A smile, 'let's just say I have gained access to more of us.'

'Us?'

'But Sophie of course us. To exhibit such fascinating abilities there is no doubt you are a member of our very exclusive club.'

'But I still live. I have not come back invincible, quite the opposite in fact.'

'What do you mean,' he asks with a frown.

'I have locked in Syndrome which often throws me into seizures and then comas. My mind and body are going fucking haywire on an almost weekly basis in my hospital room back in the UK.'

'Oh Sophie no,' the Doc cries out, taking my host's hand in his and kissing it, 'oh no. How did this happen?'

I shrug, 'a hit and run two years ago. I have travelled back to the moment the van hits but I cannot stop it. The past is not interchangeable. Step on a butterfly and a tsunami is not caused half way around the world. All you have is a dead butterfly which always died because you always stood on it. There is no version of events where that damn butterfly ever lived.'

He shakes his head and then stops, 'Sophie did you see who was driving the van when you were hit?'

I nod, 'I have gone back a dozen times, watched from every possible angle and I see shadows, a face I do not recognize, an emblem of an orange bird, an elderly woman striking the driver, and then I wake up.'

The Doc gasps, turning to me and holding out his hands for me to take, 'Sophie where are you now? Your body, which hospital are you in. It is imperative that I come to you.'

'Why?'

'Because I think I have a way of saving your life.'

48

BILLY: FUTURE DREAMS

Alan reaches across for my hand and we shake. Eric has turned to the fire with his drink and the old man moves in close to my ear, saying, 'dear Billy, it is a pleasure to meet you and nice to finally put a face to a name I have been hearing ever since I was but a boy like you.'

He then slaps me on the back and I smile, the old boy must be getting a bit tired and confused at this late hour.

As both Eric and I watch him leave the room, Eric calling out 'don't go dying on me' and Alan returning the playful jibe with, 'how rude, I wouldn't dream of it,' I try to imagine the life Alan Chesterfield has led with uncle Eric always there, an unchanging force in a forever changing world. I guess one day I will now learn what it is like to watch your loved ones grow from babies to old men and beyond. That is the curse, I get it.

'Sooooo, now what?' I ask Eric, slumping down onto the comfortable beaten leather couch and letting out a huge sigh. I'm absolutely shattered.

Eric pours us both another brandy and hands mine over, 'bedtime, tomorrow we go and see my daughter,' he says, a sad little smile appearing at the corner of his mouth. He quickly downs his drink and then nods at me, wishing me a goodnight and then disappearing the way Alan had five minutes before.

For a while I just sit there watching the fire, flames dancing in the grate, weaving in and out of each other, their majestic beauty hypnotic. Slowly I feel my eyes getting heavier and I do not fight the warm blanket sleep lays over my consciousness. I close my eyes and listen to the quiet roar of the fire, the wood hissing and cracking as I feel myself going off. A soft beeping sound entwines the crackling of the fire and when I open my eyes the fire is gone and the beeping becomes much more prominent.

I cannot move.

I am trapped.

I survey the crimson ceiling I do not recognize, a computer monitor hangs down on a bracket just to my right. It is switched off. Beyond the monitor an alarm beeping swirls around in the static which engulfs my mind. I blink a couple of times, my vision groggy and blurred, my body convulses and I feel a booming in my chest, my heart feels like it is trying to smash its way from my chest. I try to cry out but it is no use.

The room is one of shadows and silhouettes and to my right, next to my bed, sitting over me now with their hand holding mine, is one of those silhouettes.

'It's ok, just try and breathe,' the voice says, vaguely familiar but I am unable to make out who is speaking. The beeping is swirling in the air with the static which bursts into shimmers of electric in front of my eyes. The roaring is getting louder now and when I try and close my eyes they are forced back open by a slap to my face.

Eric stands over me to my left and as he moves closer I see that his mouth is full of blood, dripping down his chin and neck. Is he hurt? I want to shout out to him, to explain that it's me but I can't. I close my eyes again and another slap. When I reopen them Eric's face is inches from mine and he says, 'do not go to sleep my darling.'

The static roars on through the air like fire, its warmth freezing my consciousness. I feel the rough stubble from Eric's chin on my forehead as he kisses his daughter and then his hot tears splashing in my hair.

'It's no use,' he tells the muffled shadow to my right.

No no no no, don't say that, fight for me.

Another boom knocks my insides sideward and I can taste acid in my mouth. Uncle Eric stands, my hand tight in his and he smiles down at me again, 'I'm sorry I'm too late my darling.'

I close my eyes, waiting for my heart to explode, and when the sharp thud rips through my body my eyes are forced open by the sheer power and I jerk upwards, flying through the air and hitting the study ceiling with an almighty crash.

I land on the table with another smash and let out a well-deserved groan. What the fuck was that? I pick myself up off the floor and plonk down on the sofa just as Eric arrives, baseball bat in his hands, wearing nothing but a pair of long-johns he must have bought around the time he built this place.

'What's going on?' he hisses and I burst out laughing at the absurdity of the scene which has unfolded in front of me, Dracula himself prancing around in two hundred year old underwear wielding a baseball bat.

'Sorry Eric, I fell.'

'Upwards!' he cries out.

I nod and smile, 'what the hell are you wearing?'

'Never mind that, keep your falling downwards or even better, not at all, it's three o'clock in the morning and I'll not have Alan disturbed.'

I give him a mock salute and then wave as he disappears back upstairs. What had seemed like minutes to me had been hours. I close my eyes again and the memory of my dream floats back through my vision. I look past Eric standing over my bedside and there, hanging around the door handle is one of those do not disturb signs you see in hotels. What holds my attention for longer than the half second this piece of information should is the number 203 stamped diagonally across the sign. Sophie's hospital room.

49

ERIC: MY LITTLE MAN

I wake up to the sound of people about in the kitchen, pots and pans clanging together, the sound of muffled voices echoing up to my room and I am momentarily lost in time. Am I waking to the sounds of the boys wanting to make me and their mother breakfast in the late1940's? Is it the maid crashing about trying to find the misplaced eggs she plucked from the chicken coop we keep in the mid 1800's? Or is it Sophie inventing another chocolate and peanut butter monstrosity with jelly and ice cream in the late twentieth century?

As I lie here with my eyes shut, centuries of memories, good memories, memories surrounding this house and the families of mine which have lived here with me, engulf my thoughts. I am home.

Arriving back to the now, I can hear Sheila and Billy talking downstairs in the kitchen. They are planning a full English breakfast for us all.

'Alan is sleeping in this morning, I left him to rest when I got up at seven,' Sheila tells Billy and I jump to my feet.

Absentmindedness can affect the old. Sheila , at seventy six, can be described as old, and the fact that she has spent almost sixty years with a man who has never slept in, who even as a child, was an early riser, sends a spike of dread down my spine. In seconds I am at Alan's bedroom door and as I knock I already know there will be no reply.

'Al,' I whisper, feeling a sickening crunch in the pit of my stomach. I open the door and peer into the darkened room. Over on the far side Alan lies still in his bed, no rasping breathes, no heart wrenching coughs and cackles. He is at peace.

'Al, mate, stop it now,' I tell him as I make my way over and kneel down at his bedside. I notice there is no rise and fall from his chest and I also feel the cold of his hand when I reach for it and bring it up to my cheek.

'Oh little man,' I whisper and then kiss his hand, placing it back down by his side. Deep inside I can feel the beast stir, only this feels different. There is no red veil, I am in complete control. This is not a hunger, this is something else. Grief. Alan Chesterfield was my great grandson four times removed. He was my boy who I raised, he was my best friend and confident, he was the keeper of my sanctuary, the keeper of my secrets, in later years a father figure I looked up to, and most importantly the guardian of my little girl, and now, the little terror who I would make forts with in the woods and go fishing with in the lake at the back of the house, is gone. My Alan. My boy. Stolen from me like the rest of them.

For a while I stay with his body, aware Sheila will come up at some point to wake him up and find us here and Alan gone. In the darkened room I stay by his side and relive our life together, recalling the good times and some of the bad, all of which helped mould Alan into the great man he had been, fiercely loyal to his family and uncompromising in his will.

I feel a hand on my shoulder and turn, looking up to see Sheila standing just behind me.

'He looks so peaceful Eric,' she says, squeezing my hand as I reach up for hers. It has been close to two decades since I last saw Sheila and when I turn to hug her I see that her once gorgeous thick blonde locks have since thinned and whitened. Her cells are slowly breaking down, allowing for the natural process of her body to do the same too. Pretty soon, give it ten years, maybe even twenty, a blink of an eye which can pass so quickly, she too will dead, another generation of Chesterfields taken from this earth, buried in their plots in the cemetery, a mere headstone acting as blurb for the life which was once led.

'I should never have left,' I tell her and she looks up at me, stroking my face.

'Oh dear, dear Eric, Alan understood why you felt you had to leave. He did not agree with it but he never resented you for your decision and he never stopped loving you. You left with us the most precious gift anyone could have given, a little girl who would never quite believe her father was gone.'

'Where is she Sheila ? Where's my baby girl?'

Sheila smiles and continues to stroke my face, 'I will take you to her, but first I need to ring our doctor.' She then kneels down where I had been moments before and kisses Alan's forehead.

'Sweet dream my lover,' she whispers and turns back to me.

Feeling the tears rolling down my face I shake my head, 'how do you do it, manage to remain so composed?'

Sheila shrugs, 'Eric we have been battling his illness for months, putting on a brave face for Sophie when we would visit her. I guess now all that is left is that brave face.'

'I'm glad I got here before it was too late, that I shared a drink with Alan in front of the fire in my study, like we used to back when you two were first married.'

Sheila smiles again, 'Alan once told me you and he had been enjoying a drink in your study for far longer than that. Didn't you used to put a nip of brandy in his and his brothers bedtime cocoa to help them sleep.'

I nod at this and recalling Al and his older brother Peter always sleeping through like logs when I spiked them, I laugh, 'a long time ago yes.'

'Perhaps it is fitting then that you two had that one last drink together.'

I look back down at the old man, lean over and stroke his head, 'perhaps you're right.' I then turn and kiss Sheila on the cheek, heading out of the room before it gets too much and I breakdown.

As Lord of Chesterfield Manor and man of the house I would not embarrass Sheila by succumbing to my emotions any more than I have in front of her. Call me old fashioned but a man shouldn't express vulnerability to the fairer sex. I know this isn't very twenty-first century, but hell, neither am I, neither was my little man, Alan.

BILLY: COMA

Our arrival was well timed, the poor old man could not fight the cancer any longer. It was almost as if he had been waiting for Eric's return so that he could let go, knowing Sophie would still have a protector watching out for her. In this case she has two.

It is no secret the girl who I remember only as a child, amazes me. I wonder what she was doing with my body while I was stuck in hers, and when will this happen? It was the middle of the night at Chesterfield manor, why would Sophie have wanted to jump to this particular moment, to visit Eric? Although I have not mentioned this to Eric I am pretty sure he would have to me had Sophie visited him last night.

We wait in the kitchen drinking strong and bitter coffee. The Doctor is upstairs with Sheila pronouncing Alan dead and outside on the courtyard stands the coroner's van ready to whisk Alan away to the morgue.

I watch Eric with morbid interest. I have never seen this side to the man before, grief stricken, at loss with the world. I reach over and squeeze his hand and Eric turns from where or whenever his mind had travelled to. He smiles and squeezes my hand back. Tears fall from his eyes and he then buries his face into my shoulder and sobs.

Seeing him like this makes me want to cry also, and it occurs to me that no matter how many times you lose a loved one, the pain is always as sharp, as real. Each time is like the first time.

We hear the bedroom door close upstairs and we stand, Eric drying his eyes and composing himself as Sheila and the Doctor enter the kitchen.

He moves over and shakes the Doc's hand. The Doctor nods his head and says, 'he fought like a warrior.'

Eric nods, 'what now?'

'Now the coroner will take the body to the morgue and I will notify Alan's solicitor of his passing for the purpose of the will. Alan was very specific in that he wanted to be buried here in Chesterfield manor's grounds under…'

'Under the oak tree with the swing in it,' Eric smiles.

'So he told you of this?'

Eric shakes his head, 'no but it is fitting he wouldn't want to leave this place. He spent his entire life here.'

The Doc nods at this and then shakes Eric's hand again, 'I'll wait outside while the county coroner does his work,' he smiles and then, 'will your father be attending the funeral?'

'No, I'm afraid my father passed away some years ago,' Eric answers him.

'I'm sorry to hear that, and of course what happed to Sophie.'

Eric nods and the Doc makes his way outside.

When I guess he can't ignore my staring at him any longer he turns to me and says, 'they think Alan was my grandfather, that me twenty five years ago, which was the last time I met the doctor, was my dad, and I guess that Sophie is my sister.'

I shake my head, 'fucked up,' and Sheila begins to laugh which causes us all to start up.

'Living in this family with Eric around certainly has had its moments.'

Eric reaches for Sheila and brings her close for a hug, 'aww, Sheila, you wouldn't have had it any other way,' he says kissing her cheek.

'Right you two lets go,' Sheila tells us after our fourth round of coffees, 'I have rung ahead and the lovely nurse Bradshaw says we are more than welcome to visit Sophie.

The drive over to the hospital is one filled with silent contemplation of what awaits us in room 203. Sophie, the girl who can travel through time, who warned me of a birdy hurting her and that I must remember this, she is there, a thirty year old woman not the little girl I know. We will meet in real time, the present, the here and now, and I am nervous.

I turn to Eric and nudge him, 'you ok?'

He meets my eyes and says, 'not even a little bit.' Then, leaning forward to Sheila in the driving seat, 'who will tell Sophie of Alan's passing?'

Sheila gasps, holding up her hand to her mouth and glances back, 'oh my poor poor little girl,' she says, 'I…I don't know, perhaps I should.'

Eric nods at this suggestion and closes his eyes, conversation over.

We arrive at the hospital and park up, Sheila wandering off to feed the ticket machine, and Eric and I walk across the carpark towards the entrance. The place is awash with people mulling to and fro. Bandaged legs on crutches, with people attached of course, elderly men and woman with vacant expressions etched into their faces are wheeled about by nurses or loved ones, and standing amidst the carnage is a young lady, a nurse, who smiles as we enter.

'Mr Chesterfield,' she says as she approaches us and Eric frowns as he takes the offered hand.

'It has been some time since anyone has called me that,' he says and I then hold out my hand for a shake.

'And you must be Willy? Oh my how I have been looking forward to putting a face to the name.'

I am momentarily lost. What the fuuuuu…

'Oh Nurse Bradshaw, Pippa my dear, I see you have found the boys,' Sheila calls from behind me and I smile. 'Pippa has been with Sophie ever since she arrived here and she was always Alan's favourite.'

'Pleased to meet you,' Eric tells her.

'How is she?' Sheila asks as the nurse turns and leads us away down a corridor.

'Not good I'm afraid, she had another seizure in the early hours of this morning which threw her into another one of her comas. I have spoken to nurse Beatrix and she has no problems with the three of you visiting.'

'It's visiting hours why would she?' Eric snaps back.

The nurse smiles, unsure, and I butt in, 'you'll have to excuse Mr Chesterfield, he is very emotional.'

'Yes of course,' the nurse says, glancing back at Eric before leading us up two flights of stairs. While we walk Sheila gabbers on about how the good nurse would often read to Sophie in the early days, before Sophie's computer had been installed.

The nurse turns back and blushes a little, 'we have become very good friends, the sort who help each other and share each other's secrets.'

In saying this she glances at me and I catch a look. She knows about Sophie.

We arrive outside room 203 and the nurse stops for a moment, turning around to face us, back to the door, blocking our pass.

'Please be aware Sophie has had a tough time of it this past year, and the stresses of her condition have caused some changes to her physical appearance.'

She turns the handle and it squeaks as the door opens.

Inside is a cavern of shadows. Although the curtains are open the blinds beyond are slanted, letting little light in from the outside world. As I walk in I see the bed, and on the far side of the bed is a host of machines beeping and sucking and hissing, breathing for and keeping tabs on the little girl who runs so freely after me a life time ago. In the bed lies a tiny body which, in this poor light, could have been mistaken for a few pillows thrown together and covered with a sheet.

'Oh my poor poor dear,' Sheila says as she bustles past, busying herself with the blinds, 'what are you doing lying here in the dark, anyone would think you didn't want to get up lazy bones.'

I turn to the nurse who smiles at Sheila's words.

'It is important to carry on as though nothing is amiss. Sophie can still hear us and I think the normality Sheila is displaying is good for reviving her.'

'Well someone has to keep things ticking over while she sleeps,' Sheila says with a smile, 'I'll just pop out and rustle us up some coffees and water, won't be long.'

We all smile at the old lady as she leaves the room and I ask, 'what triggers Sophie's seizures?'

Watching Eric as he heads towards her I noticing what appears to be a scrubbed bloodstain at the foot of the bed.

'From what the tests indicate, Sophie experiences these seizures after intense mental stress. The CAT scans indicate this also. Her brain is going into overload and this is bringing on her seizures which then lead to the coma.'

He makes his way around to the side of the bed, hesitant upon his approach, and reaches out for her hand, fingers quivering as they touch. Eric then leans over his daughter and kisses her forehead.

'I'm here baby girl,' he whispers, his words carry through the beeps and whirrs of the machinery.

'How many seizures and comas has Sophie had since she arrived here?' Eric asks, stroking Sophie's skeletal face and brushing a strand of hair away from her nose.

'Eighteen. But they are becoming more and more frequent. When Sophie is comatose she is more and more at risk of going into cardiac arrest, her brain function slows down dramatically, and I am always afraid that each time she wakes the brain damage will be irreversible.'

'Brain damage?'

'Oh yes,' she says, 'Sophie risks everything when she jumps.'

51

ERIC: THE RETURNING WANDERER

Alan would have approved of being buried on such a terrible day. He would laugh as the rain poured down in torrents, having mercy on nothing and no one, and said *'even the earth weeps at my passing.'*

I know this because I know my boy, knew my boy, loved every hair on his head from the moment he was born to the moment he passed. I knew this day would come, as it comes for them all, the mortal man. The only real celebration of life *is* death. It is the yardstick on which man measures his life, reflects upon choices he made. Without that reflection is it possible to really ever live your life to the fullest? This is a question I have pondered upon for some time.

The rest of the congregation have taken refuge inside the small parish church while the weather shakes off. Friends and family I do not know. Although there were a few of Alan's old university chums who recognised me from a time long passed, they, like Alan, are old men and woman now, their memories frail. They may recall Alan Chesterfield's wedding day but they will not recall in great detail the best man. I am practised in keeping just out of view, in the shadows which keeps me and my family safe.

The rain is relentless as it batters the earth, and it has a sobering effect, sharpening the edges of what was a surreal service. A part of me always wanted, needed, Alan to be the one who would rise again. He would reawaken divine and everything would be ok, my boy would be back.

I walk through the graveyard, marvelling at how the place has changed since I buried the first of the Chesterfield line. His name had been David and he was my son. He and his wife had had four children and it was David and I who had built Chesterfield manor, with the help of a few of the locals of course.

Stopping by the side of his headstone, I run my hand across the weatherworn granite as droplets of rain splash their way down the smoothed rock to the ground. They are all here in this cemetery, my family, my blood, all gone, resting in peace having had their time and made their own small differences to those who loved them. I don't blame Alan for wanting to be buried in the grounds of Chesterfield manor and I understand why. He wouldn't have wanted to become just another slab of rock in this graveyard, just another Chesterfield long gone who no one remembers but me.

The rain eases up a little and as the deafening roar of the falling water subsides I hear someone cough. Looking around I see nothing but now the sweet aroma of pipe tobacco greets me from beyond the petrified Chesterfield dynasty.

Another cough, this one more like a train rattling along its tracks as the owner splutters through their smoke.

I make my way past the rocks, back towards the path which entwines itself through the graveyard and there, sitting on a bench perhaps a hundred yards away, umbrella up shielding himself from the worst of the downpour and indeed sucking on a pipe, sits…Alan, only it isn't. His weatherworn face with deep etched creases does resemble the boy's, but where Alan indulged himself in his later years, giving way to him gaining a few pounds, the man who sits on the bench is slim, his face taut.

'Come on Uncle Eric. Come and sit down and talk to an old man.'

I approach with care, the resemblance uncanny.

'Peter?'

The old man looks up, his tired grey eyes flashing something in them as he smiles, 'help me up,' he says, grinning and I extend my arm to him.

'My god Peter, it has been…'

'Seventy one years, three months and eighteen days since I left this place.'

I laugh, hugging Alan's older brother tight, remembering the teenager who yearned for the sea and who, on his eighteenth birthday, enlisted in the Royal Navy and never looked back.

'It's absolutely incredible to see you,' I tell him, laughing in delight. 'I didn't see you in the service.'

He shakes his head, 'I snuck in half way through to pay my respects. This is Al's day filled with people from Al's life.'

'And tell me something of your life, what have you done for the past seventy one years, three months and eighteen days?'

Peter grins, 'lived it Eric. I spent twenty five years in the Royal Navy and climbed the ranks to Captain. What fun I had, a different girl in every port, no doubt spreading the Chesterfield seed far and wide,' he laughs and I find myself laughing too, on a day like today, when I believed I would never laugh again.

'After I retired from the Navy I bought a boat and spent a few years at sea, traveling the world on my terms, helping those who needed help until I met the love of my life Annya on the island of Ceylon which is now Sir Lanka. We spent a couple of years afloat around the Maldives, Indonesia, and Thailand until Richard, our first, was born. Five children, eight grandchildren and our first great grandchild later and here I am, back in the godforsaken rain paying my respects to my baby brother.'

'And what are your plans while you are in the UK, is your wife with you, any of your children?'

Peter shakes his head, 'no they are all back in Thailand, that is where I have lived for the past thirty years, etching out a living as a fisherman on a Navy Captain's pension. I came alone because they do not know about you and they do not know of my secret.'

He sits back down and I follow suit. The rain has now stopped but the clouds are dark and menacing, promising another outburst soon.

'What secret Peter?' I ask him.

'In my time with the Navy I have worn many hats. Are you familiar with operation dynamo?'

I nod, 'of course, the evacuation of troops from Dunkirk beach in 1940. At the time I was in Germany…' I hold up my hand and smile, 'sorry, continue.'

'I was a naval medic, twenty years old and still wet behind the ears. It was my job to assist the doctors on our vessel with the incoming wounded soldiers. To this day I do not understand it, and perhaps I never will but something happened and those I treated got well.'

'That would be your medical training,' I say, but Peter shakes his head, reaching into his overcoat pocket.

'It was something else Uncle Eric, something from you,' he takes out a small pocket knife and clicks the blade upright, 'watch carefully,' he says, and then slices across the palm of his left hand. Blood instantly rises to the surface of the cut and I watch with interest. Peter shows no fear or anguish, common traits which are usually displayed when faced with the flowing of one's own blood.

'Watch now,' the old man whispers and I catch a smile. He places the blade down beside him and with his other hand rests his fingertips upon the wound, slowly rubbing away in a circular motion.

I watch beyond the blood as the gash begins to close until the only evidence of any cut in the first place is the blood stains on his hands.

'Do you see Uncle Eric? Do you understand?'

I jump to my feet and take a step back, 'all this time, you…you're one of us, of the Divine.'

Peter flashes me another grin and shakes his head, chuckling when he says, 'I wouldn't call me Divine, although I read quite recently that was the name others were using.'

He puts away his knife and pulls out a book from the same pocket, a paperback edition folded and creased to hell but unmistakably the latest print edition of William's memoir The Divine.

'And your gift, it works on other people, you heal them as you just healed yourself?'

Peter nods, 'if only I had known Alan was sick, I might have pulled that cancer right out of him.'

'So it is not just surface wounds, you can cure disease?'

'Eric, with these hands I could cure the world, but as you can see I am an old man, I do not have the time left to fix the planet.'

'You have read the book, you know what Mr E believes, that when you die you will be reborn.'

'Tell me Uncle Eric, where might I find this man Mr E?'

I shake my head, and then stop. He might not be able to cure the world but he could cure one. Sophie. I smile, and look past Peter, back at the church, at all of Alan's friends and family who have now gathered outside in the courtyard, waiting for Sheila to signal the short journey up to Chesterfield manor to lay Alan's body to rest underneath the old oak tree.

This thought, of Peter being able to cure Sophie. But would he do it?

I watch as Billy walks out from the mingling crowds, suited and booted with a folded umbrella in his hand. He waves and as I lift my hand to wave back I see that on his other arm nurse Bradshaw links him. Billy whispers something into her ear and as she laughs the sound of that laughter sticks me in the gut like a barbed spike.

Why would Billy be escorting the nurse to Alan's funeral? He wouldn't, unless…Sophie!.

52

SOPHIE: IN THE NOW

Waking up from a coma is a lot like waking from sleep. At first your mind is groggy, you forget where you are, when you are, who you are. You yearn to stretch your aching body, to get that blood pumping back through your muscles but then the memories return and you remember you are stuck, an ornament being kept alive by the machines by your side, buzzing and whirring.

When I am comatose it feels like my eyes have been forced shut, and so my mind jumps back to Africa, to the tribes, to the children, and for a while I am allowed to forget that this is not my reality, it is merely an echo of a time now passed. For a while I am rewarded freedom from my life again without having to use a host. I am allowed to be Sophie again. My comas are my only chance of living again.

Yes the doctors and nurses worry. Nurse Bradshaw, my little Pips, tells me repeatedly my next jump could be my last, that my mind can only take so much before it haemorrhages and once that happens I could well be a frozen vegetable, my mind having gone the way my body has.

What am I to do, stop jumping, hammer shut the escape hatch? My ability is now a part of me and I do not believe it has finished evolving. I believe there is still more.

Five days have passed since I spoke to the professor, Mr E, the Doc. After the encounter I met with granddad, and for the first time in my life lied to him. I told him the professor had been happy to go through the book with me, to answer any questions I had on its prose, but that was all. I do not know why I kept the professor's true identity from my granddad. Possibly because of the way I know he feels about the man who he thinks tore my dad away from his family. Revealing the professor's identity to my granddad would have stressed the old man out, something I am now glad I did not do.

I look out from the back of the car, watch the fields roll by, sheeted with the hammering rain, wanting to be anywhere, any when but in this car heading towards this destination.

I feel his hand on mine and when he squeezes I turn and smile but I am now back inside a memory, back in my room yesterday…

'Sophie, you're back,' Pip says, immediately switching on the computer monitor and slipping the glasses onto my face.

s o m e t h i n g h a s h a p p e n d

Pip blushes, I can see it on her face that something is wrong. She begins to stroke my face, squeezing my hand in hers, 'it's your granddad, I'm afraid he died two days ago.'

It is the most awfully frustrating feeling wanting to scream out in grief, to cry the tears which must be cried but your body will not allow it.

i n e e d t o j u m p t o g o b a c k

The robotic voice sounds out and Pip shakes her head.

'No, you can't Soph, you jump and you will end up in another coma, the funeral is tomorrow and…'

a n d w h a t

She turns and from the corner of my room a silhouette walks forward, tall and athletic, his smile one I have seen before, lost in a memory, lost in a dream.

'Hello Sophie, long time no see.'

'Are you ok?' Willy asks and I rest Pip's head on his shoulder.

'I wish I could be here in body, whenever I'm jumping there is always a dreamlike quality to everything. My focus is never one hundred percent and there is the constant threat of being catapulted back into my body at any moment.'

He squeezes my hand again and kisses the side of the nurse's head, 'it'll be okay,' he says, 'I'm here by your side.'

I feel sick. After all this time he is here, my dad, saying goodbye to granddad at the local church where he has buried so many of his family.

'And you didn't tell him I'd be coming Willy?'

He smiles, shaking his head, 'he doesn't even know you are awake yet. The plan is to head over to the hospital after the reception at Chesterfield manor.'

I turn to him, 'can I ask you something?'

He nods.

'Why did you stay, when dad left the hospital why did you not go with him?'

'And do what? Hang around the house while Eric and your grandma sorted out funeral stuff? I'm a stranger to these parts. I have no one but you. I am here because of you.'

I smile at this and then rest my head back onto his shoulder.

The car pulls up at the front of the church and we get out. The funeral has already ended and as the rain stops the congregation begins to file out, mingling with each other in the courtyard, waiting no doubt for grandma to lead them all up to the house where Grandad will be laid to rest.

'Where is he,' Billy whispers, more to himself than to me, stopping as he looks beyond the old friends and family of granddad's and out into the graveyard.

'What is it Willy?' I ask, linking my arm in his as we make our way through the crowds.

'I'll tell you,' he says as he raises his hand and waves over the gatherings, 'if you do me one little thing first.'

'Anything,' I say, 'standing on my tiptoes to try and see where he is looking, waving.

'Stop calling me Willy, that hasn't been my name for some twenty years.'

I laugh out loud, and as I agree to Billy's terms he pulls me close so that I can look down his line of sight. Out into the graveyard, through the trees, and standing over a man sat on a bench, is my father, his silhouette never changing, the unmistakable figurine etched into my memories.

'Daddy,' I whisper and let go of Billy's arm, stepping out of the nurse's high heeled monstrosities so that I can run to him, run to my daddy in the present, the now.

53

ERIC: SOPHIE

My heart begins to race, Peter's words muffle as the world slows down around me and I watch Billy point across to me. Nurse Bradshaw's eyes follow Billy's arm and beneath the woman's exterior Sophie peers across the graveyard, stopping and stepping out of her high heels.

'Sophie.' The whisper escapes me and is lost on the wind.

All this time, two decades, and here now she stands barely a hundred yards between us, the crying baby, the inquisitive toddler, sweet little girl, the love of my life, my daughter, my angel.

As I begin to run towards her I watch as she lets go of Billy's arm and moves forward towards me too.

54

WILLIAM: THE END OF THE LINE

I step into the room and close the door without a sound, twisting the lock so that it snaps into place, keeping us from being disturbed. I look over at the bed and let a sorrowful smile pass across my lips.

'Don't worry my girl, soon everything will be better,' I tell Sophie as she lies there watching me, and I walk towards her bed. The room is cast in shadows, the occasional flickering lights from the ventilation system and life support machine being the only source of light.

I reach for my book, The Divine, my attempt of finding others like me which has ultimately led me here, to this room. Placing it down on the bedside table I squat besides Sophie and smile. Her eyes squint to try and make out my features but the shadows are too thick, I remain a dark ghost hovering at the side of her.

'Sophie,' I whisper, tapping the cover of The Divine, 'I brought you this. I know you already own a copy but I have written an epilogue at the end of this one just for you which I would like to read to you now.'

I lean forward and kiss her forehead and then reach behind the machines to my left, unplugging them slowly, methodically, making sure I miss nothing, making sure Sophie is free of manmade intrusion.

An alarm starts to beep and above our heads a red light begins to flash. Soon staff will be knocking on the door, panicking, not realizing this is what Sophie needs, her transition from one plain to the next.

I clear my throat and begin, 'death is a part of life, the finality, the end of the line for all beings but the Divine…'

55

SOPHIE: COUNT ST GERMAIN

As I run, the years of uncertainty melt away and everything comes together. The Father, the monster, the immortal, the man, here in front of me, running towards me, his arms outstretched for me.

'*Sophie,*' I hear a whisper on the wind and as I close my eyes I see a man standing over my bed. His face is masked in shadows and he whispers something to me but I cannot make it out, his words are lost through time and space.

I race forward, towards dad.

'Daddy,' I call out and then the silhouette's words burst through into my head.

'*Don't fight this Sophie, you need to calm down, embrace the change.*'

'Fuck you,' I shriek, turning my head to see a blurred Billy running towards me. I close my eyes and there he is again. My room is bathed in a red tinged darkness and I cannot see past my bed. I am floating in the thick ooze of nowhere, searching for direction, searching for hope. The alarm bleeps continuously above my head with the flashing light and to my left I feel my attacker move back towards me. A hand appears from out of the black, delicately stroking my cheek.

'Don't touch me,' I cry out, my words echoing around the tombstones of those long passed, carrying to my dad who speeds towards me.

Billy appears by my side, and I cry to him, 'birdy…birdy.'

'Hurt Sophie,' I watch him mouth, 'room 203.'

'Run Willy, run,' I cry out, feeling the static in the air thicken, preparing to catapult me back to the hospital room and into oblivion.

I watch as Billy nods at me and then takes off at such a speed that by the time I blink he has disappeared. The static in my ears is now roaring through the air and when I turn back to dad my equilibrium falters and I begin to fall to the ground.

'Dad,' I manage, holding out my hand and feeling the warmth of his fingertips run across mine as he is there to catch my host, saving Pip from the fall.

I look up and I am back, my father stuck in an embrace with Nurse Bradshaw and having no means of getting here to me. I can feel my heart crashing in my chest, the adrenaline souring around my body with no outlet. Watching the figure I can see him more clearly now, towering over me as I lie motionless beneath him. He kneels down beside me and it is then his face meets the light and I see the person trying to end my life is the one person I entrusted with my whereabouts. The Doc.

'You needn't fear this Sophie. This has to happen in order for any of this to have happened.'

He reaches over me and flicks the switch behind my head which cuts off the ventilators which breathe for me. Next my pacemaker, and as this switch is turned off my body convulses internally. My organs are shutting down, being starved of oxygen and are now fighting to keep going but there is no use. I am dying.

I search the room, looking for an escape route, anything that will help me, will save me. The shrieking from the alarm rings inside my head and there is nothing, hope is still getting here, still running at his incredible speed to get to me, to save me. I try to concentrate, ignoring the alert, focusing for a final jump before the lack of oxygen to my brain causes me to black out, never to regain consciousness.

My intruder reaches out for my hand, no doubt to console a dying woman, I am, after all his best friend's daughter, but this bitch will not go so easily. As our hands touch I fling my psyche at him with all the force I am able to achieve, a sling shot of static coursing through him as I search for something or someone deep inside his mind.

His memories open up to me like cats eyes at the side of a winter road, only this road appears to go on for eternity. The Doc, he remembers everything. His mind is completely flawless.

Further back I move down that road, running as far away from the present as I am able before I stop and open my eyes.

I stand in front of a door, my hand held out as though I was about to knock. The window to my right has no glass to keep out the cold, and tonight is a cold night. I knock on the door and wait. What had Mr E been about to do? Had he planned to knock on this door or had he been hesitating?

The door opens and I am confronted with the man who will one day plough his white van at full speed into me on a busy street in central Manchester. His face has not changed and will not change for he is one of the Divine and he cannot die. This I realize now. This is the moment where things could be changed, what I plan to do now could be undone and then everything would change. I could save my own life if I just walk away.

The first fist I smash into his eye socket with such force that I feel my knuckle cartilage splinter beneath the skin. The man cries out as he falls backwards into his room, rummaging around on the floor, trying to find his feet.

'William, no, I have no valuables with me,' he says as he manages to find his feet, reaching beneath the light brown tunic he wears and pulling out a vintage single shot handgun, only right here and right now this weapon he holds is perhaps advanced for its time.

He fires the shot and I veer to the right. The ball bearing clips my collarbone and makes its way through my host's neck. He smiles, throwing the gun my way and revealing a knife.

'Please, William, let us sit down and talk, as we have been talking all night over dinner.'

He lurches forward with the blade and I let the doc take the hit. Groaning as the blade slips deep into his stomach, the man who will ruin my life takes a step back, out of breath, and this is when I run at him grabbing him by the neck and repeatedly head butting him as hard and as fast as I am able to. He cries out, pleading with me to stop but I don't listen. Taking his hair in my hand, I kneel him up and pull the knife from my host's body.

'No…please, William.'

As I run the blade across his neck, opening his windpipe and slicing through muscle and cartilage, my one day attacker gurgles on the blood which begins to choke him. He coughs, bending over onto all fours as he attempts to breathe.

'I am not William,' I cry out, swinging the blade in my hand and then with as much force as possible bring it down through the back of his neck. Next I take the belt from his waist and wrap it around his neck, dragging him out of the room.

'No…' he gasps, his neck wound now having healed around the knife. With one swift movement I pull the blade from the back of his neck and then thrust hard into his skull. This will not kill him but I think I know what might. I think I know how I can end all of this before it ever began.

I peer out of the glassless window. The street is two floors down. I take hold of my aggressor and fling him out into the night. He calls out as he falls through the air, landing with a sickening thud onto the ground. I follow him, jumping out of the window.

A few lights have been lit in some of the windows surrounding the main street where we both now lay. Busy bodies wanting to get a glimpse of what all the commotion is about no doubt.

I rise to my feet, ignoring the bone which protrudes from my leg. It will heal, of that I am certain. I begin to limp down the street dragging him in my wake, panting heavily, my breathing filling up the deserted street on this cold moonless night.

At the end of the road I see what I have been searching for, the local Blacksmiths, and knock.

No answer.

With a steady kick from my newly healed leg the door flies off its frame and we enter. Inside I quickly find what I need, the vice, and place his head into the contraption's jaws once he is lay out on the table, tightening and only stopping when I hear the skull creak. Out comes the knife from the top of his head and I sit and wait.

A minute passes and I watch as the dullness sharpens in his faded eyes as the connections in his brain, severed by the steel, reconnect and consciousness returns.

'What…' he gasps, trying to prise his head from the vice with little success, 'what is this?'

I make my way towards him, picking up a heavy iron hammer and then smile, 'question time,' walking around the table where he is lay out.

'What is your name?'

'William, you know very well…'

I pound the hammer into his left kneecap and he cries out in devastating agony.

'My name is not fucking William,' I scream, slamming the hammer down again into his right knee.

'This word,' he sobs, 'fucking. What does it mean?'

I laugh despite myself. He will remember this, the first ever time he heard the word being used.

'Tell me your name or you will discover what losing the means to fuck feels like,' I tell him, the hammer hovering a foot or so above his groin.

'I have had many names,' he says, spitting out blood, 'the name I use these days is Count St Germain. Who are you? You do not speak like the gentleman I shared dinner with earlier tonight but yet the physical resemblance is undeniably a mirror image. Tell me, do you take on the appearance of others friend and what is it you seek from me?'

I move in close and slowly creak the vice handle towards me. St Germain begins to scream and to quieten him I bring the hammer down hard upon his jaw, shattering the bone like frost under one's foot.

He moans, a guttural, primitive sound filling the blacksmiths and I reach for the knife again, slowly bringing it back to his neck.

'Wait,' he breathes, hoarse and crackling with blood.

I pause and wait.

'Who are you? What is it you seek from me?'

I shake my head, considering maybe breaking his jaw once more but what would be the point when he regenerates so quickly? I twist the vice handle again and watch as Germain's cracked skull begins to pierce his forehead outwards.

'Please…I have done nothing to you,' he gasps.

'But you will Mr Germain, and I cannot distinguish whether it is out of revenge for this that you come after me or if I am the one who is rightfully vengeful. On a linear timeline I attack you first but on my own line you struck the first blow. What is one to do?'

I twist again and his eyes begin to bleed.

'Please no more. Whoever you are I will promise to leave you be. I will not pursue you, just please, let me live.'

I twist the handle one final time and stop, slitting St Germain's throat and then driving the hammer hard into what remains of his crushed head.

As I walk away, backing up out of the shop, aware now why this man will run me over one day in the distant future, I call back to him.

'Living is something the Divine are experts at. One day though I promise you *will* die.'

I then leave the building, aware now that I have to make it back to his room before I jump again. William will knock on the door and find St Germain has left. This is how he recalls it because this is what happens to him. I can see it now, my ability is once again evolving. I am becoming more, I am seeing more. Things are changing. Maybe it is down to the intense stress I am under back in the hospital room, but here, in the Doc's mind I can feel his life, his memories, relive them all in a micro second. My mind is opening up, connecting with the neurons in his brain, bonding, creating a pathway into his mind. I understand this because he understands this.

I feel her presence, a little girl in the 1300s looking up to her big brother to provide safety. She waves goodbye to him and this is the last time she will see him for close to three centuries, just before where Doc's mind will darken and his memories are black, the cats eyes at the side of the winter road extinguished for decades.

His last memory of the sister is here.

I open my eyes and find myself by the side of a road, my horse and cart tied up to a tree close to where the road veers off to a track which leads into the forest. I know who lives up that track, the Witch Crawford, and she will destroy the Doc's life, entomb him in an iron coffin, because of what I am to do now.

'Nessie,' I growl and start running up the track.

56

ERIC: TWO FALCONS

'Daddy,' is the last word she cries out as she falls to the ground and when our finger tips touch I am there to catch her, watching her eyes glaze over and then reanimate.

'Sophie,' I ask, sitting her up in my arms.

'No, I'm sorry, she has gone, but there was a man in her room, I think he is there to kill her.'

I feel the beast stir and I do nothing to stop it surface, the red glaze falling over my mind. Although I still have the power of reason, am able to think as a man, my urges, once handed over to the hunger, are impossible to control until I have taken my fill. I am a primitive hunter out to protect my young.

A guttural growl escapes my lips and the nurse's eyes widen. I lift her up and then, watching the funeral's groupies take interest in the commotion from Sophie's call to me, I turn from them, running back towards the bench and an old man with the ability to heal others.

'Is everything alright?' he asks, making his way down to greet me, walking stick in one hand and umbrella in the other.

'Peter, do you recall when you were young, perhaps five or six, when Alan was just a baby, I took you out and showed you the countryside by flying over it.'

'We pretended we were falcons,' he says, his eyes brightening and the five year old inside him now brimming to the surface.

I wrap my arm around his chest and kiss the back of his neck, 'well this time we are the fastest thing in the air my friend.'

'An eagle?' he asks with an excited shriek.

'Nah mate, two bullets heading towards their bullseye,' I tell him and then power up into the air, gravity, wind resistance and the laws of physics not daring to fuck with me right now.

I listen to the shocked congregation's cries as we take off but there is no time. This isn't the first occasion I have been forced to reveal myself to the masses. Last time it didn't end well for them.

As we shoot up into the air I cloak us so that only the very inquisitive eye at two hundred feet might see a murmur in their vision. A blur that might cause them to do a double take, but by the time they look back we would be gone.

'Tell me Eric,' Peter shouts over the wind which pummels our bodies as we glide through the air towards the hospital, 'why am I joining you on this little excursion?'

'Your ability, my daughter is dying and I need you to save her,' I tell him.

'Your daughter?' he asks, 'but how, why?'

'Because of who she is, because of what she is.'

I let gravity take control and we fall towards the hospital.

As the ground shoots up to meet us I slow, taking the impact of the land which crushes a couple of vertebrae. I cry out as I help Peter into the hospital entrance, throwing him in a nearby vacant wheelchair.

'You ok Eric?' He asks, looking back at me as I feel my spine's discs correct themselves.

I smile, the beast smiles, and we move on down the corridor.

'Whatever happens, Peter, you need to get to the girl,' I tell him as I hit the button for the elevator and the doors ping open.

SOPHIE: CIRCLE

This day is a magnificent one, not a cloud in the sky, and underneath the canopy of the forest, heading up towards where Nessie told William she lived in a simple wooden hut, beams of sunlight flow and ebb down to the ground.

In the distance I hear the unmistakable thud of logs being chopped, its noise echoing through the trees. I do not know why I am here. She is the one who sits in the passenger seat of the white van, but she also appears to be fighting with St Germain every time I have gone back. Why? I know from William's memories that they both work for the Phoenix committee. Why would they be fighting, and at such a crucial moment like trying to run someone over.

I make my way through some trees and reach an opening, the small log cabin sits in the middle of the clearing. To the right stands a chicken coop and horseless cart, the left a log pile and an old lady walking towards me wielding an axe.

'So you found me,' she looks past me and frowns, 'where are the provisions, the bread and more importantly the mead?'

A memory four hundred years old comes hurtling out of the abyss. William had gone into town to fetch some bits and pieces so they might celebrate finding each other again.

'Back with the horse,' I tell her and she reaches for my hand.

'Come big brother, let me show you my home. I even have a black cat that turns up every now and again.'

I follow Nessie into the hut and she turns, placing the axe down by the door and wrapping her arms around me for a hug. I accept the show of affection and smile as William would have had he been here.

'Tell me little sister, have you ever heard of a man by the name of Count St Germain?'

Nessie turns away from me, 'can't say I have,' she says but then I hear that unmistakable sound of a sword being unsheathed, the metal on metal which would turn William's blood cold in these circumstances.

Nessie spins around holding her samurai sword which whistles through the air, narrowly missing my cheek. I stagger back, reaching for the axe behind me and bring it up to protect myself with.

'What do you want, who are you?'

'I just want to talk Nessie. I know that you are scared but so am I, things have happened and I need information.'

She swings the sword towards my neck again and I slam the axe down hard, knocking the blade out of her grasp. She screams and comes at me with her nails, digging them into my eyes, gouging as deep as she is able. I slam my fist into the side of her head and she drops to the ground unconscious. I too find myself stumbling, my legs heavy like all life from them is draining away. Both of my arms go numb, and the axe clangs to the floor. As I land on top of Nessie the beeping begins to ring in my ears. I am being pulled back.

No, not yet, I can't go back. To go back would be to accept my death, to give up.

I feel my eyes getting heavy and as they close I see the red light spinning above my head, above my hospital bed. If I go back now all will be lost. Using all the power I can muster I reach for Nessie's limp arm and with one final push I am staring at my former host. William is unconscious because I still control his psyche. Back at the hospital in the twenty-first century William is conscious and trapped in my body. He will be splayed across my bed as I am here inside his memories. I stand up and know what I must do before I try to save my own life. Grabbing some rope from the corner I throw it over the central beam in the roof and standing on the dinner table tie it tight. I then fashion a quick makeshift noose and wrap it around my host Nessie's neck.

If I am right when I jump I will incapacitate Nessie long enough for William to regain consciousness and help his sister down from the rafters. She will then attack him and lock him in his iron coffin, believing him to be a demon. Everything comes back around in a circle…apart from this.

As I leap off the table I close my eyes and time stands still. In between memories time does not exist, only the static which is the glue that holds together time and space.

I open my eyes and watch the streets of central Manchester pass me by through the window screen. Another fine day.

'Are you ok Ness?'

I turn and there again is St Germain, in a lot better condition than the last time I saw him twenty minutes and three centuries ago.

'Stop the van,' I tell him, turning to see him smirk.

'Are you crazy? Do *you* want to explain to her why we missed our opportunity?'

'Explain to who?' I ask.

He just smirks. 'What's the matter Ness, is it time for a break? You've been working yourself ragged since the boss gave us the go ahead to find your brother.'

'My brother…William.'

'Once we have finished this job I'll buy you a beach you can lie on for a couple of weeks and just relax.'

We stop for the lights and up ahead I recognize the junction. A left and then another left and we will be on the street where I was mowed down two years ago by the white van I am now riding in, driven by the man with the birdy cap St Germain, or Morris, Victor Morris if Nessie's memories are correct.

'Victor stop the car there has got to be some other way,' I shriek and this outburst makes him jump.

He starts laughing, 'what the fuck Ness, you almost made me crash the van.'

'Stop this fucking van now,' I scream as we turn onto the street and up ahead I can see the woman wearing the white cardigan and yellow floral dress approaching the road to cross.'

I Punch Morris hard in the side of his head and he retaliates by delivering an open palm strike to my nose, bursting it and causing tears and blood to blind and choke me.

'There she is,' I hear him say and I strike out once more, this time going for his eyes.

'Nessie nooooo,' Morris cries out, swerving to the left and onto the pavement. All I can do now is turn and watch from inside the van, watch as that young lady, having grown tired of western life and longed to be back in Africa with the tribes, where life made sense, steps into the van's path. For a second she turns to face us and as we connect I swing back and punch Morris as hard as I can in his head. It is too late though, Dr Sophie Chesterfield has been mown down by the big white van, but in that last moment before her world changes forever she sees the old lady attack the driver. She needs to see this because this is what I saw. Another full circle complete and now all that is left is the hospital room. I feel the warm tears splash down Nessie's face and say goodbye to the world I loved. I then close my eyes and head back to oblivion.

57

BILLY: SECOND CHANCE

Speeding through the hospital corridors and up the stairs onto the second floor I try and prepare myself for what I am about to encounter. I try the door but it is locked. As I kick it as hard as I can the door bursts open and I jump inside, the room dark other than the dim red glow from a bulb above the bed. Where are all the nurses, all the doctors?

I reach out for the light switch but none is there. As I approach the bed I see a body face down by the side of Sophie. There is something familiar about this person. I reach out to turn them over and Sophie lurches forward and grabs my wrist. I jump back.

'You're…you're ok? But how is that possible, what has happened?'

She smiles, getting up out of the bed and running to me, reaching up for the back of my neck and bringing my face to hers for a kiss.

'This is not real,' I hear her say, the words appearing in my head as I continue to kiss her.

I break off and move back, 'how, what is this?'

'You arrived here an hour ago and you attacked him there,' she says, nodding to the figure still unconscious over the side of her bed. 'My father then arrived and he killed the man. It was very messy and it did no good. I still didn't make it. With all the fighting the little old man who arrived with my dad couldn't get to me in time to save me.'

'I don't understand,' I tell her, reaching for her hands, our fingers entwining, 'how can this be, how are you still here then?'

Sophie leads me to the chairs set out in the corner of the room beneath the tv and we sit, 'I am still here because we share a connection Billy. I am still here because I jumped into your body moments before I died.'

That night at Chesterfield manor, my dream…of course.

'All this time I have been trying to change the past using big gestures, but it appeared everything I did I had already done and so would land me right back here where I am.'

'What are you saying that you are destined to die?'

Sophie shrugs, reaching for my face and stroking it with the back of her hand, 'I don't know. This is the last time I am going to be able to try and stop my death Billy and I need you to save me. In a moment I am going to send you back through your own psyche, back to where you held my hand and kissed my forehead.'

'But I haven't…'

'And when you arrive back I need you to save this man,' Sophie says, pointing to the collapsed figure. 'by saving him you will save me, my dad will not kill him and the healer can do his work.'

I open my eyes and Sophie is back in her bed. Her eyes are shut and her arm is resting next to the man whom I am to save, the man with his head down, face buried in the bed sheets. I walk around to the other side of Sophie's bed and try shaking him awake, that familiarity washing over me again. I then lift his shoulder up so that his face might turn and reveal.

Crying out I drop the shoulder and the body rolls off the side of the bed, thumping to the floor. Dad, it's my dad. William Johnson, the Professor, the teacher, the father, my father, dad.

'Dad,' I cry out kicking him hard in the ribs.

Sophie's eyes shoot open and as they do dad groans and picks himself up off the floor.

'My god Billy, what are you doing…'

I lash out with as much force as I can throw behind my fist and feel it connect with the side of his face, 'you are killing Sophie, why!'

Dad recovers from the punch like a pro and without missing a beat, holds up his hands in surrender, walking towards me saying, 'Billy, you don't understand, there are things…'

As I throw the second punch dad catches the fist and flings me over onto my back, quite a move for a tired old professor.

'Son listen to me, you don't understand, it is Sophie who came to me.'

'No, you don't understand,' I shout at him, pummelling his torso as he reaches over me to lift me back onto my feet.

With one huge fist dad strikes my face and hard, harder than anything I have ever felt before, then picks me up off the ground with one hand, snarling, 'you think you are any match for me boy, you think…' he stops and I feel the pain in the side of my face begin to lessen. He is watching me heal.

Dropping me and then stepping back away from me he reaches for his fist, biting his knuckle, 'my god Billy you are Divine.'

'And you are a murderer,' I spit out.

Behind him I watch as Eric appears from nowhere, throwing an old man with a striking resemblance to Alan Chesterfield down into the corner of the hospital room and then attacking with vicious ferocity.

'Eric no,' Dad cries out as Eric punches him with such force that he sends him across the room, denting the solid brick wall. I hear bones crack back into place as dad finds his feet but it is too late because Eric is already on top of him striking quicker than even I, with my new found speed, could match. Dad groans and yelps as his body is put under the extreme pummelling at the hands of Eric.

'Please just listen,' dad tries but Eric isn't listening. He picks dad up and slams him into the ground, digging his teeth into the side of his neck and twisting so that the vertebrae snap, wielding dad paralysed.

'Eric stop,' I cry out and he looks up at me, his eyes shining red like the blood around his mouth. Snarling at me, he brandishes his teeth and the elongated canines drip with claret. With one final twist Eric decapitates my father, throwing his battered head to the far side of the room.

I hear myself scream, the sheer horror of what is happening sending me into my own terror filled paralysis.

No, this cannot be happening, daddy...

Eric moves across to the elderly man and helps him to his feet, he too appears terrified at what he has just witnessed.

'Save her,' the beast growls and the old man rushes over to Sophie, placing his hand over her forehead.

The room holds still for a moment until the healer shakes his head and turns back to the beast, 'I'm sorry Eric but it is too late, she's gone.'

'Billy...'

I open my eyes and Sophie is sat next to me still.

'Do you now see.'

I nod. I do see. Dad needs to leave so that the healer can do his work.

I stare into her bright green eyes and smile, moving my face back in for another kiss and whispering, 'I love you you know.'

'Then save me Willy.'

58

SOPHIE: JUST THE BEGINNING

As I am pushed back into my own body all I can do now is watch and hope I am right, that Billy can change things. I open my eyes and stare at Mr E who lifts himself from besides my bed.

'It was you, all that time ago.'

I lie here, as always mute to any words put to me.

'I spent forty years locked in that iron box Sophie. Why? Why couldn't you change it so that I would be spared that?'

He leans in towards me and kisses my forehead, sitting back down in the seat next to me. My heart thumps hard in my chest, trying to work out what the hell is happening, slowing, and reducing the blood and within the blood the oxygen that reaches my brain. I begin to feel nauseous, my stomach turning once as my lungs search for the air they need to keep me going. I long to close my eyes and sit out this suffering, the suffocation from broken breathers and delirium from a derelict heart.

The knock at the door roars through the air with a deafening boom. The doc looks up and I catch the flash of fear through the crimson shadows of the room. This wasn't his idea, ending my life. Another knock, this time with the sole of his boot and Billy comes racing through into the room.

But everything is different.

Before Billy had already entered before I had jumped back from William's memories. William had still been unconscious, now he is awake and on his feet, fists clenched.

'Billy? How are you here, why son?'

'No time dad, you need to leave.'

Billy looks over at me and smiles, and I smile back in my own way before my eyes begin to fall again.

'What this looks like, I am doing this for Soph…'

I hear a crash and my eyes shoot open once more, startled by the noise. William is on the floor and Billy stands over him, blood dripping from his clenched fists.

'Leave now, go back to wherever you disappeared to and tell them you failed because I will not let this woman die.'

Quicker than I am able to follow, Billy lashes out again, pummelling the doc with body hits before delivering the haymaker to finish his father off. Just before the fist connects William catches his son's arm and flings him into the wall, using Billy's own momentum against him. Another crash and the doc walks across the room towards his son.

I can feel myself fading, the scene in front of me now like a dream, the edges softened, fluffy, ready for me to float away…

'Dad any second Eric will be here and he will kill you, do you understand!'

William scoffs at this, the very notion of death so absurd but we have seen what happens. Billy jumps to his feet and cries out, launching himself at his father, flying through the air and then through the window to my right. I watch as Billy carries his father out into the grey sky, hear his cry echo out as he then drops the doc into gravity's buxom beyond the hospital grounds.

My heart has now stopped and I feel the blood run icy through my veins, slowing, stopping my thoughts from processing, from meaning anything. I can hear something by my side but I cannot open my eyes. A whisper on the wind says *'jump'* but it is too late. My next jump is to the great beyo…I feel the hand hit me across my face hard and manage to open my eyes once more.

Billy is there, so too is my dad and the old man from the cemetery.

'Sophie you must jump now,' Billy says holding my hand, please, it is important, you need to…

I open my eyes. I am sitting on the couch in grandad's study. It is late at night and the house is silent. As a teenager I would often spend many quiet nights alone in my granddad's study, staring into the flames from the fireplace, lost in my thoughts.

I stand up, looking down at my arms, man's arms, Billy's arms. He was here, the night before granddad died. I smile. Billy knew about this because he would have been transported to my body, would now be feeling my slow frozen death.

I hear granddad's dry rasping cough and make my way upstairs to his room. Knocking quietly on the door the old man tells me enter, sitting up in bed and turning on his bedside lamp.

I notice grandma fast asleep next to him, earphones on her head, no doubt listening to the mating calls of whales or the sounds of the sea, and eye mask keeping out the light.

Granddad reaches for his glasses and frown when he sees me standing by the door.

'Young Billy what can I do for you at this,' he pauses to check the time, 'ridiculous hour.'

'Granddad,' I say, 'why didn't you tell me about the cancer?'

Granddad sits up straight and frowns, 'Sophie? When are you coming from?'

I shake my head, 'not far enough from here. Why granddad, why keep it from me?'

The old man shrugs, pivoting around so his feet touch the carpet at the side of his bed. 'By the time I was diagnosed the doctors painted a very bleak picture, the chemo would finish me off quicker than the cancer they reckoned. You had enough to deal with and I didn't want your pity or sorrow.'

'Oh granddad,' I exhale, 'we share such a huge secret of mine I wish you could have entrusted me with yours.'

Granddad shakes his head and I help him up to his feet.

'Come on. Let's take a walk as this maybe our last time.'

I help him on with his thick dressing gown and we head downstairs. At the door Granddad steps into his wellington boots and we walk out into the cold night air. He pulls me close and kisses my forehead and his touch sends tears flowing down my cheeks, Billy's cheeks.

'I die tonight don't I?' granddad asks and I nod, trying to keep from bursting out crying.

'There is nothing I can do. I can't change it because I am stuck here now with you. Time has frozen when I have come from but when I go back…'

'Why on earth would I want you to try and change anything my dear? I am eighty three years old, I've done alright. That is a decent innings. If not now, when? When I'm ninety and pissing the bed because I can't get to the toilet before my bladder goes? God knows it's a race against the clock already.'

'How is your dad taking my passing?'

I shrug, 'I don't know, I saw him but something happened and…'

'Is everything alright my dear?'

'No it's not. When I go back I think I'm going to die.'

Granddad nods at this and stands up, 'come on, walk an old man back to his room will you. The night is getting cold and anyone would catch their death if they stayed out here.' He flashes me a grin and we link arms.

'It's been a funny old life this one of mine. Uncle Eric's presence kept that sense of wonder alive in me long after I should have become a hardened cynic. I guess even now I am still that five year old boy, in awe of the world and everything in it.'

We crunch our way back up towards the house and I listen to the shortness of granddad's breath, watch the pain in his face when the cancer squeezes with its tentacles. Perhaps he is right, perhaps it *is* his time.

'Before we go in I want you to listen to me Sophie. I promised someone a very long time ago I would never tell you this secret, but I guess an old man is allowed to break a promise every now and then.' I wrap my arms around him for that final hug, grateful of my ability, grateful I have been able to see him one last time, to say goodbye.

'Who did you promise?'

The old man looks up at me and says, 'you Sophie. I don't know when you come from because you never reveal this but I have known for a long time about your gift as you have been visiting me since I was a teenager. All my life I have had a guardian angel, you. You pop into my life, your face never the same but it is always you.'

'But how would that even be possible? Traveling back beyond my own existence...' I pause, 'my dad, I travel through him.'

Granddad shakes his head, 'no, it isn't your dad.'

'It's the doc,' I continue and granddad nods.

'You got it kiddo, but be warned, keep your distance as much as you can, William is dangerous in his single-minded pursuit to find more of the Divine.

I feel like telling him how right he is, how when I come from he has just pulled the plug on my life support machines and now I am hiding out here before I head back to my hospital room, to oblivion.

I kiss Granddad and snuggle at the old man's shoulder, 'tell me about the first time you met me, in your life not mine.'

'Well, if memory serves, your dad had grounded me to the confines of Chesterfield manor after I stole a bottle of whiskey from the cellar and got completely out of it with friends.'

'You never did,' I laugh.

Granddad nods, 'I was sat by the entrance gates when this striking young lady, perhaps in her early twenties, walked right up to me and from the other side of the gates said hi...'

Remembering where I am, when I am, and what I have waiting for me back in my time I put my hand up to his lips and say, 'stop.' The old man does as asked and frowns, waiting for an explanation.

'I'll find out soon enough what happens next,' I tell him.

Granddad nods and then says, 'there's something else Soph, I need you to look inside my head my girl. There is still a piece of this puzzle left out and I need to show you before I am gone and it is too late.

The old man stops when we approach the old oak tree. Right now in my time granddad's body will be getting lowered into the ground right here.

He kicks at the dirt and then turns to me, 'a lot of secrets surround this place, and now, before it is too late, you must learn of one more.'

Grandad reaches out for my hand and closes his eyes.

What is it he wants to show me?

'When you were just a few months old late one night I was here…'

The all too familiar static begins to crackle in the air and I am overcome with sudden feeling of nausea.'

'Grandad,' I call out over the electric air and I am propelled backwards, watching as the world around me changes, grandad disappears and now I am back in my old bedroom in Chesterfield manor. I can hear shouting, a woman, not grandma, someone else. I look around my room and then see in the corner the crib where a baby sleeps amidst the racket. I switch on the night light by the side of the crib and look down at myself, reaching out with granddad's fingers and caressing my small head, the hair so soft.

Another crash, this time glass and I hear my dad cursing followed by the woman's voice again. It's my mum, the woman I never met. The piece of the puzzle, my puzzle, my origins and the mystery surrounding my mother's disappearance.

'She won't bond with me, her own mother!' I hear her scream from the other room.

'She is a baby,' dad retaliates, followed by a scream from the lady who carried me and bore me.

'That's not my baby in there Eric, and I'll prove it. She has taken your love for me away, taken everything.'

Another cry of anguish.

The baby stirs, searching with her mouth for something to suckle. I reach into her crib and find her dummy, placing it in front of her face until the baby finds it and is once again content.

'If I can't live with your love she isn't going to either,' mum shouts from the other room and I quietly close my bedroom door on the once again sleeping baby, heading down the landing to where the commotion has suddenly subsided.

Before I arrive at the door I hear the wet gurgling sound and realize instantly why grandad had to bring me here.

Crashing into dad's old bedroom I watching as he spins through the air twirling as though he and mum are ballroom dancing together. Gravity has no meaning as speckled merlot rains down on me from the body of my mother as dad holds her to his mouth,

He hears me enter, peering over her shoulder, and lets out a guttural rumble, his face stained with my dying mother's blood.

'Alan no,' he growls dropping the lifeless body to the floor.

I try to speak but no words come and he turns from me, flying across the room and out of the window, into the night.

I run across to mum, the lady I had only ever seen in photographs, and lift her head, putting pressure on the neck wounds and holding tight as blood seeps through my fingers.

'Sophie,' I hear as the wind blows into the room from the smashed windowpane.

It is granddad calling me back to him through his thoughts and memories. He had blacked out and when he had come around he had been lying in the bedroom with my dead mother on his lap.

'Granddad,' I call back to him through thirty years of anguish. I can feel his pain then and now, the guilt associated with covering up my mother's death.

As the tears blind me and I blink them out of the way I am back with grandad at the old oak tree, my swing gently swaying with the night and grandad too with tears in his eyes.

'He did it to save me,' I say and granddad nods.

'She was obsessed with Eric your mother, she had spent years tracking him down, the myth, the legend, the impaler, and when she finally had him I guess she couldn't handle what he was and what you had every chance of becoming too.'

The old man takes a step forward and stamps his foot down hard, 'I buried her here, ten feet down and the next evening when Eric returned I told him what had happened and he wept for a week. You see control that side of him as he may, the beast is and always will be there, it is a part of who he is and there has always been only one thing stronger than the urges from Eric's hunger.'

I close my eyes as he says his next words, wishing I could see my dad now, my hero, my saviour, my knight guided by blood.

'And that is his love for you.'

I smile and hug the old man as he opens his arms for me, we then head back towards the house. As we part company at the bottom of the stairs granddad leans over for one final hug and whispers in my ear, 'it's been a blast kiddo, I love you my girl.' He then turns and starts to climb the stairs back up to his bedroom.

I head back into the study and plonk myself down where I started, where Billy will wake up. I take one last look around me and then watch the last embers of the fire slowly die out. I close my eyes and feel the rushing static take me back to the body which failed me. I open my eyes again and feel my body convulse.

'Sophie, Sophie,' dad cries out next to me, shaking my body so that my head slams back and forth. I can feel Billy still holding my hand and hear the old man standing over me say he is trying, he is trying to fix it. I manage to open one eye, the blurred red shadows muting together into one electric spike through my consciousness.

'Sophie, no,' continues my dad, his voice muffling as I feel myself drift away from them on a cloud, all of the pain, all of the worry evaporating.

The static buzzing around my head drops from the air and they have all gone. I feel nothing. Peace has finally found me.

The first crash in my chest comes at me with such force that it propels my body upwards. In the shock I cry out and taste the cool winter air as it forces its way into my once broken lungs. I cough and hear the sound this makes loud, a deafening boom in the abyss of nothingness. I swallow hard for the first time in twenty six months and then taking one more deep breath cry out, 'Daddy.'

THE END

COMING SOON

CHRONOS

THE DIVINE CHRONICLES ~ BOOK TWO

ERIC: 1958

My eyes open to darkness.

It's hot.

Too damn hot to be bound to a chair with a gag in my mouth, that's for sure.

I am sat upright on some kind of stool which I can move if I thrust forward but my arms are chained to the wall.

What happened?

It was a simple hit which should not have caused too much of a stir in the criminal underworld. A small time pimp and dealer had ventured into my employer's territory and seeing this as an act of disrespect or war and to maintain his reputation, the boss had ordered the hit.

That's where I had come in, the angel of death. My job is to 'take care' of such problems and guarantee there is no come back on my employer further down the line. I am well respected and feared in equal measure for the work that I carry out, but also I am a freelance agent so if whoever took me is hoping to use me as some sort of bargaining chip then they will be disappointed.

I close my eyes and try to take stock of the situation.

'Hola?' I try in Spanish and then the same in English.

My muffled voice echoes around the room and then dies out to nothing.

I hear the cranking of a metal door or shutter beyond the echoes and wait.

Inside I feel an unwelcome acquaintance begin to wake.

The beast.

It had been two days since I'd fed before being taken. God knows how long it has been now.

Another, much louder, cranking of metal and then an explosion of light burns my eyes as my captors open the cell door. I squint and watch as two men appear in front of me and step into the room, flicking a switch which illuminates my cell.

'You're awake I see Mr Garcia,' one of the two men says, although it is impossible to determine which as they both wear black balaclavas to match their all black jumpsuits. There is some sort of crest sewn on to each man's left shoulder, a bird with its wings in flight rising out of fire. Very symbolic given who I am.

'Si Senor, quesiera te…'

'Let's just stop with the charade now to speed up the interrogation?'

'No comprehende…'

My whole body begins to tingle. Not a good sign. I am plagued with an infection, an infection which can be sedated, but when the beast inside me wakes there is just one thing on its mind, feeding.

These poor men before me have no idea. They will have just been doing their job.

Shaking my head as the buzzing in my ears starts up I feel the short, sharp crack of the cosh as it connects with my cheek. The force knocks me off my stool and I roll onto my side, aware now I have more slack with my bindings.

'Shall we start again, this time I would prefer you spoke in English Mr Garcia?'

How would these men even know I was able to converse in English?

As the blood from my cheek hits the floor my senses sharpen. The hunger is morphing my body and mind into the vessel to deliver its feed.

Number 1 reaches behind him and number 2 hands him something. He approaches me and then squats down so his face is inches above mine.

'Mr Garcia my employer would like to know the whereabouts of this man.' He holds out a small paperback book and before my eyes even focus on the title I know what book he is holding.

'How would a lonely fisherman like me know anything of this,' I growl in Spanish.

The Divine, by Mr E.

Number 1 nods and lifts me back up onto my stool, then takes off his balaclava. The man before me is in his mid-thirties, short black hair and very blue eyes, a mere baby with his big-baby-blues hired to do the devil's work. The fact that he decided to show me his face means that they are planning to either keep me prisoner or kill me, the latter making a hell of a lot more sense. He turns and nods to his mirror image, number two, and the man walks forward.

'Before we strap you to that gurney,' he says, pointing to the corner where in the shadows an old hospital bed rusts away, 'we are going to give you a chance.'

I smile and nod, 'no comprahende .'

Another strike from the cosh and I hear my cheekbone disintegrate beneath the skin.

Number 1: 'Come on Mr Garcia. You want to get out of here? Return to your fishing and scuba diving? This is your chance. Who is Mr E?'

I smile and then say in English, 'It's a mystery.'

Number two claps and then walks over to the gurney, wheeling it out into the light as number 1 continues, 'very good Mr Garcia, Mr E, mystery, the author wanted to remain anonymous which I can understand, but the trouble is my employer believes you not only know who this Mr E is but you also know where he is.'

The splash of blood from my cheek stifles the beast within. It wants more, wants to taste the red, but not yet. First I must interrogate these foot soldiers.

As I rise to my feet both 1 and 2 pause, taking me in. I want them to see that they do not scare me. That these mere toddlers are nothing compared to fights I have been up against in the past.

'Who is your employer?' I ask, leaning against the wall as the red haze lowers and the beast begins to steal my senses.

'That too will remain a mystery,' 1 grins.

Quite the cheerful one, this guy, let's see how long that lasts.

I close my eyes and listen to both of their pulses fighting each other, quickening as I take a step forward and strain at my binds.

Their fear is thick in the air and with it the beast cries out inside me. I can feel my own heart rate quicken and with it strength, the beast's strength, enriches my body. The heavy iron shackles which bind my hands together now feel like nothing more than kitchen foil, and as I brace and move my wrists apart they snap.

1 and 2 step back and I move in quickly, taking 1 by the throat and biting hard into his neck, his blood instantly gratifying the beast. A shot sounds out from beyond my victim and I watch as number 2 shakes off a further five shots, all but one missing me but the lucky bullet which finds its target embeds itself into my collar bone.

I cry out as the searing fire electrifies my nerves and drop number 1.

'w…w…wait,' is all number two manages before I snatch his throat from him and watch as the man drops to the ground, attempting to gasp for his last breaths. I then kneel down beside the soon to be corpse and feed again, crying out in delight as the beast's presence subsides and I am rewarded back my faculties.

'That's enough,' a new voice cries out from the corridor and as I turn to the door I notice a set of eyes peering in through a purpose made slit.

'I want to talk to the employer,' I shout out.

'You will Eric.'

A sharp spike slices through into the back of my mind, electric fire searing through hidden memories, bringing them once again to life. Eric. The name felt vacant but is slowly filling with equal measures of nostalgia and dread.

'Who are you?'

I watch as the eyes crinkle through the peep hole, signifying he is smiling.

'We can be friends to you or an enemy you wish you never had, now where is Mr E?'

I drop to the floor and sit down, trying to work this out but coming up short. This man knows who I am, or rather who I have been, so he must also know that me giving the name of The Divine's author is redundant because names change and people disappear to live new lives.

'Why are you so interested in this man? What do you think he can give you?'

'Information, Eric, is all we seek.'

I nod to this. As full of shit as the answer is it deserves at least a little of my respect. The truth, the brutal cold hard truth would be more acceptable but 'information' is a decent enough answer.

'So which ones are you then, the scientists or the religious nuts? Not that it matters much. The end is just the same regardless of which sect you're from. The scientists want to cut us up and 'study' us, the religious extremists want to burn us at the stake. The result is the same, it is only the reason which differs.'

'One seeks to learn more about you, the other, in fear, wants to destroy you,' the man says from behind his door, quoting the words of the man he is seeking. 'Tell me Eric, have you read The Divine?'

I stand back up and wipe the blood from my mouth, sizing up the door between us, heavy, cast iron, and impossible to breech.

'Read it?' I ask, clenching my hands into balls. The strength I had to snap my shackles is still within me. I just need to wake the beast.

'Yes of course.'

'Read it?' I repeat, only this time the words escape as a growl and the faint dum-dum, dum-dum of my captor's heart beat greets my ears. I can almost taste his blood. The beast is reawakening; I have called upon its strength and savagery so that we might escape.

'Come on Eric, we are all friends here, have you?'

I take a step back, and then another, my vision tunnels so that all I see now is that door and beyond it my freedom.

'I am the Divine,' the beast roars and together we charge towards the door, our combined strength and speed working in union so that we might survive this ordeal.

From beyond the peep hole I watch as my captor's eyes widen, and then the beast takes over and all I see is red.

AUTHOR'S NOTE

I've written a few novels in my time. Most are clogging up my WRITING folder on my laptop, silently waiting for me to click on them so they might stretch their legs, ever hopeful that they will be the next one I turn my attention to and complete. Don't worry guys, I haven't forgotten you're there and you will all get your place in the sun eventually.

This book, *The Divine* was not such a novel.

Five years ago I had an idea. I knew I would like to write about immortality of some sort and I didn't want it to be mystical. I wanted an element of science in the story, grounding the characters in real life. Or as close to real life you can get when dealing with time traveling coma patients and an invisible Dracula. The Divine is the first in at least four which I will churn out when the stories come to me.

This one took so long to write because in the beginning, having written 30,000 words and well on my way towards the half way mark, I split up with a girlfriend and she deleted my hard drive. My baby (the novel) was gone and I had to start again with just snippets of what I'd had to guide me.

I gave up.

I stopped writing for nearly four years. Everyday beating myself up because I knew I should be doing what I love, what I have had to always do.

And then after a chance conversation with a friend in the pub I was inspired to put pen back to paper and start again.

Thanks John, your telling off about me not writing this book was what I *needed* to do put the wind back in my sail, and after a year of learning how to tell a story again I believe this is my best to date and a piece of work I am very proud of.

That is why this one is dedicated to you buddy, like it or loath it this is the sum of your words, here in its entirety.

I would also like to thank my eager first reader Ian and my brother Chris. Always ready to criticize plot points, always ready to inspire me and push me when you were both impatiently waiting to read the next chapter I hadn't yet written. Cheers guys, and I hope you enjoy the end product.

And last but by no means least, you, my reader, having gotten this far it means you made it through. My most heartfelt thanks to you. I really do hope you enjoyed yourself along the way and I look forward to seeing you again here next time.

Any mistakes you catch would of course be gratefully received and I look forward to hearing from you.

I would like to invite you to please leave a review on Amazon, B&N, ITunes, hell even a scribbled endorsement on the your local park bench would be great. That way I might reach and engage with more readers like yourself, prompted by your kind words (fingers crossed on the kind words).

Feel free to drop me a line at robradcliffe.net where you can sign up to my reader's club, like my facebook page, follow me on twitter, or simply just try my next offering.

Once again, thank you for your time, and I'll see you on the other side.

Rob Radcliffe
x

Printed in Dunstable, United Kingdom